About the author

Fiona lives in the small town of Airdrie near Glasgow with her husband, Liam, and their two daughters, Erin and Sian. She works as a deafblind guide/communicator and a British Sign Language facilitator, having learnt BSL after the birth of her second daughter.

This is Fiona's second novel and she is planning on writing more.

WHAT'S MINE

Also by Fiona Morgan

Free

Fiona Morgan

WHAT'S MINE

Vanguard Press

VANGUARD PAPERBACK

© Copyright 2018
Fiona Morgan

The right of Fiona Morgan to be identified as author of
this work has been asserted by her in accordance with the
Copyright, Designs and Patents Act 1988.

A CIP catalogue record for this title is
available from the British Library.

ISBN 978 1 784653 56 9

*Vanguard Press is an imprint of
Pegasus Elliot MacKenzie Publishers Ltd.*
www.pegasuspublishers.com

First Published in 2018

Vanguard Press
Sheraton House Castle Park
Cambridge England

Printed & Bound in Great Britain

Dedication

To Liam
For everything.

Acknowledgements

I started to write this book as I missed the physical art of writing and the characters that became like friends. Again telling myself that the second book wouldn't get done, if I didn't do it! So here we are, done and dusted once again.

As with Free I wouldn't have managed to write anything without the support and advice from others, so my thanks go to the following.

Mum and Dad, thank you for everything you do for me and your unconditional love and support. It means the world to me. Dad, thank you for helping me pick the cars involved, and for reading your first novel just for me. Mum, thank you again for all the advice you gave me on the inner workings of the court. Thank you to the girls in Airdrie Sheriff Court Witness Service for their information and support too. Any mistakes are my own.

Thank you to Con McAfee for the advice on lawyers and the High Court, again any mistakes are mine, or have been smudged to fit.

Gary and Eveline, thank you for all the support you have both given me. Eveline, thank you for allowing me to carry your character over to this book. Gary, thank so much for all the advice and information you have given me, I really couldn't have written without it. Any mistakes, as usual, are my own, or I've smudged them to fit.

Another thank you to my sister Gail for my gorgeous author photographs, I still love them!

Erin and Sian, thank you for letting me use your names. You are both growing into amazing, talented young ladies who make me proud, and a little bit crazy, every day. I love you both so very much.

Liam, again I have left the best to last. Thank you for all of your love and support throughout the years; I couldn't have done half the things I've done if I didn't have it. Thank you for all of your spell checking and sorry for not believing you, (the words really didn't look right), and for answering all of my weird questions and requests. I love you with all my heart.

CHAPTER ONE

Bronagh walks from her job interview at House of Fun party planning fearing the worst, but hoping for the best. She feels she must have come across as a desperate crazy lady, and to a certain extent she is desperate. Desperate to get a start on her own wedding coordinating business. She has decided that working as a party planner is the best way to gain experience and showcase her talents before breaking out on her own. At twenty-five years old Bronagh is fed up working in retail shops and pubs, so after her best friend, Max, noticed the job advert online and sent her the link, she knew it was time to get her plans, and hopefully her life, started.

Max has always been kind and thoughtful towards her, plus he is absolutely gorgeous. Bronagh would love for him to see her in a romantic way, but he never seems to, so she has resigned herself to not being his type and accepting the fact that she will only ever be his best friend, or at least she tries to accept it.

Max is broad shouldered with sandy short hair and crystal blue eyes. He is a good bit taller than her five feet five inches. She guessed about six foot, and always seemed to have a tall blonde on his arm, which is nothing like her. Bronagh has auburn waves, that shine like copper in the sun, freckles dusting her nose and is a curvy size twelve. She loves her curves and has never wanted to be straight up and down.

She sighs as she makes her way back to her car, a green 1999 W plate Ford Fiesta that could be temperamental at best in the cold weather. She chastises herself, remembering that she needs to stop thinking about Max in a romantic way and to stop worrying about the job interview. Trying to put everything out of her mind she mutters to herself, 'Que Sera Sera', what will be will be, and what will be should be found out in a few days, or so David and Erin (the married couple who own House of Fun party planners) had said.

The weather that day is clear and bright for a late February afternoon and Bronagh is glad to see the sun after a week of rain, so much so it manages to lift her mood and gives her something to smile about. Climbing into her car she turns the key in the Fiesta's ignition, and after the second try and a few pumps of the accelerator the car roars to life.

****

Sitting in her bright red 64 plate Audi TT, Elaine glowers at the redheaded woman that has just left David and Erin's house. That is, was, her job the redhead had just been interviewed for and she has no right getting it, unless, Elaine thinks, the redhead was part of the plan to get her fired all along! In Elaine's opinion they had no grounds to fire her, she wasn't doing anything illegal and nobody actually witnessed her having sex with the child's father. They'd only seen her leaving the same shed the idiot had left seconds earlier! There was many things they could have been doing, but no, the wimp of a man had to admit to everything, and so she had to be fired, or so Erin had said. David just sat there saying nothing... god were all men wimps?

Elaine had come to the impression that she was fired because Erin was jealous of her good looks. That Erin planned for the father to seduce her, making sure they got 'caught', so having no choice but to fire her, whilst all the time having this ugly redhead waiting in the wings to step into her position! Well Elaine would make sure that that wouldn't happen; the redhead was going down! Slamming her car into drive she pulls away heading back to her house in the Southside of Glasgow, making plans as she drove.

****

Pulling into the car park at the back of her flat in Parkhead, Bronagh huffs. The bin men have left all the bins in the middle of the parking bays again. She gets out of her car and drags them onto the pavement so she can pull into her numbered parking bay. Getting out of her car, she waves hello to one of her neighbours as she drags her bin into the shared bin shed. Walking up the three flights of stairs to her flat can sometimes be a dangerous trek as not everyone who stays in the flats are legal and above board, and it wouldn't be the first time she had walked into the middle of a drugs bust on one of the landings, wholly embarrassed and confessing her apologies as she sprinted up the rest of the stairs, plus the lighting on the stairwell was never the best, if it worked at all.

Getting safely into her flat, Bronagh locks and chains the door, even though it is still light out. She loves her flat. She has worked damn hard to get it and furnish it the way she likes. To save on money when she first moved in, she whitewashed every room and then added splashes of the colours she wanted in each room as and when she had the money to do so. She knows it's not a palace, but it's hers and once she is inside with the door locked, she does feel safe. Bronagh goes about her routine of taking off her shoes and jacket, putting them away in her cupboard and tidying up from her rush to get out that morning, when her phone goes and looking at the screen she sees it is Max. She smiles looking forward to hearing his voice.

"Hey you," she answers in her usual cheery voice.

"Hey yourself." His gravelly voice comes through the phone. "I thought you were going to phone me when you got through with the interview?" Bronagh squeezes her eyes shut. She had been so wrapped up in thinking everything had gone wrong, she had forgotten her promise to Max to phone. She knew he wasn't chastising her really; it was just a thing they did with each other, kidding on they were annoyed, but they weren't really.

"Sorry, it went out my head." Her stomach growled, reminding her that she hadn't had any lunch, "Have you eaten yet?"

"No, I was too busy waiting on a phone call."

Bronagh laughs at Max. "Okay, I'm sorry. You want to go to the pub and I'll treat you, since you starved yourself with worry?" She loves the banter that occurs between them. She wishes it could be more, then reminds herself again that she isn't his type.

"Aye, that's the best way to gain my forgiveness! You want picked up?"

"Please, I could be doing with a beer to get over that interview." She winces again as she remembers how needy she came across in the interview. "I'll be ready in five?"

"Aye," Max answers. "That sounds like a plan, then I can hear all about this interview." They say their goodbyes and cancel the call. Bronagh goes into overdrive touching up her hair and make-up, making sure her deodorant is still working and giving herself another spritz of her favourite perfume, Rush. Within five minutes she hears the horn of Max's car, a well-cared for 60 plate black Volkswagen Golf. Pushing her excitement back into its hide-hole, she grabs her bag and heads back out the door, trying hard to not make eye contact with her neighbour across the hall, as she climbs into the car.

"Hey you... again." Max smiles.

"Hey yourself, again," Bronagh answers and Max pulls away from the kerb, and drives the five minutes to the pub they class as their local. Once in they find a booth to sit in and order nearly straight away. They both know the menu inside out so don't need to even look.

"So," Max starts, "how did it go?" Bronagh drops her head into her hands and groans.

"I must have come over as a desperate needy idiot! Honestly, everything they asked, I was just the proverbial nodding dog, agreeing with everything and anything they said." Max's eyes are glinting with barely held together laughter. "Don't you even think about laughing. You know how much this job would mean to me. You're the one that put me onto it!" Max clears his throat from his laugh, and tries to be serious.

"I know, I'm sorry. I'm sure it wasn't that bad. You would have just came across as enthusiastic. Were they impressed with your experiences and your references?"

Bronagh shrugs. "I think so. They said they were going to contact my references today. They also asked if I had organised any parties for anyone, and could they contact them."

Max takes her hand. "Well that sounds good. They wouldn't contact anyone if they weren't interested in you, and I hope you gave them my sister's name; she was over the moon with the wee yin's first birthday party you did!"

She nods, and smiles. It was fantastic how Max knew what to say to make her feel better; she guessed that's what friends did for each other. 'Friends' Bronagh huffs at the last thought, but manages to cover it up.

"Aye, I did. Thanks Max, you know just what to say to make everything seem better." He gives the hand he is still holding a squeeze.

"Of course, you know how amazing I think you are." He smiles at her, trying to guess her feelings and convey his. He is madly in love with Bronagh, and has been since they met five years ago, but he could never get up the nerve to tell her, so they have just fallen into friendship and stayed there. If this is all he can have of Bronagh he will grab it with both hands. Having her as a friend is more important than not having her in his life at all, so he buries his feelings, normally with some blonde he finds in a bar, and continues loving her from afar.

****

Elaine is fit to burst thinking about her job and the redhead. She needs to get out of her house, and get enough alcohol in her that she forgets she is unemployed, single and still living in the house her parents left when they died. She refuses to think of her parents so phones her 'friend' asking if they could hook up and where. It needs to be somewhere that no one will recognise them; she doesn't think his wife would be too happy if she found out they were friends with benefits! They arrange to meet at a pub in the Parkhead area of Glasgow.

Within the hour Elaine has changed clothes to a black PVC pencil skirt and tight fitting white vest top that leaves very little to the imagination. If she is going to be drinking, she is going to be having sex; she can't do one without the other, especially with this particular 'friend'. The taxi company rings her back alerting her to the taxi sitting outside. She takes one last look in the mirror before leaving the house, locking her door and strutting to the taxi, blowing kisses to the old woman who lives across the street from her and who is always twitching at her curtains.

She arrives at the pub and grimaces at the run down look of the exterior. She pays the driver and climbs out, checking up and down the street to make sure she doesn't know anyone before entering the pub. She feels the hot air bursting from the heater above the door and is thankful for that, at least; she never brought a jacket, opting instead for the coldness as a ploy to get into her friend's arms later. She looks about, trying to spot her conquest for the night but realises he hasn't arrived yet so walks up to the bar and orders herself a vodka tonic before sitting at table near the bar, but further up the back, so she could keep her eye on the front door. She turns her head slightly to the right to see what kind of clientèle the pub brings in and catches a redhead out the corner of her eye. It can't be, she thinks, as she turns round more to get a better look. A small gasp leaves her when she realises that yes it is the same redhead from that morning. Elaine smiles, now she knows something about the bitch that is trying to take her job; she has a rather hunky boyfriend and she eats in the most depressing pub in Glasgow. It's a start, she thinks, now just to get more information and she can get her plan started.

Once Bronagh and Max have finished their early dinner, they relax in one of the old and cracked leather couches. She is on her second Corona and Max is stuck on the Irn Bru.

"So when did they say you'd find out?" Max has tried his best to make Bronagh feel better about her job interview that morning, and he wanted to know when she would find out so he can put the date in his diary or a reminder on his phone. He likes to know what's happening in her life.

"Next week. Erin said the start date would be Monday the seventh of March. They have a few communions in for the May so they need someone in to start the preparations." Max has been nodding throughout her answer.

"Sounds to me they really liked you. I reckon you've got it!" Max beams at her.

"Aye, but you're biased! Right nature calls, so I'm going to the loo." Max shakes his head at Bronagh's bluntness, just something else he loves about her. She gets up and walks towards the toilets that are situated near the back door, giving Elaine a better look at her as she walks past her.

Elaine gets up and walks over to the hunk of a man that the redhead is sitting with. She slides down onto the couch as if she had been sitting there all day.

"Hi, I was just wondering, what's that girl's name? The one you've been sitting with? It's just she reminds me of someone I know, and I don't want to embarrass myself by getting it wrong, so if you could tell me, then I'll know either way without any red faces." She bats her eyelids at him, but she can tell by the look on his face that she would be getting nothing more than an answer from him, if she even got that.

Max eyes the woman sitting next to him. Normally he likes blondes, but this one is a bit too harsh looking; her make-up is too heavy and her perfume too cloying. He's trying to wrack his brain to see if he remembers her from anywhere, but keeps coming up blank. He doesn't see a problem telling the woman Bronagh's name, but doesn't want to give much more information than that.

"Eh, it's Bronagh. Bronagh White."

"Ah, not who I thought it was," Elaine quips quickly. "No matter, and you are?" Again she bats her lashes, and pushes her chest out until it is almost touching Max's arm, trying to look sexy. Max blushes at the obvious come on the woman was trying.

"Max," he states without emotion. Elaine nods. She would love to feel just how solid this guy's muscles are, but she doesn't want to get caught by either her friend or his, so she thanks him for his time and for saving her from an embarrassing conversation, then leaves to return to the table she had been sitting at. Within seconds of her sitting down her friend walks through the doors and arrives at her table.

"Hello gorgeous, imagine meeting you here." He smiles at her and she tries to suppress the groan in her throat. He greets her the same way every time they meet. He is lucky he is drop dead gorgeous because his conversational skills leave a lot to be desired.

"Lee, you're looking ravishing tonight. I do like it when you wear you suits," she purrs. "Now are you going to stand there looking handsome and sexy, or are you going to get me another vodka tonic?" Lee nods then walks over to the bar to get their drinks. She takes her vision from Lee and looks toward the toilet door and smiles as the redhead, Bronagh, walks back in.

Bronagh sits back down and frowns at the expression on Max's face.

"What's up with you?" she queries.

"What, eh, nothing. Do you know that blonde woman sitting down there? The one sitting near the back wall?" Bronagh looks over to where Max is motioning with his head. She rolls her eyes when she notices the woman in question is a blonde.

"No, why? Is she your next conquest, or has she been and I'm meant to remember her name for you?" Her eyes glint with mischief, but with an underlying twinge of disappointment, as she turns back to look at her friend. Max looks horrified.

"No! She's not my type!" Bronagh eyes him again. "I know it's been blondes for a while, but no, thanks. She came up here when you were in the toilet to ask your name, saying she thought she knew you. I told her your name, but she said you weren't who she thought you were." Max shrugs, still feeling uneasy after his encounter with the woman. "I don't know I've just got a funny feeling about her and not the good kind." Bronagh laughs, then finishes her beer.

"Right what we doing? You want to dump the car and make a night of it, or do you want to come over to mine and phone the rest of them? I mean it is Friday." The thought of being alone with Bronagh all night would be amazing, but he knows it's best for his sanity to have their other friends with them. He really wishes he could find the courage to tell Bronagh how he feels. One day he tells himself, one day.

"Aye, phone the rest and we'll make a night of it. Your house or mine?"

"Yours. That way your car is home with you tomorrow." He smiles.

"Good plan, smarty pants." Bronagh smiles back, her heart strings being pulled with Max's smile. They leave the pub and Bronagh phones their other friends as Max drives. They all agree to meet at Max's house for a night of fun and drinking.

****

Elaine and Lee have a few drinks then leave for their usual hotel that Lee had quickly booked when Elaine phoned for their rendezvous. There was never any expense spared when they got together. She was his lover, his escape, his playtime and everything his wife wasn't. She scratched the itch his wife couldn't, even if he didn't let her try.

They arrived at the hotel and went straight to the room, ordering room service of Champagne and strawberries. They made sure they used every moment they had together for exactly the reason they were together; sex and lots of it, or at least as much as they could fit in until Lee had to go home. Elaine knows she is going to need Lee to help her in her plan to take down Bronagh and then get her job back, so she starts to tell him about losing her job, or at least her version of the events.

"I've been let go from my job." They are both still lying in bed, Lee drawing circles on Elaine's arm. "Remember I told you one of my bosses, Erin, didn't like me? Well she's eventually got her own way; she fired me last week after setting me up and spreading rumours about me." Lee sits up, looking straight at Elaine as she tells him her story. "The birthday party I worked last weekend, the dad asked me to help him get more party decorations from his shed. I know I should've thought twice about going somewhere private with him, but I thought I was just doing my job." Elaine manages to get just the right amount of emotion into her voice as she continues, "but once we got there, he came on to me, trying to kiss me and putting his hands on me." Lee growls and starts to say he was going to do things to the man who had 'hurt' her and her employers who had not only let the sexual assault take place, but fired her for gross misconduct. Elaine quietens him down, before continuing, "we were both seen leaving the shed, and the wife put in a complaint about me after he 'confessed' everything. I promise you nothing happened. I told him no and said I would scream if he didn't stop trying to kiss me, so he stopped, thankfully. I left the party and went straight back home so I could take a shower, get the feeling of his hands off of me." She had managed to find tears to add to her story, which riled Lee up even more.

"Who is this man and where does he stay? I'm going to take this to my editor. We will name and shame him not only his for sexual assault, but House of Fun for firing you." Elaine puts her hand on Lee's chest, calming him from his rant.

"No I don't want that. I don't think he was really going to hurt me. I think he was told to make it look like we had, you know... done things so I would get fired. I think they, well Erin, wanted me out and had my replacement waiting in the wings. She knew she couldn't just get rid of me, so she set me up. I don't want the poor wee lassie going in after me to end up the same, with the life sucked out of her, then everyone thinking she's some sort of slapper." Lee nods, she had been feeding him stories of things that Erin had been saying about her for the best part of a year. "I was thinking, maybe we could get some information on the new girl, and you know, warn her?" Lee muses over this information for a bit, before agreeing. He would help her with anything she asked of him as long as she continued to make him feel the way she did.

"Yeah, if you can get me her name I can have a wee dig about. Now come here for more kisses. I'm going to need to go back to the wicked witch, so I want to go back with a smile." Elaine grins at him. She knew he would do what she wanted, so she made sure she paid him particular attention when they had sex this time.

CHAPTER TWO

Friday night turns into Saturday morning. The group of friends eventually fell asleep around three in the morning, but that didn't stop Bronagh being up at nine. She was always up early. She tried to sleep in, but just couldn't, so she padded her way through to Max's kitchen and popped the kettle on. Trying to be as quiet as possible, so not to wake the sleeping dead bodies sprawled about the living room. She starts to make her coffee when she hears someone enter the kitchen behind her. She spins on her heel and sees Max standing at the door, and her heart skips a beat at the sight of him. He is wearing a pair of jeans with the button fly still open, and nothing else, showing off his broad shoulders, muscles and tattoos, most of which are car and mechanical related.

"Hey you, what you doing up?" Max smiles at her, still trying to rub the sleep from his tired eyes.

"Hey yourself," she answers. "You know I don't sleep much once I've had my six hours. What you doing up? Did I wake you? Sorry, I thought I was being quiet." He laughs, as he gets his own coffee cup from the draining board.

"You were, kinda. I don't know what woke me, but once I realised you were up I decided to get up. That way I can stop you from tidying up!" Bronagh blushes. She was going to do some clearing up as she was drinking her coffee. She couldn't help herself. She wasn't a neat freak; she just always felt guilty when they had a party at somebody else's house and that person was left with the clearing up.

"I don't mind helping. It's not fair to leave it all to you. We all made the mess." Max steps over to her side and kisses her on the cheek, and her stomach flips.

"I know, and that is one of the things I love about you." Both of them take in an inaudible breath, neither of them able to take in Max's words and actions. Max takes a step back as the kettle clicks off, and clears his throat.

"Aye, you know like a friend... love." Bronagh nods her head, trying to hide her thrill at the kiss and first words and then her dismay at the last words. Max clears his throat again; the need to hold Bronagh in his arms and kiss her is pulling at him. He needs to get out of the kitchen before he acts on impulse and ruins their friendship. "I'm going to pull a top on, pour mine too?" Max nods towards the kettle and the cups, and Bronagh nods again.

"Aye, sure." They both look at one another for a second too long then Max walks away, berating himself for letting his feelings slip out that wee bit.

Once Jane, one of the friends they were drinking with, had woken up, Max went for a shower, leaving the women talking in the living room about the night before and the new job that Bronagh was hoping she had landed herself.

"Honestly, I just don't know. I guess I've got as good a chance as anybody. I really hope I didn't come across as needy as I felt I was. Anyway never mind that, how's things going with you and him?" Bronagh nods to the sleeping shape lying on the other couch. Jane looks towards the same shape and smiles.

"Yeah, we're doing good. Still in the honeymoon loved up stage, so I guess if we can make it through that and still like each other it will be grand." The women laugh and the prone shape moves slightly. They laugh again, but quieter this time.

"Right, enough about me and him, what about you and him." This time Jane nods her head towards the living room door, motioning that she was talking about Max. Bronagh's cheeks flush red.

"What do you mean? There isn't a me and him, well not unless you're talking friends, unfortunately." Jane gives her an incredulous look, and Bronagh looks shocked.

"What? We're friends, that's all. I am not his type, if you haven't noticed. He likes blondes and I am certainly not blonde!" Bronagh shakes her head, making her copper hair fly about. "But apart from that, we've known each other for so long that if anything was going to happen it would've happened by now, so shush." Jane rolls her eyes and gives Bronagh another look of incredulity and knowing.

"Are you kidding me? He can't keep his eyes off you, well at least not when you aren't looking at him. I swear to god you both need your heads knocked together. Youse are both majorly into each other, but neither of you will make the first move." The women hear noise coming from the hall so they drop the subject, and Bronagh changes it as Max walks through the door.

"Right, I better get organised to leave, before my neighbours think I've disappeared. I've not been home since lunch time yesterday." All three friends laugh at the thought of her neighbours noticing anything other than their own alcohol level. Their laughing wakes up the prone body on the couch, Stewart, Jane's boyfriend, who grumbles at them all for being too loud, and the day being too bright.

After another hour, they are all awake and ready to leave. They decide to meet for dinner that night at their local Chinese buffet at seven. Max offers to give Bronagh a lift home.

"We can give her a lift," Stewart intervenes, but quickly shuts his mouth when he sees the look Max throws his way.

"Youse are going in the opposite direction. I'll run Bre home," he says, more of a statement than anything. Jane gives Bronagh a look of 'I told you so' and Bronagh rolls her eyes, silently telling her friend that it means nothing. Stewart shrugs his shoulders, knowing there is something going on, but not knowing what. Jane laughs at her boyfriend as she ushers him out the house. Max sees them out then returns to Bronagh.

"You ready to leave just now or do you fancy another coffee?" Max hopes she will choose the coffee and more alone time with him.

"Coffee sounds great, thanks." The two friends sit for another two hours talking about everything and nothing as was their usual chats before Max takes her home.

****

Elaine had stayed in the hotel for the rest of the night, no point wasting a good room just because Lee won't stay the night, not that she desperately wanted him to stay. He might get the wrong idea that Elaine has proper feelings for him, god forbid. They had spent some more of the night talking and planning how to get to the new girl and warn her of Erin and how she treats her female workers.

Elaine makes her way back home, by taxi, which cost a small fortune, and makes a mental note to get the fare back from Lee at some point. She can't afford taxis any more now she is unemployed. Once back inside her house and changed into comfy clothes, or pyjamas to everyone else, Elaine picks up her mobile and finds the contact she is looking for, the receptionist at House of Fun. If anyone would give her the information she needs it will be her. After the third ring the receptionist answers.

"Elaine, how are you? I'm sorry to hear about Erin firing you. You were so good at your job." Elaine rolls her eyes, she had fed the receptionist the same stories she had been feeding Lee, and she was young and naive enough to believe her, thankfully.

"Yeah, honey I know, but it's probably for the best. If she can get someone to take me into a secluded shed, just think what else she could do, it doesn't bear thinking about." Elaine adds a shudder into her voice for good measure. "Anyway, I hear that they were interviewing yesterday. Do you know if they have decided on anyone yet?" There is silence on the other end of the phone. Elaine knows the receptionist is debating if she should tell her anything or not. "I mean, I was just wondering, maybe if I could find out who is going to get my job, I could maybe warn them to watch their back, you know, looking out for other females, not wanting to give *her* the chance to do the same again?" This is enough to convince the young girl on the phone and she gives Elaine some of the information she needs.

"Okay, well, when you put it like that, we don't want any other members of staff being bullied. Well, all I know is... her name is Bronagh White, and she lives in Parkhead. I'm not sure of her exact address but I can try and find out on Monday when I'm back in the office?"

"That would be fantastic honey, and remember to keep this between us. I don't want Erin turning on you." Elaine's grin is splitting her face. She now has a name to give to Lee to get a start on. The women say their goodbyes and promise to stay in touch before cancelling the call. Elaine knows she won't stay in touch. She wouldn't want a friend who is as young and naive as that girl. She heads to the kitchen for some food, thinking all the time about what hell she is going to bring down on the redhead called Bronagh!

She takes a shower then messages Lee the small details she has found out about Bronagh. Basically her name, that she lives in Parkhead, and the fact that she has red hair. While she waits on a reply, she decides to go onto her computer to do some searching of her own for Bronagh White.

Thankfully after half an hour her phone buzzes. It is the reply she has been waiting on from Lee.

*For you my darling,
Miss Bronagh White Flat 3/1 10 Westmuir St Glasgow
single at the moment, will keep looking. Xx *

Elaine does a wee jump for joy on her couch in celebration of getting some important information that she can use. She writes back a quick thank you message, then grabs her bag and car keys, thinking to herself she may as well get mission 'take the redhead down' started as she heads out her door and into her Audi.

CHAPTER THREE

Pulling up to the kerb outside the front of the flat, Elaine can see a black Volkswagen Golf pull in front of her Audi. The two cars are nose to nose. She notices that it's the same guy from the night before, Max. She pulls out her phone to check that Lee had said she was single, which he did, so she decides he's either a relation, or she's a lesbian. There is no way you could be 'just' friends with that hunk of man flesh without doing things to that body, she thinks. She starts to take some pictures on her mobile, making a mental note to maybe invest in a better camera for her mission. She sees both Bronagh and Max the hunk exit the Golf, then watches as he walks over and cuddles the lucky bitch, wrapping his muscled arms around her shoulders. Elaine realises that the embrace is more than friends, but too awkward to be lovers. It is then she realises that they both have feelings for each other, but neither of them have admitted it. She smiles. This was something that she could use to her advantage, she thinks to herself. She continues to watch as the wannabe lovers continue their goodbyes.

****

Max takes Bronagh into his arms in a hug, a friendly one he reminds himself.

"I'll see you later?" Bronagh is enjoying the embrace, but manages a nod. "You want picked up?" he asks, trying to eke out as much time as possible with her in his arms.

"No, you don't need to drive. Get a taxi and I'll meet you there." Max lets out a breath. Normally when he was drinking he would struggle to keep his feelings about Bronagh to himself, so would find a blonde to bury his feelings in, but he was getting fed up with nameless blondes, hiding his feelings and not having Bronagh in his arms. He inwardly promises himself to stay away from blondes and find the guts to open up to Bronagh.

"Okay, if you insist. So, seven then?"

"Yes, I do, so seven." They both look into each other's eyes, both seeing something there that they don't normally see. After a long second they both look away, not sure if their eyes were fooling them or not, or even if the other had seen what they had seen, but neither of them dared to ask, not wanting to be disappointed.

Bronagh makes her way up the stairwell to her flat and goes through the routine of locking the door then waving from her living room window to let Max know she had made it in safe; she loves the way he looks out for her. She goes to the bathroom and runs herself a bath. She would love a shower in her flat, but finances were always against her. As she waits on her bath filling up she looks out clothes for the night ahead. She wanted to look sexy enough that Max will notice her, but not so much that she looks desperate or like she's trying too hard. It is, after all, just dinner with friends. In the end she opts for her skinny black jeans and a red low v-neck chiffon top and her red heels with a slight platform. She checks on her bath, turning the taps off she plops her hand in to check the temperature. Happy that it is just right she climbs in and starts to analyse everything that Jane had said and everything she felt ping between her and Max when they were cuddling and looking into each other's eyes.

Max climbs back into his car once he sees Bronagh wave from the window. He can't believe what he saw in her eyes after they'd cuddled. Could it be possible she has feelings for him, he thinks, the same feelings he has for her? A bud of hope plants itself in his heart, he tries to push it down, but it refuses to budge so instead he decides to hold onto it and believes, even if it's just for that afternoon, that there could be something more between them. As he pulls back out onto the main road he notices the Audi parked in front of him, taking a look in as he passes, he notices the woman from the pub yesterday, she gives him a small wave and a wink. Having just a split second to react, he raises his hand in a gesture of a wave back. He thinks it's strange to see her parked in front of Bronagh's flat, but dismisses it to think more of what could be with Bronagh herself.

****

Elaine lets Max and his Golf pass before she pulls out and does a very inconvenient U-turn to follow him. She may as well know where the hunk stays too if he is friends with HER and if she is planning on getting him into bed, she needs to know where that bed is. She follows him back to his house which is situated in the Gorbals area. She turns her nose up at the area, but then thinks it's not the place she wants to be in bed with, but the hunk, so let's go of her snobbish attitude as she hangs back and watches him get from his car and enter his house. She sits for a bit trying to work out her next move when her phone buzzes alerting her to a new message coming in. She looks at the screen and sees that it's from Lee.

Hello gorgeous, I know it's Saturday but I have managed to get in touch with one of my contacts, I have got the girl's phone number, it's 07703987654. Hope you manage to contact her and warn her before it's too late. Stay sexy xx

Elaine does another wee dance to herself at the new information. Now her plans could really get under way. She pulls up the text messages on her phone. First she answers Lee's message with a thank you, then moves on to message Bronagh.

Hope the job is everything you hoped it would be, enjoy it... if you get it, bitch!"

She smiles. It has started, and all her new dreams will be coming to fruition soon. She is going to bombard the redheaded Bronagh with hatred and spitefulness about the job she desires and her new employees until she either refuses the job or leaves, and if that happens to bring down Erin and her precious business during the campaign of hate, then even better. Deciding she wants to see Bronagh's flat again she turns her car towards Parkhead. Elaine pulls into the kerb to watch the window of Bronagh's flat for a second. She notices Bronagh come out of the door and look at her car. Panic creeps up Elaine's neck at the thought of being recognised, but lets out a breath when Bronagh climbs into the waiting taxi. Curiosity getting the better of her, Elaine follows the taxi.

****

Bronagh's phone buzzes alerting her to a text message. She looks at the screen expecting it to be Jane or Max, but it is from an unknown number. She is normally wary of unknown numbers, but as she is waiting to hear about the job she opens the message. Reading it she frowns. Who would be sending her a message wishing her luck for the job? No one, other than Max, Jane and Stewart, knew she was going for the job, and the message wasn't from one of them. Reading the message again she notices the word 'bitch' at the end of the message. Her heart starts to pound in her chest. She puts her phone down trying to get away from the message and makes a mental note to ask the others if they recognised the number. She then goes back to getting ready, trying to push away the horrible message from her mind. She keeps the make-up on her eyes light, never one for heavy eye shadow, preferring instead to let the mascara do its job and open up her eyes. She always thought it best to let the light in to show off the emerald green of her eyes. Another must in her make-up routine is her red lipstick; she never uses any other colour for her nights out. Looking at the time, she realises that it is almost half six, so she picks up her phone and orders a taxi, asking for the ring back service. She always asks for this service as it saves her from waiting outside with all the crazies that live near her. Waiting on the taxi, she opens a bottle of Stella Artois, and goes back to thinking about the job, and her dreams of running her own wedding coordinating business. From an early age she had loved setting up parties for others, starting with her dolls, and her friends from school, then moving onto her parents and their friends when they had them over for dinners. When her dad had turned forty she was the one to organise his party. Everything from the hall and its decorations to the food and the invitations. She didn't let her mum do anything (except book the mobile bar; she was too young to do that being only twelve) and it was a huge success, everyone complimenting her on a great party, and the best of it was her dad's reaction to it all. He was over the moon with his party, he couldn't stop bragging to everyone there that it was his daughter that had thrown him the party and how proud he was of her and all her hard work. Once she'd turned eighteen, she'd started work in her local bar and always put herself forward to work any parties that were booked in. She gave her ideas out when asked, or added small extras to enhance the decorations that were already there. Eventually people were asking more and more for her input until eventually she was asked to organise the first birthday party of Max's niece. It was because of that party that she decided what she really wanted to do with her career, party planner and hopefully eventually a wedding coordinator with her own company.

Her phone rings with the taxi service's ring back, bringing her back from her musings. She takes one last look in the mirror and opens her front door. As she steps out she is faced with one of her neighbours, drunk and sliding down the wall as he tries to open his front door. Thankfully he doesn't or can't see her so she makes a quick getaway down the stairwell. Walking out of the main door to her block of flats Bronagh notices a red Audi sitting; she wonders why someone with such a nice car would be risking it by leaving it unattended in a neighbourhood like this one. She shrugs the thought off and climbs into the back of the taxi, taking her phone from her pocket to text Jane and Max, letting them know that that was her leaving. Just as she finishes the messages the phone rings in her hand, another unknown number. Still wary after the strange, slightly nasty message she wonders about answering the call, but the thought of the call she is waiting on about her job interview claws at her, so she decides to answer.

"Hello?" She uses her politest phone voice, but even she can still hear the wariness in her voice as she talks.

"Hello, hi, Bronagh? This is Erin House from House of Fun." Bronagh's stomach clenches at hearing Erin's name. Her mouth goes dry, and she has to swallow to get her saliva moving again, or at least enough to get her mouth to work, letting her speak.

"Yes... I'm Bronagh. Hi, Erin."

"Oh, good, I'm glad I've got the right number. I'm sorry to phone you on a Saturday night, but David and myself thought it would be best to let you know as soon as possible that we would like you to start your new job on Monday if that's possible?" Bronagh's stomach flips again as she takes in the information that she got the job, and they want her to start earlier than they had spoken about. Then she realises that Erin is still talking. "We were really impressed with your interview, and your enthusiasm for the business of parties. We contacted the lady who you did the first birthday party for and she raved about how seamless everything went, so... we would love to offer you the position. We have a diamond anniversary next Saturday and would like you to be part of it." Bronagh is nodding furiously in the back of the taxi. The driver gives her a strange look through the rear view mirror as they pull up to the restaurant. Bronagh signals to the driver that she will be two minutes as she continues to talk into her phone.

"That's great and yes Monday is fantastic, thank you very much."

"Brilliant, now, do you have any questions?"

"Eh, yes." She rummages in her bag to get her purse and pays the driver before he got really annoyed at her for sitting in his taxi talking, and climbs out whilst still talking. "What time do you need me to start and where? Oh and what will I wear, I mean, I know when I'm covering parties it will be smart business wear, but for other days is there a uniform, or is there a uniform for parties also? Will I go to your house where the interview was?" She stops talking realising just how much she was talking and takes a deep breath. "Sorry I know I'm babbling." Erin gives a small laugh.

"That's okay. I'm enjoying how enthusiastic you are about my baby. So, yes if you come by the house, the door to the office is at the side of the house, say about ten. When we are at the office planning you can wear casual clothes, jeans etcetera, but yes, when you are working at parties it's business smart. One thing though, when you are working parties please remember it is not your party and you aren't 'going' to the party, you are working it so I would appreciate if you dressed for work and not a party or night out." Erin knew she was being a bit over the top, but after her last employee she wasn't taking any chances. Bronagh on the other hand was confused at why she was being told the obvious, but agreed with her new boss.

"Absolutely, I understand." She sees another taxi pull up and squints to see who is in the back seat as Erin continues to talk.

"Okay, I'll go and let you get on with your Saturday night and I'll see you on Monday?"

Max steps out of the taxi and sees Bronagh standing outside the restaurant waving wildly at him to go over to her. As he approaches he hears the end of her conversation.

"Yes, and thank you again. I'll be there on Monday with bells on." Erin laughs again as they finish their goodbyes and Bronagh cringes at her words. Max stands next to her as she grabs his arm. She puts her phone in her back pocket and turns to face him, grinning from ear to ear. So much so that Max can't help but grin back at her.

"Max, guess what, guess what?" Bronagh is almost jumping up and down with excitement.

"What?" He can feel her excitement in his every fibre.

"I got the job!" Bronagh squeals with delight, and Max's grin widens. "That was Erin House on the phone, it's mine, I start Monday!" Her excitement takes over both of them as they hold each other in the closest embrace possible.

"Well done you, that is fantastic, I knew you would get it. You are amazing at parties, and everything. You are just amazing!" He gives her a kiss that brushes the side of her mouth, and they stare at each other again. Bronagh swallows hard at Max's words, hoping he meant them the way they sounded, but reminds herself that they were just friends, even though they seemed to have had two 'moments' now. Before anything else can happen or be said, another taxi pulls up at the kerb and Jane and Stewart get out.

"What youse standing out here for? It's cold!" Jane looks between the two friends.

"Good news," Max replies. "We'll explain when we get in."

"Oh good, have youse decided..." Bronagh gives her a sharp look before cutting her off.

"Inside! As you said it's cold out here." Bronagh growls at her friend. Jane nods and Stewart shrugs. He is never one to look like he knows exactly what is happening. Normally he does understand, it's just, he's not that interested.

The four friends walk into the restaurant, greeting the well-known staff, they are seated at their usual table. It takes them seconds to order their drinks and go up to the buffet table for their first round of food. Once they all have food and drinks in front of them, Jane demands to know what all the commotion was outside.

"SO... what's the big news?" Bronagh's grin spreads again.

"Well, I got a phone call when I was in the taxi coming over here, and... I got that job I went for!" Jane does a small dance and grins at her friend. Stewart manages to look happier than normal.

"Oh my god that's fantastic, well done you. That's great and means we have something to celebrate... we need Champagne!" Everyone around the table looks at her. "Well cheap fizzy wine at least." She grabs the waiter and orders the Cava. Once it arrives the friends all toast Bronagh and her new job. Max looks up to smile at her again, loving the sparkle the good news has put in her emerald green eyes. He notices the blonde woman standing at the bar staring over at the table. She catches his eye and smiles with a wink. He looks away quickly, touching Bronagh's arm to get her attention.

"Bre, is that the woman from yesterday? The blonde standing at the bar?" Bronagh goes to turn round to look, but Max tells her not to, so she rolls her eyes at him as she brings out her mobile phone, taking a 'selfie' so she can see who is behind her.

"Aye, I think so. You think she's following you? Trying to get into your trousers?" She laughs, but sees the uncomfortable look on Max's face. She squeezes his arm. "It will be a coincidence, ignore her and help me celebrate my new job." Max smiles at her and agrees, but keeps his eye on the woman who keeps smiling his way. Bronagh also sees that one of Max's eyes stays on her and a pang of jealousy runs through her.

****

Elaine had followed Bronagh to the restaurant, watched as she exited her taxi on the phone, and then watched more as she spoke more on the phone and then to Max. The jealousy she had felt when he'd held her tight, kissing her and looking deep into her eyes had her anger clawing at her throat. Elaine had wanted to scream. She was desperate to know, why was it that some people got everything and she got nothing, not even the man! The only 'man' in her life was only half hers, and even then he wasn't that much of a man. Seething with anger she thinks back to the scene outside, then watching as the one in front of her unfolds, she throws the rest of her wine back her throat and stands to leave, making sure she bumps into Bronagh on her way past making her spill her Cava.

"Oh I'm sorry," she purrs to Max, giving him her most sexy pout as she rubs her hands down his broad shoulders and arms to 'wipe off' the spilled drink. "I hope I didn't get any on you?" Max removes her hands from his arms.

"Not on me you didn't, but you did get it on my friend, so I think you should be apologising to her." Elaine glowers at Bronagh, sneering her apology at her, before turning her attention back to Max.

"I'm glad I missed you, I'd hate for you to have to take off that t-shirt. Well at least I would hate to have missed it, that is." She smiles her sexy smile at him and runs her hand back over the length of his shoulders, before turning to walk out into the cold night air, grinning to herself. She has a sneaking suspicion that she knew the other guy sitting at the table, but she hadn't had a good enough look at him.

Max shudders at the feeling the blonde woman's fingers leave on his skin. He's not sure why her touch had made him feel so queasy. It shouldn't, she was blonde after all and he's into blondes isn't he? But it did. He looks round the table and sees everyone staring at him, his face flushes red.

"What?" he asks with a shrug.

"What was that, or should I ask who was that?" Jane asks, then looks at Bronagh who is shaking her head as she speaks.

"That is going to be Max's new squeeze." She tries to keep her voice jovial, but knows it comes over as bitchy. She can't help it. She despises the fact that she wants him but won't do anything about it. Max's head snaps round to look at her.

"No it isn't, I told you yesterday she's not my type." Bronagh snorts and Jane continues to look between them like she was at a tennis match.

"So, youse met her yesterday?" Jane questions them and Max nods as he tears his eyes from Bronagh, not liking or understanding the pissed off look on her face.

"Aye, she came up to me in the pub when we were out for lunch. She was asking what Bre's name was, saying she thought she knew her, then changed her mind, said she was mistaken. Then I could've sworn that I saw her at your street earlier when I dropped you off." He faces Bronagh, who is trying hard to stop her face looking like she was eating a lemon. Jane continues to ask questions even though the atmosphere is quickly turning icy.

"So do either of you know her?" Both Max and Bronagh shake their heads. "Well she definitely has a thing for you Max!" Jane states,

"Lucky him!" Bronagh mutters and Max shakes his head again.

"I don't think so," he states flatly. Jane stares at her friends. She can feel jealousy coming from Bronagh and exasperation from Max, all the while Stewart sits eating. Jane knows she needs to save the night so instructs everyone to get more food, more drink and to be happy.

CHAPTER FOUR

"But I really want to see you." Elaine whinges down her phone to Lee, listening for a bit before answering. "I know I only saw you on Friday, but that was two days ago and I want you again," she continues. She is desperate to see Lee again, as she had spent the rest of Saturday night cursing Bronagh and fantasising about Max after she came home from seeing them at the restaurant. She would get angry about the job and then to take her mind off that she would get herself hot and bothered over the feeling of Max's shoulders and arms. She eventually managed to get some sleep after easing her building want and ache with her own fingers, but that only lead her to having crazy dreams of her and Max being together in every position possible as Bronagh watched on in tears, which then in turn lead her to wake up in a worse state than the one she fell asleep in. Desperate to get all the sexual tension from her body, plus more information on Bronagh if there was any, she is practically begging Lee to come over and help her out.

"Please darling, I need you." She hears Lee sigh which is normally a sign that she would be winning and getting her own way.

"I don't know what to say to her indoors." Elaine rolls her eyes at how pathetic the man she has sex with could be.

"Can't you say you have a meeting or something?"

"Babe, it's Sunday afternoon. What meeting would I be going to?" She huffs. Does she need to be the one with all the ideas?

"I don't know. You're a journalist, you make stories up for a living. Why can't you make one up now?" She pauses before starting on her guilt trip again. "Unless of course," she sobs, "you don't want to be with me." Another sob comes from her throat even though there is still no sign of tears, but he couldn't see that, thankfully.

"Now Elaine, that's not fair. You know I want to be with you, it's just difficult." Lee huffs again, "Fine... I'll see what I can do and I will get back to you, okay?" Elaine sobs again.

"Okay, thank you, darling." They say their goodbyes and then cancel the call. She slams her phone down on the arm of her couch, annoyed that she may not be getting her own way even though she played her part perfectly. Feeling even more angry and pent-up she goes to her kitchen and pours herself a wine, a Barolo. Knowing that this would need to be her last bottle of decent wine until she gets her job back, she savours the first taste. She is going to have to get used to cheaper makes of wine, maybe even supermarket own brands, god forbid. She goes back through to her living room, which is decorated in beige and golds, lifting her laptop as she sits, firing it up and opening up one of the many social media sites she uses. She puts in Bronagh's name and other information she has managed to glean about her into the search bar and starts to go through all the results that appear. After an hour of searching and another glass of wine Elaine finds what she has been looking for. Excitement of a different kind explodes in her body and she pours herself her third glass. She starts going through all the photographs of Bronagh and her friends. Every time she sees one of Max and Bronagh together her stomach sours another bit. She can't understand how two people who are so close can't see how they feel for each other. She can see it through the photographs. So because of that and how she is starting to feel about both of them, Elaine decides that while she is taking her job back, she will be taking herself a new man, Bronagh's man. She picks up the new pay as you go phone she bought in the supermarket and types out another text to 'Bronagh the stupid redhead'

Congratulations on the job bitch, hope it's everything you want it to be!

Seconds after she sends the text her own phone buzzes, alerting her she has a message of her own.

Be round in 10 but can't stay late sorry gorgeous xx

She smiles, she knew he couldn't resist her. She jumps up rushing to tidy up her living room, putting her new phone in her bedroom as she changes into something more revealing.

****

Sunday night and Bronagh's stomach is in knots. She has bathed and dried her hair and is now just sitting on her bed. She has done all of this whilst thinking about the woman from the restaurant from the night before, thinking about how her hands were all over Max. Also she couldn't get over how she had felt at seeing it. Never in her entire life had she ever felt so much anger and jealousy towards one person. It had taken everything in her to not rip the bitch's fingers off and ram them down her throat, but because she couldn't do that without raising suspicion, she ended up taking her feelings out on Max, accusing him of being attracted to the random woman who kept popping up wherever they seemed to be. She shakes her head, not wanting to dwell too long on anything that had happened the night before and picks up her phone to set the alarm for the morning. She notices there had been a message sent when she was in the bath. Her heart lifts at the thought that it might be Max, but it descends quickly to the pit of her stomach when she opens it up and reads it. With her hands shaking she looks to see who had sent it but realises it is from another unknown number, a different one this time. Unsure of what to do about either of the two nasty messages, she does the first thing she can think of. She phones Max, and thankfully he answers after a few rings.

"Hey you," he answers in his usual cheerful manner.

"Hey yourself," she replies as she usually does, but her voice isn't as cheery as it normally was.

"What's up? Nervous about tomorrow?" Just hearing his voice calms her a bit, and she smiles at the thought of him thinking of her.

"No, well aye, but there's something else." Max can hear what he thinks is a touch of fear in her voice.

"What's wrong, has something happened?" There is concern in his voice, and rage in his stomach at the thought that someone had hurt Bronagh, but it is his concern that brings another smile to her face and her heart beating faster.

"I've had two strange messages. One yesterday and then another one about an hour ago."

"What's the number? What does it say?" His questions come at her like quick fire.

"It's two different numbers and I don't recognise either of them do you?" She rhymes off the two different numbers and the messages but it is to no avail.

"Sorry Bre, I don't recognise the numbers. Keep a hold of the messages, just in case though, and keep me updated if you get any more. I don't like the thought of anyone sending you texts like that." He hears a whimper from the other end of the phone so decides to change the subject. "Now tell me, how are you feeling about tomorrow, apart from the troll?" Bronagh relaxes more as she talks to him.

"Sick, kinda nervous but excited at the same time. I just hope Freddie the Fiesta behaves himself and starts." Max laughs down the phone. He knows how unreliable her car can be and is always on at Bronagh to sell it for a newer model.

"Well I don't think it's to be frosty tonight so you should be fine. If not just phone me and I'll come right over."

"Thanks Max you're the best, and I am sorry about last night. I shouldn't have busted your balls over that random. I let her get under my skin for some reason. If you are into her then -" she swallows over the lump of words she doesn't want to say, "then go for it." Max's groan stops Bronagh from talking more.

"Eww, no, Bre I've told you I don't find her attractive. I think I might be over my blonde thing, plus, I'm kinda into someone else at the moment, but I don't think she knows I exist... well at least not in a romantic way." The words are out before he knew he was thinking them, never mind stop them. Bronagh takes a sharp intake of breath. She hadn't heard him mention anyone new he had met, and she really didn't want any more bad news, but she thinks, with the looks that have passed between them recently, could he be referring to her?

"I'm sure she does, but if she doesn't then, well, more fool her." This time it is Max that gasps, and the silence grows between them, neither of them sure where to take the conversation. Bronagh is first to find words.

"Right I better go, I need to try and get some sleep." Max is glad for the diversion.

"Okay, well let me know how you're getting on during the day if you can, but I'm sure you'll be amazing. You always are." Tears spring to Bronagh's eyes at the words from Max. Over the past few days they had both said things and looked at each other in ways that hinted at feelings they may have for each other. So between the hope in her heart, the anticipation of the new job and the worry the new messages were bringing, her emotions were over taking. They say their good nights and Bronagh crawls into bed, dreaming the entire night of Max and her being together.

CHAPTER FIVE

Waking up to an alarm was not the way Elaine expected to wake up on that particular Monday morning. She had forgotten to switch it off the night before. When Lee had eventually come over, they had spent the rest of the night having sex on her couch until she had fallen into an exhausted sleep. She knew Lee would've taken her up to her bed then leave once he knew she was sleeping soundly. He was not allowed to stay out, on his bitch wife's orders and she would never ask him to stay either. She didn't do the romantic side of sex, the sleeping in each other's arms and waking up entangled in each other. She didn't expect to be waking up so early though. Looking at the clock she decides to get up and pads through to her kitchen to make herself a coffee. Once she has her first sip she sits down in front of the TV in her living room and stares at the news. Her annoyance and anger of how her life is going starts to bubble up inside her again and she starts to think back to when her life fell apart the first time. Her parents had left her to live with her grandparents so they could live out their heart's desire by working in Somalia. Three years after they left her, when she was sixteen, they died of cholera. Her grandparents were devastated and both died within eighteen months of her parents. After her parents died, Elaine rebelled, trying to find solace in the arms of anyone who would have her. During this time Elaine learned how she could use her body to control the opposite sex and get her own way with the weak-willed men. She also learned not to let herself get close to anyone, and to certainly not have any feelings of love for anyone, maybe not even herself. After an hour or so Elaine is fed up wallowing in her own pity, she pushes aside the feelings of abandonment that she refuses to deal with and heads for a shower. Another hour later and Elaine has managed to wash all of her woes away, dried, dressed and is now prowling like a caged tiger. Not wanting to sit around any more she grabs the keys to her TT and leaves, heading towards the dodgy side of the east end of the city.

****

Eight o'clock Monday morning and Bronagh has been up for three hours and has changed clothes just as many times. Looking out of the window she can see the frost covering her Fiesta's windows. She huffs and pulls her jacket on. There is no way she is leaving it until half nine to see if her car will start. Opening the door she peers out first, making sure she doesn't bump into any of her neighbours, then steps into the close, pulling her front door behind her. She makes it down to her car and climbs in without meeting anybody, thankfully. Putting the keys in the ignition she turns them, the car spurts a few times then dies. She turns the keys back to the off position before trying again. Nothing, not a sound. Cursing her luck and her car she gets out the car, and back up the stairs to phone Max.

"Hey you," Max answers,

"Hey yourself," Bronagh replies. "Sorry, did I wake you?" She's not sure why, but she is feeling nervous talking to him, so she puts it down to the new job and the fact that her car isn't working, although deep down she knows that's not the real reason for her nerves.

"No, I was already awake. I got up to pee an' saw the weather. Thought you might need me." Max cringes at his over sharing of information even though Bronagh tells him this type of information all the time. Bronagh on the other hand feels guilty that he might've lost out on sleep because of her, but then she feels happiness sweep over her at the thought of him thinking of her, although doing it as he was peeing is a bit gross.

"I'm sorry, but yeah Freddie's not starting... I can get a taxi. I –" Max cuts her off,

"No, don't be daft. I told you to phone me if you needed me. So, is he turning over?"

"No, well, he did once then he died." For someone who knows nothing about cars Bronagh had learned what questions Max normally asked and what he meant when he used jargon like 'turning over'.

"Okay, I'll be right over. It sounds like he might need a new battery, but I'll jump start him and see if we can get him going at least for today." Bronagh sighs in relief.

"Thank you, Max, I really appreciate it. You really are too good for me... I mean to me." She quickly covers up the slip of her tongue, hoping that Max didn't notice, or maybe she does want him to notice, she isn't sure.

"No, I'm not. I mean, what kind of friend would I be if I left you stranded on your first day of work? So, I'll see you soon." Max hears her words and answers the first statement.

"Okay, and thanks." She cancels the call then holds the phone to her chest, wishing it was him she had at her chest, and also wishing she had the confidence to tell him how she feels. She pushes her thoughts away. She doesn't have the time or the energy to over analyse her feelings for Max, or her inability to tell him about them.

Half eight comes as does Max. Bronagh meets him at the car and they jump start it. They sit in the car for a while, letting the engine run with Max revving it every couple of minutes, then they head back upstairs to Bronagh's flat for a coffee and some much needed heat.

"Right, I better be going. I don't want to be late on my first day." They had both been sitting talking about everything and nothing, as was their usual conversation. "And should you not be at work already?" She eyes Max and he shrugs. They stand from the kitchen table they were sitting at and head out the front door to walk down the close stairs and out to the cold morning.

"That's okay, I told the boss I had a family emergency and would be in as soon as I could." More guilt passes through her at Max's blasé attitude.

"Max, I shouldn't come before your work, that's not fair." Max takes her hands in his and looks deep into her eyes. His heart starts beating hard, to the point he's sure it's trying to leave its home within his rib cage.

"Hey you... you're part of my family and I wouldn't have it any other way. This is your dream job Bre, and that means more to me than an hour's wage. Now go and start that rust bucket you call Freddie and get to work." Bronagh can feel the emotions in her going into overdrive and she is sure she can see feelings in Max's eyes. Not sure what else to do she opts for feigning outrage at his words about her well-loved car.

"Eh, don't talk about Freddie like that, I love him!" Max laughs.

"Sorry." He manages to look and sound contrite, even if it is put on. "I'll watch my tongue in future." Bronagh grins.

"Good." They laugh then look at each other for a second longer than normal. Max pulls her into his chest, holding her closer than he ever has as they stand in front of her Fiesta.

"Good luck gorgeous, I'll be thinking of you." Bronagh pulls back to look at Max and is shocked at what she sees in his eyes; desire. Before either of them can comprehend what the other or themselves are doing, their lips are crushed together in a passionate and what is most definitely a 'more than just friends' kiss. Max is first to break away, placing his forehead on Bronagh's before talking.

"Phone me later?" Bronagh is panting.

"Aye... " She can hardly speak or think after the passion she felt in the kiss. Max holds her to him, not sure what to say about what happened, feeling like he'd taken advantage of Bronagh. Then, he thinks, she reciprocated the kiss. Bronagh grasps his arms not wanting to let go, just yet.

"Max, I... we −" He pulls back to look at her dead in the eye.

"Aye. We'll talk later... but, yes." He gives her another chaste but passionate kiss. "Go start Freddie before I leave." Bronagh nods, opening her car and starting the engine, too stunned to do anything else. Freddie starts first time and Max waves goodbye before walking over to his works van. He feels like he has just won the lottery. He actually did it; he kissed Bronagh and made his feelings clear, well sort of clearer. They both drive off to their respective works, both grinning like idiots to themselves in their vehicles.

****

Parked at the front of the building on Westmuir Street, Elaine waits and watches for Bronagh or her car to leave for the first day at *her* job. She notices the Fiesta leave the car park and she starts her car. As she is about to pull away she notices a mechanic's works van pull out and in the driver's seat is Max. Elaine's blood is boiling at the thought of Bronagh and Max being together. She really thought that Bronagh had no idea of Max's feelings towards her, even though they were screaming from him. But if he is staying the night then, she surmises they must be sleeping together. Slapping the steering wheel, Elaine pulls back out into the traffic, cutting up someone driving a Mini behind her. The Mini blasts their horn at her, but she just gives them the finger out the rear window in between the head rests. She knows where Bronagh is headed so she doesn't need to follow her. She makes her own way through the traffic to the House of Fun. Once there she sees Erin and David's cars, along with other members of staff and Bronagh's. She parks and pulls out her new phone, the one she is using to contact Bronagh, and dials her number. It rings out until the voicemail kicks in, she cancels the call and tries another five times, before typing out a message.

Have a good first day bitch!

She drops that phone back into her bag and lifts her own phone, to contact the receptionist. The young woman answers the phone with her usual sing song voice that always grates on Elaine's nerves.

"House of Fun party planners. Sue speaking how can I help?"

"Hi, it's Elaine. I was wondering if you had managed to find out anything else for me?" There is a brief pause before the sing song voice comes back.

"Oh, Elaine, hi there. No sorry there is nothing as yet, but then again I've only just arrived, so not really had the time. But anyway how's things with you?" Elaine rolls her eyes. She can't believe the bimbo she is talking to, how does she think things are going?

"Fantastic, really, I mean I've loads of time now I don't have a goddamn job." Sue gasps at Elaine's words and sarcastic tone. "Anyway, I'll phone back in a few days, see what you can find out." Elaine cancels the call and sits, unsure what to do next. Annoyed, she drives off heading back to her own house via a shop for some wine – it is after ten so legally it's okay.

****

Erin walks past the reception area with Bronagh as Sue stands staring at the phone's receiver before she replaces it.

"Everything okay Sue?" The receptionist looks up at her boss, her eyes wide with confusion.

"Eh aye, I mean yes. Sorry yes... em, just a wrong number." Erin eyes her receptionist with suspicion then nods before starting the introductions she had come through to do.

"Okay then, this is Bronagh, our new planner. Bronagh, this is Sue our receptionist. She deals with all phone calls, helps with the bookings and keeps our diaries in order. Bronagh puts her hand out for a handshake.

"Nice to meet you Sue." Sue keeps her mouth shut, with a thin smile in place and nods, never offering Bronagh her hand. Bronagh can feel and see that the receptionist isn't warming to her being there, but she tries not to take it personally, putting it down to her not liking change or maybe being friends with the woman who worked there before her.

Erin looks between the women before giving Sue a stern look, then turns back to Bronagh.

"Right, well, we'll keep going and get you introduced to everyone else, then get you started on the party you will be working on." Bronagh smiles nervously, not wanting to rock anybody's boat, nods and walks on beside her new boss.

They go through the door behind the reception area which brings them out to a wide open plan room. There are four square tables in the white washed room, one in each corner, the walls at each party table are covered in plans and pictures of whatever party is getting planned. Bronagh stops walking, taking in the room in front of her, feeling overawed at the amount of activity at each table. Erin sees the look on Bronagh's face and lets out a small laugh, placing her hand on Bronagh's arm.

"Don't worry, I know it looks busy in here, but once you know what's going on it won't look so daunting... honest." Bronagh looks at her boss and smiles, warming to the kindly woman even more. Erin starts to explain what party each table is dealing with.

"So, table one here." She places her hand to the table nearest them. "This is a christening." She then goes round the room in a clockwise motion. "Table two is a fortieth birthday, three is a wedding and four is a diamond anniversary." Bronagh nods throughout whilst fighting the rising panic in her throat. Erin moves into the room slightly and starts the introductions to the other three planners then they walk over to the wedding anniversary table.

"This is where you will be cutting your teeth, it's a small party and I'm sure you'll do great." Bronagh nods again as Erin continues to talk. "Right, I have a meeting I need to get to, so I need to leave you to it." She hands Bronagh a folder. "This is where we keep all information on whatever party we are planning, and we also use the walls for photos and plans etcetera. Have a read through and get caught up. I am really sorry I'm dropping you in at the deep end, but I have faith in you." Erin says to everyone to help Bronagh if needed and to make her feel welcome before taking her leave from the room.

Bronagh sits down at the table with the folder sitting in front of her and places her head into her hands, the feeling of wanting to cry washing over her at everything she has just taken in. She feels a hand on her shoulder, making her bring her head up to see a young man standing beside her with a soft, happy expression on his face.

"Bronagh?" She looks up at the young male, taking in his tall, dark and handsome looks. His smile is full and gleaming white, something Hollywood would be proud of.

"Yes, hi." She still has a startled bunny look about her.

"Gordon," he points to himself as way of another introduction then grabs her hand in a strong handshake as he continues to talk. "Hey... nice to meet you. Listen, don't you worry about anything I'm sure you'll be just fine. Now first things first, would you like a coffee?" Bronagh smiles, her first genuine smile that morning, liking the easy, friendly way her new co-worker had about him.

"Oh my god, yes please, that would be great." Gordon nods and smiles.

"Good, now how do you take it?" He wiggles his eyebrows in the most comical way of trying to be smutty. Bronagh snorts a laugh, her anxiety easing slightly.

"White with one sugar please."

"No problem sweetheart. One desperately needed coffee coming up." Gordon walks off to the kitchen area and Bronagh starts on the folder again, feeling a lot more relaxed and positive about her job. A few minutes later Gordon returns.

"Here you go sweetheart. Get this down you and you'll be able to take on the world!" Bronagh takes the mug from Gordon and takes a sip. It is then she realises it's percolated and not instant and sighs.

"Oh god, I could fall in love with you Gordon. This coffee is amazing." Gordon has wheeled over his chair and is now sitting next to Bronagh, his hand placed on her shoulder.

"Aw, sweetheart, I could love you too if you had the right appendage." It took her a moment before the penny dropped.

"Ah, well, I'll just love you as a friend then." She smiles at him.

"Now that I can get in on." Both of them laugh. Bronagh can tell she has just made a new firm friend. Over the next few hours they go through the folder and plans for the diamond anniversary until Gordon announces it's one o'clock, so time for lunch.

Bronagh looks at her phone as she bites into the sandwich Gordon brought back from the deli next door for her. She sees another message from the same unknown number from before. She reads the message and a wave of nausea washes over her. She's not sure why anyone would be so nasty towards her. Gordon comes back through with some more of the liquid gold they were calling coffee and her phone buzzes again signalling another message coming through. She is a bit loath to look at it in case it is another nasty one, then remembers Max had said to try and contact him at lunch if she could, so she looks, hoping it will be him especially after their kiss that morning. She is relieved and excited to see that it is from him.

Hope your day's going well, can't wait to talk tonight. M x

She smiles to herself as she touches her lips remembering the feeling of his lips on hers.

"Oh, is there a lover boy on your mind?" Gordon asks, interrupting her musings.

"I'm not sure, to be honest." She has no idea why she is telling this almost stranger about her feelings for Max, but it feels right, so she does. "Max has been my best friend for years that I've loved for forever and this morning we kissed. Proper kissed. Like kissed kissed." She can't hold her smile back as Gordon looks at her like he is reading a fairytale.

"That's fabulous sweetheart, I hope it's the real deal for you." Bronagh nods in agreement and smiles.

"Me too." The two new friends spend the rest of the day working, talking, laughing and drinking coffee, taking Bronagh's mind off the unknown number and nasty messages. As first days go, she thinks, this has to be one of the best.

CHAPTER SIX

Elaine returned home after buying more bottles of wine and spent most of the day drinking and seething with anger. She goes onto another social media site and looks at everything Max and Bronagh have put on, plus all their friends and their friends' friends. She copies some of their photos and 'liked' some of them, as well as some of their statuses. All this is done through a new page she has made up. She notices someone who is a mutual friend of Max and Bronagh; Stewart. She remembers him from school, so on her own page she sends him a request to be friends. A flashback to the restaurant makes Elaine realise that Stewart was the other guy sitting at the table. A thrill runs through her at how handsome Stewart was, more handsome than Max she thinks. Desperate to play more with Bronagh's head, Elaine jumps back into her car. She doesn't stop to consider the three glasses of wine she'd consumed as she drives back to House of Fun. Once there she creeps into the car park, leaving her car parked out on the street, and sidles up to the Fiesta she knows to be Bronagh's. She takes a glass nail file from her handbag and makes a mark on the rear passenger wheel arch, before leaving the car park without being noticed. Getting back into her car she heads back to her own house, via the nearest off sales for more wine... again.

****

Max has spent the entire day thinking of Bronagh and their kiss. He didn't know he was going to do it until he felt his lips on hers, then all he felt was right. He is so glad he eventually did it, after all the years of being friends. He'd kissed the woman he loves and it felt great. He had messaged her earlier, not able to wait for her to contact him first. She hadn't replied as yet, but that was okay; he understood that it would be a hectic day for her. His thoughts then turn to the nasty messages she'd received and makes a mental note to ask her if she has received any more. A wave of anger flows through him at the thought of anyone being nasty to Bronagh. She is such a kind, thoughtful and generous person, it just didn't make sense to him. Pushing all thoughts of messages from his head he continues replacing the brake discs on the Volvo he was working on and starts counting down the hours until he sees her again.

Bronagh leaves work with paperwork to go through. She had made contact with the daughter of the couple whose party she was planning, just to introduce herself and give out her number in case they need to contact her for anything. She gives Gordon a cuddle goodbye and she thanks him for all his help and coffee throughout the day. She climbs into Freddie the Fiesta not seeing the scratch that Elaine had made earlier. Before driving off she pulls out her phone to message Max, desperate to let him know how her day has been. Her eyes glance over the unknown number, but she refuses to let it bring down her mood so she ignores it and continues with the text message to Max.

Heading home, are you coming over?x*

Her stomach flips as she thinks about what might be after their kiss that morning. Arriving home, Bronagh rushes into her flat, still desperate to not meet any of her neighbours. Closing the door behind her, her phone buzzes in her handbag. Max's name shines on her phone in the darkness of her long narrow hall, and her stomach flies again.

Aye will bring dinner as a celebration of your first day, chippy OK? Mxx*

She quickly types out a yes, then goes for a bath, needing to relax after the stress of her first day. An hour later; clean, dried, and dressed in her comfy lounge wear, Bronagh hears her door. She jumps up from her position on the couch where she is going through the paperwork she brought home, and answers the door, looking through her spy hole first, just to make sure it is Max.

"Hey you." Max steps into her hall, his hands full of food and places a quick kiss on her cheek. She steps to the side allowing Max room to get through, her breath catching in her throat at the kiss and the lingering smell of engine oil from Max.

"Hey yourself, that smells good... the food." Her stomach makes a sound of a whale just to prove her point. Max laughs as he passes her, heading towards the kitchen. Bronagh follows behind, going into the living room to tidy up her paperwork.

"There's a beer in the fridge if you fancy one," she calls through the doors that join the two rooms, "and bring me one too please." Max enters the living room juggling two beers and two plates full of fish and chips. Bronagh stands taking the plates from him, their fingers touching. They both take inaudible gasps as they stare at each other, both feeling the spark of attraction, then breaking out into grins. Still smiling they both sit on the couch and start on their dinners.

"So what's with the plates? You've just given me more washing up to do," she moans as Max shrugs.

"I don't do eating from the wrapper now it's not newspapers, doesn't taste the same. Anyway enough about me and my chippy eating habits, how was your first day?" Bronagh smiles again.

"It was daunting at first, but it turned out for the best by the end of play." Max's eyebrows raise.

"Wow, sounds like a roller-coaster of a day. You make any new friends? Anyone I should be worried about?" he asks with what he hopes is a tongue in cheek tone, but knows there is a hint of seriousness there too. Bronagh smirks at the thought of Gordon and Max being jealous of him.

"Yes I made a new friend. His name is Gordon, but no you don't need to worry about him... you will always be my best friend, and anyway I would have more to worry about if he ever meets you!" Max tilts his head in question, making him look like a confused puppy. "I don't have the correct equipment, but you do!" she continues. It takes Max another second of confusion before the penny drops for him.

"Ah, well that's okay then." He winks at Bronagh and she continues to talk again, telling him everything about her work. Max listens to her voice, loving how excited she is about her new job, and mentally patting himself on the back for giving her the advert in the first place. "Sounds like you had a great day." He pauses before asking his next question, not really wanting to bring up the messages she had received, but needing to know if there was someone out there verbally abusing her. "Have you had any more nasty messages?" Max holds his breath slightly, not wanting to bring down Bronagh's good mood, then he hears her take a deep breath. A shiver runs down his spine.

"Aye, here –", she hands Max over her phone so he can read the newer messages. The seconds pass by as Max reads. Bronagh can see all the different emotions pass over his face, before anger settles there.

"Who is this whack job?" Bronagh flinches at the anger in his voice, but understands that it's not aimed at her so shrugs, putting her dinner plate on the coffee table in front of them and picking up her beer.

"I don't know. It might be the woman who had the job before me, but how she got my number I don't know." Max nods, musing over what Bronagh has said.

"It might be two people." Bronagh's eyebrows shoot up to her hairline and Max sees the panic in her eyes.

"I'm sorry, Bre, it's just a thought, but isn't there two different numbers?" She nods, taking in what Max was saying.

"Aye, there is, an' I noticed that too, but one person hating on me is bad enough, but two…" She blows out her breath. "Am I really that bad a person?" Emotion starts to overtake her and tears fill her eyes. Max moves over to her and takes her into his arms.

"Hey you. Listen, no one hates you, and you are not a bad person. You are the sweetest, kindest, most generous and definitely the most beautiful person I have ever met." They are looking deep into each other's eyes as Max brings his hands up to hold the side of her face, bringing his lips to hers. They kiss, making time stand still. Max moves one of his hands into her hair until he is holding the back of her head, his other hand is running down her back, resting when it got to the dip in her lower back. Holding her as close as possible he deepens the kiss, their tongues dancing together in harmony. Max is the first to break the kiss, both of them are breathing hard.

"Again." Bronagh breathes.

"Is that okay?" Max asks, sounding unsure of himself for the first time ever in their friendship. It's certainly the first time Bronagh has ever seen him unsure, which she found quite sweet if she was honest with herself.

"Aye... yes, I mean... if that's what –" Max stops Bronagh from talking by putting his fingers to her lips.

"I'm glad, I've been wanting to kiss you like that for years!" Bronagh's eyes widen at his words.

"Really?" He nods, rubbing his fingers up and down her back.

"Really," He answers her.

"So, why haven't you... and why now? And... me too." Bronagh goes to hide her eyes with her hands, which had been resting on Max's shoulders, trying to hide her growing blush, but Max grabs them and holds them to his chest.

"I didn't want to risk our friendship, plus I wasn't sure how you felt or would react if I did, but as for why now... well I don't know, I just felt a change between us, so I thought why not!" Bronagh smirks.

"Me too... again, over everything you just said. So what now?" Max gives a small laugh.

"I don't know to be honest, but I do know I don't want to lose you... so, if you think we should continue as friends only then I will..." he pauses for a second, "deal with that." Bronagh never breaks eye contact with him.

"I don't want to lose you either, but I have been attracted to you since we first met all those years ago, so to hear you say that you feel the same is like..." Max nods, agreeing with her.

"I know me too. So do you think we should try, you know, being a couple, or go back to what we were? You know, wanting each other from afar?" Max pauses for a heartbeat, before spilling more of his feelings over the conversation. "To be brutally honest I really don't want to not be able to kiss you again, now I know how amazing it is. So could we try?" Bronagh tries to keep her grin under megawatt, but knows it is not possible, Max has just said her kisses are amazing. She doesn't trust her voice, so instead opts for nodding her head. Max smiles back at her, his own smile a full blown megawatt grin. Taking her back into his arms, he starts kissing her again only this time with more force and passion than the last ones.

****

Three bottles of wine later, at eight in the evening, Elaine is feeling very tired, very angry, and very sick. When she had came home from scratching Bronagh's car she was euphoric. She'd even contacted Lee to tell him how hot she was for him, even though he had specifically told her never to phone him at work. Normally she played by the rules of their tryst. She was the one who made most of them, but she couldn't help herself today. Her plan had started, even if she didn't know how it was affecting Bronagh the bitch yet and she was desperate to share her news. After the conversation with Lee, including an argument about her phoning, and with time wearing on slowly due to the fact she was on her own and with the alcohol taking hold, she was becoming more and more angry. She had gone into her downstairs toilet to ask her reflection in the mirror what the bitch had that she didn't. Then, with the empty second bottle of wine in her hand and no answers from the mirror, she threw the bottle at the kitchen wall, smashing it into smithereens. Glass slithers are all over her floor as she watched the dregs of red liquid run down her pristine white walls. Seeing double and anger getting the better of her, she then decides the way to go was back onto the social media sites. Elaine booted up her laptop, and making another two profiles, she goes about having a full blown conversation with herself on Bronagh's page, describing all the evil, and nasty things that Bronagh had supposedly done and said about one of these fictional ladies. Then the third bottle came and went. Elaine had worked herself into a proper rage. Walking through the downstairs of her property she screams at nobody and punches the wall, making excruciating pain ricochet up her arm and a string of expletives fall from her mouth. Just as the last 'fuck' leaves her mouth she feels the first wave of nausea wash over her. Dashing to her downstairs toilet, she makes it in the nick time before the first round of soured, vinegar smelling red liquid baptises the white porcelain. Her body convulses every time more of the soured red liquid forces itself from her stomach. Pain racking her ribs she cuddles the cold porcelain of the toilet bowl. Two hours later, after falling asleep on the toilet floor, Elaine wakes feeling sweaty, shivering and with the start of a serious hangover. She crawls on all fours upstairs and into her bed, still cursing Bronagh for everything.

****

Tuesday morning and Bronagh is sitting at her table in work sipping on one of Gordon's fantastic coffees. She is in a world of her own, thinking back to the events of the night before. Both her and Max had agreed to try 'the relationship thing', both thinking it's best to have lost and loved than never to have loved at all. They had shared many more steamy kisses well into the night, but nothing more. Max had said he wanted to woo her properly before taking her to his bed, so they arranged their first date for Friday after work.

Gordon walks over to Bronagh's desk. He'd seen the dreamy look in her eyes from where he was sitting. His eyebrows shoot up as she holds her fingers up to her mouth, remembering the feeling of Max's lips there the night before.

"Aw sweetheart, you have it bad for this boy of yours, don't you?" Startling her from her musing Bronagh looks up at her new friend, who's now standing right beside her, grinning like an idiot.

"Yes I do. I always have and apparently so has he. We just never knew each other felt the same." Gordon goes all dreamy eyed, loving the real life love story Bronagh was bringing to the office.

"That's great. I do love a good love story, unlike that crazy bitch who worked here before you. She would have it away with just about anyone... in fact," Gordon looks around conspiratorially to make sure no one else could hear him talking. "I know for a fact that that was why she was fired. She was caught having sex with a customer at their kids party! And apparently he wasn't the first!" Bronagh gasps, not understanding how someone could abuse their position like that. "Anyway, enough about that crazy bitch, I want to see pictures of your hunk of a man at lunch time." Bronagh laughs then agrees, before the two friends continue with their work.

CHAPTER SEVEN

Elaine wakes with a pounding sore head and her tongue stuck to the roof of her mouth. Never in her twenty-nine years has she ever felt this hungover the morning after. She tries to lift her head from the pillow, only to drop it back down after a blinding white shock of pain shoots through her brain. She knew she had to move as the nausea was back, but every time she as much as thought about moving, even just her eyes, there was pain, blinding hot pain. After five minutes of deep breathing she manages to move onto her side, but that led to the cramping in her stomach starting, which led to the retching, which brought on another bout of vomiting. Not able to move she hangs over the side of her bed as bile shoots from her mouth. Contraction after contraction, she retches and spits whatever is left in her stomach onto her wooden floor, splashing the red rag rug that lies near her bed. Too sore and tired to be disgusted with herself, Elaine slumps back onto her back and drifts back to a pain free, blissful sleep.

An hour later and Elaine awakes again. This time she's feeling only slightly better. She moves slowly, testing her head and stomach. Both are sore, especially her ribs; they feel like she has done a hundred sit ups for the first time in her life. At least the nausea seems to have eased, she thinks. Feeling hopeful she decides to try the art of proper movement. Bringing one knee up, then the other before resting for a bit, then she shuffles her bum up the bed until she is in a sitting position. She stops, letting her stomach catch up and settle before moving again. Swinging her legs round she puts them on the floor, managing to avoid the disgusting puddle of bile lying on her wooden floor. Now she knows that she isn't going to vomit any more, she drags herself from her bed and into her shower, sitting on the floor of the shower under the scalding hot water jet until she feels semi-human again. Getting out she dries and changes into jeans and a white t-shirt. She cleans the vomit from her bedroom floor, lifts the rug and strips her bed, putting into the washing machine before moving on and cleaning up the sink and toilet downstairs. Once everything is clean and she is feeling more human than she probably should be, she grabs her handbag, picks up her phone and listens to the messages that Lee had left the night before. She rolls her eyes at his warnings of what could happen if she starts to actually stalk this new girl, and that he had thought she was only wanting to warn her about Erin and David. Throwing her phone into her bag she grabs her car keys and leaves her house, heading to the House of Fun again, looking to mark Bronagh's car for the second day running.

****

The day passes by quickly again for Bronagh. She's feeling a little more in control of her job now that she is up to date with everything and has contacted everyone involved that she needed to introduce herself to. Starting with function managers, and carrying on to caterers, then the couple whose anniversary it is – having spoken to their daughter the day before, as their first point of contact for the party. Everyone thanked her for contacting them and introducing herself, and for taking over control of the party, not any of them having very nice things to say about the planner before her. She'd spent the longest time talking to the elderly couple, getting a feel for them, their likes and dislikes. The information in the folder had given her very little; colour schemes, etcetera but not much else, nothing about the couple. She asked them if they had any old photographs they would like to show at the party, explaining that she would take copies, keeping the originals safe, or if there was any songs they wanted. She'd suggested the first dance at their wedding or their very first dance together. She wanted the party to remind them what it was like to be in the first flush of love again. All through her conversation she was hoping that it would be her and Max one day. The rest of the day she spent making plans, sketches of the halls and coming up with menu ideas before calling it a day at four and heading home. She leaves the basement office and pulls her woollen coat closer round her as a fog has descended and is making the air feel damp but icy. A chill runs down her spine as the bushes catch her eye. A strange thought that someone might be hiding in them crosses her mind, but she shrugs it off, telling herself not to be so paranoid. Her thoughts turn to the messages and she is pleased when she realises that she hadn't gotten any that day. Whoever it was they must have had enough and given up, thankfully, she thinks. She climbs into her car and he proves difficult to start again, due to the weather, but after the second attempt the Fiesta eventually fires up and she drives away, promising Freddie the Fiesta a new battery as soon as she gets her first pay.

****

Cursing Bronagh even more, Elaine drags her cold, sore and scratched to hell body from the bushes. For a moment she thought she had been caught when Bronagh had stopped right in front of the bush she was hiding in and watched her. It felt like Bronagh was staring right at her, so much so that Elaine hadn't even breathed, frightened that Bronagh was so close she would hear it. She then sent up a silent thank you when Bronagh turned towards her car and climbed in, only for the thing to struggle to start. She honestly thought she was going to need to stay in the bush until someone came to fix the hunk of junk. Pissed at herself and the entire world in general, Elaine escapes from the thorns of the bushes and rushes to her own car parked on the street. She turns the car around, heading towards home via the closest supermarket for beer. Not wine today, even the thought of wine was making her stomach roll and contract all over again.

****

Getting home Bronagh rushes up the stairwell, dodging her neighbour who has drunkenly found a bed for a few hours on the stairs, the smell of stale urine pungent in the air around him. She gets into her flat and locks the door behind her, knowing from past experience that when that particular neighbour comes to, he can be disorientated, trying every door until he finds an unlocked one and somewhere softer to sleep. Dropping her handbag and jacket on the couch, she goes into the kitchen and opens up a beer, walking back into her living room she notices her house phone blinking, letting her know she had messages on the answering machine. She picks up the cordless receiver to check who had phoned, frowning when she sees Jane's number. She presses the buttons to listen to the message and sits on her couch, rummaging in her bag for her mobile at the same time.

"Bre, it's Jane, what the fuck have you been up to? Your page has went crazy. There is three lassies baying for your blood, calling you for everything. Call me when you get this, I didn't want to phone your mobile since you were at work... just phone me!" Jane's panicked tone and rapid talking send chills up and down her spine again. She pulls up her social media page on her mobile and has a look. Her stomach drops. She doesn't recognise any of the names of the people writing on her page, and none of them had any pictures so she couldn't see if she knew them. She tries to go onto their pages, but they had been set to private, not allowing her access. Closing down the app she pulls up her messages and fires one off to Max asking him to come round to hers, then she phones Jane. After the second ring Jane picks up.

"Bre, what the fuck?" Jane answers without even a hello.

"I don't know Jane, honestly, I don't know these people and I haven't done anything they are accusing me of. I haven't hit anyone or stolen anybody's boyfriend, unless..." Bronagh trails off, thinking of the blonde woman that keeps popping up wherever Max and her were, but she dismisses the thought. Nobody had seen her and Max kiss and she had only told

Gordon, who didn't know about the mystery woman. Jane brings her from her musings by speaking the words that Bronagh had just been thinking - to a certain extent.

"You thinking about that crazy bitch from last weekend?"

"Aye, but, why would she do that, and say they things? I mean I never even looked at her that night let alone smash her face off the table, and how would she know how many people I've slept with, and as for doing it for money, I am no fucking prostitute!" Bronagh's anger was building with every word she said. She really only swore when she was drunk or angry, which was why Jane was starting to laugh so hard.

"Oh, the sweary words are coming out now. Listen don't worry about it. It's just some crazy skanks who are trying to get a reaction, don't rise to it honey. Right, I better go. Stewart's just arrived." Just at that Bronagh hears her front door go, announcing Max's arrival.

"Yeah me too. Max has just arrived."

"Ooh, are youse finally getting it on?" Jane asks. Her tone is teasing and Bronagh blushes, but decides to keep her news to herself, for reasons she isn't exactly sure of.

"No, I messaged him after I read the posts on my page and he's came over. Anyway I've told you we're just friends and he's into blondes, so shush and go and deal with your own man." The friends say their goodbyes as Bronagh unlocks and opens her front door letting Max into her flat. He takes one step into the hallway and crushes Bronagh's lips with a kiss, his warm lips full of passion and concern for her. Eventually he pulls up and closes the door behind him with his foot, not letting go of her hands, looking deep into her emerald eyes.

"Hey you."

"Hey yourself." They grin at each other after their passionate, then their usual greeting. Max leads her into the living room, sitting her down on the couch next to him, still holding her hands.

"So, what's happening?" Bronagh lets go of one of Max's hands and pulls her phone out to show him. They sit in silence as Max reads then re-reads the posts and comments before looking back up at Bronagh. She can see anger dancing in his eyes and his jaw clenches and relaxes as he tries to control it.

"Who are these bitches?" Tears prick at the back of Bronagh's eyes as she shrugs.

"I don't know." She swallows back the emotion that's lodging itself in her throat. "Do you think it's connected to the messages I've been getting or that woman that has turned up the last few times we've been out?" Max blows out the rest of his anger; he can see Bronagh is fighting back tears and doesn't need him angry.

"I honestly don't know Bre, maybe. Can you copy it, the messages I mean, to keep just in case they are connected?" She nods and takes screenshots of all the messages, posts and texts before putting her phone back down and taking a mouthful of her beer. Max gazes at her, trying to work out why anyone would be harassing her like this. He decides to change the subject the only way he knows how to, his stomach.

"Right, I'm starving, you want to go out for food? My treat." He smiles at her and she scrunches her nose at him.

"No, you paid last night, so my treat tonight, but you're driving as Freddie stuttered again when I was coming home tonight." Max agrees and they leave the flat heading to the Chinese restaurant they went to the weekend before.

****

After one beer Elaine's stomach is settling but her mind is not. Fed up not knowing how her harassment is affecting Bronagh she decides to go and have a look for herself. She grabs her keys and heads out her front door, driving to Bronagh's flat in Parkhead.

She arrives in front of the flat just in time to see a black VW Golf pull out of the car park at the rear of the building with Max driving and Bronagh in the passenger seat. She ducks slightly in her seat so they don't see her as she again curses Bronagh for having everything she doesn't. Grabbing the chance she has been presented with, Elaine follows behind the Golf until they get to the restaurant. She pulls in, double parking across from them so she can watch them park and walk into the restaurant hand in hand and smiling at each other. A low growl leaves her throat and she pulls back into traffic looking for somewhere to park her Audi before heading in after them.

Opening the door Elaine steps in to the dullness of the restaurant blinking a few times to get her vision to adjust from the bright, still low hanging sun, and is welcomed by a handsome faced waiter. He escorts her to a table for one near the door that is still in view of the table she needs to see. He takes her drinks order and smiles, giving her puppy dog eyes. Any other day she would have had him at the end of his shift in the alley next to the restaurant, especially since he looks ten years younger than her twenty-nine, but not tonight. No tonight she has another man in her sights and a redhead to bring down.

****

Sitting at a different table from where they normally sit, Max and Bronagh face each other holding hands as they wait on their drinks order before heading up to the buffet for their first round of food. Once they are seated again and enjoying their starters, Max asks how things are at her new job, then he listens intently as Bronagh gushes about how everything has been great so far. Explaining everything she had done up to that day and everything she had left to do, holding Max's attention until he lifts his eyes. He looks over her shoulder and sees the blonde woman, his expression and his stomach fall at the same time. He tries to regain control of his expression before Bronagh notices but is too late. Bronagh's expression goes from happy and excited to worried and anxious.

"Max, what's wrong? You look like you've seen a ghost." He tries to smile but he knows that it hasn't reached his eyes, so he decides that telling the truth is his best course of action.

"Um, well," he pauses really not wanting to worry her, "I don't want you to freak out, but, I think that woman from the weekend is sitting behind you."

It's Bronagh's turn for her stomach and face to free fall. She doesn't want to turn round to see the woman, but needs to know if it is her or not. "Are you sure?"

Max shrugs then peers over again at the same time as Elaine looks back at him. She locks eyes with him, giving him a wave and a wink. Max nods his head imperceptibly before bringing his attention back to Bronagh and swallows.

"Oh aye, I'm sure. She's just waved at me, and winked." Bronagh's stomach falls another bit as it flips at the same time.

"Who is she?" her voice quivers. "What does she want?" Max takes her hand and squeezes, trying to support her as much as possible through his touch.

"I don't know Bre, but it doesn't matter. Don't let her get into your head." Bronagh nods, trying to make it look like she isn't affected by the woman's presence, but they both know she is. "And anyway," Max continues, "maybe she isn't your crazy person, maybe she's all mine. You know with all this irresistibility." Max smirks as he runs his hands over his body. Bronagh looks up at him. She knows he is trying to bring humour to the situation to take her mind off of everything and she is thankful for the distraction, so decides to counter his irresistibility with sarcasm.

"Really? I give you a few kisses and now you're god's gift to all women?" Max's eyes glint then turn serious.

"Not all women, but hopefully you?" He knows that it's a loaded question and that he has managed to turn the atmosphere from stressful to serious via humour in two seconds, but there is a part of him that has always wanted to ask that particular question. He stares into Bronagh's emerald green sparkling eyes as they grow wide at how fast the conversation turned, and holds his breath, counting his heart beats in his ears until she puts him out his misery with her answer.

"You always have been." She lowers her eyes and can feel her blush start at her toes as it rushes up her body and into her cheeks, until she thinks it might actually make the top of her head blow if it didn't calm down. Max smiles and lifts her chin up. He loves how Bronagh can't hide her emotions from her face. Still looking deep into her eyes his smile widens.

"You have been for me too." Blushing again Bronagh breaks eye contact, not able to cope with the emotions running around inside her. Max squeezes her hand again before dropping it so they can continue with their meal and letting the conversation continue about work and when would be best to get Freddie the Fiesta a new battery. All the time Max is aware of Elaine's eyes on them.

CHAPTER EIGHT

Elaine watches them. She knows the moment Bronagh learns of her presence, saw her shoulders bunch up, saw her back stiffen, and if she really concentrated she could almost hear Bronagh's rapid breathing as she thinks about why Elaine would be there at the same time as them... again. It made Elaine feel great to see Bronagh start to panic, and she really needed to feel great about something. Every now and then during the two hours they ate, she would catch Max's eye and would smile or wink at him, making him feel awkward and her hotter. He really is gorgeous, she thinks to herself, so much so Elaine could see them together, visualise everything she would have him do to her and everything she could do to him. She takes out her phone, firing off a quick message to Lee, asking or more like demanding him to come over to hers for a quickie. Putting her phone away she notices that Bronagh has left the table, leaving Max sitting on his own. Grabbing her chance she quickly makes her way over, sitting herself on the seat next to him.

"Hi there, I thought that was you. Imagine bumping into you again. Are you following me?" she purrs in his ear, her hands on his knee and shoulder. Max turns in his seat, removing his leg from her touch and brushing her hand from his shoulder.

"I'm sorry but who are you, and why are you talking to me?" He can't keep the disgust from his voice, there is just something about this woman and her touch that gives him chills.

"Aw don't be like that. You remember me from the last time, or are you still annoyed at my wee whoopsie when I spilt my drink on that *person*." She places her hands back on his chest and again he removes them, letting them drop, as his anger grows.

"That 'person' is my girlfriend, and I am more annoyed that you seem to be everywhere we are, so if you don't mind, please leave, now!" Elaine sees Bronagh return from the bathroom so grabs Max's hand placing it high up on her thigh, as she moves in to talk into his ear.

"You know you want this more than you want her!" She moves his hand further up until his fingers are skimming between her legs. As much as he tries to break free she holds on tighter with both hands, moving even closer she licks the shell of his ear before nipping his lobe. He jerks his head away and stands, the only thing he can think of doing to get her off of him. Standing with him she growls, letting go of his hands and grabs his face.

"I will have you." She sneers before kissing him fiercely, letting go just as Bronagh approaches them, having watched their encounter from afar. Elaine turns on her heel to face Bronagh with a smirk on her lips.

"Enjoy him while you can, bitch!" she spits at her, before flicking her hair and strutting off, throwing money onto the table she had been sitting at.

Dashing from behind the table Max grabs Bronagh. She is standing staring into the space that Elaine has just vacated, her mouth slightly agape. Panic runs itself up his spine.

"Bre, honestly she came up to me, I did nothing. I was pushing her away, telling her to leave. Honest. Bre, Bre did she say something to you? Bre tell me." Max's voice is frantic. Bronagh brings her vision back to him.

"Can we leave, please? I want to go home... please just take me home." Her eyes are pleading with him and Max nods, lifting both their jackets. He pays the bill then leads her out of the restaurant holding her hand tight in his. They get into his Golf and drive, not seeing Elaine or her Audi TT a few cars behind them.

Max parks his car behind the flats in one of the visitor spaces and walks round opening the passenger door to help

Bronagh out. She hadn't uttered a sound on the drive home, staring straight ahead for the entire journey. He escorts her up the three flights of stairs to her flat, closing and locking the door behind them. Bronagh sits on her couch, not sure what else to do, and Max sits next to her, putting his hands on her shoulders turning her slightly to face him.

"Bre are you okay?" As she looks up at him her tears start and she can't stop them as they flow down her cheeks unchecked.

"Max –" She sobs pulling him to her and holding on. He holds on just as tight until her body stops shaking and her sobs subside. "She said I had to enjoy you while I could. What does she mean by that?" Max shakes his head and shrugs his shoulders, not sure what to say to her.

"I don't know, but I'm pretty sure it's my choice who I'm with and I'm with you. After all these years of not having you, I am not letting you go. Not ever if I have my own way."

Bronagh closes her eyes, trying to take in what Max means. Opening her eyes she looks straight at him, fear giving way to excitement that has started to course through her veins. "Are you saying... forever?"

Max nods, and takes a deep breath. "Aye, if that's what you want... if you'll have me?" Bronagh nods her head slowly, still not entirely convinced of what Max is saying, and he can see her uncertainty in her expression, so he tries again.

"Bre, it's you; it's always been you. I've always wanted you." Confusion clouds her eyes.

"But I'm not blonde, or thin."

Max scrunches his eyebrows in confusion. "What?"

"It's blondes you're into, skinny blondes. Every female you've ever went home with has been a blonde, and thin and... and I'm not blonde, or thin... that's why I never stood a chance." Bronagh sags in his arms. Max flinches like he has been punched in the stomach. He never once stopped to think that she would notice who he went home with, but now he understood how hard it must have been for her to witness his flings and one night stands. He knew it would have killed him if she went home with anyone. He had mostly stuck to blondes with little or no shape, purely because they weren't Bronagh. None of them measured up to Bronagh, but then again he hadn't expected them to, they were a means to an end.

"I, Bre, they... they weren't you." He sighs. "I think I was trying to make myself like women who were nothing like you, the polar opposite to you, trying to wean myself from you, like coming off a drug, but it never worked. Nobody came near to how beautiful and amazing you are. I never fancied them, never wanted them, really, not the way I have always wanted you. Your curves are every man's wet dream. They are my perfect dream!" A sob escapes her throat, for years she has wished and dreamt and prayed for Max to say these things to her and now he is, she can't believe him. She straightens her back, trying to find confidence to say her next words.

"Prove it!" She holds herself straight as Max's mouth gapes open.

"Eh... what?" He stutters, too stunned to say much more.

"Prove it's always been me you've wanted. Prove it's me you want now and, if it's true, forever. Max, make love to me." Desperate to do just that, his manhood surges to life, but he doesn't want to take advantage of Bronagh's emotions. The silence seems endless to Bronagh and she stands to leave the living room, knowing it was too much to believe that Max really wanted her after all the years of being friends and all the gorgeous blondes. Max stands at the same time, grasping her hand and sweeping her into his arms, crashing his lips onto hers, holding her so close to his chest not even light could get between them. He breaks the kiss but keeps his lips on her skin, whispering in her ear as he presses kisses all over her ear and neck.

"Bre, it's always been you, and there is nothing I want to do more than take you to bed and have you all night, but –" he feels her sag at the word 'but', and holds her closer still, letting her feel his full arousal against her leg. "I need to know we are making love tonight because it's right for us and not because some crazy bint has gotten into your head." Bronagh pulls back knowing her decision was a bit of both, but wanting him all the same.

"I want you Max, I need you. I need to know it's me that you want." She can't believe the confidence she has started to get with her body as she stands in Max's embrace and grinds herself between his legs before pulling back, taking Max by the hand and leading them both into her bedroom.

****

Elaine followed Max and Bronagh back to her flat, the fire and spite inside her making her stomach roll again. She saw them both go inside and decides to wait ten more minutes looking constantly from the front door of the flats to the window she thinks should be Bronagh's, willing Max to leave so she could seduce him properly, but it's to no avail. Her anger getting the better of her, she grabs the glass nail file she had been using to scratch Bronagh's car from her bag and rams it into the driver's side rear tyre. She returns to her car and drives to Lee's house, breaking yet another of their rules.

Stopping in front of the house of her lover, she pulls her phone back out. Noticing that he hasn't replied to her earlier message, she punches the speed dial button for his mobile. After four rings Lee answers, his tone is panicked as he hisses down the line.

"Elaine what the hell are you doing phoning me?" She puts on her best poor me voice.

"I needed to see you my darling. Even if just for a second," she pleads.

"Well I can't get away at this time of night Elaine. We can get together at the weekend." Lee is annoyed at her contacting him, and Elaine can hear it, but she won't be put off.

"No!" The word comes out harsh as her anger gets the better of her. She takes a deep breath and tries to calm down. "No, darling, the weekend is too far away. Why don't you come out and put something in the bin, we could have a quickie in the garden?" She hears the gasp of realisation as Lee peers out of his bedroom window.

"Are you outside my house?" Elaine giggles.

"Uhuh."

"What the fuck Elaine, are you mad? What if my wife was to see or hear. I thought we said this was for pleasure, no worries, no strings, no commitment." She growls at him, her anger pitching again.

"It is, I just have an itch I need scratched by someone other than myself!" She lowers her tone so she is practically begging, but Lee stays strong.

"No Elaine, not tonight, or any night this week and most definitely not in my back garden with my wife in the house. Now go home."

"NO!" She shouts, then regains a semblance of her control. "You said you'd help me through this awful time of my life and now you're backing out and leaving me." Her anger was coming through her voice again. She hears Lee huff and she thinks she has him on the hook, until she hears his answer.

"I don't care, Elaine. I am at home with my wife. Now if you don't leave now I'll phone the police... oh, and don't contact me again until I contact you, okay?" He doesn't wait for her answer before cancelling the call leaving Elaine sitting in her car with the knowledge that she is all alone.

"You bastard!" she screams as she throws her phone back into her bag. Burning the rubber on her tyres, she screeches away back to her own dark and empty house, on her own again.

Once there she proceeds to get very drunk, again, passing out on her couch spilling her last beer all over herself as she slumps down.

CHAPTER NINE

Holding Bronagh after making love to her had to be one of the best feelings in the world Max thinks to himself. They had given themselves to each other entirely after Bronagh walked them into her bedroom, only breaking contact for Max to sheath himself in latex. He always knew Bronagh's curves were gorgeous, but to have them in his hands and pressed against him was more than he could possibly dream of. He held her, stroking her arms until she eventually fell asleep, her breathing evening out, then he continued to hold her, not wanting to let go in case she disappeared. Sleep evaded him as worry pressed itself on his mind. Worry about all the nasty messages and the crazy blonde, trying and failing to work out if they could be connected or if it was all a huge coincidence. Eventually exhaustion takes over and sleep comes, but with it comes dreams of losing Bronagh and the blonde woman taking her place.

Bronagh wakes early in the morning to Max thrashing about in bed. She holds him close, almost lying on top of him, whispering his name trying to soothe his angst. He opens his eyes, letting out a ragged breath. He grabs her and kisses her soundly on the lips, pulling her properly on top of him. She pulls up leaning on her elbows to look in his eyes, seeing fear mixed with relief there.

"What's wrong?" she asks as Max, who is still breathing hard, caresses her face softly.

"Just a bad dream. I'm okay now I've woken up next to you, now come here." He grabs her down onto him again igniting every nerve in her body and making her desperate for more.

After making love again they bathe together, cleaning each other, caressing each other until they hear the alarm clock go off in the bedroom. Knowing they didn't have time for another round they climb from the bath and dry. An hour later they leave Bronagh's flat together, stopping to kiss goodbye at Max's Golf which is parked next to Freddie the Fiesta. Max opens his door to climb inside as Bronagh turns to go back to her flat when he shouts her back. She turns back smiling, thinking he couldn't leave without another kiss, until she sees his face.

"Bre, you've got a flat tyre."

"What? How?" They both move over to the offending tyre, and Max is first to notice the gouge. All the air leaves his body.

"Someone's stabbed it." Bronagh gasps standing up and going round to inspect the rest of the car, finding the scratches on the other side.

"Max look." Her voice catches in her throat, as he makes his way round the car to where Bronagh is standing. Seeing the scratches he puts his fingers to them feeling them with his fingernails to check how deep they were.

"They're deep, and deliberate." Bronagh can't keep her emotions in check and lets her tears fall.

"Why?" is all she can choke out before Max pulls her into his chest, kissing the top of her head.

"I don't know honey, but you're not going to be on your own until we find out who and why, okay?" Bronagh nods and they both go back up to her flat. Max phones his boss explaining that he would be late in and why, then he takes Bronagh to the police station before running her to work.

****

Waking up on her couch, Elaine tries to move but every bone and muscle in her body screams at her due to the way she has been slumped over for the full night, and her head was thumping and her stomach rolling again. She really needed to ease up on the drinking she thinks to herself. Getting up and moving she makes herself a coffee and checks her phone, hoping that Lee had contacted her, but knowing he probably hadn't, and wouldn't. She had broken too many of their rules, her rules. There wasn't anything from Lee, but she smiles as she notices that Stewart has accepted her friend request. Opening up a private message, Elaine starts a conversation with him, telling him how great he is looking and asking what he has been up to. Much to her delight Stewart replies almost immediately, explaining that he's not really been doing much, and how lovely it was to hear from her after so long. Elaine smiles into her coffee as she continues to converse, realising that she might not need Lee any more, not to have sex with or to help bring down Bronagh. They make arrangements to meet for lunch that day, neither of them mentioning Stewart's relationship with Jane.

After her conversation with Stewart, Elaine jumps into the shower, the hot water cascading over her, easing her hangover and making her feel more human again. She climbs out after ten minutes and takes her time getting dried. Moisturising every inch of skin so it feels silky smooth, then, she turns her attention to her hair, taking her time to blow dry and straighten it to perfection before moving onto her make-up, then picking out an outfit, making sure her look said sexy without being slutty. There was time for that later. She knew Stewart had a girlfriend (and that she was friends with her nemesis), but she didn't know why he didn't mention her when they were chatting earlier, and she didn't care. She was planning on using him for his body and his knowledge of Bronagh.

Midday comes around and Elaine is ready to leave. She decides to take her car and stay off the alcohol, at least for the afternoon, plus she wants to stop by Bronagh's flat, or her work if she'd managed to get the flat tyre changed, to scratch up the car some more.

Starting off at Bronagh's flat Elaine grins when she sees the Fiesta still parked with the flat tyre she gave it the day before. She allows herself a small victory dance in her car at the thought of Bronagh coming out of her flat to see her car. The panic and fear that must have flooded her system. It gives

Elaine a thrill, just what she needs when she is about to go to lunch with a sexy man. She gets out of her car and sashays over to the Fiesta, removing the glass nail file from her bag to inflict yet another scratch, counting up how many days she has been following her rival.

****

In the House of Fun basement office Gordon tries his hardest to get Bronagh out of her melancholy mood. She had explained that her car had had a flat tyre that morning, but he knew there was more to it than that. Not wanting to push too much he left her to her work and her musings until lunch time. Come half twelve though Gordon can't stand the look in Bronagh's eyes any more. He takes over one of his famous coffees and places it in front of her then takes the seat next to her.

"Hey sweet pea, you've been in a funk all day. You okay? Anything you want to talk about? I'm all ears if you need." Bronagh looks up at her new friend. She knew she had been in her own head all morning, thinking about the blonde bitch last night and then the flat tyre and scratches her and Max found on her car that morning had her overthinking every last moment of her life. She had tried to push all her thoughts to the side, but her mind wasn't for it.

"Hmm, aye, well... " She shrugs, trying to smile.

"Problems in paradise?"

"What? No — no, that's fine, we're good, real good." Her eyes shine for a second before going back to the dull worried glaze that had been there all day. "No it's —" emotion catches in her throat as she thinks again about everything that has been happening to her. "I've been getting some nasty messages on my phone and through social media sites, then this morning I came out to find my car tyre had been stabbed, deliberately." Gordon gasps.

"Do you know who's doing it?" She shakes her head, fear dancing in her eyes.

"No, but for the past week or so there has been a blonde woman turning up wherever me and Max are when we're out. She keeps hitting on Max and being bitchy to me, but I don't know if they are connected or not. We went to the police this morning. They are going to look into it, but they say there isn't much they can do about it as we don't know who is doing it and it could just be a coincidence with the blonde." Ice runs down Gordon's spine at the mention of a crazy blonde woman. Surely it couldn't be the same crazy blonde that was sacked from the job Bronagh just filled, he thinks to himself. He dismisses his thoughts about the connection, but his gut keeps at him.

"Hey, listen it'll be okay, and I'm sure that big strapping lad of yours will protect you." Bronagh smiles properly for the first time that day, at Gordon's description about her boyfriend.

"Aye, he is looking after me. He says he's not letting be on my own at night, and he drove me here this morning. Thankfully he was there this morning and was the one that found my tyre flat and the scratches." Gordon's eyebrows reach his hairline with this piece of news.

"Oh, so he was at your place this morning?" Bronagh blushes at her unwitting confession.

"Aye. He stayed the night. We went out for dinner last night and the crazy blonde turned up again, trying to get Max to feel her up." Gordon gasps at Bronagh's description of the night before. Bronagh shakes her head at the memory. "Honestly you should've seen her an' the way she was grabbing at Max's hand, it was desperate." Another chill runs up his spine as he thinks of the blonde who he'd worked with before. "So, we went back to mine and... well, one thing led to another. It was all very emotional." Tears spring to Bronagh's eyes as she thinks about the night before, then a smile breaks out. Gordon settles into his seat, probing her for more information, bringing Bronagh from the darkness she has been worrying about all morning and making her giggle like a school girl. The friends spend the rest of the day in their usual coffee-filled way of work and banter.

****

Stewart had initially mentioned going to the Chinese restaurant that the friends usually frequented, but Elaine had shot down that suggestion, after being there the night before making herself known to Max and Bronagh, she didn't want to return and raise suspicions. They agree to meet in the city centre and find a pub there.

Knowing females should always be fashionably late and remembering from school that Stewart lived on his own time, Elaine made sure she was ten minutes late. As it turns out they both arrive at their meeting place of Buchanan Street Underground at the same time, greeting each other with a casual hug and a chaste kiss on each cheek. They agree on a Thai restaurant and head towards Nelson Mandela Place. They get settled in at the table they have been escorted to and order drinks, then they both study the menu, a strange awkward silence growing between them. A few minutes later they order their food and Elaine notices her heart is racing, trying to beat itself out of its cage and she isn't exactly sure why, even though she is highly attracted to the man sitting across from her. He is tall and lean, his ear length dark blonde hair always looked just the right amount of messy. He was the picture perfect surfer dude even though there isn't a sea or an ocean near him, but she is used to having gorgeous men in her company, so she dismisses that idea then wonders if it is due to his relationship status. Again she quickly dismisses the thought. She has been the 'other woman' before. In fact she is normally the extracurricular activity for the men she has had in her bed, and that's how she likes it; all the fun with none of the hassle. The reason for her nervousness unknown, Elaine pushes all thoughts aside and concentrates on being sexy and making Stewart putty in her hands.

"So," Elaine squeaks, her vocal chords obviously not getting the sexy message her brain had sent them. She clears her throat and tries again. "Have you kept in touch with anyone else from school?" Stewart looks up at Elaine and smirks. He never thought he would ever see her nervous. She was always full of confidence at school. Confident in herself, with her body and her ability to get any male she set her sights on, even to the point of rumours of an affair with a teacher in her sixth year.

"No, you're the only person I've spoken to since we left. Elaine." He pauses and takes a deep breath before locking eyes with her and continuing, "You know I'm in a relationship with someone?"

She nods. "And?" she counters. Stewart shrugs just as a waitress returns to their table with their food. Their conversation stops until she leaves, telling them she hoped they enjoyed their meal. As soon as the waitress leaves the table and them alone once again, Stewart starts talking again.

"She thinks it's serious, I'm not quite there, yet. I'm thinking one last hurrah will make up my mind for me, so if you're into that idea, and me, then I would like to have lots of fun with you. If not then we can have a nice meal and go our own way." Elaine's heart speeds up again. This time she is putting it down to the excitement of getting what she wants and the promise of having sex with the gorgeous man sitting across from her.

"Now the thought of fun sounds like something I would like to have," she purrs, her sexiness finding its way back to her voice. Stewart smirks again.

"Good, now eat up and we can go back to mine. I'm not seeing my girlfriend tonight so we will have all evening to have fun!" He winks at her and she grins.

CHAPTER TEN

Bronagh's week had continued with more of the same hassle. Max changed the vandalised tyre and she continued to check her car every day, morning and night, and at some point every day there's a new scratch. By Friday she realises whoever is doing it is counting out the days, using a tally mark for each day. Five tally marks for the five days of being harassed and five days at her new job. She wonders if it is all connected, and makes a mental note to ask Gordon. She had made sure she was taking photos each day and screenshots of all the messages she was receiving. The messages had continued, getting at least one a day, and they normally consisted of just one word, ranging from bitch to cunt and every other disgusting name, and back again. Max had been coming over to Bronagh's every night after work so she wasn't on her own and she phoned him when she reached work. He had wanted her to move in with him and said he would drive her to and from work every day, but she put her foot down on that idea. She had told him she wouldn't be responsible for him either losing his job, or at the very least him losing money from his own work. He eventually agreed to her driving herself as long as he could spend the nights with her. That wasn't really a hardship for Bronagh with their new relationship status. They made love every night, falling asleep in each other's arms exhausted but sated. Thankfully this meant all thoughts of stalkers, messages and vandalism were always far from Bronagh's thoughts when she fell asleep, although not always from Max's, as more nightmares took over some of his nights.

That night Max had brought in fish suppers for dinner again, and they sat eating, drinking beer, talking and feeling at ease in each other's company.

"Is it tomorrow you've got your first party?"

Bronagh smiles. It amazes her how much information Max remembers, most men just nod and grunt in all areas of conversation and never take heed of anything that was getting said.

"Yes, it starts at one, but I want to be there for about ten. I've got some more setting up to do. The cake and balloons and other things still need to be picked up." Max is nodding listening to every word.

"You nervous?" She puts her plate down and picks up her beer.

"Aye. But I'm organised, so as long as I get everything there before twelve and Freddie behaves, I should be fine." Bronagh cocks her eyebrow at Max and he snorts out a laugh, holding his hands up as if in defence.

"I know, I know, I will get him a battery." Bronagh shakes her head.

"I didn't mean it as a hint, kinda. He has been starting fine for the past few days." Max looks turn more serious.

"I know, but he still needs one." Bronagh takes the plates through to the kitchen as she hears Max laughing to himself, in a more light-hearted mood than he was seconds ago.

"What's up with you?" she asks as she walks away.

"You've got me talking about that bloody car like he's a human!" Bronagh snorts.

"You know you love him," she shouts through the adjoining French doors. Max stalks into the kitchen leaning on the door frame of the open door, his eyes flaring with heat. Bronagh turns round when she hears the door frame creak with him leaning on it and leans herself against the counter. Max stalks his way further into the kitchen taking his time to reach her, stopping when they are toe to toe. Bronagh gasps as he puts his hands on her hips pulling them towards his.

"I only love that car because he belongs to you and you love it, but I love you more than I love anything." Before she can react Max's lips are on hers, kissing her hard, so she does the only thing she can think of and kisses him back, just as hard. Max runs his hands from the curve of her waist under the vest top she was wearing to the curve of her breast, his hand gliding over her soft skin as Bronagh pushes herself into his palm encouraging his hand to get to its destination. Finding her nipple with his finger, Max starts to pluck, flick and roll it with just enough pressure to cause Bronagh to whimper. Desperate to feel every inch of her boyfriend, Bronagh fumbles to get to his belt and the button fly of his jeans. Max smiles into her lips and he stops kissing her, pulling back to look at her.

"Are you desperate?" There is a slight joking to his tone, but underneath there is some worry. Bronagh digs him in his ribs with her fingers.

"Getting you like this after all those years? Yes a bit, that's just how you get me," she says truthfully. The thought of her being desperate to get him fills Max with love and makes him harder than he ever thought possible, but there is also a bit of him that is frightened. Does she think this is just a fling for him? Did she not believe what he just said to her? He brings his hand back to her waist and makes sure she is looking straight at him, understanding every word he was about to utter.

"Bre you've got me! I'm not going anywhere. I'm here. With you. Forever."

Bronagh's hands had stopped in their bid to free him and were now resting on his freed manhood, as she searched his eyes, making sure that what he was saying was the truth.

"Forever?"

He nods, giving her another kiss. "Forever."

She nods, seeing nothing but love in his eyes as she closes hers to kiss him again, this time slowing everything down, knowing they have forever to be with each other, they move into the bedroom. Max lowers Bronagh onto her bed, running his hands up and down her side until he pulls off her top. Sitting back on his heels Max stops and looks at his girlfriend, relishing in her beauty and the fact that they were together. Bronagh starts to feel insecure under his stare.

"Max..."

Max grins. "You are so beautiful Bre."

Her insecurities melt as he kisses his way down her neck to her breasts. The lovers enjoy each other's bodies, writhing together until they both climax loudly. Afterwards Max holds Bronagh tight, drawing lazy circles on her shoulder. He feels a puddle of liquid growing on his bare chest so gives her shoulder a squeeze making a sob escape from her lips, which is followed by a very unladylike sniff.

"Hey you, what's the tears for?" Bronagh sniffs again, this one even less ladylike than the last and sits up slightly so she can look at him.

"I never thought this would happen, you, me, us." She motions between them before continuing. "Then you went and said words like 'beautiful' and 'love' and 'forever', making it real, but —." Max tenses starting to think the worst, then makes himself relax knowing how she feels about him without her actually saying the words. He pulls her up fully so they are facing each other.

"Listen, I know how you feel because I feel the same. I know I used the 'L' word and it's still really early days in our new relationship, but I have loved you forever and I am going to love you for forever more." She nods then shakes her head as she swipes the palm of her hand at him, slapping him on his biceps.

"Oi, what was that for?" Max asks with confusion.

"Because you didn't let me talk or let me answer you before you ravaged me." Max's eyes spark with humour.

"Ravaged?" he asks with a smirk and Bronagh nods, stifling the laugh that is threatening to escape over the emotion in her throat.

"Yes, ravaged, but that's okay, because I love you too." This time his eyes go wide. Hearing her say those four words made him let out a small sigh of relief.

"I don't think I wanted to give you time to answer. I was frightened of your reply," he tells her honestly. Bronagh is shocked at his insecure statement.

"Max, you've got me! I'm not going anywhere. I'm here. With you. Forever." She repeats his words back to him.

"Forever?"

"Forever," she whispers against his lips before she kisses him with every ounce of love she has for him.

After satisfying each other again, Bronagh falls asleep in Max's arms feeling happy, content, satisfied, safe and loved.

Saturday morning comes around, the day of the diamond anniversary, Bronagh's first party as the planner. She wakes at six thirty and knows she won't get any more sleep. She climbs out of bed as quietly as she can, trying not to disturb Max, and pads down the long hall to her kitchen. She puts the kettle on for what she knew would be her first of many coffees that day. She knew she had everything organised as she had spent most of the day before bouncing between the venue and the office, but she just wanted everything to be perfect. She had become very fond of the elderly couple over the week through talking to them about how they would like their party, and knowing this was her first with the party planners and that she had been given only a week to get it going her way, she really needed it to go smoothly. Taking a sip of her freshly made coffee Bronagh hears Max move about down the hall. The sound brings back memories of the night before. Again her emotions threaten to overtake her as she thinks of Max's words of love and forever, then, she allows herself to remember every touch and kiss they'd shared and she smiles to herself.

"You have got a very dirty smile on your face, Miss White, wish to let me in on what's going through that mind of yours?" Max's husky morning voice brings Bronagh from her x-rated memories and she blushes.

"Have I? Well I don't think I need to tell you, you were there when we made the memories." Max has made his way over to her and leans down kissing her gently on the lips.

"Hmm, and a good memory it is, but I hope we will be making more of them!"

"Me too." Bronagh blushes again, moving up onto her tipoes to give him another kiss. Max lifts the cup from her hand and takes a sip from it before giving her it back. She watches his every move, stunned that he could steal her coffee, then smiles as she realises how relaxed he is standing in just his boxer briefs and tattoos in her kitchen.

"What're you doing up this early? I mean technically it's still night time," Max asks, bringing Bronagh from her drooling over the way his tattoos move over his muscles.

"What? No it's not. You're up at this time every morning. Anyway, I woke up and couldn't get back to sleep. I've got too much going through my mind and too much to do. I really don't want anything going wrong today of all days!" Max nods his understanding.

"I know, but today will go fine. You are an amazing party planner no matter how much time you've had to organise it. Plus, I'm coming with you, even if I just sit outside in the car, I want to be there." Bronagh's heart swells, then panic hits her as Max continues to talk. "I want today to go well for you too, and I want to be there to see you being a success, so just as a precaution, even though the police don't think it's anything serious, I want to be nearby... just in case anything or anyone crazy happens." He can see the panic starting to show in Bronagh's face so before she can say anything he puts his fingers to her mouth, stopping her words on her lips.

"Nothing is going to happen. I just want to be there to support you, okay?" Bronagh nods. "So, are you just going to stand there panicking over everything that is already organised, or are you coming back to bed to make more memories?" She looks at the folder sitting on the counter top next to her mug of coffee, then back at the man she now calls her boyfriend standing in front of her with the sexiest grin she has ever seen and back again, before grabbing his hand and heading back to her bedroom.

CHAPTER ELEVEN

Elaine and Stewart had enjoyed each other's company throughout lunch, filling each other in about their lives since they both left high school and the last time they had seen each other. Once it was out in the open that they both wanted a sexual relationship, at least for a while, they both ramped up the sexual innuendos and caressing of each other. Elaine's favourite being running her foot up the inside of Stewart's leg until she reached where she wanted to be, his crotch. Both feeling hot, they finish their meal and head back to Elaine's car. The drive home was just as hot and heavy as the restaurant as Stewart used the time to stroke Elaine's thigh, not going too far up as they didn't want to crash her Audi TT.

Once back at Stewart's flat, they both gave up with the teasing and started to attack each other like animals, both of them ripping at the other's clothes until they are both naked and panting hard. Stewart leads them to his bedroom, pushing Elaine roughly onto her back on his unmade bed crawling over her. He rakes his eyes over every inch of her flushed naked body, as she lies there watching him.

"Like what you see?" she purrs at him. Stewart drags his eyes back to her face with a self-satisfied grin on his face.

"Oh aye." His voice is gravelly, "I've been wanting this since high school." Elaine gives him her own grin as she pushes her hips up to meet his fully erect penis and pulls his hips down, digging her nails into his skin.

"Well, what're you waiting on? I'm clean and on the pill, take me... NOW!" That was all Stewart needed to hear as he thrusts himself into her, loving the feeling of being inside her.

After copious amounts of alcohol and each other, again, they both fall asleep. Hours later Elaine wakes up feeling far too hot and not in a good sexual way. She looks round and sees Stewart draped over her and it feels like he had his heating on at a hundred degrees. She shifts slowly one tiny inch at a time until she is free and can escape to the toilet. She's not used to sleeping next to anyone, and she is definitely not used being with anyone the next again morning. Because of this, she is unsure of how to proceed. The flat is small so it's not long before she finds herself in the kitchen. She lifts the kettle checking if it needs water and starts it on to boil, before hunting for cups and the rest of the ingredients required for a coffee. Minutes later, with coffee in hand, Elaine moves from the kitchen into the small and very messy living room. Sitting on the only empty seat on the couch she retrieves her phone from her bag. She wanted to get her daily message to Bronagh done before the party started, hoping to put her on edge before she even gets started.

Today's the day bitch, I hope you fuck this up!

Satisfied with her message, Elaine phones the receptionist, just to double check the details, making sure they were still the same as before.

"Good morning House of Fun party planners." The irritating voice of the receptionist rings through the phone. Elaine grimaces, she really hates that woman's voice.

"Sue, hi, it's Elaine. I was wondering if everything for today's party is ready? I mean, I just wanted to double check that everything was going to plan with it, as you know, it was my party to plan after all." Her voice all sweetness and concern.

"Aw, Elaine, it's so nice to hear from you and it's just like you to still worry about others." Elaine rolls her eyes, removing the phone from her ear for a moment so she could have a second of respite from the screech of the receptionist's voice. "And yes, all the main details are the same, Bronagh just added to your planning."

"That's fantastic Sue. Well I better go, don't want you getting into trouble with Erin. Thanks again, bye." She cancels the call before the other woman has a chance to reply, or start another conversation. She puts her phone on the arm of the couch and starts rapping her fingernails over the screen, processing the information and plotting her day. She looks up from her pondering as Stewart walks into the room, wearing only his boxer briefs. Elaine looks him up and down, eyeing every inch of his naked body as he stands in front of her and grins.

"I made myself a coffee, I hope you don't mind." She says, her heart rate increasing and going crazy, and again she can't understand why he is having such an effect on her. She puts it down to being in a new situation, and carries on talking after clearing her throat. "I don't normally see the men I've fucked two nights in a row, but I have a feeling I'm going to be celebrating tonight, so how do you fancy getting together again tonight?" Looking him up and down again she licks her lips, letting him know what exactly would be happening again, and Stewart's grin grows as does other parts of his anatomy.

"Sounds like it might be fun! Why not." It's Elaine's turn to smile as she unfolds herself from the couch and sidles up to him.

"Oh it will be, I promise," she purrs in his ear before nibbling on the lobe, "I need to go just now so I can get done what I need to, so there will be something to celebrate." Stewart grabs her, crushing his lips to her, deepening it until all she can feel is his tongue in her mouth and his stubble grazing her skin, then his phone chirps to life, interrupting them.

"Hold that thought," he growls at her, then grabs his phone answering it gruffly. "What?" There is silence as he listens to the other person, "No, I need to cancel tonight, something has come up." More silence before he growls back, "I know I was busy last night, but something has come up and I'm going to be busy again tonight!" His tone was getting more exasperated "Listen Jane, we don't need to be to joined at the hip and we can have nights that we're not together." Elaine gives a small laugh when she realises it's his girlfriend on the phone and he is cancelling plans to spend the night with her. Perfect, she thinks as she starts licking, nibbling and kissing every bare inch of his skin, starting with his bare chest and going lower. Stewart hisses the lower she goes, trying to keep his tone level. "Right Jane, I need to go... fine, Sunday... aye, Sunday, bye." Cancelling the call he throws his phone onto the chair next to them, letting Elaine finish her descent down him.

****

Half nine and Bronagh is sitting ready and waiting on Max. Once they are both ready they climbed into Max's Golf, Bronagh not wanting to risk the Fiesta breaking down in the middle of the day due to the unreliable battery.

They pulled up at the bakery first, collecting the main anniversary cake and what felt like a thousand, but was actually only two hundred, cupcakes then they went onto the florist to collect the balloons, table arrangements and bouquets of flowers the couple were handing out as gifts. Driving back to the venue Bronagh was going over her list of everything that had been done and everything that was yet to be done for the umpteenth time. Max knew to keep his mouth shut about her near obsessive list checking, feeling the anxiety and stress coming from his girlfriend in waves.

They pulled up at the venue and Max jumps out, going round to open Bronagh's door. She looks up at him bewildered.

"We're here." He motions to the building and Bronagh smiles.

"Sorry, I'm a bit preoccupied."

Max laughs. "I can tell. Right you go in and get whatever sorted and I'll start bringing everything in, and you can order me about and tell me where to put everything." She gives him a kiss, then places her forehead just under his chin, taking a moment to breathe. He puts his arms around her silently giving her strength. They work together for the next hour, Max doing everything he is told, placing everything exactly where he is told to, or at least he thinks it's exactly where he is told to until Bronagh fixes it. He doesn't take offence to her nit picking, understanding what the day means to her.

Come noon the hall is looking perfect, exactly as she had planned and sketched. The couple and their children are first to arrive, they gasp at all the work Bronagh had put in. They spot the copies of the old photographs she had pinned to the wall and go over talking excitedly about who was in them and where they were taken. Before finding their seats they come over to thank Bronagh for all her hard work. She tells them it was her pleasure and it really was.

Max sidles up to her, as she greets other people arriving, standing close enough that no one else could hear them.

"Hey you."

She turns and smiles at him. "Hey yourself."

"Everything looks amazing, gorgeous. You doin' okay?"

She takes a deep breath then nods. "Aye, for now. Ask me in five hours and I'll let you know." She blows out her breath and gives him a chaste kiss.

"Okay, well, you go and do your thing and I'll find a corner to sit in and read my new book."

She nods giving him a squeeze before letting him walk out into the corridor to find a spare seat to occupy, leaving Bronagh to do what she does best, making sure everyone has a good time, and the couple get the party they paid for and desperately want.

During the setting up, Bronagh had organised for a small stage to be placed at the sound system with a microphone on it. At one o'clock she brings everyone's attention to the stage, explaining that the couple would like to have their 'first dance', the same first dance they had at their wedding reception sixty years ago. Everyone stands and claps as they take the floor for their dance. On the second song they are joined by their son and daughter and their partners, and finally Bronagh asks that everyone join them to dance for the third song of the day. As she stands on the stage watching all of the couples in the room dance to the romantic music her heart flutters with hope that one day it would be her and Max. Noise coming from the corridor brings her from her wedding fantasy. Checking that the sound system will continue playing the couple's play list of chosen music, she steps down from the stage and makes her way towards the door, and the noise, her smile plastered to her face as she prays that whatever the commotion is, it isn't anything to do with her or the party.

Arriving in the corridor Bronagh stops dead. Frozen to the spot as her eyes fall onto the crazy blonde trying to get past Max, while placing her hands all over his chest. She forces her feet to move. Pulling all her strength into herself to face this crazy person once and for all.

CHAPTER TWELVE

"Can I help you?" she asks in what she hopes is a tone that's strong and says 'I'm in control'.

Elaine turns her attention to Bronagh and snorts in disgust at her presence.

"I don't think so. You see I am the person who should be running this party, so I will be taking over from here!" Elaine steps forward, side stepping Max and going straight towards Bronagh, but she holds her ground, not letting her fear show.

"No, I think you'll find I organised this party through House of Fun party planners. Now could you explain exactly who you are and why you're here?" Max stands staring at the two women, amazed at the bare faced cheek of the blonde woman and proud of his girlfriend for her strength. Elaine takes a step back as if she'd been slapped, annoyed that Bronagh hadn't worked out who she was.

"I'm the person you stole the job from so you could play at parties!" Everything starts to click into place for Bronagh and Max; all the messages and this woman turning up wherever they were. 'Is this woman stalking me?' Bronagh thinks quickly to herself, then pushes the thought aside, knowing she hasn't time to worry about it at that moment.

"Ah, so you're Elaine are you?" She looks Elaine up and down before continuing, "I've heard a lot about you, and not all good. Now I am sorry you lost your job, but that had nothing to do with me. So if you don't mind I would like you to leave as this party is by invitation only and you have definitely not been invited." Elaine's eyes go wide. She expected Bronagh to cower in front of her, and the fact that she is facing up to her is causing her anger to rise. "And while you're here can I also make a point of telling you to leave me and my boyfriend alone, or I will be in contact with the police again, this time with a name." Elaine snarls. The thought that Bronagh had already been in contact with the police and that she would go back to them makes Elaine snap, and she starts screaming in Bronagh's face.

"You fuckin' bitch, you have everything that should be mine. The job, the hunk, everything, and I want it back. I will have it back! All of it, every last fuckin' bit of it!" Max dashes forward, getting himself in between Elaine and Bronagh, placing his hand in the air in a stop gesture. At the same time the couple's daughter makes her way towards them from the party.

"What is THAT woman doing here?" she demands. Bronagh turns to her, panic zipping up her spine. She swallows the panic away and walks towards the woman.

"I am really sorry for the intrusion, I have no idea why Elaine has turned up but she is just leaving." Bronagh turns back to Elaine, her jaw tight like it was set in steel with anger, "NOW!"

Having regained her composure, Elaine snorts a laugh at the small group. She walks past Max and leans in to whisper into Bronagh's ear.

"Enjoy your life cow, it might all come tumbling down round about you." Then she turns on her heel and leaves, swaying her hips and flicking her hair and laughing manically as she goes. Bronagh gasps, swallows then takes a deep breath. She turns to face her client again.

"I am so sorry. I can only apologise for the interruption. I had no idea she would turn up, or that —" Bronagh stops talking when the woman holds her hands up and shakes her head.

"No need. It isn't your fault. I'm pretty sure that woman has issues, and you had no way to know who she is or that she would turn up today." Bronagh breathes out, a breath she didn't know she was holding and sends up a prayer of thanks to any deity that would listen that her client wasn't pissed at her. "And anyway no one else noticed the slight disturbance."

Bronagh tries to smile, but she knows it doesn't reach her eyes. She had so wanted the day to be perfect.

"Thank you, and yes, this is very true. So shall we get back before anybody else notices. Her client nods her head in agreement. Max grasps Bronagh's hand as she goes to walk away. She jumps at his touch.

"Hey you." He pulls her into him, trying to get her close. She goes into his chest but keeps her hands by her side. "Bre, what did she say to you? Are you okay?"

"I'm fine. She didn't say anything important, it's all okay." He doesn't believe her, but also doesn't push the subject, knowing she needs to get through the rest of the party.

"Okay, if you're sure?" She nods her head, not meeting his eyes and still not relaxing into his embrace. He drops his arms. "I'm here if you need me, Bre, don't shut me out." This brings her eyes to his. She sees hurt there, and she hates herself for putting it there. She didn't mean to hurt him, she just needed to get through the rest of the day before she could contemplate what Elaine had said to her. She puts her hands on his chest.

"I know, and I don't mean to shut you out, but I don't have time for the breakdown that is threatening me, so I am going back into the hall to finish my job, and I will have it later, with you." Max nods his understanding, bringing her back in to give her a kiss on her forehead.

"Okay gorgeous, you go and make that party even more amazing, then the rest of the night I am doing nothing but holding you." Bronagh gives a short nod and gives him a chaste kiss.

Five o'clock eventually arrives and the last of the guests make their way out. Everyone had congratulated Bronagh for all her hard work and making the day so memorable. Nobody mentioned her being missing for the time she was dealing with Elaine, or hearing any disturbance, and again she sends up a silent prayer. She cleans up, convincing herself that the party had indeed been a success.

****

Seeing the party she was meant to be hosting being a success at the hands of her nemesis had been horrid, but seeing Max there waiting on her, protecting her was just too much for Elaine. How dare that bitch think she could have Elaine's life and get away with it!

Elaine had driven about Parkhead, seething with anger, unsure of what to do with her anger, but knowing she needed an outlet for it. She decides she wants to hit something, destroy something and knowing that they had taken Max's car to the party (she had recognised it when she visited them) she knows exactly what she wants to hit. With a new determination Elaine drives to the nearest sports shop, buying herself a shiny new golf club, a driver, then straight to Bronagh's flat, parking at the front of the building. Knowing exactly where Bronagh's car was, having been round earlier to gouge in that day's tally mark, Elaine climbs out, carrying her shiny new toy and makes her way to the car park at the back of Bronagh's flat.

As it was a dry bright day, a disgustingly dirty looking, rather semi-drunk man is sitting on the bottom step at the front door of the building. A half smoked skinny roll-up resting in between his dirt ingrained fingers. Elaine eyes him up before leaning the golf club on the car and strutting over to him. Putting on her most sultry voice.

"Hi there, do you live here?" The drunk lifts his yellowing eyes to hers and smiles. A vision of black and brown stumps, which Elaine assumes were teeth at some point in his sad alcohol induced life, assault her eyes.

"Aye, an' whit ae it?" His voice rough and gravelly with years of smoking and other abuse. Elaine tries to smile and not gag from the stench that has just consumed her.

"Well, I need to get on with some business with that car over there. The owner owes me and I'm reminding them of the debt, so if you don't mind either not being here or not seeing me, it would be much appreciated." The drunk nods, with a smirk as dirty as his fingernails playing on his lips.

"Aye, well see that'll cost ye hen. Ah mean, a've no got any booze fir the day or the morra, an' pay day isnay 'till Monday. So ye see, a'm gonnae need something to wipe away any memory I might have. Know whit a mean?" Elaine huffs slightly before agreeing.

"Fine, wait here and I'll see what I can do." She struts back to her car and lifts £50 from her purse. She knows she needs to start watching her money, but this she feels is worth it. Back standing at the drunk she thrusts the money at him, desperate not to touch him. He grabs the money and gives it a quick count.

"Wow, hen, you must be needing a lot of privacy!" He states with a grin.

"Well, yes, so if you don't mind." She motions with her hand for the drunk to remove himself from the stair, but he remains rooted to the spot.

"Oh naw, hen, I'm staying right here to watch your fancy arse an' tits knock fuck oot that car. The money's just to make sure a dinnay tell oanybody." Elaine huffs again.

"Fine, I hope you enjoy the show!" She spits her words over her shoulder as she struts back to the car, lifting the golf club. Swithering where to start Elaine walks around the car, swinging the club in her hand. After a few seconds of pondering she hears the gruff tone of the drunk behind her.

"I'd start wa the heidlights hen, nice an' easy like." She turns and growls at him, which brings on another smirk from the drunk. She takes his advice anyway, swinging the club at the Fiesta's headlights and flashers. Starting on one side then the other. Getting a rush of adrenaline she continues, swinging for the wing mirrors and then the windscreen. For the twenty minutes she is swinging her club, the drunk shouts and cheers from his vantage point on the steps. Eventually she stops, hardly able to lift her arms and breathing heavily from the exertion. Elaine stands back to look over her handy work. Every inch of the car is battered and scratched. She hears the drunk clapping behind her and turns, her smile beaming. The drunk stands from his seat on the steps and walks up beside her. She takes a step back, the stench wafting from him just too much for her stomach to handle at this close range.

"Well done, hen, that was some show you put oan there." Elaine gasps, not thinking the foul smell could get any worse until the drunk opened his mouth, but he isn't caring. He continues with his congratulations. "I'm sure the stuck-up bitch that owns that thing had it coming. Now if ye use this oan the tyres the job's complete. I wid say anyway!" The drunk hands her a small vegetable knife that he had had concealed on his body, somewhere. Elaine jumps slightly as he pushes it towards her.

"Ye canny be too careful these days hen," he says with a shrug, noticing her wide eyes looking between him and the knife. "It's only fir protection... and a few tyre slashes." Again he smirks as Elaine plucks it from his grip, trying her damnedest to make sure she doesn't touch the dirt infested skin, then goes to each tyre in turn stabbing them over and over again. Engraving 'enjoy bitch' into the bonnet as the final insult, she hands back the knife and thanks the drunk, wishing him a very happy and intoxicated night. The drunk wishes her the same before walking away with his £50, Elaine guesses towards the nearest off licence.

Getting home, Elaine gets herself stripped and into a well needed shower. She needed to scrub away her perspiration and the smell of the drunk. She didn't realise how much a sweat beating up a car could create. Getting out and dried she messages Stewart, letting him know the celebration is still on. His reply is almost instant.

Just got rid of the girlfriend. Going for a shower, be at yours in an hour

Elaine grins. She loves the fact that he is blowing off his girlfriend for her. She quickly sends him her address then continues to get dressed.

The hour goes quickly and just as she finishes colouring her lips with her bright red lipstick, her door bell goes, announcing Stewart's arrival. Opening the door Elaine appraises the handsome man standing on her doorstep before standing aside to let him in.

Stewart is dressed in dark skinny jeans and very tight white vest top with a dark shirt thrown over it all. His hair is tucked behind his ear. Elaine knew he was probably freezing as it is still early March, but he looked as hot as hell. He gives her a smile as he brushes past her and makes himself comfortable on her couch.

"So what we celebrating then?" Elaine closes the door and sits down beside him, placing her hand on his thigh.

"Well... there is this little bitch who stole my job and today I made sure she knew that I will be taking it back, along with other things." Stewart's eyes flash with uncertainty then settle, before heating with desire. He liked a woman who wasn't afraid to take what was hers and stood up for herself, and if that included her being a little bit crazy, well that wasn't any of his business. He wasn't going to be with her for long. This is a bit of fun until he made up his mind over Jane.

"So, she take the hint then?" he asks fishing for more information.

"Oh aye, the ginger nut couldn't get me out of the party quick enough. I could see she was frightened I would lose her her job even though she tried to hide it." Stewart's head shoots up.

"Why did you call her that?"

"What ginger nut? She has stupid red hair."

"And she was working at a party today?"

"Hmm," Elaine smirks inwardly. She knows that Stewart is starting to connect the dots that link her and Bronagh, but she has decided to play dumb.

"Her name wouldn't happen to be Bronagh White would it?" Elaine makes her eyes go wide with feigned shock as she lets her hand fly to her mouth.

"Yes, it is, do you know her?" She really was a good actress even if she did say so herself. Stewart snorts.

"Aye, if it's the same woman. She's my girlfriend's best pal." He looks at her hand which has been rubbing up and down his thigh, then back up to her eyes and smiles.

"Oh, and...?"

"And... she's a stuck up cow. I asked her out about a year and a half ago, before I went with Jane and she turned me down, saying I wasn't her 'type'. I mean who has a type when you're banging? But now I know why she knocked me back, she is infatuated with that dick Max. They're perfect for each other, stuck-up and far too serious!" Elaine grins and slides further over to him, taking her finger and running it up and down the side of his face then brushes his lips.

"You don't need her when you've got me," she whispers as she launches herself at him, kissing him all over until they are both naked, writhing and screaming their release.

CHAPTER THIRTEEN

Once the party finished and was everything cleaned up, Bronagh and Max head out to Max's Golf. Bronagh felt dog tired and Max could see it. Once both of them in are the car Max turns to her.

"Home?" Bronagh shakes her head vigorously.

"No, yours, please." Max gives her a look, asking why without words. "I know there is going to be another gouge in Freddie and I know I'm going to need to look for it, and I just don't have the energy or the strength for it just now. I just want to go back to yours and do nothing." Max nods his understanding.

"Okay, my bed it is!" She gives him a tired smile, but at least it's a smile he thinks. They arrive at Max's house in Dalmarnock and he pulls into his driveway. He looks over at Bronagh again. She had been very quiet on the drive from the party, looking out of the passenger window, exhaustion covering her face.

"Hey you." He places his hand on hers bringing her focus to him.

"Hey yourself," she answers softly.

"You okay?" She gives him another tired smile, and shrugs.

"Honestly, I don't know. I'm tired, I'm scared, I'm glad the party is over and I'm ecstatic that it all went well, kinda." Max nods agreeing with everything she was saying. "I really just want to enjoy my first party being a success and ignore the 'incident'." She makes air quotations round the word incident. "I don't want to think about crazy blondes and just kid-on everything is normal." Max squeezes her hand.

"We can do that." She squeezes his hand back as her thanks and they climb from the car. Getting into the house Bronagh's phone rings to life. She pulls it from its pocket in her bag and shows it to Max.

"It's Erin, my boss."

"Well answer it." She nods and presses answer.

"Hi Erin." She tries to make her voice sound light and happy, and can only hope it comes across that way.

"Hi Bronagh. Just checking in, see how the party went." Erin's tone is light and happy Bronagh notices and she really doesn't want to tell her about the 'incident', but she knows she needs to so gets on with it, taking a seat on the stairs so she doesn't fall down in the hall.

"Yeah, it went well... well mostly." She hears a noise from the other end of the phone, but continues. "A woman called Elaine tried to come in and take over but my boyfriend, who had given me a lift this morning, stopped her and I managed to get her out." Another noise from the other end before Erin speaks.

"Did the client see the altercation? And why was your boyfriend there?" Bronagh pinched the bridge of her nose. She was really starting to fear the worst of this conversation.

"Yes, no, well, the couple's daughter came out from the hall as I was trying to get Elaine to leave. I apologised profusely, but thankfully she said it was all right, that I wasn't to know Elaine would turn up and that I had dealt with it all professionally." She takes a deep breath before continuing, her stomach knotting with every passing second. "And as for why my boyfriend was there, well... I, we, have been having some problems with someone harassing me. I have been getting nasty messages and my car has been vandalised every day for the past week, and had the tyre slashed. Plus when I am out with Max this same woman keeps turning up. Max doesn't want me to be on my own and he wanted to be in the vicinity today, just in case anything happened, and thankfully he was there." There is a short silence before Erin talks again.

"Oh, Bronagh, I am so sorry. I didn't know anything like that was happening to you. Do you know who the woman is, and is she connected to the messages and vandalism?" Bronagh lets out a very unladylike snort.

"Well, we didn't, but we do now. It's Elaine. We can't say for certain that she is the one doing the messages and stuff but she has approached Max a few times, coming onto him and being slightly threatening to me, like today she told me I had to enjoy the things I had. Like I wasn't going to have them for long." There is a sharp intake of breath from Erin.

"Again, I am so sorry. I knew she didn't take getting fired well, but I didn't expect her to do anything sinister, and I understand why Max wanted to be there, and like you I'm glad he was. The client seems to have taken it all okay, I certainly haven't had any complaints. When you come in on Monday we can have a chat about the party and Elaine more, but from what I'm hearing congratulations are in order for making sure the party was a success despite the circumstances, so thank you, and I'll see you on Monday." Bronagh is shocked that she wasn't getting fired, but grateful all the same. She thanks her boss and wishes her a nice weekend before cancelling the call.

Max is still in the kitchen, having stayed in there to make a start on the stir fry they were having for dinner and to give her some privacy. He looks up when she walks in. He watches her for a second trying to get a read on how things went from her expression, but it was blank.

"Hey you." He decides keeping things normal between them is the best route to take, so hands her a beer.

"Hey yourself." She sits at the small four seater round table in that sits in the corner of the kitchen.

"How'd that go?" He nods towards her phone that's still clutched in her fist. She looks at the phone then up at Max.

"Em, aye, okay, I think. I told her about Elaine's visit and she thanked me for keeping the party going." Max nods.

"That's good." Bronagh nods back, still a bit bemused.

"Aye, I mean, there was more to it and she wants to talk to me on Monday, but she didn't fire me, so aye, that's good." Max continues to nod as he moves the food from the heat to walk over to her.

"And why would she fire you? The party was a success, and all because of you!" He kisses her forehead then goes back to the food.

"Well, I guess. Anyway enough of that, what you cooking? It smells great." She smiles, her first real smile since she saw Elaine standing in that hallway.

"Stir-fry." Bronagh's phone buzzes as a message comes through. Her heart leaps a bit, then chastises herself for it, she doesn't want to start living her life in fear.

Hope today went well, things cooling off between me and Stewart, talk later J x

She frowns at the message before sending her reply.

Went well although some craziness. Meet tomorrow for coffee? xx

The friends organise to meet the next evening for drinks, Max insisting on taking them and picking them up.

Once dinner is ready Max serves and sits at the small kitchen table, the couple enjoying their 'normal' quiet night together.

Sunday comes as does the rain. Bronagh hears it rapping on the bedroom window and burrows further down into the bed, getting closer to Max. He stirs.

"Hey you, what you doing?" His voice croaky with sleep.

"Hey yourself, and I'm trying to get away from the rain." Max pulls himself up onto his elbow, looking at her like a confused puppy.

"You know you're inside don't you, and the rain is outside? It canny get you." She rolls her eyes at him.

"I know, cheeky, I was just... I don't know. It's just warm and cosy in here and it sounds horrid out there. Anyway, shut up and give me a cuddle." Max puts his arm around her waist and pulls her closer still, nuzzling her shoulder.

"Mmm, that I can do," he mumbles as he squeezes her tight and nuzzles her neck. Bronagh groans.

"Oh I've changed my mind don't squeeze." Max sits up sharply.

"What?"

"My bladder didn't like it!" Max groans and laughs as Bronagh jumps from the bed heading to the toilet.

Climbing back in quickly, she manoeuvres herself back into Max's arms, and he envelopes her, placing his lips back on her shoulder.

"Better?"

"Hmm, much thank you." Max continues to kiss and nip down her jaw and neck to her shoulder.

"Bre?" The atmosphere changed from the laughter of earlier.

"Mmm?" She can hardly think straight with everything Max was doing with his tongue to her skin, her brain and vocal chords not really being connected at that moment.

"Don't ever doubt how much I love you!" This time it's Bronagh's turn to pull up, looking deep into Max's crystal blue eyes and seeing nothing there but pure love and desire.

"Forever?" He nods.

"Forever." They kiss each other fervently, everywhere all at the same time, each of them pouring every inch of love, passion and desire they have for each other into their kisses. Their hands move fervently over each other until they are moving together as one, connected by their love making.

They spend all of their morning and most of the early afternoon lazing about, enjoying the peace and quiet and each other before they return to Bronagh's flat.

****

Saturday is just a haze as Elaine wakes up feeling entirely too warm, again. Stewart is wrapped around her again, for the second morning in a row, something unheard of for her, although she didn't feel as uncomfortable as she did the morning before. This she puts down to her waking up in her own bed and not a strange one. As she lays there she slowly remembers the events of the day before.

Seeing Bronagh and Max at the party had incensed her, and she knew she had shown them her hand perhaps a bit too early, but she didn't think that would matter. They couldn't prove it was her doing all the messages and vandalism. All they could be sure of was she ate at the same restaurants as them. As for the things she had said to Bronagh? Well that was one word against another, she always made sure no one other than Bronagh could hear her when she passed on her thoughts. Elaine goes to move her arms and winces at the pain shooting through them. This time her pain isn't from alcohol, no this is muscular. She must have used muscles she didn't know she had yesterday when she beat the hell out of that crappy car! She smiles, pleased with herself and the carnage that Bronagh would go home and see.

Stewart smiles in his sleep, reminding her of their second night together. The man is amazing, she thinks to herself. She had never had anyone who knew so many tricks of the trade when it came to having sex. She had thought Lee and her had had good sex. Stewart blew him out the water!

After their first round, starting when Stewart admitted his dislike for Bronagh and finishing on the living room floor, they had gotten ready to go for dinner. Both of them opting for Italian. They couldn't keep their hands from each other all throughout dinner, and even more so the more they learned of each other's dislike for Bronagh. The discussion about Bronagh and their mutual hatred for her evolved over dinner, until they were planning her downfall, neither of them taking it entirely as a joke. In the taxi back to her house Elaine confided in Stewart everything that she had done to Bronagh's car earlier that day, making him happier in every sense of the word. Elaine couldn't believe her luck when she realised he was desperate for her all because she had beaten up that car. The rest of the night had been spent pleasuring each other, drinking, and hating Bronagh. Bliss! Elaine thinks.

She looks down and realises she is running her fingers through Stewart's hair, in a very loving manner. It is slightly damp from him sweating, but she didn't mind. They had both worked up a sweat the night before. She had never felt like this for anyone before, and certainly didn't expect to have any feelings after just a few days. Not one to do emotions she pushes all thoughts of feeling from her mind, but doesn't stop stroking his hair. Stewart stirs again and wakes, smiling as he sees Elaine watching him.

"Like what you see?" She really likes his confident cockiness.

"Oh aye I do!" she answers, just as cocky. He grabs her down on top of him as they go for what feels like round ninety.

****

Thankfully the rain has stopped as Max drives round the back of Bronagh's flat and parks in the visitor parking bay next to the Fiesta. He is first to see the car as Bronagh is busy on her phone organising her night out with Jane.

"What the fuck?" he roars. Bronagh jumps and her head snaps round to look at Max.

"What? What's wrong?" Bronagh's blood is rushing through her veins as fear creeps up her spine.

"Bre, your car, look at Freddie." Confused Bronagh looks round.

"What's wrong with Fred –" There is silence as she spots the battered heap that was her beloved car. Her hand flies to her mouth as she squeaks out Max's name, the fear she was feeling growing tenfold. Max is out of his Golf and over at the Fiesta, walking around it slowly, checking every inch of metal and taking in every inch of damage. After what seems like hours, but is only actually seconds, Bronagh stumbles from the Golf. She stands at the driver's door looking at the mess. The windows had been smashed and the doors had been caved in so much the hinges are showing. Tears run down her cheeks unchecked.

Max walks up to her, standing by her side; he places his arm around her waist and pulls her into him. She stumbles into him, but doesn't fold into his embrace as she would normally, too shocked to think or move.

The drunk walks past them, stopping at Bronagh's side.

"That's a pure mess you've git there, hen!" They both turn to look at him. Max notices the strange smile playing on the drunks thin cracked, dirty lips.

"Did you see anything?" Max knows it's a long shot asking the drunk, but he had to take the chance anyway. The drunk sniggers.

"Me? Ah never seen nuhin!" Another snigger and another strange smile pass the dry cracked lips.

"Okay then..." Max utters, not believing a word the drunk just said.

The drunk resumes his journey to wherever it was he was headed, only this time there is a spring in his step and a whistle on his disgusting lips. Max turns to Bronagh, who only moved to look at her car again.

"Bre, honey, you okay?" He places his fingers under her chin and moves her head so she is facing him. Her head moves without resistance but also without reaction. Eventually she drags her eyes from her car to Max. All he sees there is panic and fear. It's written all over her face, with the fear taking over and filling her eyes. She stares at Max, not talking, not moving, just standing looking at him.

"Bre, please say something." Max almost begs. Bronagh opens her mouth but nothing comes out. She closes it and tries again. Still nothing. She starts to shake her head. Max puts his hand on the small of her back trying to guide her away from the car and towards her flat, but she doesn't move. He pulls her into his arms, placing his mouth at her ear.

"Hey. You. I'm here! Now let's get inside away from this and take it from there okay?" He squeezes her in a hug and kisses her cheek. She manages to nod her head imperceptibly. Max takes her hand, giving it a gentle tug to get her moving. This time her feet comply by moving and continuing to move as they enter the communal stairwell, up the stairs and into her flat.

As soon as they get into the flat and the door is locked behind them, Bronagh's legs give out. Max catches her before she hits the floor easing them both down gently. They sit on the carpet in the hall, Bronagh clinging onto Max as if her life depended on it, sobbing. Max holds her like his life depends on it too.

Half an hour later they are still sitting in the hall entwined in each other, but Bronagh has calmed, only giving the occasional shuddering breath. Max talks first.

"Bre, do you want me to phone the police?" Silence engulfs them again, before she nods and murmurs her agreement. They stand, Max helping Bronagh and holding her until they reach the couch, neither trusting her legs just yet. Once seated Max brings his phone out and dials the 101 police number.

Max explains the situation, then listens for a minute. He answers some questions, and then thanks the operator, cancelling the call and placing his phone on the couch.

"Officers will be round as soon as they can. They'll have a look and then come up to ask some questions."

Bronagh nods, but nothing more.

CHAPTER FOURTEEN

Monday morning arrives and with it a roaring gale. The rain lashes the windows as the wind howls against the house. The weather is perfect for Bronagh's mood that morning. She had hardly slept the night before, and when she did drift off she dreamt of Elaine beating her car, and her helpless to do anything about it. A few times she woke up to Max having nightmares too. Thrashing and shouting out her name. She would calm him by stroking his hair and saying his name, but he never seemed to fully wake up.

Yesterday when she saw her car her stomach sank, the feeling of fear and panic was horrendous and clawing, shock ricocheting through her veins rendering her immobile.

The messages and Elaine's words had affected her to a certain extent, made her worry some, but she knew she could continue to live her life relatively unscathed. Then yesterday happened. Yesterday Elaine upped the ante. Showing up at the party, threatening her, then destroying her car, all of it together made everything very real and very scary. Yesterday showed that Elaine could get to her and do a lot of damage.

After she had broken down and released everything in a very long, very cathartic cry, she knew she had to involve the police, having already made a complaint about the messages, but didn't know if she had the voice to do so. Thankfully Max was there, giving her strength and doing everything she couldn't at that moment in time, like dealing with the police, phoning Jane to cancel their plans, and more importantly, making her feel safe in the one place she should feel safe, her own flat.

Then Jane came over. Bronagh thinks back to her friend's reaction.

"What do you mean you 'think' you know who's behind this? Why are we no pounding down their door?" She stalked up and down Bronagh's living room, anger radiating from her as she wore a tread into the carpet. Bronagh just sat, shaking her head. Max had had the good sense to go and organise some food and drinks for them.

"We can't do that Jane, the police are dealing with it." Bronagh's voice was small, but there.

"Is it that weirdo, crazy blonde? It's her intit?" Bronagh nods.

"We think so. Elaine, her name's Elaine. She used to work at the party planners, but got sacked, allegedly for sexual misconduct, and I got the job." Jane stops pacing and stares at Bronagh, her mouth hanging open.

"Sexual misconduct? Seriously? Who was she banging?" Then a twinkle comes into her eyes. "What kinda parties you plan? I always thought it normal celebrations, you know like birthdays and shit, not..." Jane leaves the rest of her sentence hanging in the air, both of them knowing exactly the type of parties Jane was referring to.

"Allegedly it was some of the clients she was having it away with, and no I don't plan *they* types of parties, get your mind out the gutter!" They both smile, the atmosphere lightening slightly before Jane plummets it back to depression again.

"That's okay, I don't think I've any need for they kinds a parties any more. Stewart is going off me!"

Bronagh remembers why they were meant to be going out that night and chastises herself for being pre-occupied, but guessed her friend understood.

"What's happened?" she asks, and Jane tells Bronagh about all the cancelled plans, the missed calls and even how desperate he was to get rid of her earlier that day. The friends continue talking for hours, both of them supporting each other. Max, again, chooses to be sensible and goes to the bedroom to read.

****

For Elaine the weather didn't interpret her mood on the Monday morning. Stewart had blown off his girlfriend on the Sunday, getting rid of her as soon as she had asked him to. Now that was a man in control, she thinks to herself, not a wimp like Lee was. An emotion raced through her heart, but she didn't examine it; she was just happy he wasn't a wimp and hated Bronagh as much as she did. What was even better was, he was willing and desperately wanting to help Elaine bring her down.

They had spent most of the night planning their next move and toasting every idea they had, which is why Elaine was once again searching for paracetamol.

Stewart had woken her about five that morning saying he had to leave, something about needing to get ready for work. She had no idea what he did for a living, so she shrugged and fell back asleep. She woke around nine with another pounding head, but not too warm, this time.

Having found the painkillers and made herself a coffee Elaine settles on her couch, flicking through the TV channels until she finds the trashy morning talk show, her dirty little secret. Minutes into her programme there is someone rapping on her door. She groans. Putting her coffee down, she pauses the TV and goes to answer the door.

Two police officers stand looking expectantly as Elaine opens the door. She notices the male officer first and smiles, her best flirtatious smile as she fiddles with her satin dressing gown, not to pull it closer, but to open it just a little further, revealing more flesh than is strictly necessary. The female officer notices everything and rolls her eyes before clearing her throat and speaking.

"Miss Ashton, I'm WPC Young and this is PC Loughran. We have some questions for you regarding your whereabouts on Saturday. May we come in?" Elaine takes her eyes from the male officer and looks WPC Young up and down with disgust, then huffs.

"If you must." She draws her eyes off of the WPC then turns and gives PC Loughran a beaming smile, then turns and leads the way into her living room. The two officers look at each other, WPC Young glowers at her partner, who shrugs, lifting his hands in a defensive motion before stepping over the threshold.

Elaine is sitting on one seat of the two seater couch, leaving the other seat and a single chair for the officers to choose from. WPC Young claims the single chair, leaving the seat next to Elaine free. PC Loughran stands. There is no way he was opening himself up to anything Elaine would do or say. WPC Young is first to speak again.

"So Miss Ashton, we have received a complaint of harassment towards a," WPC Young refers to her standard issue notebook for a second then continues, "Miss Bronagh White." Elaine looks shocked for a millisecond, but covers it, she hopes, then answers.

"Well now, this is a turn up for the books," her tone innocent, "I admit I popped my head into the party she was hosting on Saturday, but only to ensure it was all going as planned." She turns her attention to PC Loughran, putting on her best poor me voice paired with her puppy dog eyes. "You see, I had started planning the party before I was unfairly dismissed from my job, and I just wanted to check all was going well... you know for the client. Bronagh didn't take too kindly to my presence and, well, she threw me out. I wasn't there to upset anyone." She bats her lashes at PC Loughran again who has started looking everywhere but directly at Elaine. WPC Young clears her throat once she has finished taking notes of what had been said.

"Okay, Miss Ashton, now could you tell us where you went after you left the party?" Elaine fiddles with the tie of her robe again, still looking at PC Loughran.

"Well, I met with my close friend and we came back here." WPC Young nods.

"Could we have this friend's name please?" A flicker of panic crosses Elaine's face and again she tries to cover it.

"Eh, yes. Of course. It's Stewart McMillan. He was here for the full night, leaving about five this morning." The officers share another look, then WPC Young continues her questions. Elaine answers them all as innocently as possible, batting her eyelashes at PC Loughran often. As they finish up, the officers advise Elaine to stay away from Bronagh, her flat and her place of work. Elaine feigns worry and gushes that she doesn't understand why Bronagh would complain, but yes she will absolutely stay away. She sees the officers to the door, thanking them for bringing it to her attention. The officers nod then walk away, both of them glad to be out of the house, especially the PC Loughran.

Behind the closed door Elaine is livid, screaming into the empty house as she goes from room to room, for no particular reason other than to use up the adrenaline surging through her system.

"The fuckin' bitch actually went to the coppers," she screams. "The boot, the fuckin' cow! Unfuckinbelievable!" Shaking with anger she lifts her new mobile, stabbing out a message.

You fuckin' cow I will fuckin' get you!

She threw the phone down, picking up her own phone, sending a message to Stewart this time.

Hi babe, the bitch had the police at my door. She needs to be taken down another notch, I was thinking about the flat? Let me know what you think. Would love to see you later, need cheering up xx

His reply comes back quickly.

Need to see her indoors for a bit, don't want her getting too suspicious, be over after that, then we can plan x

Getting Stewart's reply calms Elaine somewhat. She is so glad he isn't a wimp like most other men. She goes to the kitchen to make herself another coffee then settles back onto her couch, pressing play on her TV control to continue her show.

CHAPTER FIFTEEN

Max goes into work as normal for eight thirty, promising to be back in time to take Bronagh to work. He hadn't left her side after Jane left on the Sunday night, and was loath to leave her that morning, but Bronagh had insisted. She didn't want him to lose his job because of her, plus they had both agreed, late the night before, that they should continue with their lives normally; well as normal as they could.

At ten o'clock Bronagh is sitting at the table she is used to working at in the House of Fun office and Gordon is handing her one of his amazing coffees.

"So, how did it go?" Bronagh looks up at Gordon, a dazed look on her face. Eventually it clicks that he means the Diamond anniversary party.

"Aye, aye, good. I mean it nearly wasn't but it all ended up good." Gordon looks at her confused, but before he gets the chance to ask any questions Erin walks into the main workroom and Bronagh stands as her stomach drops.

"Ah Bronagh you're in. How you doing?" Her tone is light and friendly, but it still doesn't assure Bronagh that she isn't about to get fired.

"Yeah, fine, thanks."

"Good, well, why don't we have that chat just now." Bronagh's stomach drops even more. Gordon looks between the two women, then turns to Bronagh giving her a tight smile. Bronagh lifts her cup and follows her boss to her office.

They settle in Erin's office, Bronagh's heart trying to thump its way from its home inside her chest. Erin smiles, trying to put her at ease.

"I see Gordon's made you some of his liquid gold." Erin points to Bronagh's cup. She nods, not trusting her voice, "He's a master at making coffee, I don't know what he does, but it is amazing." Bronagh murmurs her agreement, still not trusting herself to speak. Erin senses her worry and smiles, "Bronagh please don't worry, I've not brought you in here to tear strips off you." Bronagh starts to nod, slowly. "I phoned the couple whose party it was, and their daughter. All of them sang your praises, they had an amazing day. They couldn't believe the amount of work you put in, and in such a short space of time." Bronagh can only stare at her boss. "I asked the daughter about the, eh, interruption by Elaine, and she explained that you dealt with it all professionally and discreetly." Another nod, then a big breath out. Erin smiles, she could feel how anxious Bronagh had been, so leans across her desk and grasps her hand. "You did an amazing job, even if there wasn't any complications, you surpassed yourself." Tears sting at the back of Bronagh's eyes.

"Thanks," she squeaks.

"Now tell me, what's been happening with Elaine?" The emotion that Bronagh had been trying to keep under control all morning explodes from her as soon as Erin mentions the problems she has been having with Elaine, and she sobs.

Taking a second to compose herself Bronagh starts tell Erin the whole sorry story. Starting with the messages on her phone and the messages on the social media site, then continuing until she reaches the vandalism of her car. Erin holds her hand to her mouth, looking like she might be sick.

"I'm so sorry Bronagh. I had no idea, and you say your car was trashed between Saturday and Sunday?" Bronagh nods.

"Yes, he was fine when I left Saturday morning, and I didn't want to go home after the party, I don't know why. I just wanted a normal night without having to look for more scratches, so I stayed with Max, and when we returned on the Sunday he was... destroyed." Another round of tears well up in her eyes as she swallows another sob.

"And you've reported all of this to the police?" Bronagh nods her head as she talks.

"We had reported the messages a week or so ago, then Max phoned them on Sunday after we found Freddie... I mean my car. I call him Freddie," Bronagh explains. Erin gives her a smile.

"How are you getting to work?" Bronagh sags slightly at that question. The constant feeling of being reliant on Max bringing her down slightly.

"Max is taking his break from work early so he can pick me up, but I can't expect him to continue like that. I guess I'll need to rent a car until my insurance gets through the paperwork."

"Well, if there's anything me or David can do please don't hesitate to ask." Erin clears her throat, signalling the change in conversation that is about to happen. "Now, we have another two parties we want you to work on." Bronagh's eyes widen at her boss's words. "One is a communion, so it's not until May, but we've been booked just now so have a look at it and get a head start on it." Erin hands her a folder similar to the one she had for the Diamond Anniversary only in blue. "And the second party is an Engagement party. This one is on the third weekend in April, so a bit closer." She gets handed another folder, this one is red. Bronagh places both folders on the desk in front of her, lifting the red, engagement party one first opening it. A wistful notion fleets through her thoughts and heart, a want or wish that maybe one day she would be planning her own engagement party with Max. Erin starts talking again, explaining everything Bronagh had to work on, bringing her from her fantasy. Bronagh thanks her boss then leaves to get on with her new work load.

****

After lounging about for most of the day, Elaine decides to soak in a long hot bath. She had been plotting and planning all day, everything from an unfortunate road traffic accident to death and destruction of Bronagh and everyone she knew except for Max. In every scenario Bronagh ends up maimed or dead, Elaine ends up with Max, Stewart, her job back and lots of money. Coming back to reality after yet another fantasy, Elaine climbs from her bath, enveloping herself in one of her fluffy white bath towels, then her dressing gown. She makes her way through to her bedroom to get dried. Pulling on her comfy lounge wear, leaving the sexy stuff for later, she goes and makes herself some dinner.

Shoving her ready meal for one in the microwave, Elaine pulls out a bottle of wine. She's managed to eventually get over the horrendous red wine hangover. Five minutes later the microwave beeps, alerting her that her dinner is ready. Taking her dinner into the living room, she settles in front of the TV to eat and wait on her lover.

Stewart arrives at ten, breezing into the house without knocking, stopping in his tracks when he sets eyes on Elaine. She had fallen asleep waiting on him, wine glass in hand. Gently he removes the wine glass, placing it on the coffee table, then he brushes a stray strand of blonde hair from her eyes.

"Elaine sweetie." He rubs her shoulder, trying to waken her from her slumber. A few seconds later and in a very unladylike manner, Elaine stretches and snorts as she comes to. Looking at Stewart sitting over her, she blushes. She had planned on changing into something far less comfortable and a lot more sexy than her pyjama bottoms and a vest top.

"Stewart... what, how? Hi."

"Hi, you know you shouldn't fall asleep when you haven't locked your door. A bad man could come in!" Elaine's eyes widen, then sparkle.

"Are you a bad man?" Her voice is husky with desire. Stewart gives her a wink.

"I can be if that's what you want." Elaine thinks for a second.

"Hmm, maybe." She wriggles herself up to a sitting position. "But first let's get some planning done, so I can see how bad you can be. Drink?" He nods and helps her get up.

Once they both have glasses of wine and snacks they sit to plan Elaine's next and their first step together in the downfall of Bronagh.

"I want to hurt her, physically, although maybe not quite yet, but eventually," she states quite matter-of-factly. Stewart nods and smiles.

"So, *eventually,* we will be hurting her, physically?" Stewart asks for clarification. Elaine looks like she is thinking for a minute then nods.

"I want her to know she can't go about stealing other people's jobs and being Miss Perfect. Like you said before, she needs taken down a peg or six!" Stewart nods again, then a wistful look crosses his face. He had spent many nights fantasising and dreaming about how he would teach her a lesson for turning him down. He never thought he would get the chance to do anything about his wishes and dreams, then his fairy god-lover arrived and all his dreams have started coming true. Both of them excitedly talk about all the nasty things they could and eventually would be doing to Bronagh. Stewart calms, putting on his sensible head for a bit.

"Okay, so we know what we want to do, eventually, but for just now I think we should rein in what we are doing, like the messages and shit, just for a month or so." Elaine goes to protest but Stewart places his hand on hers quieting her, before continuing, "I know you're desperate, but listen to me, if we go off high on the thought of getting revenge and do something we could probably be arrested for in the next week then Bronagh, and the police are going to know it was you. So the next time the police come over it won't be for a friendly chat, but if we wait, make her think it's all finished with, lull her into a false sense of security, then hit her, it will be twice as hard on her." A slow smile spreads over Elaine's lips as she agrees wholeheartedly with the gorgeous man beside her. She puts her glass down, takes his face in her hands and looks deep into his pale blue eyes.

"You, my lover, aren't like any other man I have ever known. You are not a wimp like them, you are an evil genius, a fuckin' evil genius!" Stewart's smile grows as does other parts of his anatomy as Elaine launches herself at him, kissing every inch of her lover.

CHAPTER SIXTEEN

Bronagh makes her way back to her desk with her two new folders, still a bit stunned from the meeting.

"You okay sweet cheeks?" Gordon enquires.

"Hm? Aye, I'm fine. Been a rough weekend, and it looks like it's going to be a busy few months, but yeah, I'm okay." Gordon perches himself on the edge of her table.

"So, you going to tell your Uncle Gee what happened at the party that made it all nearly not good?" Bronagh smiles at her new friend, then recalls the crazy tale of her first party working for House of Fun.

"Wow," Gordon stares wide eyed at her. "That is a busy weekend for sure." Bronagh snorts a laugh.

"That's one way of describing it."

"And you think the messages and your car are connected? That Elaine is behind it all?" She nods.

"Aye, I think so." A few seconds silence envelopes the friends as they take in what that could mean.

"She really is something else!" Gordon states. "So how you getting to work and back?" Bronagh explains the arrangement she and Max have, and Gordon can see she has issues with it.

"You don't like him picking you up and dropping you off?"

"No, aye, I mean yes, I am happy, kinda. It's just... urgh, I can't keep relying on him like that. It's not fair on him or his boss and work mates. Plus I have never had to rely on anybody as much as I'm relying on him just now and I'm just not used to it. Then there's the fact that we've just got together and now we are in the middle of this crap and he has went all over-protective on me. It's not healthy for a relationship to start out like this."

"I know what you mean honey." He pauses for a second, thinking. "You live in Parkhead?"

"Aye, why?" Gordon's smile covers his face.

"I'll pick you up."

"What? I can't ask you to do that."

"You're not asking I'm offering. It's on my way here, and it will take a bit of pressure off of you worrying about Max and his work. Now go phone that hunk of yours and let him know I'll drop you off tonight, so I know where I'm going tomorrow." Tears sting the back of Bronagh's eyes at the kindness of her new friend, her emotions still a bit whacked out with everything going on. She nods then picks up her phone.

Max arrives at Bronagh's just as Gordon drops her off. He walks over to Gordon's 15 plate Mazda 6 TS and opens the passenger door holding onto Bronagh's hand as she climbs out and gives him a kiss.

"Hey you."

"Hey yourself." She smiles, feeling more relaxed than she had all day. Max dips his head into the car to thank Gordon.

"Hey, thanks for giving Bre a lift. You sure you don't mind picking her up?" Gordon shakes his head, warming to Max and his protectiveness.

"Not at all, I pass by this way going to work." Max drums his fingers on top of the car.

"That's great. I've looked at getting Bre on the insurance for my Golf, but I just don't want her on her own." He shrugs, feeling slightly embarrassed at his babbling and he's not sure why he feels the need to explain himself, but he does. Gordon holds his hands up.

"I totally understand. If I had a girl as gorgeous as Bronagh I would do everything in my power to protect her too. Well, you know if I liked girls, but you know what I mean." Max nods and laughs, understanding exactly why Bronagh likes her new friend. The men say their goodbyes and Gordon drives off, beeping his horn as he goes. Max turns to

Bronagh and takes her hand before they walk up the stairs to her flat.

"He's nice." Max flops onto the couch as Bronagh brings them through beers.

"He is. I told you you'd like him, and he makes the best coffee in the world!" Max rolls his eyes at her.

"You lady are a coffee fiend!"

"Oh aye, you know it! Right, dinner. Take away?" Max nods, loving how normal the night was.

****

One month later

"So are you going to finish with her?" Elaine is lying in Stewart's bed, her heart beating hard in her chest, partly due to their energetic love making, but mostly because of the question she has just asked. Her and Stewart had been seeing each other nearly every day since they met up a month ago. Never in her whole adult life had she been in a relationship where she wasn't the 'other woman' and she certainly never saw any of her conquests on a nightly basis. She never allowed any of them to make her heart feel anything, but then again, she thinks, they were all wimps and not worth her time. The surfer looking hunk whose bed she was lying in was certainly not a wimp, and he is making her feel things, emotions she had thought she had shut down many years ago after her parents left her. He was also making her do things that she never had thought possible, like forgetting she wanted Max as part of her annihilation of Bronagh and ask the question she just asked and is now currently holding her breath waiting on the answer.

"I don't know," Stewart answers. Elaine blows out the breath she had been holding, disappointment surging through her. Stewart feels her slump and smiles. He had never thought this affair would turn into a relationship of sorts, or that he would want a relationship with this crazy blonde, but he did, and he knew she felt the same.

"Hey, it's not like that. I just think it might be more advantageous to us if I'm still part of their 'group' and close to our target, you know, be able to keep an eye on her." Elaine settles for a minute thinking through everything Stewart was saying. She understands what he's saying and knows that it's a good idea to keep Bronagh close, the whole friends and enemies and keeping them close thing springs to mind, but she just couldn't help being jealous of the girlfriend he would be spending time with – another first she thinks. Stewart pulls her into him. "Believe me, I'll keep sex with Jane to a minimum and I'll only think of you." He kisses her forehead and Elaine chuckles then gives in.

"Okay, I understand, just make sure you come back to me and get properly satisfied!" Stewart laughs.

"Oh don't you worry my darling, I will." They smile at each other as Elaine takes his earlobe in her mouth and tugs. Stewart growls his response and flips her onto her back kissing her hard. He moves his mouth slowly down her neck to her chest, taking each of her breasts in turn. He moves further down, kissing each inch until he finds her core. Elaine feels him smile as he licks and suckles her until she screams his name.

An hour later they are both sitting in the small kitchen at the back of Stewart's flat, drinking coffee and eating rolls and lorne sausage.

"So you think hitting her flat is the next step we should take?" Stewart nods his answer, his mouth full. He swallows.

"Aye, she might not connect the dots, seeing as you've done radio silence on the bitchy messages and her 'life has gone back to normal', her words by the way." Elaine's eyebrows shoot into her hairline. She didn't like the quote or Bronagh's life being described as 'good'. Stewart reaches over and clasps her hand in his. "All in good time my love, we will get her, all in good time." Elaine smiles, well grins like a lunatic if she was being honest with herself and wonders at just how far in love she had fallen with the man in front of her.

****

The month after Elaine gatecrashed the party she was working, had been busy for Bronagh on the job front, having been given two different parties to organise, and all quiet on the harassment front, which she was thankful for. All the nasty messages had stopped and Elaine was nowhere to be seen when they were out. Her and Max's relationship had also settled, Max easing up on being the helicopter boyfriend. Then, after two weeks of Gordon running her to work, Max organised the car insurance for her to drive his beloved Volkswagen Golf. She was extremely honoured at the gesture as no one but Max got to drive that car!

The only thing that hadn't gone back to normal was Jane and Stewart's relationship. Stewart had been getting very distant, coming up with excuses or reasons of why he couldn't see Jane, or if he did why he couldn't stay. Bronagh and Jane had had many conversations about his behaviour, Jane convinced that he was having an affair while Bronagh was trying to get her to entertain other reasons behind it, even though privately she agreed with Jane, as did Max.

"I didn't like him much when they first started seeing each other," Max states. It's Monday night and they are lying in his bed, both of them getting settled for the night.

"That's because you thought he was lazy."

"He is lazy." Max stares at her with disbelief. "And he has eyes for you." Bronagh looks at her boyfriend with confusion written all over her face.

"No he doesn't. I mean he hung about with people I knew and asked me out once, but that was years ago." Max's eyes widen, jealousy rising in his throat.

"He asked you out? Why am I only hearing about this now?" More confusion passes over Bronagh's face.

"Well we weren't going out when he asked me, and I said no. He's not my type, and I was in love with someone else. Then by the time Jane and him got together, I guessed he would be over it." Max smiles, the jealousy taking a back seat, and wraps Bronagh up in his arms, pulling her closer to him.

"Oh aye, and do I know this man you were in love with?" He starts rubbing slow circles on her back.

"I'm not sure, but maybe. You might've met him." Max starts kissing her neck to her shoulders talking and nipping with his teeth as he went.

"And do you still love him?" Bronagh's senses are on high alert with every kiss.

"Very much so, it seems to be a forever thing." Max stops his travels and looks deep into her eyes.

"Forever," he states, then takes her mouth in a searing kiss, part of him proving to her that she made the right decision picking him and not Stewart.

Tuesday morning comes and Max gets up for work. Bronagh wakes as he moves from the bed. She pulls him back down.

"Hey you." Max murmurs their greeting.

"Hey yourself," she answers as he kisses her forehead.

"You go back to sleep, I'll reset the alarm." She leans up slightly and gives him a kiss before worming her way back into the covers.

"I need to go back to mine after work. You fancy going out to dinner?" she says sleepily.

"That sounds like a plan. I'll come back here and get changed then get you at yours about seven?" She nods, her eyes closing, sleep starting to reclaim her. Max gives her another kiss on the forehead before getting up again.

CHAPTER SEVENTEEN

Just found out from Jane that Bronagh and Max will be out tonight, so you up for some fun?

Elaine reads the message from Stewart and does a wee happy dance in her living room, as does her heart.

They had spent the last few weeks getting their arsenal of equipment ready for the day they would do the housebreaking. Elaine pulls out the holdall, their first purchase, which was currently living under her bed with everything they needed in it already. Taking everything out to double check they hadn't forgotten anything, again.

Black T-Shirts x2 Black Gloves x2
Black Hoodie x2 Black Hat x1
Black Cargo Trousers x2 Black Wig, Female x1
Black Trainers x2 Black Bandannas (for masks) x2
Crowbar x1 Golf Club x1
Box of Condoms (minus 2) x1

Pleased that they had everything they needed she sends back her answer.

Yes please. Can't wait, see you at mine at 7 x

She grabs a beer, just the one for her nerves she tells herself, then tries to relax on the couch, thinking back to the day they started their spending spree for house breaking equipment.

The day had started out with them waking up in each other's arms. Stewart getting up to make them breakfast in bed, before they both climbed into the shower. Two hours later, once they eventually got ready, they headed out the door. Their first stop was a supermarket, buying the holdall, dark clothes and trainers. Adding in a few bottles of their favourite red wine for later that night, all paid for by their new joint credit card. After that they treated themselves to some lunch, with wine, then continued their shopping. The gloves, masks, and wig for Elaine were all bought online and delivered.

They spent the rest of the night in bed planning then re-planning everything they wanted to do to Bronagh's flat as they drank the bottles of wine.

Elaine smiles at the memory.

The door opens and Stewart walks in, spotting Elaine grinning away to herself like the proverbial Cheshire Cat on her couch.

"I hope you're thinking about me with a smile like that on your face." Elaine turns her head to look at her lover, her smile widening at the sight of him leaning against her door frame.

"You better believe it. I'm remembering the day we bought everything." Stewart smiles and stalks over to the couch, towering over her.

"Hmmm, aye that was a great day."

"Yes it was." He leans down and kisses her hard. "You ready for this?" she asks, apprehension clouding her voice.

"Most definitely, you?" Hearing Stewart's strong and unwavering voice Elaine nods, any worry she had dissipating.

"Bring it on!" Stewart grins and kisses her again.

They both get changed into the dark clothes and repack the crowbar, golf club and condoms back into the holdall and leave for Bronagh's flat. They decide to use Elaine's Audi TT, as it's the least known in the Parkhead area out of their cars.

They pull up at Bronagh's flat, parking on the street, as night finally descends. The security door is lying unlocked, as was normal, and the landing lights were out, casting dark shadows on the stairs. They climb the three flights of stairs quietly until they are both standing outside Bronagh's flat.

Stewart places the holdall down and they retrieve the bandannas, gloves and weapons, kissing each other good luck before putting on their masks and getting down to business.

The crowbar makes quick work of forcing the door, making it pop and crack with the satisfying sound of splintering wood. After a quick pause to make sure no one was coming out of the surrounding flats to catch them, the lovers enter Bronagh's flat. They quickly go from room to room making sure the flat was empty before making a start.

Grinning at each other they start in the kitchen. Pulling open every drawer and cupboard door, they empty all the contents onto the floor smashing everything they could get their hands on or weapons to including doors and walls. Once they were finished in the kitchen there wasn't a plate, cup or glass left intact or a door sitting properly on its hinges. They move into the living room, Elaine putting her golf club through the TV and Stewart taking his crowbar to the coffee table and mirrors. Elaine goes back to the kitchen to get a chopping knife. She comes back into the living room with a glint in her eyes, then goes about stabbing and slashing every inch of every cushion on the couches and chairs until every part of them is destroyed. Dust and stuffing float about the living room like a scene from a cheesy romantic pillow fight. Urging each other on, they turn their attention to the spare bedroom. Again they wrench open every drawer and cupboard, pulling out every item of clothing and bedding from its home. Elaine starts with the knife again, slashing and stabbing her way through the bed until there was another pillow fight scene, this one looking a lot more sinister. One thing Elaine was thankful for was not coming across anything of Max's on her rampage. As much as she was falling head over heels in love with Stewart, to the point that she could hardly concentrate on anything but him, it still annoyed her that Bronagh had her own gorgeous sandy haired hunk. Elaine was hoping that Max and Bronagh weren't as close as she had once thought, until she entered the bathroom.

There for all to see were two toothbrushes, men's deodorant, shower gel, razor and all other sorts of paraphernalia relating to men and Max. Incensed by the thought of Bronagh and Max happy and almost living together, Elaine swings her club, making contact with the mirrored cabinet on the wall. Mirror shards and wooden splinters explode into the air as does the scream that Elaine lets rip from her throat. Stewart comes running in.

"You okay babe?" Concern is etched on his handsome features. Elaine composes herself and smiles. "Fantastic my lover, I'm just enjoying myself loudly, as you know I like to do." Stewart grins broadly.

"Well, carry on and I'll meet you in the master bedroom." The heat in his eyes is unmistakable and Elaine grabs him, crushing her lips to his.

"I'll be there as soon as I've finished in here." He gives her backside a quick squeeze then a hard slap before leaving her to destroy the rest of the bathroom. Spurred on by the promise in Stewart's eyes, Elaine smashes her golf club into the tiles, sink and bath. Swinging the club until she was out of breath and panting.

Entering the main bedroom, Elaine sees Stewart lying on top of the bed naked as the day he was born.

"Seeing you enjoy yourself so much is a sight to behold, and the thought of having you here and now is beyond anything I've ever wanted or needed." He pats the bed next to him. Elaine's eyes widen as a smile creeps onto her lips and grows until she can't hold back a full blown grin.

"You look good enough to eat," she smirks, and Stewart winks at her.

"Well what are you waiting for then?" Elaine stalks over to the bed, climbs on and crawls until she is exactly where she needs to be. Dipping her head she licks up the full length of him and smiles.

An hour later they are both sated and the room is destroyed. Everything smashable is smashed and all Bronagh's clothes ripped and slashed and the bed looks like it's spewed out its innards. On top of one pile of Bronagh's underwear Stewart opens and dumps the condoms, tearing one packet slightly open. Elaine watches as Stewart makes it look like the condoms were mixed up with the underwear and smiles. The car getting destroyed brought Bronagh and Max closer together, but the suggestion of Bronagh having another man should be enough to at least start the destruction of their relationship.

Satisfied that their work there was done, that there wasn't a spare inch of floor that wasn't covered with debris and destruction, and hot for each other all over again, they leave the flat. Tired, sweaty but happy.

As they step outside they both take a deep breath of fresh air. They had repacked their weapons, gloves, bandannas and Elaine her wig, letting her bottle blonde hair flow free. They clasp each other's hands and walk down the stairs. The drunk decides at that moment to make an appearance in front of them. Swaying slightly but not so drunk that he can't focus on Elaine and recognise her.

"Haw, hen, you're that wumin' that fucked up that stuck-up bitch's car a couple a weeks ago." Elaine stands frozen to the spot. Out of everything the drunk had probably forgotten, he hadn't forgotten that or her. Stewart tightens his grip on her hand.

"I thought you said you weren't seen doing that?" he growls into her ear. Elaine clenches her teeth.

"No, I said I fixed it so no one remembered they saw me. I handed him fifty quid, by rights he shouldn't remember anything from that night, now shush." She turns her attention back to the drunk.

"And I thought you had been told that you didn't see anything!" The drunk looks about the empty hallway.

"Nobody here to hear me, so..." He shrugs as if everything was good, then he points to the holdall in Stewart's hand. The head of the driver sticking out of it.

"Looks like you've been busy again." He licks his dry, cracked, dirty lips and wiggles his eyebrows, suggesting he knew everything that had gone on in the flat. Elaine huffs. This was not part of their plan, but she had made a slight contingency plan of her own for this particular interruption.

"Fine." She growls at the drunk and pulls out fifty pounds from her back pocket and shoved it into the drunk's filthy hands, trying her damnedest not to touch the grime engrained skin. He smiles, showing off the black abyss and small yellow stumps that was his smile.

"Ah hen, you know how to look after an auld man... an yirsel," he adds with his tongue firmly in his cheek.

"Aye well, just you forget you saw anything, and we'll all be fine." The drunk nods.

"Aye, we will that. God Bless ye." Elaine nods, bemused at the blessing.

"Right, well okay then, but that is your last so from now on you are the proverbial three monkeys, see no evil, hear no evil, speak no evil, get it?" The drunk salutes her and mumbles his agreement and thanks then heads up the stairs, a slight spring to his step now he had another fifty pound pay off.

"That was close!" Stewart growls as they climb back into her Audi. "How did you know to bring the money?"

"I didn't, it was a 'just in case' thought I had yesterday." Stewart places his hand on her knee as the engine roars to life.

"Well, well done you." She blows out a breath. She was worried that Stewart was going to be angry at her for being spotted twice, but thankfully, he wasn't. If anything he seemed to be proud of her, even praising her. Her heart swelled at his words.

"Why thank you." Stewart squeezes her thigh, and she smiles, not wanting to look from the road too much as they drive back to Elaine's house to open the bottle of Champagne they had been saving for this particular night.

****

Their dinner at the Chinese buffet was up to its usual standards of amazing. They both had eaten their fill and enjoyed every morsel of food that'd passed their lips. Their conversation had been easy as usual, talking about everything and nothing. Nearer the end of their meal Max turned the conversation serious.

"You really think that crazy bitch Elaine's finished harassing you?" Bronagh stills at the mention of that name, then she cocks her head to the side, thinking for a second.

"I don't know to be honest, but I hope so. I mean I can't live my life in constant fear, so I'm just going to carry on like nothing is going to happen, like it has been for a while and hope that it doesn't start again." Max nods his agreement.

"You heard anything from the insurance company?"

"Aye, they're going to pay out for a new car, thankfully, so I need to go look at cars. You fancy going car shopping with me later in the week?" Another nod as Max eats his last bite of cheesecake.

"I'm sure we can do that, what you looking for? Please go for a brand new car this time and not a second hand one." Bronagh looks at him quizzically. "I'll feel happier knowing the car is reliable." This time Bronagh smiles and squeezes his hand.

"I appreciated everything you fixed on Freddie, but yes I'm going to buy a new car." She pauses for a second. "You loved him really!"

Max snorts at her statement. "Only because he was yours. If he was brought into the garage by anyone else I would've hated him." Bronagh laughs and shakes her head at him. "Right, you ready for home?"

"Oh, yes please, I'm knackered." Max stands.

"Moan then." Bronagh drains her wine glass and smiles.

"Hmm, but I need to pee, so, hang on two minutes." Max shakes his head then walks over to pay the bill as Bronagh makes her way to the ladies. Most people would find it strange or even annoying, but Max loved the way she announced when she was going to the toilet.

Climbing into Max's Golf he turns to Bronagh. "Yours or mine?" It's a question they have both gotten used to asking as they had started to spend every night together since her car had been destroyed. Max had been thinking about asking her to move in with him, but hadn't found the courage as of yet, so they continued with the nightly question.

"Mine, your van's already there for the morning. And, that way it's only you that needs to get up early in the morning." Bronagh grins at her reply and Max groans at the thought.

"That's not fair, but I suppose it makes sense. Right yours it is then." He gives her a quick kiss, then starts the drive back to Parkhead.

The drive back only takes five minutes as the traffic was light. Max pulls into the numbered parking bay and cuts the engine. They both climb out and head towards the flat, unaware of the destruction waiting for them.

Bronagh is first to climb the dark stairs and arrive at her door. Her head is practically inside her handbag searching for her keys. Max squeezes her hand at the same time the light coming from the broken open door catches her eye. Fear seeps through her system again as Max pulls her behind him. He pushes the door with the toe of his Doc Martens and it swings freely. The light shining from the hall shows them the splintered wood of the broken door and then the chaos that litters the hall floor.

"HELLO?" Max shouts through the door, trying to gauge if anybody remained in the flat. Silence. He looks back at Bronagh, who has never dropped the death grip she has on his hand, her expression unreadable. "You stay here. I'm going in."

She shakes her head at him vigorously.

"Don't leave me." She croaks out. Max drops his head, thinks, then gives her a sharp nod.

"Okay, but stay beside me." She nods vigorously again. They both step inside the flat and Bronagh gasps as she sees the extent of the wreckage that is now her home.

Room to room they go together taking in every inch of the annihilation. When they started their walkabout Bronagh was gasping, then whimpers, but by the end, as they walked into her bedroom she is silent with the shock of it all. Max's anger grew with each room they went into, culminating to a rage when he saw the bedroom. The hatred that had been conveyed to them in the cutting and slicing of Bronagh's clothes and bed was almost unbearable.

Taking her into his arms, Max tries to embrace her, but she is stiff; he guesses with shock. He takes her face in his hands and tries to get her to look at him, or get some sort of emotion from her. Anything but this stiff silence.

"Bre? Bre, look at me." Eventually she drags her eyes to his.

"What?" Her voice flat.

"Are you okay?" She starts to laugh at what she thinks is a ridiculous question, but stops when she sees Max's features harden. "What's that?" Max is looking over her shoulder at a pile of her underwear. The pile that the condoms are mixed up in. Bronagh is confused at his change in tone and body language. Going from worried to angry in a split second.

"What's what? The flat? The flat's been ransacked, can't you see?" Her tone going sarcastic. Max shakes his head.

"Of course I see that," he snaps, "that's not what I mean. I mean them, the condoms. Why do you have condoms?" Bronagh's eyebrows knit together in confusion, her stomach flipping with fear.

"I don't, why would I?" She searches his face for answers.

"You do." Max's tone has turned accusing. He knew he was sounding like an arsehole, but he couldn't help himself. They didn't use that form of protection since Bronagh started on the Depo Provera injection. The thought of anyone else sleeping with his girlfriend burns at the back of his throat. He places his hands on her shoulders, turning her around sharply so she could see the offending items for herself. "They must have been in your knickers drawer, look," he demands. Bronagh's eyebrows knit some more and her stomach flips then drops as she spots them. She had never kept condoms in that drawer. On the few occasions she had bought them she kept them in her 'sexy underwear drawer', which was on the other side of the room. She starts to shake her head.

"They're not mine." She whips back round, fear and anger crossing her face.

"Well if they're not yours, whose are they and why are they in *your* drawer?"

"I don't know." Her anger grows. "But, *when* I used them, *before* us, I didn't keep them in *that* drawer!" Her tone was getting frostier with every word as her anger grew at Max's non-accusations. "So I'm guessing that whoever did this," she sweeps her arms around at the disaster area that was now her bedroom, "left them. Maybe they wanted us to argue. I guess that part of their plan has worked." Max flinches at her words. He had never witnessed her going home with anyone, so stupidly thought she wasn't with anyone. The realisation that she had been having sex with other men made bile rise up from his stomach to his throat. He knew he had no right to be jealous of her being with other guys before they had got together. He had been with his fair share of women. So he pushes the thoughts to the side as he starts to think about her hypothesis that the condoms were planted. Taking a deep breath he sags his shoulders, conceding that she may have a valid point. Especially if Elaine was involved. Taking her hands in his he looks into her blazing emerald green eyes.

"I'm sorry. I didn't mean to be a dick. It's just..." He huffs out a breath then carries on, "The hatred put into destroying your flat is horrific, then seeing, *them*." He shrugs, not sure how to convey the emotions that are crashing through him. Bronagh nods her understanding. Well she thinks she understands his outburst. She takes him into her arms.

"I know, I can't believe what I'm seeing either, but I promise you, they are not mine." Max searches her eyes. He sees nothing but love and fear shining from them. He squeezes her tightly, trying to squeeze away any lingering doubt.

"I guess we should phone the police again." He pulls away from their embrace as he reaches for his phone in his pocket. The severity of the break-in hits Bronagh square in the stomach. Looking up at Max with startled eyes she runs from him, over the debris, to what is left of her bathroom, making it to the toilet (which thankfully is intact, which is more than can be said for the sink) just in time as the contents of her stomach projects itself onto the white porcelain again and again until there is nothing left in her stomach, not even bile. Once her retching stops she places her head on the cold tiles of her broken wall. With thoughts of why me racing through her head she starts to cry.

CHAPTER EIGHTEEN

Max holds Bronagh in his arms as they sit amongst the debris in the hall waiting for the police to arrive. After the vomiting and the crying had stopped, the panic sets in. Bronagh struggles to breathe as she asks out loud why would anyone be so evil to her and what she did to deserve such an attack, and the most important question of who? Max's heart and mood drops lower with every hard fought breath that Bronagh takes. He hates that he couldn't do anything to make the situation better and all his words of reassurance sounded stupid and hollow, even to his ears.

After half an hour Bronagh had calmed, other than the odd shuddering breath, and they sat in silence amongst the rubble of her hall. Max rubbed her back as he promises himself he would get whoever was responsible for the break-in and the attack on Bronagh's car. Every so often his thoughts would return to the condoms scattered on the bedroom floor. The rational side of him understood that they could have been planted, especially if it was Elaine who orchestrated it, or even been left over from before he and Bronagh got together. The irrational side of him, the insecure side that never believed he stood a chance with Bronagh, however, is telling him otherwise. This side is convinced that the reason for them being there is more likely something that was going to tear them apart.

There's a knock on the broken door, which pushes it open, pulling Max from his destructive thoughts and Bronagh from her almost catatonic state. A strong voice booms through the door, announcing the police officers' arrival. Bronagh and Max scramble to their feet and open the door wider letting the officers get an eyeful of the destruction strewn over the floor. The officers' eyes widen at the sight in front of them but manage to cover it with their professionalism quickly.

"Miss White, this is WPC Sian Young and I'm PC Ben Loughran, can we come in please?" PC Loughran asks and Bronagh steps forward slightly.

"Yes, come in, please, sorry about..." Her emotions catch in her throat and Max steps up to her and pulls her into his arms, trying to give her some strength from his embrace. He also needs her touch to calm his anger.

The officers wave away her apology and start their questions. Once they had finished talking with both Max and her the officers start to look about the disaster zone that is now her home. All of them going from room to room inspecting what had been destroyed and asking questions about theft.

All finished with their walk about and questions, the officers return to Bronagh and Max.

"Miss White, do you have anywhere you can stay for a while? The Scene of Crime officers will need to comb through everything." Max is first to speak up.

"Aye, she's staying with me." Bronagh can only nod.

"Okay. Do you have insurance?" Again Bronagh nods.

"I'll phone them in the morning." Her voice is strangled, but there.

With promises to be in touch and condolences at the state of her house, the officers take their leave. Once they are away Max takes her into his arms again.

"C'mon we'll get home." Too tired to correct him that she is home she follows him out to his car. Neither of them bothering about securing the front door.

Once they got to bed neither of them slept much again. Both of them tossing and turning most of the night, although they never seemed to be awake at the same time. When Bronagh was lying awake Max seemed to be in the middle of another of his bad dreams as he thrashed about the bed. She would soothe him as she did the first time, whispering his name and stroking his hair, but again he never seemed to wake up, just become calmer. She made a mental note to ask him what his dreams were about, and hoped that he would confide in her.

The alarm sounds at its usual time of seven a.m. Max and Bronagh groan at the incessant buzzing. Max pulls her into his arms and nuzzles her neck.

"Are you planning on going in today?" The concern he felt was evident in his tone. Bronagh shrugs.

"I need to phone Erin and see what the protocol is for a crazy person trashing your house." Max snorts a soft laugh against her shoulder. "I've just got so much to do for the two parties I'm working on. I don't want to let anyone down, but I also need to get things organised, like phoning the insurance company and starting to clean up the flat... if the police are finished with it that is." She huffs. When did her life become so complicated? Turning to look at Max he sees that she is fighting her emotions to keep them under control. He places his hand on her cheek, stroking away a lone tear that has escaped.

"I'm sure the work will understand, and if you want I can drop in and pick up your folder thing and bring them back here. That way you can get some work done in between getting things for the flat done." Her heart swells at his generosity.

"That's a lot of running about for you." Max shakes his head.

"I'm not going in if you're not going in. I am at your beck and call today." She looks up at him confused.

"Why?"

"Why? Well firstly you've got lots to do. Contact the insurance, the police, go shopping, and secondly I'm not ready to leave your side today." Max wasn't sure if the last part was due to the fact he was worried about her safety or to his own stupid thoughts of mistrust, or even a bit of both. But either way he was staying with her as much as possible. Bronagh lifts her hand and strokes his cheek.

"Thank you. For everything." Max shrugs away the praise and dips down to kiss her.

****

The night of the break-in had been euphoric and erotic for both Elaine and Stewart, and they took full advantage of both feelings on more than one occasion during the night. Firstly at Bronagh's flat, then when they arrived home to Elaine's house and then again once the second bottle of Champagne they had opened to celebrate had been finished.

Waking up the next morning was a bittersweet feeling for Elaine. The memories from the night before bombard her. Everything from the message Stewart sent letting her know the break-in was happening to falling asleep in the arms of her partner in crime/lover, and everything in between. She smiles as she remembers the events of the night before, but it quickly turns to a grimace as the headache and stomach pains of yet another hangover threatens to overtake her body and senses. Thankfully Stewart had had to leave in the early hours of the morning for work again, so he wasn't there to witness the green pallor that was Elaine's face, or hear the god awful noises she was making as she vomited and heaved her way through the morning.

Come late afternoon, Elaine decides to try and eat something. Waiting on her toast to pop her thoughts turn to the police. Part of her slightly worried that there would be a knock at the door, the police coming to talk to her again. Then part of her relished the idea. She could claim stomach flu alongside the alibi her and Stewart had devised the night before.

"We were together the whole night, here. You made dinner, we drank champagne, made love all night then fell asleep."

Stewart's words rang in her head. She had to admit, for the most part it was true, except she never makes dinners.

Come four o'clock, and with the toast staying down, Elaine opens a bottle of Barolo red wine to breathe, then orders in her dinner. The local Italian restaurant was always a good choice.

Her first sip of wine went over like she had just swallowed some of the broken glass from last night, but that's what happens when you have a hair of the dog. Her phone buzzes, alerting her to a message from Stewart.

Been thinking about you and last night all day. Need to see Jane tonight, she's getting suspicious so will see you tomorrow. X

Her heart drops at the thought of not seeing her lover, but understood his need to keep suspicion to a minimum, sort of, but that didn't stop the tears from falling after her third glass of wine.

Nine o'clock comes and the bottle has been finished. Elaine decides on an early night. Climbing into bed she cuddles into the pillow Stewart had been using and breathes his scent in deeply, making fresh tears spark in her eyes. Never in her whole adult life had she felt this way or cried this much over a lover. With the thought that maybe Stewart was becoming more than just another lover she drifts off into a fitful dream filled sleep.

CHAPTER NINETEEN

Two weeks had passed and Bronagh hadn't been harassed again. The insurance had worked hard at pushing through her claim due to the extent of damage. She had no flat, no clothes or belongings to her name, and she continued to stay at Max's.

Her next party was booked in for the next weekend and she knew she had to be on her toes after the 'excitement' of the last party. She had managed to settle herself at work and to a point in her relationship with Max, although he was being helicopter boyfriend again. Not letting her from his sight unless she was at work (then Gordon took over). One part of her life she wasn't settled in was her friendship with Jane. She was beginning to feel like the worst friend in the world. She knew Jane and Stewart were going through a tough patch in their relationship. Stewart was pulling back and starting to use every excuse in the book to not see Jane or cancelled their arrangements at short notice. He used everything from illness to having to work away for the weekend. They all knew he was having an affair. People who work in call centres aren't known for their business trips, but Jane just couldn't bring herself to admit it. That would mean giving up on the relationship. Bronagh knew Jane understood her not having a lot of time or money at that particular time, but it didn't stop her from worrying about it.

"I'm going to arrange a girlie night out with Jane, just the two of us for the weekend after the party." She was tidying up the kitchen after dinner. Max was opening up a bottle of Shiraz.

"Is that a good idea?" Bronagh squeezes her eyes shut at his words, glad that her back was to him. She knew he wouldn't like the idea of her going out without him, and to a point she understood his need to keep her safe, but she needed time with Jane, and maybe a little time away from him and his helicopterness.

"Well, the police don't think there's any threat towards my person, that it's all just scare tactics. Plus there hasn't been anything for a fortnight now." She finishes off the dishes and dries her hands then walks over to Max, putting her arms around his waist. "I need to be able to live my life, which means going on a night out with my friend." Max places his forehead onto hers. He really was trying to not be the controlling, suffocating boyfriend he knew he was turning into. If only Elaine would fuck off and leave Bronagh alone for good and the thought of those damn condoms, and the thought of his girlfriend being with other guys, would leave his head he could go back to being the boyfriend he knows and wants to be for Bronagh.

"I know, Bre, I understand, I do. Honestly... but, I just want you to stay safe." He feels her slump slightly in his arms and he hates it, but continues with his need to keep her safe. He tries to compromise. "Can we see how the next week goes, and if there is still nothing from Elaine then we can organise something?"

Bronagh grinds her teeth, not wanting to start an argument, but not wanting to give up either she relents, slightly.

"I suppose. But I'm not going to give up on wanting to go out with Jane."

Max swallows his protestations, not wanting an argument either.

"I know you won't, but please, for me?" He knew it was a low blow using her emotions, but uses them anyway. Bronagh blows out a huff.

"Fine. We'll discuss it next week." She gives him a quick kiss, but they both feel a slight frost enter the room.

****

146

The two weeks after the break-in had gone slowly for Elaine. She and Stewart had seen each other as much as possible, although not every day. They wanted to keep Stewart in touch with Bronagh so they knew how she was reacting to everything, plus they needed to keep Jane's suspicions to a minimum, if possible.

Elaine was starting to feel cooped up sitting in her house every day. She had very little reason to go out now she wasn't scratching up Bronagh's car or going to work. Most days she didn't even get dressed until Stewart was due over, and if it was a day he wasn't coming she just didn't bother. She had even let her snobbery in wine slip and had started buying it by the box! It worked out cheaper. Knowing money would soon be an issue, Elaine had bitten the bullet and sold her Audi TT. It broke her heart to sell it, but, until she got her job back (which would happen once she got Bronagh out the way), Elaine had to generate money by other means. So, she thinks, if selling her car and drinking boxed wine is what she had to do she would do it. Anything to get her own way in the end.

With the feelings of anger and suffocation starting to take over, Elaine peels herself from the couch and up to the shower. Once she was washed, shaved her legs and under her arms, and starting to feel human again, she shuts off the water and climbs out. Enjoying the feeling of doing something, she goes about drying and styling her hair, then continues to pamper herself by doing her make-up. An hour later she's picked out her favourite red dress and is admiring herself out in her full length mirror. Realising how sexy she is looking she decides not to waste her effort, or her good mood and phones a taxi.

Remembering the mechanics that Max works at was also a second hand car dealers she asks the taxi driver to drop her off there. She had been meaning to go car shopping, and getting to Max without Bronagh could only be a good thing. Paying the driver, she shimmies out the back of the silver Skoda. Feeling eyes on her she wiggles her very short dress down so it actually covered her backside.

"Oh aye, look at the piece of arse that's walking this way." One of the mechanics Max is working with comments to him.

"Aye, I'm sure she is, but, I'm not interested, and I'm busy, just like you should be." The mechanic rolls his eyes at his workmate.

"You've turned into a complete bore since you got wa that girlfriend ye yours." Max looks up from the wheel he's removing.

"No, I've stopped being a dick is all." Well to all other women, but started being one to Bronagh he thinks to himself. He knows he's turning into an over protective arsehole, but he just couldn't help it. He needed to keep her safe, and his girlfriend.

"Ach, c'moan an' have a wee look." The mechanic pushes on. "Look she's blonde and everyhin', just your type." Max's heart stutters in his chest at hearing the woman's hair colouring. He turns his head further out to see the woman his workmate was talking about. His eyes settle on her and his heart stops, then drops.

"Ah, fuck!" The mechanic's head snaps round to look at Max.

"Don't tell me she's an ex?" Max slides himself to the driver's side of the car to hide. The mechanic's eyebrows shoot into his shaved hairline. "Oh, shit. She is an ex an' a crazy one at that. Spill. Now!"

Max shakes his head. "She's not an ex. That's the crazy bitch I was telling you about, the one that's been harassing Bre."

The mechanic takes another quick look then turns his attention back to Max. "Wow, but, she's hot."

Max growls. "Get rid of her, and if she asks, I'm not here."

The mechanic sniggers. "Okay, okay, gees a minute." The mechanic strolls over to Elaine. "Awright hen, how can I help?"

Elaine rolls her eyes at the man approaching her, but manages to plaster on her sexy smile.

"Hi there, I'm looking for a new car, and Max Stevenson."

The mechanic's eyebrows head upwards again.

"Well hen, ye see, I can help ye wa the car an' that. We've git loads ow'er there," he points towards the car lot. "But I canny help ye wa Max, sorry, an' that." She glowers at the man before her. Idiot!

"Well, *hen,*" she spits back his endearment at him, "I'm sure you could help me with picking a car, but I've asked for Max to help me, and I know fine well he's here. I can see his feet under that beat up piece of shit car he's working on. So why don't you run over and tell him I'm waiting... *hen.*" The mechanic chuckles and walks back over to Max.

"You're right, that bint's crazy, an', she wants you... so, time to man up and face whatever shit she's bringing." Max glowers at the mechanic and throws down the tools he was using. Walking past his workmate Max growls.

He starts walking over to Elaine and makes eye contact with her. For some reason this woman was making it her mission in life to bring the love of his life to her knees and maybe their relationship with her.

"What d'you want?" Max snaps, and Elaine pouts.

"Is that any way to talk to a customer? And a sexy one at that," she purrs. Max rolls his eyes.

"I've got nothing to say to you, so please leave." She stalks over to Max, closing the space between them. He stands straighter, not wanting to give her any reason to think she is affecting him.

"Now, now, Max, I don't think your boss would see it like that. I want you to show me some cars." He huffs.

"I'm a mechanic, not a salesman. Wait here and I'll get..."

"NO! I want you!" Elaine has closed the gap between them enough that she can draw her fingernail over his chest through his overalls. "I want you to be my personal shopper, and help me try out the suspension... if you know what I mean." She winks at him. She realises that she's no longer attracted to Max now she has Stewart satisfying her every desire, but she knows how much it must affect him so continues running her fingernail over his chest. He pushes her hand away. He doesn't want to show her how much she was affecting him, but he had to get away.

"No shit any of that's happnin'!" He looks her up and down then turns on his heel and walks away, his anger bubbling under his skin. Elaine smiles in triumph.

Max's boss picks that moment in time to exit the staff area and smile at Elaine, who's teetering her way behind Max. He puts his hand up to stop Max in his march.

"What's happening?" The boss looks between Max and the teetering woman trying hard to keep up with him. Max just glowers.

"She's looking for a car, so I'm going for a salesperson." Elaine eventually catches up with Max, and rests her hand on his shoulders. She feels him tense his muscles at her touch and smiles.

"Wow, you walk fast," she looks about her, as if she had no idea where she was going, "I thought you were taking me to see cars?" She manages to look confused, and innocent (all without laughing). Max swings round, pinning her with a stare.

"I told you. I. Am. Not. A. Salesman and I will not be anything to you today or any day... ever," he growls. Turning back to his boss he tries to get his anger back under control. "I'm going back to what you pay me for, you deal with THAT." He hitches his thumb over his shoulder to indicate that Elaine is the 'that', then storms off, slamming every door between the work bays and the staff area.

Pacing the floor of the staff kitchen Max manages to calm down, getting his anger back to a level where he doesn't want to hit something, he can breathe and get back to work, properly.

Walking back to the car he was working on Max needs to pass the sales area and spots Elaine sitting there. She sees him at the same time, giving him a wink and blowing him a kiss. She laughs. Anger bubbles under his skin again. Knowing he can't do anything else as she is now a paying customer, Max stalks back to work, changing the brake disc of the car with more force than was absolutely necessary.

****

Getting back to Max's house, Bronagh parks the Golf and bounces into the living room. Her mood light and airy, for the first time in what feels like forever, after a very fun and productive day at work. She can hear Max in the kitchen rattling and mumbling away to himself as he makes dinner. Making her way down the corridor and into the kitchen Bronagh hears that the rattling and mumbling is more than just dinner making.

"Fuckin' cow, fuckin' bitch, fuckin' boot, at my fuckin' work..." Bronagh made her way up to the kitchen door and listens to her boyfriend's rant before she enters and interrupts. Opening the door, she slides in and clears her throat before talking.

"Who was at your work? And why are you swearing so much?" Max stops mid rant at her voice and turns to face her.

"Bre... eh, well, maybe you should take a seat." A chill runs up her spine, judging by the amount of swearing Max was doing she wasn't going to like whatever he was about to tell her. Taking a seat at the small kitchen table Bronagh looks up at him.

"Max, what is it? What's happened? Are you okay?" The more she asks questions, the more visions are flying around her head, making her panic more. Her stomach rolls as she runs her eyes over every inch of him, making sure there were no injuries. Max sees her searching his body, and he takes her hands in his.

"I'm fine, just angry, but calming down now you're in." Bronagh gives him a worried, confused look and Max takes a deep breath before talking again. "Elaine came to my work today, and asked for me... she wanted me to sell her a car." Bronagh's face drops, then twists in anger.

"She knew where you worked?" Max nods. "And she asked for you?" Another nod. "So she came looking for you... and?" Now it was Max's turn to look confused. Bronagh swallows hard, trying not to panic, or let her anger get the better of her. "What did you do, did you sell her a car?" He kneels before her, looking up into her eyes.

"No, I told her to leave. She refused, so I went to get a sales guy and then my boss took over. Bloody loved it too so he did. Then I went back to work." Bronagh takes a few deep breaths, trying to clear the anger flooding her system. She really is fed up of that woman. Fed up with allowing Elaine to have power over her. Well no more, she thinks.

"Well, I guess she must've needed a new car." Max looks up at her bemused. Pulling a chair out he sits beside her, never letting go of her hand as she continues to talk. "I mean it could be a coincidence that she arrived at your work. Probably not, but I can't let her every move affect me." She pins Max with a determined look. "I am not going to give her power over me any more... and she will not stop me from living my life, which means being able to go out with Jane next weekend." Max opens his mouth to argue, but the stern look on Bronagh's face stops him. He hasn't the energy to argue anyway after the day he'd had.

CHAPTER TWENTY

Getting Max's mobile number from Stewart, Elaine starts to message him from the unknown number.

Where's the girlfriend?

Elaine sniggers as she puts the phone down. She missed messing with their heads. She understands the need to lie low, but the thrill she got out of going to Max's work and seeing him get angry and annoyed was worth every penny of the taxi fare and the two thousand pound she paid for the crappy second hand 2006 plate Vauxhall Corsa she ended up buying.

Pouring herself another wine from the new box she starts to wonder where it all started to go wrong, but she quickly pushes the thoughts away. What she had to remember was none of it was her fault, and all of it was Bronagh's. Which is why she was teaching the bitch a lesson.

The unknown phone buzzes. An answer coming from Max. She's intrigued, so opens the message.

Who is this? Is this Elaine? What do you want?

Her heart lifts. She can't leave Bronagh with anything. She has taken her car, wrecked her flat, and now it's time to take her relationship, even if she isn't wanting him for herself any more.

I know the condoms are important to you.

Elaine knows they would probably suspect it is her behind everything, but she knows they can't connect her to anything. So far, legally, all they can prove is she turned up at the party, and the police have already dealt with that.

A wave of nausea washes over her and she steadies herself on the kitchen counter. She pushes the feeling aside and pours herself another wine, then goes to phone Stewart.

****

"Who the fuck is this?" Max shouts to the empty living room. He had dropped Bronagh off at Jane's, so the friends could have a catch up. He was hoping that by having this night with her friend, would mean Bronagh would give up on the idea of going out next weekend, but he highly doubted it.

Throwing his phone to the side, he goes to collect his gym bag. He needed to do some weights to burn off the excess energy he was feeling, plus he really needed to get his thoughts about those damn condoms under control before he picked Bronagh up, or he might just end up saying something he would later regret.

After two hours working out and with his muscles shaking, he heads over to Jane's to pick Bronagh up. Walking up to the front door, Max walks in without knocking as was normal for the friends. Hearing the women talking as he reaches the living room door, he stops to listen for a bit.

"I honestly don't know where they came from. The last guy I slept with, before Max, was about six months ago, and I got rid of the box..." She pauses in thought. "No, in fact I gave the box to the guy telling him to keep them for next time." Hearing Bronagh talk about her having sex with another man was turning his stomach, but he continued to listen. "Then I just avoided him. I didn't like him enough to make the same mistake twice." She huffs, "And he just wasn't Max... god that makes me sound so sad, but there you go." Max's heart swells at her words and he coughs making his presence known before entering the room. He looks between the women, then his gaze rests on Bronagh's tear filled eyes. She looks up seeing Max smile and a slight panic grabs her throat.

"Max..." she croaks out, "how long have you been there?"

"Long enough, Bre, at least long enough to know I've been more of a dick than I had thought." Jane snorts and Bronagh throws her a dirty look.

"All men are dicks!" Jane slurs and Bronagh shakes her head.

"Shush you, you're just drunk and annoyed at your man."
She stands up and takes her friend in a hug. "Right I'm going,
will you be okay for the rest of the night?" Max looks at his
watch, trying to judge how long Bronagh thought the 'rest of
the night' would be, as it was nearly midnight. Jane shrugs in
her friend's embrace.

"I'll just need to be, won't I?" Max rolls his eyes at the
drunk woman, and Bronagh pulls her in for another hug.

"Get rid of him, I'm telling you he's not worth your time
or love, and you are worth so much more." Bronagh looks her
friend in the eyes. "Promise me you'll at least think about it?"
Jane looks up at her best friend and gives her a watery smile.

"I'll think..." She hiccups then wobbles. Bronagh walks
her friend over to the couch and plonks her onto it, then turns
to leave with Max. "Love you Jane," she says over her
shoulder as they leave the living room, but she only gets a
drunken mumble back in return.

Once they are back at Max's house, he decides he wants
to talk about what he overheard.

"Bre, can we talk?" Worry flashes through her eyes as she
takes a seat next to him on his bed.

"What's wrong?" Her heart beats a fast tattoo as she waits
on his reply.

"I heard what you said to Jane about those damn condoms,
and I'm sorry." Bronagh's eyes widened at his apology.

"Sorry for what?"

"For thinking the worst." Her heart slumps.

"What d'you mean, 'thinking the worst'? What were you
thinking? I told you I didn't know where they came from, that
they weren't mine. Did you not believe me? Did you think I
was cheating on you?" She pauses for a second, until another
thought comes into her head. "Do you still think I'm
cheating?" Max closes his eyes. This was not the way he
expected this conversation to go.

"No, I don't think you're cheating. You're with me all the
time. I know you're not. It's... I don't know. I guess I stupidly
didn't think you were ever with anyone, or in a relationship. I

mean, I never seen you go home with anybody." Anger quickly sweeps over Bronagh at Max's words.

"No shit! I wonder why that is?" Max winces at the profanity she uses against him. Bronagh only swore when she was drunk or angry, and at that moment she was tipsy and furious.

"I know, I'm sorry. I'm stupid. I just didn't think, or to be honest, I didn't want to think about you being with anyone, at any time. So seeing them sitting there was a reminder that yes, you probably did have lovers before me, so I got a bit jealous." Bronagh blew out a breath and her anger receded. She knew the condoms had annoyed him that night, and had suspected that they had been playing on his mind since. Maybe, she should've spoken to him about them before now.

"I never let you see me with anyone so you wouldn't think I was taken, and I was never in a relationship with any of the guys I slept with. I never wanted them, I wanted you. It was always just a means to an end for me, and now I have you, why would I want anybody else?" Max lowers his eyes and shrugs, feeling even more of a dick than he did when he was overhearing the conversation. "Is that why you don't want me going out next weekend? In case I cheat?" Bronagh's tone had softened, until she asked the last question, when her anger threatened to rise again.

The thought had flitted through Max's mind, but he knew the main reason he didn't want her going out was her safety, so he kept the confession to himself.

"No, of course not. I just want you safe, and if it is Elaine behind everything, then, I don't know, she just has a knack of turning up wherever we are." He puts his hands on her shoulders so she could look him in the eyes. "I need you safe." He pulls her into his arms, loving the way she felt there. Hopefully, he thinks, that would be the end of his thoughts running rampant over what the condoms could mean.

Bronagh knew what Max was saying was because he loved her, but she really needed this night out. Deciding one heated conversation was enough for the night she holds her tongue.

"I understand, and thank you for worrying about me." He squeezes her, "and I'm sorry for swearing at you." Max laughs.

"That's okay, I'll get over it, and I guess at least I know you love me enough to get pissed at me."

"That I do, and more... forever." Max kisses her,

"Forever."

CHAPTER TWENTY-ONE

Waking up the next morning with Stewart by her side made Elaine feel a hundred times better than she had been feeling when she woke up over the past week or so. Every morning she had been waking up with what felt like a hangover. Head down the toilet for the first half hour of the morning, praying to any god listening that she would stop drinking, if they would stop the racking of her ribs as she heaved dryly. But, come five o'clock each night she's become bored and occasionally lonely so out would come the wine glass and the boxed wine.

She moves over to get closer to her lover and his warm body which sets off waves of nausea crashing over her, nausea she thought she was skipping that day. Desperate not to throw up over Stewart, or have him hear her vomit, she rushes to the bathroom, closing both the bedroom and the bathroom doors behind her as she went. Trying to be as silent as possible, but managing to make more noise than a whole pod of whales, Elaine throws up last night's dinner and wine. Again she swears off drinking and begs her body to stop heaving. Mentally she wonders if she should be due a six pack after all the 'exercise' her stomach muscles had been getting, but, somehow she doubted it. Hearing a noise from the hall she quickly gets up to wash her face and brush her teeth, but getting to a standing position sends her into a head rush and she needs to grab the sink to stop herself from falling down again. Getting her vision back Elaine decides that her blood sugar level must have plummeted after her purging everything in her stomach. She turns on the tap and sticks her mouth under the running water trying to take away the disgusting taste that was lingering there.

There is a gentle tap on the bathroom door and Elaine freezes.

"Babe, are you okay?" Panicking, Elaine wonders if she'd locked the door. Shakily she takes a deep breath in to answer.

"Yeah, I'm okay." She can hear herself that her voice sounds croaky, but there is nothing she can do about that other than hope Stewart isn't very observant.

"Are you sure?" She rolls her eyes at the closed door. No she's not sure. She feels like death, but she's not going to be admitting that to her lover.

"Aye!" it comes out sharper than she intended. "Sorry, I mean yes, I'm just... eh... brushing my teeth."

"Okay, well, hurry up 'cause I need a pish." Another eye roll at the door as Elaine inwardly berates Stewart for being so crude and insensitive, even if she was the one telling him she was fine. She catches herself and realises how irrational she was being, but she really wasn't caring due to the way she was feeling. Grabbing her toothbrush she loads it with toothpaste again then throws open the door, growling at Stewart. Stewart's eyes widen when his sight rests on Elaine. She is almost green in colour.

"You don't look okay." He places his hand on her forehead to check her temperature, but finds it normal. "You go back to bed and I'll bring you up a cup of tea." Tears spring into her eyes at his kind words and she starts to feel guilty over her thoughts of him being insensitive. Finishing her teeth she reaches up and gently kisses him on the cheek, her tears threatening to spill over her eyelids.

"Thank you," she manages to squeak out over the lump of emotion in her throat, then goes back into her bed.

Downstairs Stewart starts making himself a coffee and Elaine a tea. He hears his phone ring in the living room and walks to get it before the voicemail clicks on.

"Aye?"

"Stewart, it's me, Jane." Stewart closes his eyes. He never checked who it was before he answered. He really didn't want to talk to his girlfriend whilst standing in only his underwear in his lover's house, with his lover upstairs.

"What is it Jane? Shouldn't you be at work?" He hears a huff on the other end of the phone.

"I'm just about to start, but I had to get this over and done with, now I've made up my mind." She takes a deep breath before continuing. "I'm done being being second best in your life Stewart. I know you're cheating on me. I don't know who with and I don't care. I spoke to Bre at length about this last night and she thinks it's for the best if I just finish it between us, and after thinking about it all night, I realise she's right. I'm better than this relationship, so, I'm done. It's over." There's silence as Stewart takes in everything that Jane has just said. Anger at Bronagh's input into his life and relationship bubbles over.

"So, because fuckin' Bronagh wants you to finish with me you do it? She controls you now does she?" Jane is taken aback at Stewart's anger at Bronagh.

"What? No. She just pointed out a few home truths, but this is my decision." Stewart scoffs.

"You spend one night with her and the next day you're fuckin' dumping me? She gets with someone and is happy and now you're not allowed to be, is that it?" Jane growls.

"NO! Stewart you are the one having an affair, and I don't hear you denying it, or asking me to reconsider. All I hear is you blaming Bre for making me break up with you." Stewart snorts down the line at her.

"Well, this seems to be all coming from her, does it not?" Jane blows out exasperated breath.

"No, it's not, I've told you. This is me, all me. I'm worth so much more than how you treat me, so... it's over."

"Really? You think? Well if you'd rather have that cow in your life other than me then fine. I hope you like being alone with only that bitch to keep you company when she deems fit to pick you back up." The hatred in his voice incensed Jane, making her scream down the phone at him.

"Don't speak like that about Bronagh. You're the bastard here Stewart. And you've still not denied having an affair, so it's over. Goodbye." Jane cancels the call before Stewart has a chance to reply so he sends her a message.

This isn't the last you'll hear from me!

Seething with anger he stomps upstairs to rant to Elaine.

"Babe, you'll never guess what that bitch Bronagh has done now." Elaine had been resting when she heard the phone ring downstairs. She couldn't hear the conversation, only muted tones, then she heard the tones getting louder and angrier until, eventually, there was silence. After a few seconds of the silence, she then heard the stomping of Stewart's bare feet on the carpeted stairs.

She was trying to sit up without vomiting when Stewart barged through the door. Looking at him, standing in her bedroom in only his underwear, with anger rolling from him in waves made Elaine feel so much better. God he was sexy, she thought. Finding her voice she asks him what happened.

"That fuckin' bitch has made Jane dump me! I mean seriously, what the fuck has it to do with her?" Elaine's heart lifts hearing the news that Stewart was free to be hers and hers alone – something she never thought she would want with anyone – then it dropped like a stone in water, when she realised how annoyed he was at not being together with Jane any more. She pushes herself further up the bed. Whether to put more distance between her and her potential hurt, or to make her look bigger and so stronger than she was actually feeling, she didn't know, but she guessed that it might be a bit of both.

"So... where... eh... where does that leave us?" Stewart's eyes widen at her insecurity.

"Us? It doesn't change us. It just makes things harder for us to know what's going on... plus, it cements what we know about her. She's a stuck-up cow that always gets what she wants, even if it means hurting others, or taking from others." Stewart had made his way up the bed and takes Elaine in his arms. Tears prick at the backs of her eyes again. She really was emotional today. "No, gorgeous, it doesn't change anything with us." He kisses her soundly, then pulls back with a glint in his eye. "It does mean that she isn't learning her

161

lesson, so, we need to take it to the next level." Elaine's heart speeds up in her chest at the thought of what they had discussed would be the 'next level'.

"You mean, take her, hurt her?" Stewart nods, as he places gentle kisses over her jaw line.

"Aye. I mean taking everything from her hasn't worked. Trying to split her and that dickhead Max up hasn't worked, so, I think it's time we changed tact and take her from her life." He grins at his lover. A grin that starts out mad with a hint of evil then turns sensual and sexual. "You game?" All thoughts and feelings of nausea and hurt leave her, replaced by excitement, exhilaration, maybe even something that's verging on delirium. Elaine nods her head vigorously.

"Oh, god aye!" They grin at each other then take each other's mouths roughly. Both of them turned on by their next plan to abduct Bronagh.

****

Friday morning and Bronagh lies awake in Max's bed as she had been doing every morning. Just lying there wondering why, now, she had a man she loved, a job she loved, did life seem to be harder? Why were things like the messages happening, or her car being wrecked, or her flat being ransacked happening? And was it all connected to Elaine? Her thoughts turn to Elaine and what she had ever done to her? All Bronagh had done was get a job, so why had that made Elaine take such a hatred towards her and her life. That was, if it was Elaine behind everything. They had no proof that she was involved and the police hadn't been back in touch to say either way. She made a mental note to contact the police, check up on her case. From there her thoughts turn to getting her flat back in order and moved back in. She enjoyed being at Max's house, but felt it was too early in their relationship to take it to the level of moving in together. She knew it was a forever relationship and she knew she loved him with all her heart and soul, forsaking all others, but they hadn't had a chance to 'date' before everything started happening, forcing these living arrangements on them. She didn't want it to be forced. She wanted everything to take its own natural progression.

The flat had been cleared and cleaned, and she had even been looking at furniture, but was still waiting on the insurance money so she could go shopping. As it was, most of the car insurance money had gone on buying new clothes after everything she owned, bar a few things she had had at Max's, was destroyed, so she still didn't have a new car, again relying on Max.

Just as she was starting to think about her job and the engagement party Max wakes up and cuddles in.

"Hey you." He knew she would be awake before he opened his eyes. He knew she woke early every morning and worried. He could feel her become more tense with every passing minute, like she had to work up the courage to face the day. He knew she needed time out from him and the shit storm that her life must feel like some days, but he just couldn't let her go, anywhere, alone. He tells himself it was for her own safety, with Elaine and everything, but part of him knew it was a fear of losing her now he has her. The condoms spring to his mind again, and again he pushes the thoughts away. They've dealt with that and Bronagh has explained them and he believes her... doesn't he? Of course he does, he berates himself mentally.

"Hey, yourself." She smiles at him, and before he can think any more about anything he pulls himself onto his elbow and presses a kiss to her temple.

"Penny for your thoughts?" Bronagh turns to her boyfriend.

"Just going through everything I need to do. The party's tomorrow and I need to chase up the police and the insurance company." Max's heart restricts at the thought of Bronagh moving out, but he ignores it, at least he tries to.

"You know you can stay here for however long you want. There's no time restriction." Bronagh smiles and his heart lifts. Maybe she will stay, forever, he hopes.

"I know, and I appreciate everything you do and have done for me."

"But?" Bronagh eyebrows go upwards. He knows his tone was bitchy.

"I didn't say 'but'. I do appreciate everything." Max scrubs his hand over his face and sits up properly.

"I know you didn't, and I also know you appreciate everything. I just felt a 'but' was coming, like there was something else you wanted to say, but were holding back." His tone was more defeated now. Bronagh sighs.

"There is a small 'but'." Max takes a deep breath, waiting on her bombshell. "I think once I get everything organised in my flat I should move back in there and we should get back to dating." Tears sting the back of her eyes as she witnesses all the different emotions cross over his face before he shuts them all down.

"If that's what you want." He moves up the bed, putting some distance between. Bronagh notices the gap and blows out a breath as she pulls herself up the bed.

"Max, look at me." He drags his eyes to hers. "I'm not wanting to leave because I don't want to be with you. I want to get back to my own flat so I can be with you." Max scrunches his eyes.

"Bre, that doesn't even make sense." Bronagh shakes her head.

"I know. I mean... it was just a few weeks ago we didn't even know that we liked each other, I mean other than being best friends, and now I'm staying here and we're in love." Max shuffles closer and takes her hand, "And we've actually only been on one 'date'." Max sniggers at her use of air quotes and she playfully slaps him, never once dropping his hand. "Which ended horrendously." Max nods his head thoughtfully. He did understand her reasons for wanting back into her own home. He just couldn't help but feel they were going backwards.

Not wanting an argument, and really surprised that this conversation hadn't turned into one, Bronagh kisses Max deeply.

CHAPTER TWENTY-TWO

Elaine and Stewart lie in bed breathing hard after their strenuous love making. Elaine marvels at how relaxed she is in Stewart's arms. Normally she would be desperate to get away but not with Stewart. With Stewart she wants to lie there forever. A small gasp escapes her lips and Stewart pulls back so he can look at her.

"Hey, what's wrong?" Tears run down her cheeks unchecked.

"I'm okay, it's ... I've just realised that you are the first lover I've had in my bed." Stewart sits up more.

"What d'you mean?"

"I don't have anyone in my bed. I always make sure if we're here we stay downstairs, but I prefer when we are at hotels. I don't do this." She waves her hand between them indicating their situation.

"So, why the change with me?" Thankfully the tears had stopped, for the moment, but her heart was still hurting with the amount of emotion running through it.

"I don't know, we just feel different... right... complete." A sob escapes from her throat as more tears flow. She had never thought she would feel anything other than abandoned ever again and certainly never complete. That piece of information was something she would never admit, not out loud anyway.

"Aw, babe, you don't need to be upset over that. I feel the same, and I am honoured that I'm in your bed." Elaine smiles, wipes away her tears, and tries to sniff delicately.

"You really feel the same?" Stewart nods.

"Oh aye, and do you know what else we agree on?" Elaine shakes her head.

"What?"

"Kidnapping Bronagh." A grin spreads over both their faces. "So, d'you want to start planning?" Joy floods her system. They had had so much fun planning the break-in, she couldn't wait to see what fun they could have with the abduction plan.

"Oh, yes please," she giggles, another thing she never did until Stewart came into her life.

For the next few hours the lovers start on their plan.

"So, what do we need to think about?" Elaine asks, trying to contain her excitement.

"Well, we'll need to work how we are going to take her, where we'll be taking her from and when we are going to do it. Then we need to think about where we are going to keep her, and for how long." He pauses to think for a bit. "Things like that."

"Hmmm." Elaine watches Stewart as he thinks. She can almost see the electric pulses shoot through his brain as an idea comes to the forefront of his thoughts.

"Come to think of it, I have a garage across the road from my flat. We could maybe clear it a bit, throw in a mattress, put fixings on the wall that we can chain her to." Elaine stares at her lover in awe for a moment, totally amazed at how quickly he came up with all the ideas, then she grins inanely.

"Have you been thinking about this?" Stewart looks down, almost shyly, like he had been caught out.

"Wee bit." Elaine laughs, hard and loud, and Stewart joins her. They both laugh maniacally for long minutes. Eventually they calm down and get back to the matter at hand, planning Bronagh's abduction.

Elaine starts to muse about things they may need to buy. "We should be able to get most things on-line, or at local shops, or between us we might have some stuff." Stewart looks at her bemused.

"You have something in particular in mind?" Elaine's eyes glint as she gets off the bed. She walks over to her dresser and opens up the top drawer. She retrieves what she was looking for and turns back to face Stewart. Walking back to the bed she dangles a pair of leather restraining cuffs from her fingers, then climbs back in, handing them over to Stewart for his appraisal.

"Damn woman, why didn't I know about these?" She grins at him, then shrugs.

"Not my thing I'm afraid. They're leftovers from an ex..." She grimaces at the memory. "Didn't work out well." Stewart nods knowingly as she speaks.

"Ach, that's a pity, it would've been fun to play, but as it is they will come in handy. We can get chains connected to these." He fingers some of the metal hoops hanging from leather cuffs. "Then connect them to the wall fixings and voilà we will have, for all intents and purposes, a fully functioning dungeon for our abductee." More grinning from both of them as they continue their planning and start on ordering some more of the equipment that they were going to need.

****

Getting into work Bronagh flops into her blue roller chair, making it roll against her table. The morning had been very emotionally charged. She felt that Max was starting to come round to her way of thinking on the issue of her moving back into her own flat, but she still wasn't sure he was in agreeance with her over her night out.

Gordon comes into the room holding two coffee cups.

"Oh my princess, you have arrived." Bronagh looks up at her friend and smiles instantly. She takes the offered coffee cup and sips the black liquid gold. Feeling better instantly, Bronagh sighs.

"Ahh... Gordon, you are my hero. Do you know that?" He sniggers.

"For sure, my darling." He bends and kisses the top of her head. "Now, how are you today?" Bronagh thinks for a second, remembering her morning in bed with Max and smiles. "Oh, honey, I don't need the details that are flying through your head, a 'good' would suffice." Bronagh blushes at being called out, then laughs.

"I'm good. Getting a bit antsy about tomorrow, but I guess since Elaine doesn't know about this party I can be assured she won't turn up." Gordon scrunches up his nose, like he has smelled something nasty at the mention of Elaine's name, then snorts out his disdain for her.

"Very true my gorgeous girl. That blonde bit of crazy won't be there messing with you this time. Have you got everything organised for tomorrow?" She nods.

"Aye, just about. I'm going to start getting things and props over to the venue tonight then it's all hands on deck tomorrow."

"Is your hunk helping you again, or do you fancy having me?" He wiggles his eyebrows comically and Bronagh smiles at her friend.

"He's working in the morning, but if you could stay on call that would be great... please?"

"For you my darling, anything." She squeezes Gordon's hand and smiles again.

"Oh I love you. Now stop distracting me, I'm trying to work!" Chuckling, Gordon walks over to his own desk leaving Bronagh to get on with finalising everything for the engagement party.

Come one o'clock, Bronagh had everything finalised and her stomach demands to be fed. Sitting in the staff kitchen with Gordon, eating their lunches Bronagh's phone rings to life with an unknown number. Feeling uneasy over unknown numbers Bronagh swithers about answering, but decides to bite the bullet and presses the green phone icon.

"Hello?" She answers quietly. Gordon holds his breath as the silence from Bronagh stretches on. "Aye... I mean yes... hmm... ihih... yes" Gordon is near bursting at only hearing the one side of the conversation, desperate to know if it is Elaine or not. "That's fantastic, yes... thank you... amazing, thanks... yes... okay, bye." She cancels the call and grins at Gordon, who is trying to look calm.

"Well, I guess that wasn't Elaine?" His tone is slightly sarcastic, but not in a nasty way. Ignoring his sarcasm she shakes her head and is almost bouncing in her seat with excitement.

"Nope. That was the insurance company... they're paying out! I can go shopping!" She pauses, then scrunches her nose. "Well, I mean, I can go shopping on my credit card as they're sending out a cheque." Gordon bounces with her as he claps his hands together like an excited seal.

"Oh honey, that's fantastic. Good news for you at last. Well, we can start having a look this afternoon, if you want?"

"I don't think Erin or David would be chuffed if they knew we were furniture shopping for my flat... but, I guess, I'm up to date with the party for tomorrow... so... okay." The two friends grab each other in a tight hug then bounce back to the main work room and huddle round Bronagh's computer.

By four o'clock Bronagh had purchased a new king size bed and bedding, to be delivered on the Saturday she was due to go out with Jane. Perfect, she thinks. I can sleep in my own house, in my own bed after the night out. Then a pang of guilt hits her. She wonders how Max would take that piece of information. She knew he was worried about her and she understood why, but she was beginning to think he didn't understand her need to get things back to 'normal'. Pushing all her thoughts aside she tidies up her desk and says her goodbyes to Gordon on her way out.

CHAPTER TWENTY-THREE

After the amazing morning he shared with Bronagh, Max managed to get through his entire day at work without his mood dipping; a feat not normally achieved at the garage. There was always some problem with a car, or an annoying customer that made his mood plummet. Over the past few years, since he and Bronagh had became friends, the only thing to get him through the day was when he knew he was meeting up with her, and now they were involved, romantically, his moods were lightened at the end of every shift. The thought of her not being there, in his arms every night, if she moved back into her own flat, weighed heavy on his heart. He understood her need to have her own space, and he guessed she might be starting to feel a bit reliant on him, which probably didn't sit well with her, considering how independent she was before all the stalking and vandalism started. Plus he knew they hadn't had the most traditional of starts to their relationship, but he loved having her all to himself every night.

Knowing the end was probably nearing for him and Bronagh living together, at least for a while, Max decides to woo her (maybe even convince her to stay) with dinner. Stopping at the local supermarket Max goes in to buy the ingredients he needs for his romantic steak dinner.

Collecting everything he needs in record time, Max heads to the checkout. A blonde-haired figure catches Max's eye and his heart starts a tattoo in his chest. Praying that it's not Elaine, he forces himself to put one foot in front of the other until he is close enough to pass her. The woman turns to face him and smiles.

Max's heart and stomach free fall from their respective positions in his body. It's her, he realises. It's Elaine.

Recognition registers in her eyes at the surprise meeting, giving her a chance to play with him some more.

"Ah, Max!" she announces. "What a surprise." Closing the small gap between them she drags him into an embrace, planting a kiss on his unwelcoming lips. "How are you and that pitiful girlfriend of yours?" Rage bunches in his shoulders as he shrugs from the death hold she has on him. He really wants to scream at her to get the fuck out of their lives, but, knows he would be the one to come out of that scenario as the baddie. Screaming and swearing at a lone female in a shop is not a good idea, so instead, he keeps his voice low and his anger behind his clenched teeth.

"DO NOT speak about Bronagh like that... in fact don't even speak about her full stop. Just leave us alone and get on with your own life." Elaine hitches a finely plucked eyebrow at him.

"Tsk tsk Max. I only said hello. No need to go all protective and predatory on me. I mean, it's a supermarket, you tend to meet people all the time... don't they?" She grins, knowing she had planted a seed of doubt in his mind. Did he just bump into her and the meeting is all innocent and just a coincidence, or, has she orchestrated the whole thing? She loved the wariness that crossed over his features. And is going to love it even more when she takes his precious girlfriend from him. She knew that for the rest of the night he would be worrying about the crazy woman. The one who always seemed to be in the exact same shop, restaurant or car sales as them. This important titbit of information came from Stewart. He had told her that Max had admonished Bronagh for going out on her own. Telling her she had to be more careful with everything that had been happening in her life. Knowing she was getting to them made everything they were doing all the more exciting.

Growling at her Max takes his leave and walks past her. Two steps away he spots Stewart. He's standing stock still with wide wild eyes. The random thought that he could be there with Elaine slips through Max's mind, but he dismisses it quickly, opting instead that his deer in the headlights stare was more to do with his guilt over Jane and how he treated her. He growls his acknowledgement of Stewart as he storms past, resuming his quest to woo Bronagh, although his mood is now at an all time low.

On his arrival home he sees his Golf parked squinty. He snorts out a laugh at the mess of Bronagh's parking, which for some reason eases the tension and anger he has been feeling since seeing Elaine in the supermarket. Desperate to see and hold her after his encounter with the crazy blonde, he rushes into his house, through to the kitchen and dumps the bags on the floor, all the while shouting her name.

Bronagh hears all the shouting as she finishes drying herself after her shower. Pulling on her tartan jammies she makes her way downstairs.

"What is it? I'm here." Max turns and stares at her. She's standing in her slightly too big pyjamas, her hair wet, leaving the auburn waves hanging down her back, looking completely gorgeous. He rushes her, taking her in his arms and kisses her soundly and desperately. Once they separate she looks at him expectantly, not sure why he felt the need to be so desperate with his kiss. Another show of how their relationship has gone too far too quickly. They've only been together a month or so, so they should still be at the desperate for each other stage, not the old married couple, together forever, so we don't need to try any more stage, she thinks to herself as she looks at her jammies.

"Hello to you too." She pants as he smiles at her, taking in every detail of her freckle covered face.

"I've got stuff for dinner." He grins at her.

"Oh, what's the special occasion?" He shrugs.

"Nothing, I just wanted to make you dinner, so steak and wine it is."

"Hmm, sounds yummy. You need a hand?" Max shakes his head.

"Nope, just you sit there with a glass of wine and look gorgeous." He declares as he sits her down at the small kitchen table.

She watches on as Max washes his hands to prepare their steak and (shop bought) dauphinouse potatoes. The smells permeating were mouth-watering. Max really was a talented cook.

"Do you want me to go change before we sit down?" Bronagh realises that Max had a full night of romance planned and she was still sitting in her jammies.

"No, you're gorgeous as you are." He smiles over at her. In his head he had a big showy night of romance planned, but after his meeting with Elaine he didn't care about any of that. All he wants is Bronagh in his arms, safe. No matter what.

Sitting eating at the dinner table is nice, Bronagh muses, they really should do it more often. Max asks her about her day and she relays everything about her getting the finishing touches ready for the engagement party she was working the next day. Then, almost as an afterthought, she remembers the phone call from the insurance company.

"Oh, and the insurance phoned, they're settling my claim. The cheque's in the post." Max grins, hoping it looks genuine, but inside his heart deflates ever so slightly.

"That's good."

"I know," Bronagh continues excitedly, not registering Max's slight drop in mood, "I was a bad girl at work and had a look online at some things and ended up buying a new bed and covers and stuff. It's getting delivered a week tomorrow... sorry." His heart deflates another bit at hearing she has started to buy things, then it aches that she felt the need to apologise for it. He really was turning into the controlling boyfriend he hated, but again, he thinks, she needs to be safe and he can't keep her safe if she's not with him.

"That's okay," he lies, "You don't need my input." It comes out bitchier than he intended and he sees her physically flinch at his words. Guilt claws at him.

"I know that, but we haven't really discussed me moving back into my place, and all of a sudden it's starting... and, yes,

I would like your input. I mean we will be spending time there as well as here... won't we?" A slight panic passes over her.

"What...? Of course we will... I was just hoping you would... " He shrugs. Bronagh closes her eyes. She knew he wanted her to stay, and a part of her wanted to stay too. She really did. She enjoyed sleeping beside him every night and waking up to his morning scowl every morning, but the more independent side of her, the side that needed to assert herself again needed her own place back, her own space, her individuality, knew she needed to stop being Bronagh, the girl who HAD to move in with her boyfriend due to a crazy person vandalising her property. She needed the decision that she and Max would live together to be made out of love and commitment and not necessity.

"I know you're hoping I'll stay, but this is something I need to do... for me. It's not going to change anything between us." Max hangs his head. He knows, he understands everything, but he's not ready to give in... yet.

"I bumped into Elaine, again, today." He states trying to obtain the reaction he desires. Bronagh's breathing stalls slightly at the mention of that woman's name, but her resolve to lead a normal life kicks in again. She will not let that crazy bitch win, she reminds herself.

"Do you think she followed you, or did she just happen to be in the same place at the same time as you?"

Max shrugs. He really was undecided on the questions. "I honestly don't know... I hope not, on the following bit. I really do. I want your life, our lives, to go back to normal, well what should be normal for us." Bronagh gives his sentence a small nod.

"Well, as there's still no proof that she's anything to worry about, we can carry on with our lives as we would normally, which means getting back to my own flat and going out with Jane next week." Max finishes the last bite of his steak and pushes his plate aside. He really doesn't want an argument tonight. Not since he had planned nothing but romance, so he swallows his words of dismay and just nods.

They change the subject and the rest of the night passes with polite chit chat that had an undertone of frost.

****

Saturday comes and Elaine and Stewart go out shopping. First they go to the local DIY shop to look for the chains to truss Bronagh up, then the wall fasteners to secure her to the wall and lastly the buckets for her bathroom needs.

Grinning like a couple of lovesick teenagers, they put everything they bought into the back of Elaine's Corsa. They had told the sales assistant they were wanting the chains for their personal dungeon - which Elaine thinks, wasn't really a lie. The young sales assistant rolls his eyes. This wasn't the first time he'd heard a story about sexual dungeons. It was the first time plastic buckets were involved, but he was so over hearing about other people's sex lives he didn't care what they were using the buckets for.

"Did you see the look on that guy's face when we told him the chains were for sex. I thought he might explode." Elaine is hyper and read the assistant's expression all wrong. Stewart could tell that the assistant couldn't care less about them or their sexual adventures, but couldn't bring himself to burst Elaine's bubble, so agreed with her.

"I know... if only he knew the real reason he really would explode." Elaine's excitement increases at that thought.

"Oh, god I know. Right where next?" She is literally bouncing in her seat.

"Bed shop for a mattress. We need to get it delivered to my house. I'll pull my old one down to the garage and I'll pay for the new one." Elaine bobs her head up and down then pulls him in for a crushing kiss.

"I'm so excited about all of this. I actually can't wait to take that bitch down. Stewart grins at her.

"Well, drive on then." With a quick nod Elaine drives to the other car park in the retail park in Parkhead. They purchase a double mattress to be delivered on the Friday of the next week. From there they go to the nearest discount shop, purchasing packets of dried pasta and bottled water. They may be holding her against her will, but they would feed her... sometimes... if she was there long enough to be fed.

After their spending spree, and satisfied they had got everything they came for that day, they decide to go for an early dinner. They choose Elaine's favourite Italian restaurant and get seated quickly. Stewart's phone rings to life and he pulls it from its resting place in his pocket. Staring at the screen he sees Jane's name and tries to process why she would be phoning him.

"It's Jane." He announces to Elaine quizzically. She shrugs. She's trying for nonchalance to cover the jealousy that's zipping through her like an electric current. Stewart thumbs the answer button and puts the phone to his ear.

"Jane, what can I do for you? You phoning to get me back?" Stewart sniggers and Elaine gives him a tight smile, making that current become stronger.

"Aw, so you do remember that it was you that broke up with me. I'm so glad to hear Bronagh's still controlling you." Elaine loosens the tension in her shoulders at hearing the sarcasm in Stewart's tone.

"Why would I care if you're going out, and I'll talk about that stuck-up bitch any way I want." Stewart pauses for a heartbeat before his expression changes from bored, almost pissed off, to smiling like a lunatic. Elaine feels her shoulders stiffen again.

"Oh, really, okay. I am so glad you phoned to tell me how you're getting over me by going out next Saturday with Bre. I'll be sure to stay away from your usual haunts. The Lock-In I'm guessing?" Elaine's excitement starts to increase again at hearing the one-sided conversation. "Yes Jane... okay... bye." He cancels the call and places his phone on the table. "Well that was interesting," he states, and Elaine lifts her eyebrows, urging him to continue. "A rather tipsy Jane thought it would be a great idea to let me know she has arranged to go out next Saturday with the bold Bronagh to let 'their hair down'. A cleansing night out for her to get over me and for Bronagh to get over everything that has been happening to her." Elaine smiles. "So that means we have our 'when'." Elaine's eyes widen with Stewart's words.

"A week today?" she asks, breathless. Stewart nods. "It's on then?" He nods again.

"Oh aye, it's on!"

CHAPTER TWENTY-FOUR

The engagement party went without a hitch. Bronagh sailed through the night, enjoying every 'thank you' and accolade that came her way. She had decorated the hall in silver and a sparkly blue, with white fairy lights adorning the walls and the ceiling, giving off a twinkly light. She had brought in balloons that morning and smiled wistfully as some of the younger children played with them, kicking them up and down the vast hall. For the whole night she felt like she was walking on air, able to do anything and everything. Invincible even. Gordon helped her bring over some of the decorations and props the couple had requested, then stayed until everyone arrived and was settled in. Before taking off he informed Bronagh that he was going on a hot date. She gave him a kiss and a cuddle, thanking him for all of his hard work then wishing him luck for his big night. Max dropped in at ten o'clock to make sure everything was going well and to steal a kiss from his girlfriend. The couple, whose party it was, noticed Max and insisted he stay for some of the fish supper buffet that had just been delivered. Bronagh really felt blessed as the night came to an end. Max had stayed to help with the clear up, the only part of the job Bronagh could see far enough. The party had gone without a hitch and, more importantly, there were no interruptions from the infamous blonde.

She fell into bed around two on the Sunday morning, falling into a deep peaceful sleep.

Both her and Max had wanted to do nothing when they woke late on Sunday morning. They lazed about watching films, eating junk food and drinking wine. They both knew they would need to talk about Bronagh moving back into her flat after the subject had been broached a few days before. She needed Max to be more accepting over that, and her up and coming night out with Jane. But every time either subject was brought up the atmosphere got frosty, so they would drop it, neither of them wanting an argument. That was exactly how they both felt that Sunday, so they ignored both subjects and kept the day fun and light hearted.

Monday morning came and Bronagh went into work loving life. Erin called her into the office to congratulate her on a 'perfect party'. After her meeting, Bronagh went back to the main work room beaming with pride. Gordon handed her another coffee and the friends chatted for most of the day about the party and Gordon's date, which apparently had been the best date ever. Bronagh thought that whatever guy Gordon ended up with they would be the luckiest guy ever.

The rest of the week went by with Bronagh feeling the same as she had that Monday morning. Full of life. Full of love and full of happiness. The two conversations she needed to have with Max were always buzzing about at the back of her mind, but that's where she kept them. She was enjoying life too much. Her and Max were in love, Jane seemed to be getting over Stewart, her job was everything she dreamt it would be, all the nasty messages had stopped, as had all the violence towards her and more importantly there had been no sign of Elaine. Yes life had sorted itself out.

Friday morning arrives as does a few text messages. The first one from the bed store reminding Bronagh that her new bed, mattress, covers and all other the paraphernalia that comes with a new bed was going to be delivered. She smiles at how excited she is to get things started in her flat, but it was quickly dampened down with the guilt at the thought of how Max was going to take the news. She pushes the guilt aside. She shouldn't be thinking like that. Her relationship with Max should still be fun.

The next text, from Jane, brings up the second conversation she needed to have with Max at some point that day.

You ready for tomorrow night? So need this! Xx

Bronagh really needs the night out too. She needs to blow off some steam and have fun with her best friend. She sends a quick text back.

Aye. Might even get to sleep in my own bed! Meet you at the Lock-In about 7?

Jane's agreement comes through almost immediately and Bronagh jumps into the shower before leaving for work.

Getting into the House of Fun office, Gordon has her coffee sitting waiting on her, as usual.

"You are my dream man, do you know that?" Gordon's eyebrows go up in mock shock.

"I don't think your hunk would be happy to hear that!" She sniggers.

"He would understand, he knows how much I love my coffee."

"So, what you're saying is you only love me for my coffee?" he sobs dramatically, which makes Bronagh snigger even more.

"No, not just your coffee. I love you for the amazing advice you give me too, and right now I need both." Gordon rolls his chair over, sitting close enough to her that their knees are touching and he takes her hand hands in his.

"Is this about tomorrow night and Max?" She nods as tears threaten to overwhelm her.

"I shouldn't be so worked up over one night out." She takes a deep breath trying to control her emotions.

"I know gorgeous. But, I also understand why he's against the idea." Bronagh's eyes flare in annoyance that her friend is taking Max's side and not hers. Gordon puts his hands up in defence, without dropping hers. "He loves you and wants to protect you... but, ultimately, I agree with you, one night out shouldn't be hard to get. Especially since it's been quiet on the crazy front."

"Aye, that's what I think. I need time out from 'us'." Bronagh uses air quotes when she mentions her and Max. "I need my own space... and our relationship back on track. We need to be at the just together point, not the old married couple stage."

Gordon listens intently, and thinks before he answers her. "Have you told him any of this?"

Bronagh shrugs. "Kinda... not really. Not entirely. We've both been ignoring the elephant in the room for fear of the frost and argument that we know would ensue."

Gordon rolls his eyes. "Well that's been a healthy and helpful way of dealing with it!" Sarcasm is evident in Gordon's tone, so Bronagh picks up a scrunched up piece of paper and throws it at him.

"Shut it smart arse!"

Gordon's 'shock' eyebrows happen again. "Oh my, swearing from my princess." She sticks her tongue out at him. "Charming. But seriously, talk to him, it'll be fine. I promise."

Bronagh smiles warmly at her new friend. "I will, but if it all goes to hell in a hand basket I'm holding you personally responsible."

Gordon stands and gives her a kiss on top of her head. "Not a problem my dear."

The friends get back to work with their usual banter, even though Bronagh's thoughts were on the conversations she was going home to have with Max.

****

A Friday night in was thought best by Stewart and Elaine. They were staying at Stewart's flat for the night so they could take delivery of the new mattress (and try it out) plus they wanted to make sure that everything was set for their plan for the next night. They had gone over everything numerous times, but Elaine was still feeling antsy. They would only have one shot at abducting Bronagh, so they had to get it right first time.

She had still been feeling sick most mornings, but she hadn't been physically sick, at least she hadn't been that morning. She had tried to cut down on drinking and on the days that Stewart wasn't staying at hers she did manage it, so she put the lessening of the hangovers down to that, or maybe it was her tolerance levels for alcohol was increasing, either way she was glad for the slight respite.

"You okay babe?" Stewart's voice brings Elaine from her musings.

"Hmm, yeah, I'm good. Just thinking about tomorrow night." She's lying in her favourite position. In Stewart's arms. "You ready for it?" Stewart turns her so she's facing him and she climbs on top of him to straddle his lap.

"Absolutely. I can't wait to take the bitch down after everything she's took from you and because of the way she treated me... definitely. Then, once we've got her I'm going to bring you back up here and make love to you for the whole night to celebrate." The timber of his voice and the words he was saying send a shiver down Elaine's spine. No one had ever told her they made love to her. It was always sex or fucking. She smiled and ground herself into his crotch.

"That sounds like a good plan." She smiles at Stewart. "But just so we know what we're doing tomorrow, let's practice the love making part one more time." Stewart grins up at her.

"My pleasure." Sitting straight up he grabs Elaine's bottom lip in his teeth and growls.

Saturday morning arrives, as does another bout of throwing up for Elaine. She really didn't need a hangover that morning and hadn't thought she had had that much to drink the night before, but still, she needs to dash. Thankfully she manages to get out of bed, make it to the toilet, throw up, silently, brush her teeth and get back to bed without waking Stewart up. Once he wakes, the lovers spend the full day going over all their equipment, making sure they had everything. Packing and re-packing. Then making sure they both knew the plan and generally geeing each other up for the night ahead.

CHAPTER TWENTY-FIVE

Bronagh wakes early on Saturday morning, as was usual these days. She and Max had spoken some about her moving back into her own flat the night before. Max agreed to help decorate, but refused to be happy about it, any of it. They managed to have the conversation without an argument ensuing, but Max had been quiet for the rest of the night, blaming it on tiredness, but she knew otherwise.

Pushing her thoughts to the side, she lies there mentally working out her outfit for her big night out. She had bought a few new things for going out, knowing she didn't have anything to wear after her flat was destroyed, along with everything else she owned. The thought of what had happened in her flat and to her car sends a shiver down her spine.

Max feels her shiver and pulls her in.

"Hey you." Bronagh smiles. If he is using their special welcome for each other then he can't be in a mood any more, she muses to herself.

"Hey yourself." She automatically answers as she cuddles into his heat.

"You okay?"

"Aye. Was just thinking about what I'm going to wear tonight, which led me to think about why I didn't have any clothes not that long ago." She feels his muscles stiffen and wasn't sure if it was the mention of her night out or her flat. Either way she wasn't giving in or giving up her night on the town. She had to get her life back to normal, which meant being able to go on a night out with her friend.

"Are you sure you're doing the right thing... going out?" Bronagh pulls out of Max's embrace and shoves herself up the bed, crossing her arms in defiance.

"Yes!" She knew this was a touchy subject, but Max needed to get over it. Max huffs and sits up too, copying her defiance.

"I don't want to stop you from going out..." He really hoped Bronagh believed his words, as he wasn't sure he believed himself.

"You could've fooled me! That's exactly what you want." Crap, Max thinks. He didn't fool her or himself.

"Look, Bre, I just want to keep you safe, and... well, we don't know who was behind everything that's happened with your car, or your flat. I mean they could still be out there, waiting on you. Plus —" He was on a roll and no amount of interrupting that Bronagh tried would stop him. He was going to have his say. "Elaine is still sniffing about." Bronagh rolls her eyes at her boyfriend.

"One, we don't know that it was Elaine behind it all." Bronagh is using her fingers to count off her points. "Two, Elaine is sniffing about you, so maybe it's you that needs keeping safe, not me." This time it's Max's turn to try and interrupt, but one glower from Bronagh makes him shut his mouth tight. "Three, there has been no messages, no one following me and no violence towards me for weeks. Four, and most importantly, the police haven't been in touch about any of it so they can't be that worried about another attack." The last point she wasn't a hundred percent sure of, but she decided to put it into her argument to beef it up. Now Max rolls his eyes.

"That's a pile of shite and you know it!" This time it's Bronagh that's thinking crap to herself, but she refuses to show it.

"I don't care, Max, I need a night out with Jane, on my own, for both of us to let our hair down and get some of the crap out of our system after everything that's went on with both of us. I'm not going to be on my own and you're acting like a mad possessive, controlling boyfriend and I didn't sign up for that," she fumes. Her bladder has started to groan at her so she goes to get up from the bed but stops when Max grasps her wrist gently.

"I know that's how I'm coming across and I've been fighting with myself for weeks over it, but I need to keep you safe... end of." He blows out his cheeks. "I've just got you where I need you in my life. In my heart, and in my bed, so I don't want to lose you, I can't lose you Bre." Bronagh sags. She can understand his argument, to a point, but she needed the space, they both did.

"I know, I do, but there's nothing to worry about. I'll be back here on Sunday night." Max's head snaps up.

"What d'you mean Sunday night. You'll be home on Saturday night, after the night out." Bronagh closes her eyes. She knew this part of their conversation wasn't going to go down well.

"Well, no, I was thinking that since my new bed is being delivered today I would just crash there."

"WHAT? NO WAY! NO FUCKIN' WAY!" Max roars and Bronagh flinches, then rights herself.

"DO NOT shout at me." She demands as she straightens her spine.

"You are not sleeping in that empty flat on your own Bre, it's not happening." Bronagh takes her wrist from his grasp and gets up out of the bed standing at the side.

"Yes it is! Even if Jane needs to stay with me, I will be sleeping in my new bed tonight. It needs to happen at some point so tonight it is. Anyway we will be closer to my flat than here, so less time in the taxi." She smirks at him. Max stares at her like she has lost her mind.

"I'm picking you up." He stabs his fore finger into his chest, then he pauses. "If Jane sleeps over that would mean she would need to sleep in bed beside you. Is that really happening, do women really do that, is that a thing?" Bronagh blows out an exasperated breath.

"No you aren't. I'm getting a taxi home. I'm a big girl, I've managed to stay on my own for a long time before now, and... grow the fuck up!" She storms from the room headed to the bathroom. Max fumes at her retreating back.

"Don't walk away from me when we're discussing this," he roars behind her.

"I'm going for a pee, for fuck's sake," she shouts over her shoulder as she slams the bathroom door behind her. Max sits stunned. Bronagh swore at him... his girlfriend who doesn't swear actually said the word 'fuck', to him, no, at him, twice! After the initial shock wears off he gets up and stomps to the the closed bathroom door.

Bronagh finishes washing her face and doing her teeth then opens the door to see Max standing there, waiting on her. He looks gorgeous standing in nothing but his boxers, his tattoos and a scowl, but she forces her thoughts to the side, reminding herself that she's too angry with him to find him sexy.

"What are you doing standing there?"

"You swore... at me. Why did you swear?"

"Because you pissed me off, that's why." She passes him by and heads back to the bedroom. "Now I'm going to get dressed as I've got a bed being delivered at noon." Max clenches his teeth and his fists as he enters the bathroom to relieve himself and try to get his anger under control.

Going back into the bedroom he starts to pull on his black jeans and a Foo Fighters t-shirt.

"Where're you going?" she asks, slightly hopeful that he's going to offer his help with the bed, but still pissed at him for turning all controlling and demanding on her. He looks straight at her.

"I may not like the idea of you staying in your flat tonight, but I'm not going to let you humph a king size bed on your own. I'm not that bad a boyfriend." She rolls her eyes, but smiles, glad he was coming to help.

"Thank you," she says quietly. Max smiles too, glad she wasn't swearing at him any more.

The lovers take delivery of the new bed and get it set up and dressed all mostly in a frosty silence. Max takes Bronagh in his arms.

"Bre, I'm sorry about this morning, and the fact that everything that has happened has turned me into someone I don't want to be. Over protective and slightly controlling." Bronagh places her forehead to his and nods at his apology. She doesn't trust her voice as her emotions build with his apology. "Why don't we christen the bed?" He looks over to her bed then back at her.

Bronagh grins, glad that he's coming round to her way of thinking about her going out.

"That would be good." She manages to get the words past the lump in her throat. Max grins back at her.

They take their time enjoying each other, making love like they had all the time in the world until they both come, screaming each other's name. They enjoy lying together, just being together in each other's arms.

"I'm glad we made love," Bronagh starts. "At least the first couple to be in it had fun and it wasn't two drunk women trying not to throw up." She was trying to lighten the thought of her staying away from Max for the night. Max kisses her shoulder.

"I've been thinking about that. I could drop youse off at the pub, then I could pick you up when youse are ready to come home. That way I can drop Jane at hers and we could come back here and stay. How does that sound?" Max holds his breath. Bronagh takes a deep breath and huffs it out slightly then shakes her head.

"No, Max, that's not what's happening. Why can't you just let me have a night out?"

"I am, I just want to —"

"Aye, I know, keep me safe. But no. You can drop me off if you want and I'll text you throughout the night, but I'm not having you waiting about for the whole night just to drive me home when I can get a taxi with my friend. End of." Max starts warming up to argue his point when Bronagh sits up and out of his embrace, for the second time that day. "Take it or leave it Max. I can get ready here and leave in a taxi from here, or I can get ready at yours and you can run me there. Your choice." Max sags and lets out his breath. He's fed up arguing and certainly doesn't want to be swore at again, although the passion in her when she was angry was quite sexy, so he agrees.

"Okay, get ready at mine and I'll run you in. But promise me you'll phone or text throughout the night." Bronagh searches his eyes, making sure he isn't angry any more.

"Okay, but I'll contact you. You don't need to be keeping tabs on me. That's a deal breaker Max. I will turn my phone off if you keep contacting me." Max feels his anger rise in his throat at her words, but he swallows it down and agrees to her terms. He wanted to keep the peace between them and make sure she would contact him if she needed.

"Fine," he huffs, "but if you need me I will come and get you. Just phone, at any time, okay?"

"Okay, and Max, thank you." He nods then kisses her.

"Just promise me, please?"

"I promise." She kisses him deeply, sealing their deal before they get up from their love making.

CHAPTER TWENTY-SIX

Bronagh takes one last look at herself in the full length mirror. She was wearing her shin length black pencil skirt, which hugs her shapely hips and backside to perfection, paired with a red v-neck three quarter sleeved satin blouse. Finishing off her outfit she chose a pair of killer red heels and her usual sexy red lips.

She always felt her size twelve curves when she went out. She especially felt it when she witnessed Max walking from the pub with a tall leggy blonde on his arm for the night. Pushing her insecurities away she reminds herself that he was currently waiting downstairs for her and not a blonde in sight. With that thought she feels a stab of guilt about their argument earlier and that she made such a fuss about going out, but she pushes the feelings away next to the ones about her body. She refused to feel anything but fun and happiness tonight.

Hearing the not so ladylike clunk of high heels coming down his stairs, Max turns and looks up to see Bronagh making her way towards him. His breath hitches in his throat at the sight of her. He has never seen anyone look so classy, gorgeous and sexual in his entire life. He mentally berates himself for not letting her know his feelings before now. All the wasted years with nameless, faceless blondes when he could've been with the woman of his dreams come crashing down on his shoulders, so much so he can hardly breathe. By the time his brain can recover from his regrets Bronagh is standing in front of him, looking at him expectantly.

"Well?" she asks, her tone wary. He blinks, trying to work out why she seems so nervous. Then he remembers the conversation they had about her looks and body compared to the women he used to take home. Then he realises that he hasn't said or done anything but stare at her. He swallows, trying to get his brain and his voice working in partnership again.

"Wow," is all he can say and Bronagh sags. Whether it's from relief that he said something or disappointment that that was all he said, he wasn't sure. He steps forward and holds her hands, trying to back up his next statement.

"You look absolutely gorgeous Bre. Stunning." He pulls her in towards him and wraps his arms around her, wishing he didn't need to let her go.

"Are you sure?" He gives her a kiss, trying to convince her of his words.

"Absolutely. I was just shouting at myself, internally, at the length of time I took letting you know how gorgeous you are. An', I don't mean just tonight. I mean all the years I was in love with you and never said anything." She smiles.

"I don't look fa—" Max places his finger on her lips, stopping her before she can finish her sentence.

"Don't you dare say that word. No you are not, you are gorgeous and mine!" He pulls her tighter. "I love every inch of you inside and out okay?" She nods, tears pooling in her eyes at his determined, but loving tone.

"Okay... forever?" Her voice quivers.

"Forever." She gives him a nod, and he kisses her again before they leave the house.

Pulling up outside the pub, Bronagh waves at Jane, who's standing waiting on her (part of the agreement that Max insisted on). She makes her way over to the car and pulls open the passenger door, reaching in to pull Bronagh from the car.

"You ready?" Her tone excited. Bronagh nods back at her friend, just as excitedly, then turns back to say her goodbyes to Max.

"Right, I'll text you during the night and let you know when I'm back at mine, okay?" Max closes his eyes, takes a deep breath and nods, trying to ease the death grip he has on his steering wheel. "And, I'll be extra careful, plus Jane will have my back." She places her hand on his cheek. "I'll be back in your arms by Sunday afternoon." That thought eased him some, but not enough to stop him worrying completely.

"Fine." He takes another deep breath before continuing. "I'm still not a hundred percent sure that this is a good idea though." Bronagh throws him a look that could only be described as the 'glennie blink'. Communicating that he was best shutting his mouth, but he continues, "I know I can't stop you. Just promise me you'll be careful and you'll come back to me?"

"I promise." She leans over and kisses Max soundly.

"Argh. Let her go for god's sake." Jane's patience with Max was wearing thin. Max looks over at Jane and growls low, but not low enough as Bronagh still hears it.

"Don't!" Bronagh looks between them, "just don't, okay?" Max nods then looks away and Jane sighs and takes a step back from the door.

"I'll see you tomorrow. Please try and not worry."

"Well that won't happen, but, whatever. Remember if you need picked up, or if you need... anything just phone okay?"

"I will. I love you."

"I love you too." Bronagh gets from the car and waves to Max as he pulls away, then turns and hugs her friend.

"Oh, I am so looking forward to this night out," Bronagh gasps.

"I know, me too. It's going to be wild!" Bronagh laughs with her friend and they enter the pub to start off their night.

Max watches as his girlfriend walks into the pub and out of his sight. An uneasy feeling settles low in his gut as he drives away.

****

Ten o'clock couldn't come quick enough for Elaine or Stewart. They agreed that they would leave Stewart's flat at ten, park at the back of the pub and, weather permitting, which it was that night, they would sit in the beer garden connected to the pub. They would get one drink each and get a feel for the place. They needed to find Bronagh and Jane, get them separated and get Bronagh out of the pub without Jane or anybody else noticing that she's getting taken against her will or that she's drugged. No mean feat, they knew.

They arrive at the pub and park up. They both turn and look at each other, expectantly.

"You ready?" Stewart is first to break the heavy silence that's settled between them.

"Hell yeah!" Elaine grins at him, feeling like a giddy teenager in love.

"'Moan then." Stewart winks then gives Elaine a passionate kiss before he steps from the Corsa.

Elaine has worn the black wig she bought for the break-in, so it's decided that she would go in to buy the drinks and place Bronagh, safe in the knowledge that neither of the friends would recognise her. She spots them sitting near the toilets in the corner at a table for four. She notices a man sitting next to Jane, pawing at her and her reciprocating his actions. Elaine makes her way back outside to the beer garden to give Stewart his drink and fill him in on their situation so far.

"So you think Jane might be a bit too pre-occupied?" Stewart's eyes twinkle at the thought of their task being easier. Elaine shrugs.

"I hope so, or we're going to need to get rid of her too." Stewart nods, deep in thought. "Anyway, they are sitting near the toilet, so I'm going to hover there and see if I can gauge the mood." Stewart nods again as Elaine leaves their table again.

Getting behind the table the girls are sitting at, Elaine hovers with her phone in her hand, straining to hear what was being said round the table. The man, who was sitting next to Jane, vacated his seat to go to the toilet, so all of Jane's attention was back to Bronagh, and she sounded rather inebriated.

"Bre, can you hear the stuff he's sayin' ae me? He pure loves me. He's sayin' I'm pure gorgeous and wants to take me home." Bronagh smiles a tight smile before speaking.

"Jane is that a good idea? I mean, you don't know this guy, he's a random. And you are meant to be coming home with me, so I'm safe." Jane slaps her palm on the table.

"Bre, Bre, Bre. Let me have some fun. I mean I'm young, free and single. I'm not an old married wumin like you." Bronagh bristles at the truth of her friend's words, but also the way Jane says them. The pissed off tone came through loud and clear.

"Jane, that's not fair." Jane brushes her friend's words aside with a sweep of her hand.

"Whitever, an' anyway, you can phone your knight in shiny car to come an' pick you up... oh, hiv ye texted him this hour yit, ye know, tae check in an' that?" Bronagh's face feels like it's glowing red as she clenches her teeth so she doesn't shout at her friend.

"Jane, please, we are meant to be having a nice night out, *together*." Jane snorts out a laugh.

"Well, I am, don't know about you. Your face has been like a bulldog chewing a wasp all feckin' night."

Elaine does an internal dance at hearing the friends bicker and makes her way back to Stewart, desperate to relay the information. She's sure this turn in the friends' evening will play into their hands nicely.

CHAPTER TWENTY-SEVEN

The random man chatting up Jane returns and the pair of them get back to groping each other, which leads them to sucking on each other's faces. Bronagh has had enough and announces that she's going to the toilet. Neither of them respond so Bronagh huffs and storms off. In the toilet Bronagh washes her hands and checks the time. Eleven thirty. Returning to the table she sees that Jane and her random hasn't come up for breath. She blows out her cheeks and taps Jane on the shoulder.

"Whit?" Jane's face is smeared with her lipstick. Not a pretty sight Bronagh thinks.

"Wow... really?" Bronagh responds. Jane seems to be overly annoyed at being interrupted and it's the last straw for Bronagh.

"Bre, seriously, just get your Maximus to pick you up. You know, you've been nothing but a wet rag aw night." Bronagh swallows her hurt down, refusing to let her friend see how much the words were affecting her.

"I am just about to... and thanks, this has been a great *girls'* night out." She turns on her heel to leave but still manages to hear her friend's 'whatever'. Fighting back tears Bronagh walks out to the beer garden, relishing the cool night air.

****

Stewart is first to notice Bronagh walking outside and he motions to Elaine to look behind her.

"Heads up, I think it's show time." A volt of electricity zaps through Elaine as she looks round to see Bronagh standing at the wall taking in deep breaths. Turning back to Stewart she grins.

"'Moan then." She reiterates his earlier words back at him.

They both stand from the picnic style table they were sitting at. Stewart walks towards Bronagh and Elaine follows slightly behind him with the chloroform, rag, and car keys in hand.

Bronagh is checking her pockets for her phone and is dismayed to realise she must have left it inside. She starts to turn, heading back inside when she hears her name being called out. A shiver runs down her spine as she turns back to see Stewart walking towards her.

"Bronagh? Is that you?" She takes a deep breath as Stewart gets a lot closer than was strictly necessary in a few long strides. She tries to step out from his imposing stance, trying to get him out of her personal space, but he grasps her arm and pulls her in. He brings his arm around her waist and closes the minuscule gap that was between them so Bronagh is flush to his chest. He reaches behind him and Elaine drops the rag drenched in chloroform into his hand. He holds the rag to Bronagh's mouth and nose, then angles her head so it looks to the outside world that they are locked in a very passionate kiss. After a minute he feels Bronagh's rigid limbs loosen in his arms, the fight leaves her body as unconsciousness takes over. Between Elaine and Stewart they 'walk' Bronagh back to the Corsa and into the back seat, laying her down unceremoniously.

****

Bronagh realises she is awake when the pounding in her head is the only thing she can concentrate on. She opens her eyes but sees nothing but darkness. She concludes that it must still be the early hours of the morning. Thinking she must have fallen asleep with her arms over her head, she tries to move them back down. She knows they are going to cramp up and hurt like hell, but she needs to get them moving so she can pull the covers over her. She's freezing. As hard as she tries she can't get them moving. She then tries to remember how she got home, but everything is a bit foggy. All at once fear and pain surge through her and she lets out a piercing scream that burns her parched throat. She pulls at her arms again, only this time she registers the clank of metal. She moves her legs and is thankful that they are free to move. Her memories start to fit themselves together, bombarding her all at once.

Jane getting very drunk very quickly. Jane taking up with the random man. Jane telling her to leave. Going out to the beer garden for some fresh air and to phone Max. Feeling like crap at needing to disturb him that late at night. Being annoyed at Jane for being a shitty friend after everything they had both been through over the past few weeks and months. The dismay at leaving her phone inside. The odd feeling of panic as she heard her name being called. She remembers recognising the voice as Stewart's and the spike of adrenaline in her blood with her fight or flight instinct tries to come into effect as he came towards her. She remembers not being able to think of what to do or what he would want before his arms were on her. Then, before she could comprehend the dark-haired woman behind him she had handed him something. That something was then squashed onto her mouth and nose making it hard for her to breathe. Fear clawed at her throat, terror turned and churned in her stomach making her want to vomit. Her lungs burning from whatever Stewart was holding over her nose and mouth, making her face feel wet. She felt something cloying in her nostrils. Her limbs starting to feel heavy as everything went black. Then, there was nothing until she came to here, wherever here is. Panic and terror set in again and she lets out another scream, bucking against her restrained arms.

The screaming makes her dry, slightly hungover throat raw and scratchy, and the movement makes pain rip through her shoulders and up her strung up arms. With her energy spent and nothing but pitch blackness surrounding her,

Bronagh breaks down. Burning hot tears run down her dry tight face, sobs rack her body, causing more pain in her arms and her stomach to lurch. She has worked out that she must be on a cushion or a mattress as she feels her legs on something soft and slightly springy. With another lurch from her stomach she tries to move away from the soft furnishing. If she's going to be sick, she didn't want to be sick where she was sitting/lying. She scrambles up onto her knees, fighting to get onto her feet. Pins and needles start shooting up and down her arms and legs. She lunges on one foot then stumbles, she feels herself falling forward then her knee lands on the hard cold concrete floor. She guesses the floor is concrete going by the feeling of it scraping on her cold skin. More pain, this time shooting up her knee, but she doesn't have time to register it too much as she starts to vomit. She retches and gags for what feels like an hour, but in reality was only a few minutes. Panting from the excretion she sits with her back against the wall and her legs on the mattress. The damp coldness of the brick wall seeping through her blouse. The sweat covering her body starts to chill her skin and she starts to shake.

Feeling like a wrung out rag Bronagh closes her eyes, wishing for sleep to take her away from whatever hell she was in, but instead her brain decides to go into overdrive with questions;-

Why did Stewart abduct her?

Who was the woman? She looked familiar, but Bronagh couldn't work out from where.

Was it Stewart behind everything?

Where was she?

Why her?

And the one that was praying on her mind more than any other... why hadn't she just listened to Max?

The last question is enough to break her and she starts to cry again, silently, wishing with everything in her that Max would work out she was missing, come and find her and forgive her for going out.

A loud clunk of metal echoes through the garage, then the screech of rusty metal followed by bright blinding light streaming through as the shutter is pulled up. Stewart walks in with Elaine close behind him.

"Good morning Bronagh. I hope you slept well." Bronagh registers that it's Stewart talking and she can hear the glee in his voice, but she can't see him. The daylight streaming in is too much for her dark adjusted eyes. She yelps and turns her back to the light, like a vampire hiding from the burning sun.

"Wow, it stinks in here. I guess you took unwell at some point?" Bronagh's head snaps up at hearing the different voice. She recognised that voice. She whips round, squinting against the light, her eyes streaming from tears of pain as the light burns her eyes.

"Elaine?" she manages to croak out. Elaine gives a small laugh.

"Of course, bitch, I wouldn't miss this for the world." Bronagh lowers her head. The same thought running through her head on a continuous loop.

'I should've listened to Max.'

CHAPTER TWENTY-EIGHT

Max spent most of Saturday night holding his phone and staring at it. He put on the television to try and take his mind off of things, but it was to no avail. He just sat staring at it watching the shapes move on the screen but not taking in what they were doing. After a few hours staring at the screen he turned it off, putting on some music instead. He picks up one of his many car magazines and started flipping through the pages, but still not really taking in any of the articles.

Bronagh's first text came in about nine o'clock.

Had food. Jane didn't eat much and is drinking wine, but all's well. Love you xx

He smiles then grimaces. He is glad that she's having a good time, but he would rather Jane behaved. He knew she could get a bit wild when she had a good drink in her, especially when she was drinking wine. The second text came in around ten thirty, which caused him to worry even more, which he didn't think would be possible.

Jane's found a random man to snog and had a lot of wine. Need to get her to calm down on both fronts. I'm OK though can't wait to see you tomorrow. Love you xx

His stomach acid hits the back of his throat when he read that message. It sounded like Jane was out for herself, and guys didn't normally pick women up on their own. Was there a friend hitting on Bronagh? He really wanted to text her back, telling her he was on his way to pick her up, but he knew that would only cause another argument which he didn't want and he really didn't want to be swore at again. He needed to show her he trusted her after everything with the condoms. He waits until midnight before going to bed, making sure his phone is by his bed, plugged in and on the highest ring level. Just in case he fell asleep, although he highly doubted he would.

After seeing every hour on the clock Max eventually falls asleep at three. He had texted Bronagh at one to check if she had made it home and if Jane was with her, but there had been no reply. He had thought about phoning, but due to the late hour he swithered. Come two o'clock he phoned, not caring for the time. No answer. Waking up with a start he looks at his phone, still no word from Bronagh. He had slept for three hours, which was three hours too many as far as he was concerned. Deciding he didn't care about the time, he calls Bronagh again. Still no answer. He hangs up and tries another three times, but every time the voicemail clicks on. He tries to convince himself that she was just sleeping and couldn't hear the phone, or her phone had run out of battery, or maybe, she had left it in her bag when she fell asleep. He prays that any of these were the reason behind Bronagh's radio silence, but the ache in his gut tells him otherwise. Pissed off and afraid he phones Jane and again he is listening to a generic voicemail message. Not willing to wait any longer for answers, Max gets up and pulls on his jeans and t-shirt from the day before. Quickly he drags his toothbrush around his mouth then grabs a can of Irn-Bru, knowing it's going to taste like crap when it mixes with the toothpaste. He opens it and heads to the door, grabbing his keys from the bowl that sits near the door.

First stop is Bronagh's flat. Thankfully at six thirty on a Sunday morning the roads around Dalmarnock and Parkhead are quiet, so he makes the journey in record time. He runs through the always unlocked security door and nearly trips over the drunk sleeping on the stairwell. Cursing him out Max steps over the prone figure and heads up to Bronagh's flat. Getting to the front door he tries the handle, locked. He pulls out his own set of keys and is through the front door, shouting her name as he enters. The silence returning to him is deafening. His heart has started a double time tattoo in his chest and panic is sliding its way through his veins.

He goes around checking every other room in the flat first, until Max finds himself standing outside Bronagh's bedroom.

Throwing up another prayer he pushes open the door and steps in whispering her name. The sight that confronts him is gut wrenching. The bed still perfectly made up, exactly the way they had left it the day before, after they'd made love in it.

Ripping his phone from his pocket he stabs his fingers into the screen, pressing Bronagh's number again. He listens into the phone and the room at the same time, willing his ears to hear the sound in the phone marry up with a sound in the flat. There's nothing but silence from the flat. Stabbing at the phone again he cancels the call to Bronagh then phones Jane, but again there is only the voicemail. Anger and panic fill his chest making it hard for him to breathe. He heads back out into the stairwell, closing and locking the door behind him. Getting back down to the main door, he sees the drunk still lying there. Max nudges him with his toe, shouting at him to wake up. Groggily the drunk peers at Max through half shut eyes.

"Whit the fuck you wantin'?" Max stands back as the smell emanating from the drunk reaches him.

"Have you see the girl that lives in three-one?" The drunk groans as he tries to sit up, making the smell permeate more. Max starts to breathe through his mouth, trying to reduce the amount of the disgusting reek he was taking in through his nose, but that just led to him tasting the smell.

"Eh? The fuck you talkin' about?" If the drunk wasn't so disgusting looking or smelling, Max would have had him by the throat screaming in his face, but there was no way that was happening.

"Bronagh, the redhead that lives here, did you see her last night?" The drunk huffs.

"Naw, a've no seen naeb'dy, now fuck aff!" Max growls but leaves the drunk alone. Getting back outside into the clean air, Max takes big breaths trying to rid his senses of the drunk's smell. He gets back into his car and goes to his next stop, Jane's house. The roads are still clear so the journey only takes five minutes. Walking up her path he notices one of her windows lying open, which he takes as a good sign that she is in and if she's not awake, well, she soon will be.

Jane lives in a maisonette flat, so Max reaches her front door without going through a security door. He crushes his thumb into the door bell then smashes his fist against the wooden door. Even though it was now nearly eight in the morning Max is aware that it was a Sunday and felt bad for the neighbours, but that was quickly pushed aside when a man wearing nothing but a pair of white low rise briefs, (the random from the night before Max guesses) opens Jane's door.

"Who the fuck are you, and where is Jane and Bronagh?" Max demands before the random can speak. The random stares at Max with a sleepy shocked look on his face. Taking a minute before he replies.

"Eh...? Who the fuck are you...? You better not be the boyfriend. Jane said she didn't have a boyfriend."

Max groans and steps into the flat, pushing the random aside as he went.

"She doesn't. I'm Bronagh's boyfriend. Is she here?"

"Is who here?" the random asks, confused. The rather loose grip Max had on his anger snaps and this time he does have the guy against a wall as he shouts in his face.

"Bronagh, my girlfriend. Is she here?" The random can only gasp like a fish out of water as Max holds his hand against the random's throat, fear running through his eyes at the crazy man holding him against the wall. Jane takes that moment to walk from the bedroom, wearing nothing but an oversized t-shirt.

"Max, what the fuck man? Put him down." Dropping the random Max stalks over to Jane.

"Where's Bronagh? Is she here? Tell me she's here?" He is almost pleading with her. His anger quickly turning to fear again.

"No, she left the pub with you..." Realisation crosses her features. "At least I think that's what happened." Jane drags her hands through her, still in place from last night, bed hair.

"What?" Max growls.

"Well, I mean, she went to phone you and then I left wa him, so I assumed you came an' got her. Did you not?" The question was out of Jane's mouth before she could stop it.

"Are you fuckin' kiddin' me? Does it look like I fuckin' picked her up and that I know where the fuck she is right this fuckin' minute or that I know if she's fuckin' safe or not? Does it fuckin' look like that Jane?" The random finds his feet and his mouth as Jane just stands there staring at Max, horror plastered on her face.

"Hey, hawd on—"

"Shut up!" Both Max and Jane shout at the random. He puts his hands up in surrender, walking away leaving them to their semi-argument.

"Fuck Max, I honestly thought you'd picked her up. She never came and said she was away, but I put that down to her being pissed at me." Jane takes a deep breath as she remembers her behaviour on their night out. "I was being a right bitch and basically," she blows out a breath, "well, I told her to go away." Jane puts her head down in shame and Max grabs handfuls of his hair trying to get his anger back under control, but he really was struggling.

"Seriously Jane, what the fuck? This was a night for the two of youse. Bre an' me had a massive argument about her going out... she fuckin' swore at me over it! Jane's eyes widen when she hears how much the night out had meant to Bronagh. Guilt floods her system.

"She swore at you?" Max nods. "I'm sorry. I'm guessing you've phoned her and been to the flat?" Max gives her an incredulous look.

"Naw, Jane of course not! What d'you think? I even spoke to that drunk that stays in the flat under Bre, but he was of no fuckin' use." Jane nods. Max's sarcasm impounding her guilt even more.

"Right so what now?" Max runs his hands through his hair again. He felt like pulling it out just to give his hands something to do. He also wanted to shake Jane like a rag doll but he knew that wasn't an option.

"I'm going to the police. I've got a horrible feeling about this." Jane looks up at Max, guilt and confusion covering her face.

"What about the twenty-four hour thing, is that not a thing?"

Max shrugs, dragging his finger through his unruly hair again. "I don't know, an' I don't care. I'm letting them know something's not right. Especially after everything else that's happened to her, I might be best telling they two officers that spoke to us after the break-in at the flat."

Jane didn't think she could feel any more guilty about abandoning Bronagh, but remembering everything that had gone on over the past few weeks had her guilt ricocheting up, taking over her stomach and her heart.

"Right, give me five minutes to get rid ae him, and pull clothes on an' I'll come with you."

Max raises his chin towards the kitchen. "You even know his name?"

Guilt spikes again in Jane as she shakes her head. Max lowers his head to the cream carpet in the hall, not trusting himself to look at Jane. As far as he was concerned she had abandoned Bronagh for a night of drunken sex with a random guy. He knew he couldn't give much thought to Jane's behaviour or he would end up saying something he may or may not regret plus he knew now wasn't the time. He needed to get Bronagh back, then he would deal with Jane.

CHAPTER TWENTY-NINE

"Surprised to see me?" Elaine sneers at Bronagh. Bronagh squirms at the sound, her mind running in a million different directions, but the main question was, how did Stewart and Elaine know each other? As if reading her mind Stewart answers her unasked question.

"Aye, me'n Elaine went to school together, then we reconnected the other month. Turns out we love and hate the same things... lucky us eh?" The lovers giggle and kiss each other which makes Bronagh's stomach lurch again.

"Why are you doing this?" she croaks. Her throat still scratchy from her screaming, crying and increasing hangover. She guessed part of it is from the alcohol she consumed and part of it must be from whatever Stewart had held over her face. Elaine lets out a snort before answering.

"Why? Why? I'll tell you why... you took everything from me. YOU HAVE EVERYTHING THAT WAS MINE!" Elaine's temper was getting the better of her as she hovered over Bronagh screaming down at her. "YOU HAVE MY JOB FOR FUCK'S SAKE." Bronagh is cowering, trying to get away from Elaine and her screaming. Stewart puts his arm around Elaine's waist and pulls her into him, calming her.

"Ssh babes, it's okay. It's all going to get fixed now." Bronagh stares at them.

"Are youse actually together? Is this who you were cheating on Jane with?" Bronagh looks between the lovers.

"Yes we are," Stewart states proudly, "and yes. Elaine opened my eyes to how life should be lived... to the full." The lovers kiss again, both of them getting very involved in it. Bronagh makes a disgusted sound and turns her back on them.

"What? You don't like watching us Bre?" Stewart asks, "Or is it just me you don't like?" Bronagh turns back to face them, confusion written all over her face.

"What are you talking about Stewart?" Stewart gives her a derisive snort.

"You know exactly what I mean, you bitch. You knocked me back, laughed at me, made me feel like a fool, then went back to lusting after that fuckin' dickhead that is now your boyfriend." Elaine rubs Stewart's back throughout his rant, consoling him like he did her. Bronagh continues to stare at him, totally bemused.

"What the hell are you... are you talking about years ago when you asked me out? Really?" Bronagh knew she was treading in dangerous territory using a sarcastic, mocking tone but she was too gobsmacked that Stewart was still holding a grudge about something that had happened nearly three years ago. Stewart reared back as if he had been slapped.

"Don't you dare talk to me like you're so much better than me, you little bitch. I opened my heart to you and you stood on it, squishing it under your five inch heels!" His rage has taken over and he raises his hand. Bringing his fist down he strikes Bronagh hard, connecting with her eye socket. Pain erupts in her temple and washes down her cheek. Her head snaps round from the power of the blow but she clenches her teeth to the pain, refusing to let them see how frightened and sore she is. Lifting her head up she straightens her back.

"I never laughed at you. You asked me on a date and I said no. I even apologised for not having romantic feelings towards you."

Stewart snorts again. "Aye and that was the worst of it all." He puts on an accent mimicking her. *"Oh Stewart, I am sooo sorry I don't think you're* fuckable." Bronagh gasps at his brutishness. "Shut up you fuckin' tease. So now you're never going to know what you missed out on. I wouldn't touch you with a barge pole, and there is every chance you'll never see or have Max again either." Bronagh gives a strangled cry as the meaning of Stewart's words start to ricochet round her brain.

Elaine gives a small laugh, but her stomach gives a lurch as she starts to question Stewart's words.

"Max will find me," Bronagh states with more gusto than she actually feels. Stewart laughs, long and hard.

"HA, aye, good one Bre. I'll crack the jokes. Guess we'll just need to see what happens... won't we?" He pats her cheek making a slapping sound as Bronagh flinches. The pain from the slap tingling under the rough taps of his hand. Taking Elaine's hand they start to walk away. Stewart pauses and turns his head over his shoulder. "Mind and pray for your escape or life... oh and just so you know, I've soundproofed this place. No one will hear you scream." Bronagh swallows back a whimper as Stewart laughs.

Walking out of the garage Stewart pulls down the shutter sealing out the light once more. He takes Elaine into his arms and kisses her, pulling back when she doesn't reciprocate.

"You okay babes? I thought you'd be over the moon at seeing your, our dream in the flesh." Elaine pulls out of the embrace slightly.

"I am... kinda... I think we should talk inside." Stewart frowns at her, but agrees and leads the way back to his flat. Once in the flat Stewart gets himself a beer then sprawls on the couch, taking a long slug from the can.

"Well?" Elaine doesn't sit, instead she paces the small, cluttered, messy living room. After a second lap of her pacing she stops and looks at her lover like she has never seen him before.

"What did you mean when you said about her never seeing or having Max again? I mean I get that she's never having you, but... I mean... do we have a plan... you know, for what we're going to do... with her?" Stewart listens attentively as Elaine panics her way through her questions, then pats the couch next to him, indicating for Elaine to sit.

"Babes, c'mhere. I guess we never spoke about this part of our plan did we?" Elaine sits down next to Stewart and grabs his hand like it's a life line, then shakes her head. "How d'you want this to end?" She shrugs and he continues. "Think about it. We can't let her go. She'll head straight to the polis and we'll head straight to the jail... an' we don't want that now, do we?" Elaine shakes her head vigorously, the enormity of what they are doing settling on her shoulders. Stewart could see her panic and that she had started to waver so he pulls her into him. "Listen babes, we're going to be okay. If it comes to it and we need to delete her, then I will take on that responsibility, but for the now we'll just teach her a lesson. Okay?" Elaine nods, her eyes still wide. "And we'll organise a get out of jail plan. Okay?" Elaine lets out the breath she had been holding onto. The thought of a getaway plan calms her and she grabs Stewart into a bear hug.

"Thank you for being so level headed. I'm sorry I panicked. Sometimes I feel like I'm just all over the place." Stewart rubs her back, soothing her.

"That's okay babes. I know we've got each other's backs and you would do the same for me." Emotion catches in Elaine's throat. She realises that, yes, she would do exactly the same for him and that no matter how this situation ends, she isn't going to let him do any of it on his own. They are in this together, come what may.

"I love you!" The words fly from Elaine's mouth before she can stop them. Her epiphany and emotions taking down her guards. She holds her breath again. Having never said those words and meant them, she has no idea how vulnerable they would make her feel.

"Aw, babes, I love you too... more than anything." She blows out the held breath again as her emotions take over and her tears flow unchecked.

****

The darkness descended again when Stewart and Elaine pulled down the shutter. It encroached on Bronagh, covering her and everything around her until there was nothing but inky blackness, fear and pain. Her cheek and eye throbs with each beat of her pulse where Stewart struck her. Knowing who was behind her abduction and their bizarre reasons for doing it wasn't as comforting as she thought it would be. If anything it disturbed her more, knowing she had been friends with one of her abductors. Stewart had seen her in all types of situations and through all different emotions, happy, sad, sober, drunk, laughing, crying, everything. He had shared special moments with her. Birthdays, Christmases, the bells on Hogmanay. Even on nights where she got angry or cried when she didn't cope seeing Max going home with yet another of his nameless blondes. She wonders what he was feeling then, if he was planning things even back then. The feeling of betrayal taking over her, Bronagh drops her head and weeps again. Wishing she had done so many things differently, sometimes wishing she hadn't gone against Max over the night out, but mostly wishing she hadn't given Stewart so much inside knowledge of her. Despair taking over from the betrayal she curls up against the wall as much as her strung up arms allow and closes her eyes, trying to transport herself away from the dark, dank prison that is now her home.

CHAPTER THIRTY

Walking into the police station on London Road, Max presses on the counter bell announcing his arrival to the officers in the room behind it. Jane is close on his heels breathing hard and swallowing harder as she tries to rein in her hangover.

"My god Max you're fast." Max throws her a look that's almost murderous. Thankfully before he can throw out a retort or act out any of his thoughts a police officer walks through the door that joins the reception area to the rest of the police station. Max looks at the officer and smiles. It is one of the officers he wanted to talk to.

"PC Loughran, I'm so glad it's you." Max rushes out his words. The officer looks at him expectantly.

"Mr Stevenson, how can I help?" He goes for a cheery tone as he can tell by Max's demeanour that something isn't quite right.

"It's Bronagh. She's went missing." PC Loughran's eyebrows shoot up at the statement, then tries to ask some questions, but Max doesn't stop talking. "I know it's not been twenty-four hours, but this isn't like her and there was all that other stuff before with that crazy bitc... woman, Elaine. I'm really worried." The officer nods his head.

"Okay, why don't youse come through to an interview room and I'll take some details." Max looks directly into the officer's eyes, shocked. He didn't expect to be taken seriously; if anything he expected some resistance. Thankful for the officer's support, Max and Jane follow him through grubby magnolia and poster covered corridors and into a small, dingy, cramped, nicotine-stained foul-smelling room. Max crinkles his nose as Jane actively covers her mouth and nose with her hand, trying to control her stomach from the nauseating smell.

"Oh god. Wow, this place is stinkin'," Jane states as PC Loughran shrugs his shoulders.

"Aye, sorry about that. They were interviewing someone who didn't understand the concept of showering or washing... or any kind of personal hygiene for that matter. Normally we spray air freshener when there's been a, eh, ripe person in... I guess we're out." He shrugs again and shows them where to sit before taking his own seat on the other side of the cigarette burned Formica table.

"Okay, so tell me, why do you think Bronagh is missing?" Jane ducks her head, her guilt sweeping over her as much as her nausea from the hangover, maybe even more. Max takes a deep breath, praying that he would be able to get his point across without breaking down or getting angry. He desperately wanted to be taken seriously.

"She never went home last night. She went out with Jane. I didn't want her to go out because of everything that had happened, but she insisted and so she was texting me throughout the night, letting me know she was all right, but Jane here," PC Loughran notices that Max's tone sours and Jane squirms in her seat, "got together with some random guy and thought Bre had phoned me to go collect her and that I had picked her up... but she didn't." PC Loughran was furiously taking notes as Max spoke. "I last got a text from her about half ten saying she was okay, but Jane was ignoring her, then nothing." Jane bristles at the accusation, but she knew she had no come back or defence so went back to squirming. "I've been to her flat, but it doesn't look like she's been home." More nodding and note-taking from the officer. "I even asked the drunk that lives below her, but he was as much use as a chocolate fire guard." PC Loughran snorts out a laugh at Max's words but covers it up with a cough, trying to stay professional. "I've *obviously* phoned her mobile." A glowering look is thrown in Jane's direction, and again the officer notices. "But it was ringing out, then going on to voicemail." Max lets out a sigh, conveying he has poured out his soul.

"Okay," PC Loughran puts empathy into his professional tone. "I understand why you're worried. As you say it's out of character for her, and then there is the recent history of crimes being committed against her, so I'll start a missing persons enquiry. If youse can give me all her details, we'll check her bank account, see when there was activity on it. Did she take out money yesterday?" Max nods. "Okay, well all information you can give us will help. Here's some paper and a pen. Write down everything. I need to know things like what she was wearing, hair colour, eye colour, height, weight, build. When and where she was last seen. Anything you can think of okay?" Max and Jane nod in unison and PC Loughran offers them a drink then leaves them to their writing as he goes to make them their beverages.

Max takes the paper and starts writing Bronagh's description. After a few moments of writing he turns to Jane.

"Did you notice what time she went out to phone me?" He tries to keep his tone level but he never managed to get it above bitchy. Jane takes a deep breath, regretting it as the smell hits her lungs and tongue again, then turns to Max. Hurt, anger and tears mixing in her eyes.

"Max, I'm sorry. I never thought anything like this would happen. I never meant to ignore her..." Max tensed his jaw to control his anger before answering.

"You knew everything that had happened to her. You knew how I felt about her going out..."

"I know!" She winces at the pain shooting through her head as she spits the words out. It was hard to hear, Max was pointing out all her failings.

"And you knew how much the night out meant to her. So why Jane? Why did you pick some random over your best friend?" Feeling her guilt push down on her Jane can only shake her head.

"I don't know... I mean I know all of that and I still don't know why I told her to go. It just felt nice having someone from the opposite sex pay me some attention. I'm sorry Max.

I really am sorry. If I could go back and change it all I would." Max holds his hands up to stop Jane from talking.

"Stop, just stop, please. I know you're sorry and you would change everything, but that's not really possible now, is it?" Jane dips her head again then shakes it.

"No, it's not. I'm sorry." The anger towards Jane leaves Max in a whoosh when he hears how guilt ridden and broken she is.

"Okay, let's just put all that to the side for just now and concentrate on getting Bre back. So, was it the Lock-in youse went to?"

"Aye we got food, then just settled in for the night. We were sitting near the back at the toilets. You know, because of how ridiculously small Bre's bladder is." They both snort out a small laugh, lightening the mood in the room for a millisecond.

"True." Max clears his throat, reality settling back on his shoulders. "Right, so, we've got her description, what she was wearing, where she was last seen. I've put down Elaine's name and how much money she lifted yesterday... anything else?" Jane takes the list from him and scans it.

"I... don't... think... think... so..." Jane breaks down, sobbing into her hands. Knowing he needs to be the bigger man, he pulls Jane into his arms and rubs her back whilst making shushing noises, trying to comfort her. PC Loughran walks back into the interview room with their drinks. Seeing the scene in front of him he gives a slight cough to announce his presence. Jane breaks away wiping her tears and snot on the sleeve of her jumper.

"Sorry. It all got a bit much," Jane explains.

"That's okay, you don't need to apologise. It'll have be a tough time for you both." He places mugs down, both of them cracked and stained. "Sorry about the mugs, normally you'd get the polystyrene cups, but I thought I would push the boat out, you know, considering youse are in here with the smell an' all." The officer smiles, trying to break the tension with his humour and Max gives him a tight smile as thanks back. "Is this the list?" He motions to the piece of paper sitting on the table and Max nods, then pushes it across the table to where PC Loughran has sat himself.

"Aye." After reading over the list the officer nods.

"Okay, well I've got the ball rolling. WPC Young is starting on some paperwork. I've asked her to be included as she was involved in the previous incidents. It will probably be passed onto CID as it'll be classed as a major incident. We're going to talk to the staff in the pub and look at any CCTV they may have and the ones on the street too. You could maybe think about putting something on all your social media sites. See if you get any hits that way." Max had been nodding his way through everything that was being said and Jane sniffled.

"Will you be talking to Elaine?" Max asks the question as his heart tries to leave its place in his chest again.

"Yes, probably. We will need to rule her out."

Max snorts and mumbles under his breath. "Aye, right!"

PC Loughran chooses to ignore the mumble.

"Okay, you and Jane head home and stay by your phones. If Bronagh walks back in or calls, she will need a friendly face or voice." Max huffs in frustration PC Loughran faces Max and places a hand on his shoulder. "Max, let us do our job. You're best being at home, or at Bronagh's... and Max, please, stay away from Miss Ashton." The officer gives Max a stern look. Max takes a second before answering, then he slowly nods, feeling defeated. Draining their mugs, they stand, thank PC Loughran then leave the station.

Standing outside they both take deep breaths of fresh air, glad to be away from the stale smell of BO and urine that seemed to make the very small room even more claustrophobic, even if it was raining a misty rain.

"I'll drop you off."

Jane looks at up at Max. "Why? Where're you going? Don't you dare go to that skank's house." Jane gives him a look full of warning.

"I'm not. I don't even know where she stays. I was going to go to the pub, see if anyone there remembers her, then go back to her flat, see if she returned."

Jane looks at her watch. "Listen, Max, the pub won't be open yet. Leave it to the police like PC Loughran said. They know what they are doing. We'll both go to Bre's and see if she's there okay?"

Deflated and all of a sudden very tired, Max agrees and heads towards his Golf, Jane falling into step beside him.

CHAPTER THIRTY-ONE

Seconds lead into minutes which lead into hours. All of them taking an eternity in the endless blackness. Bronagh goes through her fateful night out, over and over again in her head and out loud to nobody but the darkness. Trying to work out where she could change that one thing that would give her a different outcome. But, no matter what scenario she played out, it always came back to the one decision she made that now she wishes she hadn't. Going against Max and insisting she went out in the first place. With no more tears left in her dehydrated body she starts to knock her head against the cold brick wall. Feeling the wall with her forehead then her bound hands she realises that the brick is the same as the ones used on the outside of houses. Not smooth or plastered like somewhere inside, or decorated. That information coupled with the cold and dampness that is seeping from the walls to cover her thin blouse and into her bones makes her realise she is being kept in some sort of out-house or garage. She remembers Stewart going on about the garage that came with his flat and deduces that that is where she is being kept. The thoughts send dread flowing through her system. April in Scotland is still cold, even with May chapping at the door. During the night it can still fall below freezing. Visions of her not being found until she is blue and frozen in situ float around her mind. Terror takes over her body and mind as she starts to scream.

She screams until her lungs burn with the lack of oxygen, her parched throat is sore and raw with the harsh sounds coming from it and her head, eye and cheek pound in pain with each heartbeat.

The screech of the old eroded shutter cuts off Bronagh's scream in her throat. A strong beam of torch light penetrates the blackness with its long reach. Bronagh surmises that it must be about half seven as darkness is creeping in fast. The beam gets closer and brighter to Bronagh as the holder of the torch walks into the garage.

"Good evening Bre, you're still awake I see. Now so you don't think we are entirely evil I've brought you some water." Bronagh can hear the smugness in Stewart's voice. "I've also come to show you where your bucket is." Bronagh's eyes snap up to Stewart's but is blinded by the torch light so drops her head quickly to protect her burning eyes.

"What d'you mean bucket?" She doesn't want to speak; her throat is raw from the screaming and her voice harsh, emotional and breaking. She doesn't want to show him any emotion, but her confusion wins out. Stewart gives an evil chuckle.

"Your piss bucket of course." A whimper tries to squeeze itself from her throat, but she refuses to let it out. Stewart sniggers as he hears her swallow it back down. He bends down until he is face to face with Bronagh. She squirms, trying to get away from what feels like an intrusive touch, but it is to no avail as her back is already against the wall in more ways than one.

"Ah, Bre, does that not sit well with you? Pissing in a bucket? Eh? Too degrading for such a princess? Well too fuckin' bad, it's about time you got brought down off of your pedestal."

Bronagh's head snaps back up. This time she doesn't flinch away. "Fuck you Stewart! I've never fuckin' liked you. I turned you down as nicely as possible, but inside I was screaming for you to get your dirty, skanky hands off me. Then low and behold six months later you turn up with my best friend. It made me sick. I spent every second of your relationship with Jane trying to be supportive, whilst dreading seeing you, praying that you were the Greek god Jane continuously told me you were and not the bastard I thought you were. But here we are... I was right... you are a bastard. A cheating, woman beating, kidnapping bastard!"

The back of Stewart's hand comes crashing down on Bronagh's already swollen and bruised cheek before she could comprehend the shadows moving. The scream leaves her dry lips without her permission. Before she can bring her head back round, Stewart's boot finds a place in her ribs with a kick any striker would be proud of. All the air rushes from her lungs as her shoulders scream in protest at the way the kick made her body convulse. Stewart pulls back his foot, landing another kick to Bronagh's side. Over and over again he draws his boot back and kicks Bronagh up and down her body whilst steadying himself with his hands on the wall above her.

Bronagh's ability to scream is kicked from her during the barrage of strikes from Stewart's boot that he rains down on her. Thankfully it ends. She can hear his breathing harsh as he tries to gain control of it. He bends down again, his breath hot on her tear stained cheek.

"Ye'll no talk to me like that again, now... will ye?" he growls and she can hear the amusement dance in his tone. "Now, here's your bucket." He thrusts the plastic bucket into her side. She winces with pain. "Although going on the smell, I have a funny feeling you're too late to use it. I remember how useless your bladder is." Embarrassment burns Bronagh's cheeks knowing Stewart is right. "And I'll just leave this bottle of water next to the bucket. Now if you're a good girl the next time either Elaine or I come down we might give you some, you know, since you can't do it yourself. Being a wee bit tied up and that." Laughing to himself he stands and walks over to the shutter, pulling it up.

"Mind and try get some sleep." Bronagh hears him laugh as he pulls the shutter down, taking the light and her hope with him.

Still chuckling to himself, Stewart locks the shutter and says hello to a passing neighbour.

Getting back into his flat Stewart is met by Elaine at the door. She takes him by the shoulders and brings him into a tight embrace. He returns her cuddle then pulls back to look at her.

"You okay babes?" He searches her face and sees worry lingering in her eyes.

"We need to talk." A slight panic zaps through him as they walk into his messy living room.

"You're scaring me babes. What's up? Have you changed your mind over Bronagh? I told you I would take care of everything." They sit down and Elaine faces him.

"No, no... I'm right beside you on all of that. No it's nothing like that... but I'm not sure how you're going to take this." Stewart motions with his hands for her to get on with it, not sure what he is expecting to come from her mouth. "Okay, well, here goes nothing. I'm... well... we're, eh, pregnant." Stewart gapes at her trying to work out if he heard her right or not.

"Eh? What do you mean, you're pregnant?"

"We're going to have a baby." Stewart's reaction isn't ecstatic, and more worry eats at Elaine.

"How? I mean I know how... but, I thought you were on the Pill?"

"I was, I am. I wasn't well for a few days so I'm guessing that must've knocked it out, I'm sorry. I know we haven't planned for this, but I'm happy, and I really want us to be a family and happy too." She waits holding her breath and Stewart's hand for dear life. After a long few seconds Stewart relaxes and grabs Elaine into him, holding her tight against him.

"We will be. We will be a family and happy."

Elaine pulls back. "Really? You're happy?" Tears stream down her face.

"Aye. I mean I'm shocked and stunned a bit. I mean, it's something I never thought would happen to me, but now it has and that it's happened with you, the person I love more than anything else in this world... then yes, I'm ecstatic." More tears fall from Elaine's eyes, her emotions taking over her.

"Oh god Stewart, I love you too. But you know what this means, don't you?" They both sober and Stewart nods.

"This thing with Bronagh needs to end with her dead, and sooner rather than later." Elaine nods her agreement.

"We'll need to get away from here. So… how do you want to do it? We could just leave her to die or kill her and bury the body before we leave?" Stewart shrugs.

"I'm not sure. I need to think about it, but I don't want to do that just now. I want to celebrate the life we've made by fucking its mother until she can't see straight." Elaine squirms at the thought, then leads Stewart to his equally messy bedroom.

CHAPTER THIRTY-TWO

Max and Jane arrive at Bronagh's flat and Max lets them in with his key. They go around checking all the rooms again. As everything was as it was when Max left the night before and that morning, they come to the conclusion that she still hadn't returned. With a heavy heart Max locks up the flat again. They climb back into his Golf and head for his house.

Once they arrive at the house, Jane goes into the kitchen to put the kettle on as Max flops onto his couch, exhaustion trying to take over. He forces it away as he takes out his phone from his pocket and opens up the first of his social media apps. Jane walks in with two cups of coffee and hands one to Max.

"You putting a post up about Bre?"

Max takes a sip of the strong coffee before answering.

"Aye, we need to get it out there. I took a picture of her before we left so I'm going to put that up too."

Jane sits down next to him. "I'll do the same, but with a different photo. Do you think I should contact Stewart?" Max huffs at the mention of Stewart, and his gut gives a dip.

"Probably, aye. The more people who know that she's missing the better, don't you think?" Jane nods as she pulls up her contact list and phones her ex-lover.

"It's just ringing out, then going onto voicemail. He might be ignoring me, or he might actually not hear his phone. I'll try again later." Feeling defeated slightly, Jane starts her own post.

The next hour is taken up with both Max and Jane answering phone calls and messages from concerned friends. Max's phone starts ringing in his hand.

"It's Gordon." He announces to Jane before connecting the call. "Gordon, what's up?"

"Oh, Max, I've just seen your post. You must be out your mind. Are you okay?" Hearing worry in Gordon's tone was quite reassuring to Max, which takes him by surprise as he has only met Gordon once or twice, but he knew Bronagh and he had grown close since she started her new job. He winces at the thought of her job, realising that that is where all this craziness started.

"I'm not great to be honest Gee. I'm worried sick I just want her home, here, with me."

"I understand Max, I really do... so, I'll be over in twenty minutes with food. I'm guessing you haven't eaten anything today? Is Jane with you?" Emotion catches in Max's throat at the kindness this almost stranger is offering. He clears his throat before answering.

"Eh... aye, she's here. You know, you don't hav—"

"I know I don't. Bronagh's became a great friend to me and I want to help, so if that means keeping you fed and sane until she returns, then so be it. I'll bring Chinese." Max says his goodbyes and cancels the call. He closes his eyes, trying to control the emotions crashing through him, which seems to be a losing battle for him. Opening his eyes he sees Jane staring at him.

"Gordon's coming over with food." Jane grunts and looks away. Max can feel the atmosphere chill slightly around Jane. Not having a great amount of patience left, Max asks her about her change in demeanour.

"What's up with your face...? Why don't you want Gordon here?" Jane straightens, trying to look undisturbed.

"I didn't say anything!" Max gives her a look.

"Listen Jane, I don't care about any jealousy you have over Bre's friendship with Gordon. He's her friend, he's worried about her and he wants to help. So any hang-ups you have about the different friendships needs to be put aside, at least until later. I don't have the energy or the wherewithal to deal with it at the moment." Jane lowers her head, guilt crashing through her again. She knows she doesn't have any reason to be jealous of Gordon. She just needed to be the 'good' best friend and not the one who abandoned her on their night out, leaving her to be abducted.

Half an hour later Max answers the door to Gordon and two bags full of Chinese food.

"Gee, come in, kitchen's through there." He points Gordon towards the kitchen and closes the door behind him.

They divide up some of the food and sit down. Max starts to explain what they know about Bronagh's disappearance. Jane stays quiet.

"So, that's where we're at. Just waiting and praying." Gordon looks between the two friends.

"And you've still not got Stewart on the phone?" Jane shakes her head.

"I'll try him again." She grabs her phone, pressing the screen until the ringing starts, then ends. "Nothing, just his voicemail again." Max lowers his head. A heavy feeling pushes on his heart and his gut. He didn't like the thought that Stewart had any knowledge of where Bronagh was or what had happened to her, but there was a niggle in his gut that he couldn't ignore.

"Has anybody seen Stewart lately?" Gordon asks them both. Jane is the only one to answer.

"I've not seen him since we broke up, but I think I might have spoken to him." Max looks up, but it's Gordon who asks the question they are both thinking.

"What do you mean you *think* you've spoken to him?" Jane squeezes her eyes shut, remembering bits and pieces from her drunken phone call with Stewart.

"Well... I was rather drunk one night last week... and I phoned him. I didn't mean to phone him, but I wanted him to know that I was moving on. So, before I knew what I was doing I was on the phone to him telling him about my plans for the night out with Bronagh." Max is out of his chair pacing the floor trying to get his anger under control as the niggle in his gut increases.

"But am I right in thinking that Bronagh didn't like Stewart?" Gordon quizzes. Jane is first to answer her tone indignant.

"NO! Well... at least not until we started to believe he had cheated on me." Max stops pacing to look at Jane, disbelief contorts his features.

"What the fuck Jane? That is total shite and you know it!" Max could feel his anger get the better of him. "She never liked him. She put up with him for you and he knew it. In fact, six months before you and him got together, he asked Bre out and she turned him down. You just chose not to see the tension between them." Jane stares at him shocked and stunned at his outburst. She knew Stewart had asked Bronagh out and she knew Bronagh had turned him down, but she didn't realise Bronagh disliked him as much as Max was making out... or did she? She starts to think back. She could feel the tension, sometimes, when the four of them were together, but she always put it down to Bronagh and Max's undeclared feelings for each other. Putting her head in her hands Jane groans.

"You don't think he has anything to do with this do you?"

"I don't know." Max sits down and starts to pick at his food again. "But my gut says maybe." Another groan comes from Jane.

"God I'm a rubbish friend." Gordon rubs her back, trying to console her.

"Listen, even if Stewart is involved, nobody could've known he would abduct her. No one could've foreseen this." Max snorts.

"Guessed maybe." Gordon throws him a look. "BUT, not known for sure! Now, as it is we don't know if anybody *is* involved. All we know for sure is, she has disappeared." Max's phone buzzes to life. He grabs it with desperation.

"Bronagh? Eh, sorry... aye, that's me." Gordon and Jane sit in silence as Max talks. "Okay, thanks. Can I add a name into the mix...? We, well I, think Stewart McMillan might have a grudge against Bronagh... okay... I will, thanks bye." He cancels the call and looks around the room before filling everyone in. "That was Sian, eh, WPC Young. She said that they've looked at the CCTV at the pub an' seen Bronagh walk out the back door to the beer garden, like you said Jane, and she didn't walk back in. Then there's three people walking out the back gate. It looks like the person in the middle is getting held up, but they can't say if it's Bronagh or not. Although they say the height and build suggests it could be. An' her bag and phone were found this morning in the pub. The police have them just now, something to do with evidence." The two friends stare at Max trying to take in his words.

"So what now?" Jane asks, her tone betraying her desperation.

"I'm giving Stewart 'till tomorrow to return our calls, then I'm going to his flat to find him." Gordon and Jane agree with his plan.

CHAPTER THIRTY-THREE

Waking up in each other's arms was something Elaine didn't think she would get used to, but she wanted to spend the rest of her life trying. Turning round onto her back brought on the nausea. She was thankful that the physical vomiting had mostly stopped as she could control the feeling of nausea with her breathing which she was doing when Stewart turns to face her.

"Babe? What're you doin'? Are you okay?" Panic sounds in his voice which touches Elaine's heart. She nods, not trusting herself or her stomach to speak, just yet. After a few minutes the wave of nausea eases and she manage to smile at Stewart.

"I'm okay, just some morning sickness but it's easing now. I'll need to make an appointment with the doctors, get the pregnancy confirmed and booked in with the anti-natal clinic." Stewart has taken her into his arms, trying to soothe her nausea and keep her calm when he brings up Bronagh's demise.

"You canny do that babes. Mind, we said that we're going to need to leave here... you know, after we get rid of her outside." Elaine stiffens then relaxes again.

"So we do. Well wherever we end up I'll need to get booked in." Stewart kisses the top of her head.

"No problem babes. Now we need to discuss what the plan of action is." Elaine takes a deep breath.

"Whatever you think is best. I'm here, with you, no matter what." Stewart manoeuvres Elaine round so they are face to face and kisses her soundly.

"I know we didn't plan to kill her, but needs must now, and I'm here with you too, no matter what. I love you." Tears spring to Elaine's eyes.

"I love you too. I just need to say, the only thing I don't want is to leave her to die, that's just too cruel. But other than that I'm fine... "

"Okay, so what does that leave us? We could shoot her." Stewart starts counting off the ways they could kill their abductee on his fingers. "But I'm not sure where we would get a gun." Elaine thinks for a second.

"What about poison?"

"Again, I don't know where we would get it, and it could take too long to work. So that's shooting her and poison out. What about stabbing her?" Elaine screws up her nose and Stewart snorts.

"What's wrong with stabbing her?"

"It could get messy."

Stewart laughs. "It's all going to be messy... unless we strangle her, or snap her neck."

Elaine shivers. "You would be best doing that... you know with your strength."

"Hmm, that's true... but it would be me that done the actual deed no matter what we choose. I don't want you or the baby put into any sort of danger."

Tears spring to life again in her eyes and Stewart kisses them away. "I think that's the best way, snapping her neck, if you're okay with doing it, less mess. I really don't want to throw up in the garage when we're cleaning up."

Stewart squeezes her. "Okay, I'll snap her neck then." He pauses, thinking and relishing the thought. "You know what? I think that's the best idea too. Less stress for you and the baby and I get to live out something I dreamt of doing when she first turned me down." Another shiver runs down Elaine's spine but she ignores it and cuddles in deeper to her lover.

"You want some breakfast before we get started on packing and organising our future?"

The mention of food sets off a gurgle in Elaine's stomach and she giggles.

"I guess that's a yes then?" Stewart gives her another kiss then goes to make them food.

****

Standing in his kitchen waiting on the kettle to boil, Max hangs his head in his hands. It was a long night. One where not much sleep happened and a lot of anger was felt. The three new friends managed to eat most of the food Gordon had brought, although Max had eaten the least. They then spent the rest of the night answering messages on all their social media posts and trying to think of different reasons for Bronagh's disappearance. Everything was making Max's anger increase and no scenario came close to what his gut was telling him. Stewart was involved. Thinking back to the night he saw Elaine in the supermarket, he remembers seeing Stewart there. He had dismissed the idea he was there with Elaine, but now he wonders if he was too quick to dismiss the idea. He berates himself for not listening to his gut back then.

Gordon walks into the kitchen and coughs, bringing Max out of his dark thoughts.

"You look like you need some good coffee."

Max looks up and tries to smile. "I hear you're the man that makes damn good coffee."

Gordon smiles back, knowing that Bronagh must have been singing his praises.

"I am that, my dear... and I knew it would be needed at some point here, so, here I am your coffee god." Gordon brings out a percolator, a bag of coffee and gets to work.

Max takes a sip of his freshly brewed coffee and groans.

"Oh my god Gordon, Bre wasn't lying, this is amazing."

"Ah Max, I'm just glad I could do something. So what's the plan of action for today?" Max takes a second to compose the emotions running through him. Jane walks in rubbing her tired eyes. Nobody had slept much.

"Is that coffee I smell?" Gordon offers her a cup.

"It is and here is yours." She takes the cup and adds her sugar and milk before tasting it.

"Mmmm, Gordon—"

"I know, I know, I'm a god!" Jane rolls her eyes, but then smiles. She can't stay jealous at Gordon. He hasn't done anything but be a good friend to all of them.

"Right, so, who wants to visit Stewart with me?" Both Gordon and Jane readily agree to go. "Okay, well if we all get ready and meet back here about midday?" They all agree and finish their coffees then leave, promising to return at noon.

****

The darkness, pain and fear never ceased for Bronagh throughout the night. Her arms were numb from being strung up, but her shoulders, her ribs, legs, stomach, chest, face and backside all had pain shooting up and down them every time she adjusted her position, and when she didn't move she throbbed and ached all over. She had abandoned trying to work out how to get out of her predicament or what she could have done differently for her abduction to not have taken place. Instead she concentrated on praying. She prayed to any and all gods. She prayed that somehow she would get out of the garage, that Max or the police would find her. She prayed that Stewart or Elaine would come back and give her some of the water that they had left for her, then praying that they wouldn't come back, in fear that she gets another beating, or worse. But mostly she prayed that she would die before anything more horrific than another beating happened. She didn't want to die, or lose hope, but the darkness seemed to engulf her and her soul.

A rattle at the shutter makes Bronagh's heart skip a beat and she holds her breath. Seconds tick by as she waits on the squeal of rusty metal grinding against rusty metal as the shutter is pulled up, but it never comes. Just silence, which she breaks by shouting into the endless darkness.

"Hello…? Is anybody there? Hello? Help, anybody." She sags against the cold wall, all her energy drained from what it took for her to shout, and the memory of Stewart telling her that the garage was sound proofed. Her throat is still sore from her screaming the day before and the dryness of being so dehydrated. She tries to stop the tears from coming, knowing she could ill afford losing any more moisture from her body, but some still come anyway. She shivers again as the tears dry on her tight skin. Shivers take over her body again, her body shaking uncontrollably, as they had during the night until sleep eventually took over with exhaustion. Thankfully the temperature hadn't dropped as much as she'd feared during the night, but it was still cold enough for Bronagh to worry about hypothermia. Feeling exhaustion taking over again she closes her eyes, praying for the escape that would come with the oblivion that was sleep.

CHAPTER THIRTY-FOUR

After Stewart throws most of his meagre clothes into a rucksack, the lovers drive to Elaine's house. Entering the house Stewart reminds Elaine not to take too long getting things together as they needed to get back to Bronagh and 'fix' her. He also mentions not to pack too much, just the essentials. After half an hour of waiting Stewart walks upstairs in search of Elaine.

"Babes, what are you doing?" He is met with silence as an answer. Stewart's heart starts to speed up with a slight feeling of panic. "Elaine!" More silence greets him until he reaches the top step and a mumbled sob reaches his ears. He walks into Elaine's bedroom and sees her sitting cross-legged in the middle of the rumpled super king size bed, sobbing. Tears flowing freely down her cheeks, along with the snot from her nose.

"Babes, what's the matter?" She shakes her head, then shrugs her shoulders.

"I don't know... wh... what to take... take with me." Stewart stands at the side of the bed and starts to pick through the bundles of clothes strewn around Elaine. The panic he felt gives way to anger.

"Elaine, it doesn't matter what you take. We can come back for everything else later on, once we're settled, or we will buy you more things."

"But how?" she wails, then rubs her running nose on the sleeve of her jumper leaving a wet silvery trail of snot where she'd rubbed. "We won't have any money and neither of us will have a job. Where are we going to stay? How are we going to buy things for the baby? Stewart, I'm... I'm scared!" She sobs again.

"I know you're scared, but we don't have time for this shit. So could you please get your crap together so we can get out of here!" His words come out far more sharper than he intended, but he needed to get his point across. He needed Elaine organised and then back to the garage. He didn't want to put off the inevitable any longer than was absolutely necessary. He knew they wouldn't be able to move the body until after dark, but he wanted to get the main event over and done with as soon as possible. Elaine starts to wail again.

"Don't shout at me... I'm scared, and... emotional!" Biting back his anger Stewart climbs onto the bed and pulls Elaine into his arms.

"I'm sorry babes, I didn't mean to shout. I'm just a bit anxious about the next bit and would like to get it over and done with. Listen I have a friend who works in a hotel in Dumfries. We can drive down there and get a room for a few nights. Then we can start looking for a flat to rent and new jobs, or sign on or something. We can put your house up for sale and I'll get my deposit back from my flat. So we'll be sorted, okay?" Feeling a bit better after hearing Stewart's plan, Elaine nods and sniffs loudly.

"Will we be able to come back for the other stuff... once we're settled, when we're putting the house on the market?" Stewart smiles at her sympathetically.

"Of course we can, I already said as much. Now, get some essentials into a bag and let's get going." Elaine manages to pull herself together enough and packs a bag. Getting into Elaine's Corsa they head back to Stewart's flat without realising they have left the one item that can connect Elaine to Bronagh and Max... the pre-paid mobile phone she used for the nasty messages.

****

Gordon and Jane arrive back at Max's house at the arranged time and the three friends set off to Stewart's flat in Parkhead.

Max parks his car near a row of garages, making sure not to block any of them. Then they all cross the busy road.

Arriving at the security door Max presses the corresponding flat number buzzer. No answer. Trying his luck Max presses the service button and then pushes the door, but it doesn't budge.

"This isn't Bre's door, the security system on this one actually works!" Jane states flatly. Anger gets the better of Max and he slams his hand into the intercom system.

"So what now?" Jane asks, rubbing her arms from the chill in the wind.

"I don't know, to be honest." Max sighs with despondency, the anger leaving him. Gordon looks up and down the long street.

"Does he work nearby?" Jane shakes her head.

"No. He works in a call centre in Airdrie, but he doesn't work on Monday's, which made me think he would be in." Jane answers as she blows into her hands, trying to heat them up. Max rolls his eyes at her.

"It's not that cold!" Max snaps. Jane starts to retort back when the security door opens and the neighbour walks out.

"Jane, how are you? I've not seen you around for a while." Jane gives the neighbour a tight smile.

"No, eh. Me an' Stewart broke up. We happen to be looking for him, have you seen him lately?" The neighbour thinks for a second before answering.

"I've not seen him today. I heard him leave earlier... but, I did see him yesterday. He was coming out of his garage, and d'you know, I thought I heard a female's voice, but then I thought that can't be right. I mean he wouldn't have anyone in there, plus he was laughing and pulling the shutter down, so I guessed the noise was the shutter. You know how old they are. Anyway, I need to shoot, I've got a bus to catch into town. Don't be a stranger. Bye now." The neighbour waves and walks off leaving the three friends standing in disbelief at his words.

"It's fuckin' him, I knew it!" Max shouts, "He has her in his garage." His tone is disgusted. He turns to Jane. "Did you know he had a garage thing?" Jane nods her head slowly.

"I did, but I've never been in it. I didn't even know he used it or remembered he had it. Why didn't I think about that, why didn't I remember about it... god I'm such a stupid, useless friend." Gordon takes her into his arms. She wants to protest and hate him for being a better friend to Bronagh than she had been, but she couldn't. She needed his support, both moral and physical at that moment.

"Princess, we don't know for sure that she's in there." Max growls at them both and crosses the road again, dodging buses and cars. Looking up at the numbers on the outside of the garages Max finds the one that corresponded with Stewart's flat number.

"Is this it?" He turns and asks Jane as her and Gordon catch up with him.

"Uhuh." She mumbles. They all turn to look at the shutter that is sitting slightly open.

CHAPTER THIRTY-FIVE

Stewart and Elaine walk over to Bronagh, leaving the shutter open for some light, even though they had brought the torch. They weren't too bothered about the sound as the plan was to snap Bronagh's neck quickly, smoothly and with as little resistance as possible. Bronagh got a fright when the shutter was pulled up and had scrambled to her knees.

"Hello?" She hears her own voice thick and scratchy, then she hears them giggle. Her heart plummets.

"Good afternoon Bronagh. Did you sleep well?" Elaine asks in a tone that sounds like genuine concern. Bronagh's panic escalates.

"What do you want?"

"Nothing," Stewart answers. "We're here to bring this to an end is all."

Bile rises in Bronagh's dry, raw throat.

"You're letting me go?" She puts all her hope in to the question, but deep down in her sore chilled bones she knew the answer. She was even more convinced that the ending wasn't going to be with her escape when Stewart started to laugh.

"No, you silly little bitch. I'm here to end you. You know, finish you off... I'm going to snap that plump little neck of yours."

Fear overtaking her, she tries to get to her feet, but between the lack of food, pain and numbness she doesn't make it and crashes against the cold brick wall. A scream manages to make its way through the dryness in her throat and out into the empty space of the garage. Stewart is on her within seconds, crushing her with his weight.

"Shut the fuck up bitch. Don't make it any harder for yourself."

Refusing to give up without a fight and doing her best to ignore the pain taking over every inch of her body, Bronagh starts to buck and thrash her body, kicking out with her pain laced, leaden legs.

"Fuck you Stewart!" she screams, tears running down her cheeks. Stewart tries to grab hold of her but fails as she manages to buck and kick him off. She doesn't know where she was finding the energy to fight him, but she was grateful for every ounce of it.

"Fuckin' sit at peace!" He lunges for her again.

The shutter is thrown up and the bright midday sun streams in making Bronagh scream and thrash again. Stewart's concentration and patience is broken with the sound of the shutter going up.

"BRONAGH?" Max shouts in and Stewart twists round.

"What the fuck? Max?" Stewart groans.

"MAX... I'm here," Bronagh croaks out, relief coursing through her.

His eyes adjusting to the to the dullness, Max sees Stewart grabbing at Bronagh who is chained to the wall. Rage rushes through his veins and he charges forward, grabbing Stewart away from the love of his life. Elaine stands further back, trying to blend into the shadows.

Max knew he had the upper hand physically over Stewart. They were similar in height, but Max kept himself fit and was physically stronger than the lanky frame of his opponent. He pulls Stewart forward and the two men exchange blows, scuffling until they were at the open mouth of the garage.

Hearing that Bronagh was in the garage both Jane and Gordon are on their phones talking to the emergency services, doing their best to explain the situation unfolding in front of them before running into the dark garage to find Bronagh.

Max swings and makes contact on Stewart's cheek bone. He feels the satisfying crunch of bone shattering under his fist and he hears the pain in Stewart's grunt. Stewart hits the ground and Max is on top of him punching him anywhere he can. Max sits up and Stewart takes the advantage. Planting his feet solidly on the ground, Stewart pushes his hips up and twists them to the right, using Max's own weight against him, he tips Max over and off of him. Max lands on the pavement with a thud, all the air rushing from his lungs. Stewart lifts himself up from the pavement and starts to kick Max.

Elaine walks from the garage and shouts at Stewart. He stops kicking, looking up at Elaine then starts to walk away. Without hesitation he breaks into a run. Max drags himself up, pushing away the pain in his lungs from being winded and his ribs where he was kicked, and watches as Stewart runs. After a few feet Stewart looks behind him, checking to see how far away from the carnage he was. Eventually he looks round to concentrate on where he was running to, but not in enough time to see how close he was to the edge of the pavement. He trips over the kerb. Arms windmilling as he falls head first into the path of an oncoming double decker bus. With the sounds of Elaine screaming and car horns blasting, the bus hits Stewart. Its full twelve tonnes, going thirty miles per hour ploughs into him, dragging him under its wheels and taking him for a fifteen metre journey before coming to an eventual stop.

Max holds Elaine back from running over to the accident, telling her he would go and check on Stewart. Walking over to the bus, he knows it wasn't going to be good news. Seeing the driver come round the bus Max runs over to catch him before he collapses onto the pavement. All colour has vanished from the driver's face, shock taking its place.

"I... I never seen him son. He was just... just... there." The driver motions with a shaking hand to his bus. Max sits the driver down on the pavement with words of assurance and walks closer to the accident. Gingerly he looks under the bus. His stomach comes up to meet him at the bloody sight greeting him. Stewart's head has been smashed to a pulp under the wheels. Brain matter is mixed with skull fragments and blood spread over the underside of the bus and the pavement next to the rest of Stewart's limp, lifeless body. Turning away Max vomits everything from his stomach into the gutter. Through the haze of shock he hears the sirens of many emergency services vehicles and someone shouting his name.

Gordon is by Max's side lifting him up, steadying him on his feet and talking to him all the time, even though he knows that Max isn't hearing him. Gordon thinks that between finding his girlfriend chained to a wall by someone who he thought was a friend, the fight that ensued, the accident that killed that so-called friend, and the sight he must've witnessed under the bus, Max was more than entitled to have shock take him over. He leads Max back to the open garage and sits him down. Looking straight into his eyes Gordon continually says Max's name, trying to bring him back from wherever he was.

"Max? Max? It's Gordon. The police are here. Max?" Eventually Max looks at Gordon with a bit more clarity in his eyes. He looks around him. Everyone who was on the bus had come out and was standing on the pavement in huddled groups. People passing by stopped and whispered loudly at what they had seen happen. He turns back to look behind him seeing Jane holding Elaine up as she screams and howls for her dead lover. He wants to feel like he should be shouting and swearing at Elaine, but he can't, he doesn't have it in him to say anything. Instead he gets up and rushes past her into the dullness of the garage. Into Bronagh.

He finds her still chained to the wall and crying. He rushes to her side and puts his arms around her in a fierce embrace. She utters a groan.

"I'm sorry. Am I hurting you? I'm so sorry." He feels her shake her head even through the shivering that is racking her body.

"What's happened Max? I heard screaming and horns and... and a bang." Max rubs her back, trying to get heat into her damp clothes but also trying to calm the shaking he can feel convulse through her.

"Sshh, it's okay, it's over. Stewart's dead." A strangled sound comes from Bronagh.

"What do you mean Stewart's dead? How?" Relief washes over her at hearing the news of Stewart's death, but it is quickly followed by guilt. "What about Elaine?"

"He ran out in front of a bus. Elaine is still outside, but she can't get to you now. The police and that are here now. They'll get you out of here. Bre, I'm so sorry. Are you okay... Of course you're not, that's a stupid question, I'm sorry... I'm just so sorry." His voice breaks as tears choke him and spill over onto his cheeks and down into Bronagh's hair. The lovers stay exactly the way they are, Max holding on tight, mumbling how sorry he was until a police officer and a paramedic arrive and ask for Max to stand aside. The paramedic kneels down to Bronagh and starts to treat her. The police officer leaves to find a fire-fighter to cut Bronagh free of the chains.

CHAPTER THIRTY-SIX

Hours after the accident Max, Jane and Gordon sit in the drab waiting room of the Royal Infirmary Hospital accident and emergency department. The hard plastic orange chairs doing nothing to ease the bruises and scrapes Max earned during the fight with the now late Stewart. The harsh fluorescent lights sting his eyes and annoy his growing sore head, but every time he closed his eyes to block out the garish light, the gruesome images of Stewart's mangled body and pulverized head swim behind his lids making his stomach turn again and his guilt push down heavier on him. Opening his eyes he shakes his head trying to literally shake the images from his memory. Gordon looks at Max, concern a mask covering his face.

"You okay Max?" Max looks up at him.

"Aye…! Aye... well..." he blows out a breath, "I need to see her."

"I know. Hang in there it shouldn't be too long." Gordon gives Max a tight smile. Just as Max smiles back a nurse enters the waiting room asking for who was waiting on a Bronagh White. Max is on his feet and at the nurse's side before she can finish her sentence. Jane and Gordon weren't far behind him.

"Can I see her? Is she okay? Tell me she's okay. She is okay isn't she?" Max is almost begging and the nurse smiles sweetly at him, placing her hand gently on his arm to quieten him.

"She will be okay. She has a touch of hypothermia and is very dehydrated, but there shouldn't be any lasting *physical* damage." Max blows out another breath.

"Can I see her?" he asks again, this time calmer and the nurse nods.

"Only one of you though. She's asking for Max?"

Relief sweeps through him. He hadn't realised how worried he had been about her rejecting him. He turns and looks at Jane and Gordon.

"It's fine." Jane answers the unasked question. "Tell her we're here and we love her, and we'll wait for you." Tears run freely as Jane starts to break down. Gordon places his arms around her and leads her back to the uncomfortable chairs, gesturing to Max that he would support Jane.

Max follows the nurse to the cubicle where Bronagh was in bed. Before leaving she informs them that a doctor would be round to discuss Bronagh's injuries and care as soon as he was free, then she closed the plain light blue curtains giving them a semblance of privacy.

Max stands for a long second drinking in the sight of his girlfriend lying in the hospital bed. It hurts him to see her so battered and bruised and vulnerable. Drips connected to each of her arms, her face swollen where Stewart had rained down blows from his fists. Her lips dry and cracked from dehydration. He could see more black and purple bruises on her neck and more colour peeking out from the edge of her hospital gown. He guessed there was even more over her body where the hospital gown and blankets covered her. Seeing past all of that, Max thought she was the most beautiful sight he had ever set eyes on. She was alive, she would heal, she was safe and, he prayed, she was still his. She wouldn't hate him.

Panic started to mask Bronagh's features the longer Max stood, just staring at her. She thought she must look horrendous.

"Max?" Her voice cracks as her throat is raw, and Max is by her side, holding her hand and caressing her face with feather light fingers, frightened he might hurt her or even break her.

"Hey you." His tone is soft and loving as relief courses through him. He leans over the bed to kiss her forehead, trying not to pull any of her drips or press on any of her injuries. But still she grimaces. "I'm sorry." Max panics and Bronagh looks at him with tears flowing from her eyes. In her darkest moments in the garage she had thought she would never see Max again. Now he was standing next to her looking concerned, frantic even, guilt crashes through her.

"Why are you sorry? I'm the one who's sorry, I was selfish —" She manages to get her words out over the pain in her throat. The rawness had reduced some but it was still sore to talk. Max stops her talking by gently laying his finger on her dry lips.

"Sshh. You've got nothing to be sorry for; all you did was go on a night out, like a million other people that night. I'm just glad you're safe, and... and, well... are you okay?" Before she can answer a doctor announces his arrival and hunts for the split in the curtains. Finding them after a few seconds he makes his entrance smiling.

"You'd think I'd know how to get through they things," he jokes, then coughs when he feels the atmosphere in the small semi-private cubicle. "Okay. Well..." He checks his notes. "Miss White, here, was held in a garage is that right?" Max makes a sound low in his chest at the reminder and Bronagh nods, not trusting her voice not to crack with emotion. The doctor continues, "so, because of this, you have a touch of hypothermia, and dehydration. We have started you on a heated saline drip to help with both of these. The other drip is an antibiotic drip, just as a precaution, for your cuts and splits. There seems to be no internal injuries, broken bones or anything, but I would assume your ribs will be bruised inside as well as out, looking at the mass of bruises you have on your torso. But other than that, you are, physically, okay." Max and Bronagh have been listening to the doctor intently, neither of them breaking the contact they have with each other through their intertwined hands.

"When will she get home?" Max is first to speak, desperation lacing his words. Bronagh winces. The thought of going home sends a stab of fear through her. She didn't want to be alone, but she also didn't know if Max would want her back with him.

"It'll be a few days," the doctor answers. "We'll transfer her to a ward tonight and keep her on a saline drip for at least another twelve to twenty-four hours. The hypothermia was mild, thankfully, but still enough to cause Miss White to shiver, be fatigued and have slightly slurred speech. Although the shivering is starting to subside I see. We want to make sure her core temperature increases and stays at normal levels and that nothing else pops up, like a concussion. Hopefully by Friday or maybe the weekend she will be ready for home." Max nods, then squeezes Bronagh's hand. The doctor takes his leave with their gratitude and thanks, leaving Max and Bronagh alone again. Max is first to break the silence that has descended.

"Gordon and Jane are in the waiting room, but only one person was allowed in." Bronagh's heart lifts.

"You wanted to see me?" Max looks at her with a strange look, making her stomach flip.

"Why wouldn't I want to see you?" Before she can answer him a nurse and a porter arrive in the cubicle.

"Time to move darlin'," the stout porter announces in his gruff Glasgow accent, and ushers Max out of the curtains. Fear courses through Bronagh at Max not being by her side, worried that if he left he would never return. She asks the nurse if Max could remain with her as she goes to the ward. Relief floods Max again as he hears Bronagh ask for him. Her questioning tone about him wanting to see her sits heavy on his mind. Knowing he needs to let Jane and Gordon know what's happening he returns to the waiting room. Quickly he explains how Bronagh is feeling and that she will be staying in hospital for a few days. They both send her their love and take their leave for home. Max returns to Bronagh's side and they both let out a breath of relief.

****

Sitting in her dark cold living room Elaine couldn't make sense of her emotions. She couldn't believe her luck at getting away from the scene without her being arrested or anyone noticing. Once she was home and sat down, every other emotion she was feeling washed over her, crashing into each other making her dizzy. Not knowing if she wanted to laugh or cry or both. She and Stewart had been so together in their plan when they arrived to kill Bronagh, then, once they had been found by Max and the others she could see and feel Stewart distance himself from her. Forget about her. Then, she realised, he was literally running away from the scene, without her! The abandonment she'd felt her whole life, and when he had looked back at her rushed through her again. Without warning the images of Stewart falling in front of the bus burst to life behind her closed eyelids. Grief engulfs her. Tearing her heart out as it rips through her every cell. Hot fat tears bounce from her tired eyes, not taking their time to run down her cheeks. She has never felt pain like it in her entire life, not even when her parents left her, or when her entire family had died and she was on her own. Grief quickly turns to anger as she thinks about living her life without him, raising their unplanned child on her own. He ran away from her, from them. Before she could shout after him or follow he was gone, taken from her under the wheels of a moving bus. Leaving her alone. The sound of the bus's horn blaring and the squeal of the tyres skidding along the road, ring through her memory and she cries out, hoping the scream that rips from her lungs would drown out the noises in her head, but it doesn't. If anything they increase and mingle until they are all one. Trying to stand up on legs that refuse to support her was a challenge that Elaine had never before experienced. Twice her legs gave way from her, landing her back on the couch dazed and confused. Taking deep breaths she tries again. Success. Holding onto the walls, Elaine makes her way slowly to the dark kitchen. Switching on the lights she winces at the harshness of it. She takes a second to wonder if that was how Bronagh had felt when they let light into the garage, but she pushes the thought aside, not wanting to ponder Bronagh or what they did to her. She had decided that, because Stewart had left her, she could distance herself from everything they had done, leaving the blame firmly at the dead man's feet entirely.

Picking up an unopened box of wine and a glass, Elaine sits at her kitchen table, not sure that her legs would make it back to the living room. She knew she shouldn't be drinking now she knew she was with child, but she couldn't think of anything else that she needed at that particular moment in time. Pouring herself a large glass, Elaine starts to think about her future and what her best plan of action would be.

Coming to with banging sounds followed by muffled shouting, Elaine tries to move. Groaning with pain she realises she had fallen asleep, slumped over her kitchen table after too many glasses of wine. The banging and shouting increases and Elaine drags herself from her chair and into a standing position. The movement sends a wave of nausea and dizziness washing up and over her as her head threatens to explode with the movement and noise, but still the banging and shouting continue.

Gingerly she makes her way through the house to the front door where the entire racket is based and opens it. The fact that her front door was unlocked registers somewhere in the back of her consciousness, but she couldn't find the energy to care. Standing on her doorstep are the two police officers from before.

"Miss Ashton, you remember WPC Young and myself, PC Loughran. We met a couple weeks back." Elaine groans as the PC's voice rattles through her pounding head. "We were wondering if you had a moment. We need to ask you a few questions regarding an incident that you were allegedly involved in yesterday." Elaine stares at the two officers, trying to think of what to say. She opens her mouth to talk when her nausea turns into something much more. Clamping her hand over her mouth she turns on her heel and runs up the stairs, making it to the bathroom just as the vinegar smelling, putrid, soured wine makes its way through her fingers and into the pristine white sink. The two officers look at each other and roll their eyes then step inside the house, closing the door behind them.

CHAPTER THIRTY-SEVEN

Once settled into her single room on the ward Bronagh and Max sit holding hands. They both know they have many things to discuss, but neither of them wanted to break the comforting silence that had descended upon them. After what felt like an eternity Max takes a deep breath to ask the question that has been burning in his throat.

"Bre... are you okay?" Bronagh looks deep into Max's red rimmed tired eyes. Her heart restricts at the sight before her. She had put that tiredness there by being selfish, she inwardly tells herself. Tears roll down her cheeks as she answers him.

"No, not really." Max's heart breaks.

"What can I do? How do I make you better?" His questions are almost pleading. Bronagh shakes her head imperceptibly. Not knowing what to say as she didn't think there was anything he could do.

"There's nothing you can do —" Before she can finish her sentence a nurse comes into the room letting Max know that he needed to leave. Both Max and Bronagh ask if he could stay, but the nurse is adamant. He had to leave as it was an hour after visiting time, so with a heavy heart Max raises from the hard plastic chair he had pulled over to the bed, and leans over Bronagh. She looked so pale and scared laying in the hospital bed it made his heart ache. Her eyes were pleading with him not to leave her, which made his mood darken and his heart hurt more.

"I'm sorry Bre. I'll be back first thing tomorrow, I promise." He holds her face in his hands and notices her shivering had stopped. Leaning in, he grazes his lips over hers, unsure if she would let him kiss her. Bronagh hesitantly kisses

Max back. Gingerly she lifts her aching arms until she can clasp her hands behind his neck, then pulls him down more. Max takes the invitation and deepens the kiss, finding her tongue with his.

Knowing Bronagh is still weak, Max uses all of his self-control and breaks the kiss after a minute or so, but keeps their contact by resting his forehead on hers. Pulling back he looks into her eyes, noticing the fear dancing in them.

"I'll be back as soon as they let me in okay?" Tears run down her cheek as she nods, still grasping her hands behind his neck. Gently Max loosens her grip and brings her hands to his lips, kissing each knuckle individually. "Try and get some sleep, and I'll see you tomorrow. I'm so glad you're back with me and safe... I love you." Bronagh releases a gasp then a sob as everything she had been hoping for and holding in came out in cleansing, cathartic sobs. As Max holds Bronagh close he hears the nurse re-enter the room, then turn and leave closing the door behind her when she hears the crying.

Once her sobs have subsided and she could breathe again Bronagh pulls back from Max's embrace.

"You still love me?" Tears glisten in Max's eyes as he fights his emotions to speak.

"Of course I still love you; I'm never going to stop loving you." He gives her another kiss. "We'll talk about everything tomorrow, but as far as I'm concerned nothing has changed between us. Now try and get some sleep." They say their goodbyes with more tears and Max leaves the hospital, emotionally wrung out like a used dish cloth.

A different nurse enters Bronagh's room and introduces herself as Nurse Bale, then she gives a slight snort.

"My badge still says Nurse Masterson. Bale's my married name. I keep forgetting to order a new badge, so just call me Eveline." Bronagh looks at the nurse and takes an instant liking to her kind smile and warm eyes.

"Have you been married long?" Bronagh is glad for the change in conversation, although she felt weird at having what could be classed as a 'normal' conversation at that moment.

"We're just coming up six months." Eveline busies herself checking Bronagh's drips and vitals. "How are you feeling? Your shivering has stopped and your temperature is getting there." Bronagh nods.

"I don't know how I am, to tell you the truth. Sometimes I think it was all a bad dream, then I remember Stewart, the guy who kidnapped me, is dead and then it all comes crashing back around me. After that I feel relief that he can't get me again and then I feel guilty for feeling relieved that another human is dead." Eveline stops what she is doing and listens. "At least Max is still with me." She sighs, tears catching in her throat again.

"Was that the man that's just left?" Bronagh nods. "You thought he would leave you? I don't mean to probe, but, it wasn't your fault someone abducted you." Bronagh shrugs.

"It's a long story, but, he warned me not to go out as we thought I was being stalked, but I still went." Eveline nods slowly.

"I don't think he would blame you. He looked worried and somewhat relieved. Have you had a chance to talk about what happened?" Fear flashes in Bronagh's eyes.

"No, not yet. I'm a bit frightened to talk about what happened, to him. I don't want him to think any worse of me, or hurt him any more than I already have."

"Hmm. I understand. It will help to talk to someone about what happened, preferably a professional counsellor as well as your boyfriend. But believe me you will be best having a conversation with Max about how you're feeling in the relationship too. If he loves you, he'll support you through everything without it changing too much between youse. Talking to each other and being truthful is the best way to get through things like this. I have friends who went through some bad times and between their love and talking they got through it, in fact they are getting married next year." Eveline finishes up her checks and gives Bronagh's hand a friendly squeeze, "Try and get some sleep. Everything feels better when you're not as tired... okay?" Bronagh nods again and wriggles down into her bed, taking care not to pull her drips.

Max pulls his Golf into his driveway and turns off the engine. He slumps forward, resting his forehead on the steering wheel. Every emotion known to man crashes through him, starting with relief, then carrying on to joy, love and anger, but mostly guilt. Guilt that he wasn't there to stop Stewart from taking Bronagh and guilt that Stewart was dead, even if he did feel a hint of gratitude for his death. Taking a deep breath he pushes open the driver's door and climbs out, closing it with a little more force than he would normally treat his beloved car. Getting into his kitchen he grabs a beer from the fridge and sits at the small table to think. He starts by thinking about the night of Bronagh's abductions. Could he have stopped it? Should he have let her go? The rational side of his brain knows there was no way he could have stopped her going out. He tried, so there was no way he could've stopped the event, without turning into a stalker himself. But the guilt stays with him. Next he thinks about the behaviour of Jane which gave Stewart and Elaine the opportunity to abduct Bronagh. Anger flares in his chest. He wonders for a second if Jane was also involved, but dismisses the question immediately. He knew in his gut that Jane knew nothing about it by her actions when she found out about the abduction. No, he muses, her only crime is making a bad friendship decision that happened at a convenient time for others. He drains his bottle and retrieves another one, trying to get a grip on his anger. Then he thinks about finding Bronagh chained to the wall and Stewart standing over her. Fear sours in his stomach. He was sure Stewart was about to do something to Bronagh. Another beating or worse. A shiver runs down his spine at the thought. Grabbing his third beer, Max vows to himself, Bronagh, any god listening and his empty kitchen that as long as he lives, nobody and nothing would hurt Bronagh ever again. Taking his beer to the living room he sits on the couch, staring at the blank TV screen until exhaustion takes over and he drags himself up to bed.

CHAPTER THIRTY-EIGHT

As she sat waiting on her duty solicitor in the stale interview room in Parkhead Police station, Elaine couldn't believe what had happened. After she had spoken to the two officers and they'd left, she was sitting in her living room grieving for and being angry at her dead boyfriend, then, an hour later the officers return and arrest her for the alleged abduction of Bronagh White.

The grubby door to the interview room opens and in walks a tall, slender, well dressed, but harassed man. Elaine assumes it to be the duty solicitor. Seeing his sharp but rain dampened suit and clean shaven jaw, Elaine straightens herself up, dragging her fingers through her hair, trying to get it to sit in a less hedge dragged backwards way. She starts to get up from her seat, but the solicitor motions for her to remain seated.

"Miss Ashton, I'm the duty solicitor. I understand you are under arrest for an alleged abduction of Bronagh White? Is that correct?"

Elaine nods. "It wasn't me though; I mean it wasn't my idea." She tries her best to look contrite and convincing as the solicitor eyes her for a second before looking deeper into her eyes. Elaine felt like he was looking deep into her memories, trying to read them.

"Okay, well, why don't you tell me in your own words how Miss White ended up chained to Mr McMillan's garage wall and what you were doing there when she was found."

Elaine looks startled for a second before covering it up with a furlong look. "He made me do it!" Elaine makes her statement with a crack in her voice. The solicitor takes out a notepad from his briefcase and starts taking notes as Elaine talks him through her version of the events leading up to the abduction of Elaine and thereafter.

"Okay," the solicitor starts, "so you're saying you're not guilty as you were under duress to go through with the plan, and you were actually against it all?" Elaine makes a show of dabbing her dry eyes and sniffing.

"Yes! Stewart made it sound like we weren't going to do anything that bad. Then, when I found out I was pregnant he used our baby to get me to help him."

"Okay, well—" The solicitor is interrupted by a sharp rap on the interview room door. Two burly CID officers enter the already small room making it so much smaller.

"Miss Ashton, you ready to tell us what happened?" Elaine throws a frightened look towards her solicitor then back to the officers as they sit down and start recording the interview.

****

A bright light shines straight into Bronagh's face, blinding her to the point of pain. Behind the light she hears a man's voice laughing at her, taunting her. Telling her she'll never be free again. The light intensifies, blurring her vision and burning her eyes until it blinks off and she's back in the darkness. The terrifying, endless blackness. She can hear a voice whimpering, softly to start with, then growing increasingly into a worried, panicked female's voice, asking not to be left alone, they don't want to be on their own again. She thinks the voice sounds like her own, but she can't be sure. Behind her she can hear a third voice; this one is saying her name over and over. She tries to turn around but she's stuck. Her body unwilling to move under her command. She strains her neck trying to look behind her when Stewart's face flashes in front of her. His smiling face hovers in the darkness, grinning at her, until he starts to laugh, throwing his head back into the darkness so all Bronagh can see is the back of his throat exposing his uvula. His laughter turns into a piercing scream. The scream fades and eventually there is silence, leaving only

Stewart's distorted face. His mouth gaping open. Slowly his face distorts more as his skull starts to cave in. His eyes start bulging from their sockets. The pressure of his skull imploding making his eyes push their boundaries until, inevitably they pop from their sockets aiming themselves at Bronagh, landing in her open hands.

Screaming and thrashing Bronagh wrenches herself from the nightmare to see Max leaning over her, saying her name repeatedly, stroking her hair, trying to bring her back from whatever horror she was dreaming about. Realising it was just a dream Bronagh lets out a gasp and grabs Max. Pulling on her drips she grimaces, but refuses to let go. Max holds on just as tightly.

"Hey you, sshh. Bre, it's okay, I'm here, it's okay." Continuing to hold on to Max, she sobs into his shoulder, making haunted, desperate sobs until there was nothing left inside of her but hollowness.

"Oh, Max... "

"Sshh, it's okay. You're safe, it's over." She pulls back, eventually, and takes a deep shuddering breath. Her eyes are red rimmed and bloodshot, and Max can still see the fear from her dream dancing in them. He sits on the edge of the bed so she doesn't need to stretch to reach him and holds her hands as she speaks.

"I was back there, I was in that darkness again... he was... there and laughing and... and..." Tears start running down her cheeks again as she starts to shake all over and hyperventilate. Max moves up the bed more, taking her back into his arms he rubs her back, trying to soothe her.

"It was a dream Bre, it's over. You'll never be back there again. I promise." After a few minutes, and once she had calmed enough Bronagh manages to speak.

"What happened to Elaine?" Max stops rubbing her back, wondering why he hadn't thought about Elaine. He had seen her in the garage, then the fight started and before he could think about what was happening, Stewart was dead. He knew he had held her back from going to see Stewart under the bus, and went himself but from that moment onwards he didn't remember much other than the vision of Stewart's mangled head and body. Once the police were finished talking to him he was too worried about Bronagh to think about anything or anyone else.

"I'm not sure." She stiffens under his hands. "I'll find out, but everything will be fine. I promise." Max spends the next few minutes settling Bronagh down until she is fully back in control of her breathing and her grasp has loosened enough for him to breathe.

The door to the single room opens disturbing their almost tranquil moment. Nurse Masterson walks in with a friendly, but worried look on her face.

"Bronagh?" Bronagh looks up and smiles.

"Eveline, this is Max, my boyfriend." Max smiles at the nurse and inwardly relaxes at being introduced as her boyfriend.

"Hi Max... Bronagh, there is two police officers wanting to talk to you. Are you feeling up to talking to them?" Bronagh and Max share a look before Bronagh looks back to the nurse nodding her head.

"I'll be fine... Max can stay, can't he?" Fear tinges her question. Eveline looks at them both.

"I don't see why not, but remember I never let Max in!" Eveline winks at the couple then lets the police officers in.

"Miss White, I'm WPC Young and this is PC Loughran. We met a while ago. We've been asked to come and ask you some questions about the events leading up to and including your abduction, plus the day you were found and the events that unfolded then." Bronagh looks between the officers taking deep breaths readying herself to talk.

"Can Max stay? Please?" Bronagh almost begs the officers. WPC Young's eyes flick to Max then back again.

"Okay, but we may need to ask him to leave when we discuss certain things." Max holds Bronagh's hand tightly as he watches her fear play out on her face and feels the white-knuckled grip she has on his hand even though she agrees with the officers. For the next two hours Bronagh talks about her life since taking her new job, the messages, the feeling she had that she was being watched in the car park, the destruction of her car and her flat tyre. Everything until the present day, managing to get through most of it with her emotions intact.

CHAPTER THIRTY-NINE

The week building up to Stewart's funeral was a tough week for Elaine. Being arrested for stalking and the abduction of Bronagh came as a shock, but getting remanded in prison was an even bigger shock. She was sure that she would be released on bail due to her defence of being under duress and her pregnancy, but the Advocate for the Prosecution played the flight risk card perfectly since the police had found both her and Stewart's packed bags. The day she got the information of Stewart's funeral and permission to attend it her spirits lifted. That was until the day of the funeral arrived and she stood in the funeral parlour's chapel of rest, then by the graveside handcuffed to a female prison escort. She has never felt embarrassment so intense in all her life. All of Stewart's family glowered at her and whispered to each other about her. She noticed there weren't many people in attendance, about ten, and wondered if this was due to Stewart not knowing many people or because of his behaviour and life choices at the end of his life. The fleeting emotion of guilt passes over Elaine that it may be her fault, that she made him choose to get involved with her plan to bring Bronagh down, but she dismisses the notion quickly. Stewart had been all the man he was ever going to be. He made his own choices. He chose to meet her for lunch, chose to be in a relationship with her, chose to work with her in her plan, chose to have his own gripe with Bronagh and he chose to abduct her and plan to murder her. Her mood sours as she remembers his choice to run away from her. Yes, he made his own choices and if he was willing to abandon her and their unborn child in life, then she wasn't going to feel guilty about using him as her pawn for her defence in death.

Turning round on her very uncomfortable bed in her prison cell, Elaine wipes away her tears and her memories. She knew she needed to sleep as it was the first day of her trial in the morning, but sleep so far had eluded her. She had noticed her stomach had started to swell more with her and Stewart's baby growing inside her. She was planning on using her 'condition' to her advantage. She had thought about getting the pregnancy terminated. She even went to the prison doctor to discuss it, but in the end she decided she couldn't go through with it. She couldn't lose the only connection she had left with the only man she could love. Yes she was angry at him, with him. Yes she was using him and blaming everything on him as her defence, but she still loved him and needed their child to hold onto that love. Turning round again she tries to get into a more comfortable position, hoping sleep would take her soon.

****

After another eventful night full of bad dreams, night terrors and an unfortunate slap to Max's jaw, Bronagh stands in her towel staring at herself in the mirrored wardrobes in the bedroom she was sharing with Max. Not one night since leaving the garage where she was being held has Bronagh had a peaceful night. Every night was filled with fear and images and dreams.

Seeing herself in the mirror she is shocked at the amount of weight she had lost. Her face was pinched and pale looking, the dark circles under her eyes were proof of her sleepless nights and worry. The only time she had worried about her curves was when Max had gone home with a skinny blonde, but, seeing herself now she decides she is definitely better looking with them than without.

Max stands leaning against the door frame watching his girlfriend scrutinise herself in the mirror. The weeks that had passed since she had come home had been hard on them both.

He was up every night with her when she had a nightmare, but he knew when he did sleep it was mostly restful and hers wasn't. The bruising that Stewart had inflicted on her had faded or disappeared. Walking up to Bronagh he places his hands on her hips which makes her jump. As much as they were sharing a bed at night, and she had, eventually, let Max hold her, they had yet to be intimate fully. Max flinches, hating that he couldn't hold her without it causing some fear.

"Hey you." She places her hand on top of his to keep him connected to her. She wanted to give herself to him again, rekindle their sex life again, but she was frightened she would take another panic attack if she felt trapped in their embrace. She had spoken to her counsellor about it and they had advised her to take her time and to listen to her body and her heart.

"Hey yourself." She answers, loving that they were still together enough to have their idiosyncrasies.

"How you doing? You ready for today?" She turns in his arms to face him.

"Not really. I don't know how I'm going to react when I see Elaine for the first time, or what the lawyers are going to bring up, or ask me, or expect me to say, or if I'll break down, or... or..." Max could feel her tensing up and see the panic set in her features. Gathering her into his arms he kisses her forehead. Aware that she is only wearing a towel he concentrates on getting her calm, pushing all other thoughts from his mind.

"Hey, it's okay. Remember what your counsellor said. No matter what your reaction is, it isn't wrong. It will be completely normal for you... and no matter what, I'll be there with you, okay?" Holding on tight to his neck, Bronagh does her breathing exercises as she listens to Max's soothing voice. It amazed her that not once had he ever gotten angry at her over her abduction or blamed her. He has always been there by her side, not letting her be alone, even to the point of nearly losing his job.

"Thank you... and, I'm sorry." Max places his index finger on her lips to quieten her.

"I've told you, you've got nothing to apologise for."

"But, your job."

"I've fixed it with my boss. I'm going to work weird hours for a bit until the court case is over with, and if need be you can come in with me to the workshop. You know so you're not on your own. It's all sorted. I'm not going to lose my job, or lose hours or money, so please don't worry." Bronagh holds his gaze for a heartbeat before crushing her lips to his in a breathtaking kiss.

Breaking the kiss, they are both breathing hard.

"I'm sorry." Bronagh whispers through her pants.

"Please, don't apologise for kissing me like that... ever." Bronagh grins and her cheeks grow red.

"Okay... well, I guess I'd better get ready if we're to get to court." Max gives her another, more chaste, kiss then leaves her to get dressed, fixing his trousers to a more comfortable position.

****

Climbing out of the prison escort vehicle at Glasgow High Court, Elaine's embarrassment returns. As much as she was allowed to shower and wear smarter clothes, she still felt grimy, like a second class citizen almost. Lifting up her chin she tries to put an emotionless face on as she lets herself be led into the courtroom.

Bronagh is sitting in the prosecution witness room, holding onto Max's hand like her life depended on it. Their passion from that morning long forgotten as she uses all of the breathing exercises she'd learned to keep the threatening panic from taking over her. Max looks on feeling completely useless. He desperately wanted to take away every last second of pain that Bronagh had been through and was about to go through with the looming court case, but he knew he couldn't, which only made him feel even more useless. Over the weeks since Bronagh had returned home they had had many conversations, mostly highly emotional ones, about the fateful night of her abduction. They had spoken about how they both wished they could change the past, but neither blamed the other. After every conversation Max inwardly vowed to himself that he would never let Bronagh go, or let anything hurt her again. Especially, if it isn't beyond his control.

Gordon and Jane walk back into the small wood panelled room holding two polystyrene cups each. Max looks up as they approach and gives Gordon a quizzical look.

"What's wrong wa your face?" Gordon rolls his eyes and flashes Max with a look of disgust.

"I refuse to call whatever is in these cups coffee! Honest to god if I'd known I was going to be forced to drink this swill I would've closed my eyes at that bloody garage and saw nothing!" Gordon hands over one of the cups to Max and Jane hands the other to Bronagh. Bronagh sniggers at Gordon's statement, glad for the comic relief, but it's Jane that's first to respond verbally to him.

"Haw, I'm sure Bre's freedom is worth a crappy cup of coffee or two." Bronagh smiles as Gordon softens.

"Of course it is, but Bre knows I just hate bad coffee." He winks at Bronagh and takes another sip of the coffee, making another face full of disgust. "That's it, tomorrow I'm bringing everyone a flask... or my whole damn percolator!" Bronagh tries to smile but it doesn't reach her eyes as the humour from seconds ago had vanished. Replacing it was guilt, which was pushing itself against her panic.

"I'm sorry," she whispers and Gordon drops to his knees in front of her instantly.

"Hey, there is nothing to be sorry about sweet cheeks, you've not done anything wrong. I would go to the ends of the earth with bad coffee for you, do you hear me?" Tears glisten in Bronagh's eyes as she manages a nod of her head.

"I'll buy you one of they fancy machines that make all coffees when this is over, as a thank you... if I still have a job at the end of it, that is." Panic rises in her throat again at the thought of her job. Erin and David had told her to take all the time she needed and not to worry about her job, but she knew they were a small business, so couldn't afford to have staff earning without working, so she continued to worry. Gordon could see her panic.

"Erin told me your job is there for you, no matter how long you need off. So don't worry honey, okay?" She tries to smile again, and manages a one sided lift to her mouth. Max has sat in silence, feeling even more helpless than before.

CHAPTER FORTY

Sitting in the dock, Elaine can see her defence lawyer and her advocate sitting with their heads huddled together, deep in discussion. They had both pointed out a name on the witness list and asked if she knew who the person was. Her answer both times was no. It was not a name she had ever heard before. She dismisses their worries over the unknown witness. Instead she tries to boost her slow growing baby bump by pushing out her stomach more. The idea being to appeal to the jury's sensitive, family side. No one's going to send a pregnant mother-to-be to prison... are they? She had instructed her lawyer that her plea was to be not guilty through coercion. The lawyer had looked at her with mistrust, but she swore that that was the truth and the whole truth, at least as far as she was concerned (although she never admitted that part to her lawyer).

Within two hours of arriving at the court from her cell, Elaine is sitting listening to both advocates opening statements. Hearing the prosecution's, Elaine tries to keep calm. She has such a different view of the events leading up to and ending in Bronagh's abduction. She had told her lawyer everything and most of it was the truth. She had had to smudge the time she'd got together with Stewart and make it sound like he was already working on his vendetta towards Bronagh before involving her. She had made sure her lawyer and the advocate understood she was as much a victim as Bronagh was. After all she was the one who was pulled into Stewart's warped love and then felt trapped, similar to how Bronagh was, when she found out she was pregnant.

Listening to her advocate speak to the jury about her life crumbling around her, how she lost her job through no fault of her own, having to sell her beloved Audi TT, just to make ends meet, then how Stewart had managed to manipulate her, using her vulnerability as a hook to reel her in. Making her fall in love with him, making her do his bidding of hatred towards Bronagh and then leave her, literally run away from her and straight into the path of a double decker bus. Ultimately leaving her to clean up his mess and bring up his child. It was extremely hard for Elaine, being made to relive the moments of pleasure Stewart and she had shared together and then the pain she felt when he ran and hearing him being killed was almost torture. Throughout it all the only emotion Elaine allowed to show on her face was grief. She wore no make-up, feeling that it added a more devastated look, adding to her grief stricken look. She gives herself an internal pat on the back for her clever plan of action.

****

The days sitting in the witness room were tedious. Max and Bronagh sit together, Max not letting go of Bronagh's hand, hoping that by holding onto her he can take away all her pain and stress and worry. Even when they get home they sit the same, Max always holding on to her.

Gordon is the first witness to be called for the prosecution. Bronagh's heart hits the floor when she hears his name being called. She stands and gives him a hug, mumbling how sorry she was that he had been dragged into her mess. Taking her face in his hands he kisses her on her forehead then whispers in her ear.

"Don't you worry my princess, we'll all get through this. That crazy bint will be behind bars and you can get back to living your life to the full again." He gives her another kiss then leaves with the Macer. Max swallows away the stab of jealousy he feels when Gordon took Bronagh into his arms. He knew it was irrational. He knew Gordon was gay so would never look at Bronagh in a romantic light. He knew he and

Bronagh were still a couple, but the jealousy came anyway. The need he felt to keep her safe before she was abducted had grown tenfold since he had gotten her back, and as much as he tried to hold onto the overly controlling, suffocating, helicopter boyfriend, he couldn't help himself.

Jane noticed Max's jaw twitch as he watched Gordon and Bronagh's embrace, and made a mental note to talk to him about it and his tight hold on Bronagh.

Bronagh sits back down and starts her breathing exercises again. Max immediately puts his arm around her and holds her hands in his free one. She stiffens for a second, which Max feels, then relaxes again. Jane watches all of this with worry, so asks Max if he could do a coffee run. Max starts to complain, but Jane gives him a look that would freeze water and he caves, giving Bronagh a chaste kiss before leaving the women alone in the small room. Jane changes seats so she is sitting in front of Bronagh.

"You okay?" Bronagh stops counting in her head and looks at Jane, wondering where the question had come from.

"In here, with all of this? Knowing that it's because of me youse are all here, going through this? No... not really." Bronagh slumps in her chair. She hadn't meant to sound bitchy, she hadn't meant to snap, but she did and it brought a fresh wave of guilt over her. "I'm sorry, Jane. I'm just..." Jane takes her hands.

"I know. I'm sorry too. But please believe us when we say this isn't your fault. If I hadn't been so wrapped up in myself or that random it might not have happened." Bronagh shakes her head.

"We've been through this. They would've still got me, and maybe you too, so please, don't think like that. I am starting to believe that it's not all my fault. My counsellor is working with me on that. I think maybe once this is all over, and if the jury believes me, it will help me move on... I hope." Jane gives her friend an encouraging smile then starts to ask about Max and his clingy behaviour when he makes his reappearance. Bronagh gives Jane an imperceptible nod acknowledging what she was about to say before taking the coffee that Max was handing her. Then he takes his seat beside Bronagh again, resuming to hold her hand.

****

Every time Elaine looks at her lawyer and advocate her heart sinks another bit. Their faces have gone from professional but jovial to stern to downright pissed off during the progression of the hearing. She had been surprised and perturbed to hear about the prosecution's statement that they were going to prove her harassment of Bronagh had begun before meeting Stewart, and that it escalated after they were together. Not that she'd been coerced into the harassment and abduction as she was claiming. She couldn't understand how they would prove that until they brought out the pay as you go mobile phone she had bought. In her haste to pack and being in the middle of having an emotional breakdown, Elaine had forgotten all about it. She had also forgotten about the messages she had sent to both Bronagh and Max. The realisation that she hadn't mentioned the phone to her lawyer also zaps through her as she dares a look at them. Their heads are stooped towards each other and both are shaking them furiously. They both look up at Elaine, complete exasperation written all over their faces as they lock eyes with her. Keeping her face semi-emotionless she lowers her head. Seconds later another shock reverberates through her and her legal team. The mystery name is called. In walks an impeccably clean, well dressed, entirely sober man and the penny drops as to who the man is... the drunk that lives below Bronagh and who Elaine bribed twice, once when she vandalised the car and then again when her and Stewart broke into the flat. The courtroom closes in on Elaine as she realises her future will probably be in a six by eight prison cell for the foreseeable future.

CHAPTER FORTY-ONE

Every morning during the court case Max asked Bronagh if she was ready and every morning she gave him a smile and told him she thought so. Every morning she didn't think she'd make it through the day but every day she did, and every night she felt exhausted but more confident that she would get through this part of her life, confident that her life would get back on track and confident she would end up with her dream of owning her own company.

The support Max had given her since he found her chained up in the garage had been consistent and unwavering. She had panicked that he wouldn't want her after everything she had been through. He had always reassured her that he wanted her just as much as he had before the abduction. That panic returned when he was called as a witness before her. He was going to hear about the events running up to her abduction and be questioned on them. Would that change his mind about her choices, she wondered. It also meant she was going to be on her own in the witness room, but thanks to her counselling, breathing exercises and the ladies volunteering with the witness service supporting her, she managed to be without Max. A massive step forward, she thinks.

The night before she was due to give evidence she was sitting in the 2016 Mustang that Max was doing a service on. She sat with her eyes closed, feeling the softness of the leather seats and breathing in the scent of the gaudy tree air freshener swinging from the rear view mirror. Thankfully she could also smell the oil that Max was changing. She'd always loved the smell of Max when he was working on cars. Feeling more confident after her step forward that afternoon, and with the smell of oil reminding her of her attraction to Max she steps from the car. Max is lying under the Mustang so she taps his foot to get his attention.

Wheeling himself out from under the car Max looks up at Bronagh and registers the look in her eyes. His heart starts beating hard as other parts of his anatomy go the same way. He hasn't seen her look at him like that for a long time.

"Hey you, you okay?" His voice is husky as he looks up at his girlfriend, desire flashing in his eyes and growing in his overalls. Bronagh moves so she's standing straddling him.

"Hey yourself. Aye, I'm good... in fact, for the first time in a long time I'm more than good." She gets down onto her knees, sitting on top of him. "Have I ever told you how sexy you smell when you're working?" Max moves his head to the side like a confused puppy, but he refuses to move, terrified that he might change whatever is about to happen. Instead he opts for smiling and hoping.

"I can't say that you have. You like the smell of sweat and grime?" Bronagh snorts.

"No. I like the mechanical smell. Oil and hard work." She starts to unstud his overalls as she talks. "Have I told you how sexy your tattoos are?" Max's throat is dry at the thought of Bronagh undressing him.

"I think you may have mentioned it." He blushes despite himself.

"I think I want to see them again... just now." Max swallows again, trying to get his brain to work in partnership with his voice box.

"Right now?" He berates himself for questioning Bronagh, fearing she might change her mind. He blows out a breath when she answers him.

"Right now." She stands and pulls Max up by his unstudded overalls and pulls him to her, kissing him like it was the only thing keeping her alive at that moment. Max pulls back, panting hard from the power of the kiss.

"Your clothes will get stained... " Bronagh grins at him.

"Better take them off then." Max takes off his nitrile gloves and takes her face between his hands, looking deep into her eyes, searching them.

"Are you sure?" Bronagh grins and kisses him again.

"More than anything. Please, Max, make love to me." Max doesn't wait to be asked again as he lifts her up and presses her against the Mustang's closed door, kissing her with every ounce of love he has for her.

Deciding his customer wouldn't be happy if they had sex on their car, in case they make scratches in the paint, amongst other reasons, he moves them to the waiting area. Taking his time Max pulls up Bronagh's t-shirt, her skin erupts in goosebumps as he runs his fingers over her breasts. She moans into his neck and it spurs him on. He unbuttons her jeans and pushes them down, taking her underwear with them. With another moan from Bronagh and her hands on his clothes, stripping him, Max struggles to control his need for her. He shrugs the last of his clothes off and takes Bronagh's breast in his mouth, removing her bra to give him more flesh to enjoy. He turns them both so he is sitting on one of the chairs. Bronagh licks and nips her way up his neck as she grinds herself into him. Neither are able to wait any longer. Bronagh lifts herself up so Max can position himself before she slides back down, both of them groan in satisfaction of being together after everything that Bronagh had been through. Holding on tight to Max, Bronagh starts to move her hips, grinding herself into him until they both climax neither letting go of the tight hold they have of each other. Breathing hard for many long minutes before either of them can talk or move, Bronagh shifts slightly and Max holds on tighter. She pulls back to look at him, worry tingeing her heart.

"You okay?" He smiles at her and brings her lips down for another, slower kiss.

"I'm better than okay, you?" A slow shy smile crosses her lips.

"Same as you. I can't believe how okay I am. I love you so much." Max's breath hitches in his throat at her words. He had started to wonder if he would ever hear those words from her again.

"I love you too Bre... more than life."

"More than your Golf?" He laughs.

"Well, hold on now..." Bronagh squeezes his ribs with her knees and he laughs with a wince, "Of course more than my car. Forever."

"Forever." They kiss again before untangling themselves and cleaning up. Not feeling up to working any more Max and Bronagh grab some takeaway for dinner and head back to Max's house. The lovers hold on to each other, not letting each other go, this time it's for better reasons other than fear.

****

Every time another witness or another piece of evidence is produced for the jury, Elaine can feel her freedom slipping farther and farther away. Her cell closes in on her, even as she sits in the dock. She knew her lawyer and advocate were doing their best with what she had given them, and she knew they still had to put forward her evidence, but if she was being honest with herself she knew that wasn't really much and it certainly wasn't going to be enough to secure her freedom, especially when they shouted Bronagh's name as the last witness for the prosecution. Elaine had hoped that Bronagh would be too traumatised to be of much use to her prosecution and when Bronagh walked into the court and stood in the witness stand, Elaine could see worry etched all over her face, fear dancing in her emerald green eyes, panic in her stiff posture as she walked through the courtroom. She thought she had gotten her wish, but her hope was short lived. Bronagh walked into the room with all of those traits that Elaine could see showing, but she also had her head held high and a determination in her stride as she took the stand.

Even through all her panic and fear Bronagh manages to keep her voice strong, determined to not let Elaine see how broken she could sometimes be, and equally determined to see Elaine jailed for her part in the abduction. She didn't have the chance to face Stewart as a free woman, so the only comfort she could take was that she stood up to him whilst he had held her captive. Even though she just swore at him, she knows she made her feelings towards him perfectly clear.

The prosecution advocate stands and gives Bronagh a reassuring smile before she starts her questions. Bronagh repeats the oath then forces herself to lower her shoulders in a bid to relax, even if it's just a tiny bit. She is taken through some questions to settle her in before the advocate starts with the more emotional questions.

"Now, Bronagh," the advocate starts, "I know this is going to be difficult, but I need you to tell me why you were at the pub, the Lock-In, on the night in question?" Thoughts of the night out flash through her mind, and a longing of what should have been pulls at her, but she swallows away all her what ifs and answers the question.

"I was there for a girls' night out with my friend Jane."

"Just you and Jane?"

"Yes."

"Did you know that the accused and her boyfriend, Mr McMillan, were there?"

"No."

"So it was a surprise when you saw them?" She takes a deep breath, knowing that the time had come to relive her abduction out loud.

"I didn't see them. I only realised Stewart was there when he shouted on me."

"Where were you when Mr McMillan shouted on you?"

"I had gone outside to the beer garden to phone my boyfriend, Max, but then I realised I had left my phone at the table."

"And is that when he approached you?"

Another deep breath. "Yes. He came in close to me and held me to him, then he held a cloth over my mouth and nose. I could feel it wet against my skin as he held it."

"Did you know why the cloth was wet?"

"No, but I've been told it was chloroform."

"Okay, could you tell the court in your own words what happened after that please?"

Bronagh had been dreading this question, dreading the words leaving her lips, baring her soul to the full room.

"I felt weak then passed out. The next thing I remember is waking up cold and in darkness. I tried to move my arms, but I couldn't and eventually I worked out that I was chained up. After a while, I don't know how long, Stewart and Elaine came into where I was being held. They told me why they had abducted me, explaining to me that it was all my own fault. I had stolen Elaine's job and turned down Stewart's romantic advances towards me about two years ago." Bronagh catches Max's eyes. He looks pained at what he was hearing. She looks away quickly, not wanting to see his pain, not able to cope with it at that moment, knowing that if she tried she wouldn't get through her evidence. The advocate instructs Bronagh to continue, so without hesitation she does. She relives in detail the sordid tale of her abduction and the beatings she received during it. The courtroom was silent as she spoke. Bronagh could still see Max from the corner of her eye. She could see all the pain and guilt he felt as he listened to her evidence. She finishes her evidence and her cross examination and the judge dismisses her from giving evidence. Panic rolls off of her as she walks from the court, worried that now Max knew the brutal truth he wouldn't want her again.

CHAPTER FORTY-TWO

Arriving home after court that night, Max and Bronagh collapse on the couch, both of them exhausted from the continual strain of going to court every day and emotionally drained from the line of questioning that Bronagh had been put through. Max knew she had been held against her will, chained to a wall in a garage, nothing to keep her warm and beaten by Stewart. But hearing her talk about it, going into the intimate details of her beatings, of hearing every nasty unjustified thing said to her, by both of her captors, was nearly more than Max could stomach. Several times Gordon or Jane had to stop him from storming the dock to confront Elaine. Max reigned in his anger, barely, knowing that once Bronagh was released from the witness box she would be back in his arms forever.

Inching round on the couch Max watches Bronagh as she half sits, half lies with her eyes shut and her breathing steady. She looked more at peace in that moment than she had since she returned home. He lifts his hand, and with a feather like touch he places his fingers on her cheek.

"Hey you," she mumbles, still not opening her eyes.

"Hey yourself," Max answers with a smile. "Thought you'd fallen asleep?"

Bre smiles, still relaxed. "Hmm, no, well, not yet... you?"

Max continues to stroke her cheek then tucks a loose strand of hair from her face. "No, too busy watching you."

Bronagh peeks open one eye. "Creepy much?"

He blushes, despite his smile. "Sorry, I can't help it, you looked so peaceful and so beautiful."

Bronagh's breath hitches in her throat at his words. "Really?"

Confusion passes over Max's features. "Really what?"

"You think I'm beautiful... still?" Emotion squeezes in her throat making the last word come out more of a squeak. Max sits up pulling Bronagh up with him.

"What do you mean still?" Worry crashes through him and Bronagh for different reasons.

"Well, I mean, after everything you heard. What happened to me... what I had to do... because of the lack of facilities." Pain lances through Max's heart as he realises Bronagh's thoughts. He closes his eyes and pulls her towards him, holding her face in his hands, his thumbs rubbing her cheeks as he presses his forehead to hers. He can feel her panic emanating from her in waves, feel her tremble under his fingertips from the emotion she was barely holding in.

"Bre, what makes you think I wouldn't think you were beautiful any more... I mean, I understand... kinda, but..."

"But nothing Max. I... I threw up where I had to sit. There was nowhere... nothing for me to..." Anger and embarrassment fight inside Bronagh to get their place as she continues to talk, her voice raising with every word until her anger won out and she was shouting. "I WET MYSELF! I HAD TO, THERE WAS NOTHING TO USE!" Her voice softens. "Then he gave me a bucket, telling me it was a piss bucket, but he didn't uncuff me. He told me he knew it would've been too late, that he remembered how crap my bladder was... then he laughed because he knew it was true, I had pissed myself." Tears are coursing down her face at the confession. "I'm dirty, tainted." The last words came from her in a broken sob. Tears break their barriers of Max's eyelids as he hears Bronagh's brutal confession. He knew that what had happened to her must have broken parts of her and reliving it all in court would have shattered those parts. He didn't know what to say to lessen the shame she felt. He also knew that no matter what he said it would come out wrong and cause Bronagh more pain, so he did the only thing he thought would get his message across. He kissed her. He poured all his love for her, all his desire for her into it, in the hope she understood he didn't think she was dirty or tainted.

Pulling back Bronagh stares at Max, eyes gleaming with the tears not yet spilled, searching Max's face.

"Bre, I love you. With everything I have, every fibre of my being. I love you, and nothing can stop me from loving you!"

"So you don't think I'm dir—"

Max shakes his head vigorously making her stop speaking before she can finish her sentence. "No! Not in any way shape or form. I think you're beautiful, stunning, strong, resilient, brave and so amazingly sexy."

Bronagh blushes at his words, but it doesn't last as he takes her mouth in another smouldering kiss the function of which is to erase all the self-depreciating thoughts from her mind.

Lying in bed after making love, Bronagh thinks back to her confession with Max, and feels it was cathartic. Feeling brave, she finds her voice and asks Max a question that she thinks he might not like.

"Max, after the court case is finished, do you think I... we could maybe go back to my flat?" Max had been rubbing slow lazy circles on her shoulder and stops when he thinks about the question.

"Why?"

"I've not been back since... and well, it's something I think I need to do." Again Max takes a second to think over what she was saying.

"Well, I was thinking... why don't you just sell the flat. You know, move in here permanently?" A panicked feeling zips through Bronagh and she's not sure why. She's lived with Max since her flat had been vandalised by Elaine and Stewart, so it made sense, but it wasn't sitting right with her. She wanted to face her demons so she could move on before she moved in, properly and permanently.

"I..."

"You don't want to?" Max sits up, worry and maybe anger flash over his face.

"No, yes, I... I, yes I want to, and I know that that is going to happen, but there's some things I need to do first. I need to be me again first." Max closes his eyes, getting his emotions under control. He understands what Bronagh is saying, but in his mind she is better drawing a line under everything and moving forward. Not looking back. And it would be better for him too.

"I want to keep you safe. I need you to be safe. So I think we should maybe move forwards, not backwards. I think going back to the flat might be a step backwards." Not strong enough to face an argument Bronagh nods then turns onto her side to sleep. Max holds in his huff and wriggles back down into the bed.

****

Getting ready the next morning for court there is a frost in the air between Bronagh and Max. He had tried to speak to her, offer her breakfast and coffee, but she'd declined, quietly. Not sure if the atmosphere was due to the way they had left things the night before or the thought of listening to the defence and Elaine's evidence, Max decides to try and broach the subject.

"Bre, are you okay?" Bronagh stops putting the last of her minimal make-up on and looks at Max through the mirror she was standing in front of. Anxiety, anger, confusion, disbelief and many more emotions battle within her. She takes a breath and clears her throat before talking.

"Not really. I need to go and listen to *her* lies and hope that the twelve people listening to them believe me and not her. I need to remind myself to breathe every second of every day and I just want this the fuck over with!" Max winces at her use of the swear word, but he understands, so wraps his arms around her from behind, continuing eye contact in the mirror.

"I'm sorry this is happening. I wish I could take it away. I want you to be safe and happy and I will do everything in my power to make that happen."

Bronagh turns in his arms. "I know you will, but there's some things I need to go through so I can put my demons to rest, then, once that's done you can ask me to move in with you... properly."

Max smiles, knowing she was referring to their conversation from the night before. He understood that he needed to let their relationship take its natural progression. He didn't want to let her go through with some of the things she thought she needed to go through, but he also knew if he tried to stop her he would end up being the controlling boyfriend he was fighting against becoming. He nods at her, not trusting himself to talk, giving her a quick kiss and they both resume getting ready in a slightly thawed out atmosphere.

Meeting at one of the ball-shaped bollards in front of the High Court building, Gordon hands Bronagh and Max their coffees. Bronagh takes the travel mug from Gordon as he pulls her into a hug.

"How you holding up my princess?" Bronagh holds Gordon close, enjoying the friendship and strength he offers her.

"I'm getting there Gee. Thank you for asking... and thank you for my caffeine fix!" Gordon smiles his answer and gives her a kiss on the top of her head. Max watches the embrace with pure jealousy written all over his face. Jane watches Max then pulls him aside.

"What is your problem?"

Max looks stunned at Jane's question.

"What d'you mean, problem? I don't have a problem."

Jane gives him a pointed look. "Don't talk shite, Max. You do have a problem and it's with Gordon, now spill it!" He goes to deny the accusation again, but changes his mind. He admits to himself as well as Jane his problem.

"I don't want anybody else near her... well any other man." Jane's face contorts into something like disbelief as she looks at Max.

"You get that he's gay, right? He's not into Bre sexually. She's like a sister to him. You do know that... *right?*" She eyes him and he shrugs, then slumps his shoulders.

275

"I know... I know it's stupid, and unreasonable and they see each other as family, but..." He huffs and scrubs his hands over his face. "She relaxes when he holds her." He slumps his shoulders, again, at his confession. "There's still times she jumps when I reach for her." Jane places her hand on his shoulder and squeezes.

"Give it time. Give her time, it'll get better. She loves you, youse are made for each other. Just don't push her too far, and don't smother her, okay?" Jane's tone is kind, but there is a hint of a warning in the undertone. Max shrugs again, but holds back anything he was going to say as Bronagh and Gordon join them.

"Everything okay?" Bronagh looks between her boyfriend and her best friend. Jane beams a big smile at Bronagh.

"'Course," Jane says breezily. "We ready to do this, listen to her crap?" The happiness wipes itself from Bronagh's face and she grabs Max's hand, and taking a deep breath she shrugs.

"Ready as I'll ever be." Max gives her hand a squeeze as his heart splits between his need to pick her up and run away with her from everyone and everything, and his duty of being her boyfriend and supporting her to get to the end of the court case.

"'Moan then." Max smiles at them all as the four friends walk into the court building.

CHAPTER FORTY-THREE

Elaine's defence and evidence only takes one day to get through. When she took the stand she tried her hardest to be the downtrodden, used, weak female that she had told her lawyer and advocate that she was, but she ended up trying too hard and laying it on too thick. Her advocate tried not to roll his eyes every time she spoke, and sometimes he managed it. He also, sometimes, managed to hold in his sighs and his head shakes. The judge, however, didn't try to hold his exasperation back and rolled his eyes continuously. The prosecution table smiled. She turned the tears up from the odd one slipping down her cheek to pouring out of her eyes as her advocate finished up, but they soon dried up and were replaced by anger as soon as the first question was asked by the prosecution.

Every day her pregnancy became more real to her. Her stomach was expanding and she was starting to feel some movement. With each passing day in court she was beginning to wonder if she would be giving birth in prison. She had broached the subject with her lawyer. They had spoken about the ins and outs of being pregnant and giving birth in prison but he refused to give his opinion on whether or not she would be doing it or not. She had also spoken to some of the women in the prison and the general consensus was that she would probably be made to give the baby up for adoption. The thought of losing her last connection to Stewart broke her heart as much as seeing him run away had. In the middle of her sleepless nights she sometimes tries to convince herself that he hadn't run away from her, from what they had done, but she knew she was only lying to herself. She was angry with him. Once upon a time she had thought all men were wimps, then she met Stewart and he changed her mind. She never once thought he was like all the other men she'd had affairs with, until he ran away from her and his responsibilities, just like a wimp. Elaine was desperate to hate him for that, but she couldn't. He was the first and only person she had ever loved, who had got through the emotionless state she had become and that was something that broke her heart even more.

Just before the judge adjourns the court for the day he explains that the next day would be the summing up from both the defence and the prosecution, then it would be time for the jury to be sent to the jury room for their deliberations. A sense of foreboding falls over Elaine. She turns in the dock until she finds Bronagh. Her anger bubbles up and over at the sight of her. Before she could comprehend what she was doing she was screaming at Bronagh.

"You fuckin' bitch! You stole everything from me! Everything that was mine! If it wasn't for you I would have a fuckin' job and Stewart wouldn't be fuckin' dead! You, you..." The judge was roaring from the Bench for there to be order in his court and if Elaine didn't control herself she would be found in contempt of the court. The prisoner guards on either side of Elaine lurch forward and grab at Elaine's arms to stop her from climbing over the dock then wrestle her into handcuffs, all the time being aware of her pregnancy. Throughout her outburst her lawyer and advocate sit with their heads in their hands.

Elaine is removed from the courtroom, taken back down to the cell block to calm down to await her transport back to prison. The judge apologises to the court then adjourns for the day. Everyone in the court stands as the judge is escorted from the Bench, a stunned silence hanging heavy in the air.

Bronagh sits stock still throughout Elaine's tirade at her, too shocked to move or breathe. Max had jumped to cover her, trying to protect her should Elaine have managed to break free and attack her. Even though the judge had dismissed everyone then left the room, Bronagh and her friends fell back down into their seats and remained there. Bronagh wasn't sure her legs would carry her and they hadn't wanted to leave her, so they all sat in the stunned silence that lingered.

****

The next morning everyone was back in the courtroom sitting in the exact same spots as the day before. The only difference was the extra police presence; it had been doubled. Bronagh's nerves were more on edge that day than they had been on any other day of the hearing. This was partially due to Elaine's outburst the day before and partially due to neither her or Max getting any sleep. They had discussed the incident and Max had held her close for the rest of the night, but it hadn't settled her. Elaine's words of blame, Max's talk of selling her flat, plus all the work she had been doing with her counsellor rattled around her brain. Some of the things going around and around her head weren't sitting right with her.

The judge starts to speak bringing Bronagh from her musings about her feelings. He apologises again to the court for the disruption the day before, then warns Elaine that that type of behaviour would not be tolerated in his court and she should think herself lucky that he wasn't holding her in contempt of court. After his words of warning and a rather arrogant grunt from Elaine, the judge hands the proceedings back over to the advocates for their summing up.

The prosecution advocate stands and walks over to the jury to start their summing up. They recap all of the evidence they'd produced during the trial. They reminded the jury of everything that Bronagh had been put through, allegedly, by Elaine and Stewart. Starting with the abusive text messages sent from the phone found at Elaine's house and one from Elaine's own phone, then continuing with the damage to her car and flat, then culminated with her abduction and imprisonment. All through the prosecution's summing up the court is silent. Hearing it all again makes Bronagh shake. Max brings her into his side more, asking if she wanted to leave. She shakes her head. Max holds her closer still, hoping to take away some of her fear and vowing to himself again that he would never again let her go.

The defence advocate stands and tries their best to salvage what they could from the case, which, if they were asked 'off record', wasn't really salvageable. After a paltry amount of time summing up, the defence advocate sits down. The judge advises the jury of their duties and gives them some directional advice before releasing them to start their deliberations.

The four friends file out of the courtroom. They all agree that they all desperately need a coffee, but don't want to leave the building. They buy some of the swill from the coffee machine and find a quiet corner to discuss the end of the trial. One sip from his coffee makes Gordon's face contort with disgust. Bronagh laughs out loud. A genuine relaxed laugh.

"Wow is it that bad?" she asks as she sniffs her own cup. Gordon swallows then grimaces.

"Naw..." She laughs again. Max tries to stamp down on the jealousy that's creeping up his spine at Gordon managing to get a real laugh from Bronagh, but it was to no avail due to the next statement from Bronagh.

"You know I can't wait for all this to be over so I can get back to work where you can make me my proper coffee again." Gordon winks, then feigns being offended.

"Is that all I am to you, your personal coffee maker?" Bronagh feigns shock back at him.

"Not at all. You're my fairy coffee mother." Jane laughs alongside them but Max just glares into his swill.

"Bre, you sure you're ready to think about going back to work? I mean you don't want to push yourself too much and end up worse off." A strained hush hovers over them at Max's tone which was almost condescending.

"Well... aye, I think I will be, once this is over. My counsellor tells me I should do things when I feel the time is right, not to put them off. I know not to rush things, but I am ready for this to be over and my life to be back." They all agree that the trial should be over soon and they were all looking forward to that day. Jane changes the subject to the summing up and the strain of Max's question eases.

****

After a swift two hours, and to the surprise of everyone involved, the jury announce that they have arrived at their verdict. Elaine is brought back up from the cells and stood in her usual place in the dock between two guards. She could feel her legs tremble and her heartbeat increase. Her breathing caught in her throat every time she tried to take a deep breath in. Closing her eyes she takes a moment to compose herself, not wanting Bronagh to see her break down.

The four friends file back into the court to take their seats, all of them holding onto Bronagh in some way or another as she grasps Max's hand with all her might, mentally telling her feet to move one in front of the other. Once seated she closes her eyes and starts her breathing exercises, trying to keep her panic and fear at bay. Max can feel her emotions as his own, making him take more vows to keep her safe.

The judge is seated then brings the court to order again. He instructs the clerk to the court to start. He stands and in a clear, booming voice he asks the foreperson to stand. He continues and asks the foreperson if they have come to their verdicts for all of the charges. The foreperson answers that yes they had, then the clerk continues,

"To the charge of abduction, how do you find the accused, guilty or not guilty?" There is a pregnant silence in the room as the foreperson takes in a breath to answer.

"Guilty." There are gasps from round the room, but the clerk of court ignores them.

"Is that by a majority or unanimous?"

"Unanimous." There is a brief pause, as everyone takes in the words they were all waiting for, but it is shattered when Elaine starts to scream.

"WHAT THE ACTUAL FUCK!" The guards at her side step forward but she raises her hands, gesturing that she would calm down. She puts her hands on her knees trying to get her breath back after her shock and her outburst.

"To the charge of assault how do you find the accused?"

"Not guilty." More gasps are mouthed round the court, but none of them cover up Elaine's laughter. The judge asks for order again, and again warns Elaine with contempt of court, then he motions for the clerk to continue.

"Is that by a majority or unanimous?"

"Unanimous."

"To the charge of stalking how do you find the accused?"

"Guilty."

"Is that by majority or unanimous?"

"Unanimous."

"And to the charge of harassment and causing fear and alarm, how do you find the accused?"

"Guilty."

"Is that by majority or unanimous?"

"Unanimous."

The judge settles everyone down again then starts to talk to Elaine. He tells her how despicable she is, putting an innocent woman through months of harassment and two days of being held against her will in what could only be described as a freezing damp dungeon. He continues his diatribe by calling her a callous woman who'd only thought of herself when she'd concocted her plea of coercion. At no point, the judge points out, did her counsel prove she was under any coercion. If anything she was the one who'd started the ball rolling then included Stewart in her plans until they both fed off each other's unfounded hatred for Bronagh. Winding up, the judge adds, that due to her horrendous outbursts he would indeed be holding her in contempt of court.

"I want this wrapped up with today, so I will be handing out the sentencing just now." The judge glares at Elaine. "I sentence you to two years for the harassment and stalking and five years for the abduction of Miss White. These sentences will be served consecutively, with parole not to be even considered until five years have been served." Elaine stumbles in the dock, catching herself just before her legs give out entirely.

Her world closes in on her. A vision of her cell in her mind's eye is the size of a postage stamp, and she's sure that's how it's going to feel every day for the next five years. She doesn't realise that she's being led away until her feet start moving on their own accord. For once she was glad for the guards on either side of her, holding her up and manoeuvring her to where she never thought she would end up.

CHAPTER FORTY-FOUR

Standing outside the court building in the strong June sunshine Bronagh is in shock. Around her Jane and Gordon are gushing about her winning and how wonderful it was hearing the words 'guilty' being uttered. Max stands holding Bronagh under his arm, watching her. Worry etched on his face.

"Hey you?" He turns her so she is face to face with him, making her look at him.

"Hey yourself," she answers after a beat.

"You okay?"

She thinks for a second before a grin spreads over her face. "Aye, I think I am. Actually I think I'm better than okay...I think I'm fuckin' great... now. And yes I did swear without being drunk or angry."

Jane grabs her friend in a bear hug and whispers in her ear. "That's my girl, and I am so sorry." Bronagh hugs her friend back.

"There is nothing to be sorry about, honestly." The friends break their embrace with tears running down their cheeks. Gordon claps his hands to brighten the heavy atmosphere.

"Right, well I suggest a celebratory drink. Who's up for it?" Max starts to decline when Bronagh speaks up.

"I think that's a great idea, but we'll need to drop off the cars." Max turns to her.

"Are you sure Bre? I mean you've not wanted to go out since..." Bronagh turns to him with a smile.

"I know, but it's officially over now, so... as long as it's not the Lock-In, then I don't see why not. I won't be on my own, youse are all going to be there... won't you?" Gordon and Jane agree fervently as Max swithers.

"Well, if you're sure?" After a grin and a nod from Bronagh, Max is made to give in. The friends part to take their cars home, agreeing that they would meet at another of their local pubs.

Once back at the house Max takes Bronagh in his arms and kisses her soundly, pouring every last ounce of love he has for her into it. Bronagh is taken aback by the strength of the kiss to begin with, then she relaxes into it. Allowing herself, for the first time since the night of the Mustang, and the soul wrenching, cathartic confession, to feel how much she loves kissing Max and being in his arms. With her feelings awakened and realised, she pushes Max against the wall in their bedroom. Kissing him with all the excitement and relief she felt when she heard the the verdict.

Loving the feeling of having Bronagh in his arms and relaxed, Max moves them so Bronagh is against the wall. He lifts her and Bronagh wraps her legs around his waist. Her old fears of who Max used to date assaults her thoughts, the skinny, waif like blondes. As if reading her mind Max pulls back to look at her.

"I've only ever wanted you." Relief once again floods her system and she crushes her lips back onto his, desperate for everything to be back to the way they were before her abduction. Nipping at Max's lip, Bronagh urges Max on. She loves the feeling of her legs wrapped around him and his hands on her skin. Max takes his time, enjoying Bronagh being in his embrace, knowing she wants him as much as he wants her, relishing in the feeling of having her safe in his arms. Before long they are both desperate for each other, and give themselves to each other entirely.

Holding Bronagh against the wall, after having the most intense orgasm he'd ever had in his life, Max doesn't want to let go. He holds her between him and the wall, holding on tight, feeling like everything he ever wanted was in that minute, and if he let go, let the celebration night happen, he would fail again. Fail at keeping what he desperately wanted safe.

"Do we need to go out?" Bronagh takes a deep breath, feeling more tired, but more restful than she'd felt in months. Her first thoughts were no they didn't need to go out, they could stay in bed for the rest of the night. But then the need to go out and enjoy herself, free of fear has her answering Max.

"For me to start my life again, yes, we need to go out." Max slumps and Bronagh feels it. She steels herself for an argument about keeping her safe, but it doesn't come. Thankfully. They had started having more arguments, although Max called them disagreements. Mostly they were about Bronagh and her wanting to get out of the house. She had needed to go to court every day, but Max constantly tried to talk her out of it. She had mentioned going back to her flat again only to be told to wait and see if she still felt the same after the trial had finished. She understood that Max was behaving like an insecure teenager due to what had happened to her which brought on his need to keep her safe. She also knew that at the start she had clung to him like an oasis in the desert, but now she needed to start letting go, start getting her life back. She needed Max to understand that meant him letting go of his fears too. She makes a mental note to talk to him about his behaviour another day, wanting this day to be about being believed, about celebrating, about getting back what is hers... about getting her life back. Max gives her another kiss before putting her down.

"Okay, we'll get sorted then phone a taxi, but please, stay with me." Bronagh pushes back the odd sense of deja-vu of being trapped. Plastering on a smile she gives Max a short nod then heads to the bathroom.

****

The celebratory drinks turn into a meal and more drinks. Bronagh muses to herself about how relaxed she is feeling. There had been a huge weight lifted from her shoulders that day and she felt every part of the lightness. The only thorn in her side, she thinks, is Max's constant watching of her. Every time she moves, his head snaps round to see her, asking if she was okay. At the start of the night she'd thought it was cute, but after the third hour it had started to grate on her.

Not wanting the night to end, Gordon invites everyone back to his for more drinks, but Max puts his foot down, insisting that everyone return to his. Gordon and Jane share a concerned look at Max's behaviour but nothing is said. They all hail a taxi in the balmy night and head back to Max's house. Bronagh sits in the back of the taxi, warm from the alcohol, the warm temperature of the summer's night and Max's body heat and for that moment in time, she is happy.

The morning after was full of groans of sore heads but happiness. Jane and Gordon say their goodbyes after some coffee with promises to contact Bronagh later. Bronagh and Max were alone.

Bronagh tidies up the full downstairs of the house. She told Max, and herself, that there had been nothing done when they were at court, so she was just catching up, but if she was being honest she was putting off the conversation she knew she needed to have with Max. Not sure how to tell him she was returning to work and that he was being too possessive. She finishes cleaning the toilet, and then puts everything away. Taking a deep breath she sits beside Max who's been snoozing on the couch.

"Max?" Her voice is hesitant. He opens his eyes and smiles. The smile slides from his face when Bronagh's worried features come into focus.

"You okay?" Another deep breath.

"Aye... no... we, I, can we talk, please?" Worry and a slight panic fills Max as he pushes himself up into a seated position.

"Okay... what's up?" His words are guarded, but laced with worry. Giving her eyelids a quick squeeze together Bronagh starts with the subject that she thinks might be the best (or worst, depending on Max's reaction).

"I want to start back work." She holds her breath waiting on Max's reply.

Max blinks a few times. Relief that she wasn't asking to move out, or worse, end their relationship, floods him, but worry and his possessive need to keep her safe tramples over the relief.

"No." The word is out of his mouth before he can lessen the harshness of his tone.

"What? What do you mean no? I wasn—"

"I don't think you're ready. Give it another week or so. I mean, see how you feel being on your own in here when I'm back at work. Then, we can think about it." Anger spikes in her veins. Was the love of her life really telling her she needs to be a forties housewife and wait for him to come from work?

"Are you kidding me? When did we transport back to the forties Max, where I get to keep house and wait on you? And anyway I wasn't—"

"That's not what I said, Bre. I just think—"

Bronagh raises her hands to stop Max from talking any more.

"I am not sitting in this house on my own everyday just to see if I can. I am ready to get my life back. Erin and David said I could go in a few days a week to start with. A staggered return, before returning full time. I will be with people who will look out for me, like Gordon, so nothing and nobody will hurt me, and as I have tried to say —"

Max interrupts her again.

"You spoke to Erin and David about this before me? Why Bre? I'm your boyfriend. This is not something I should be finding out after everyone else."

She stares at him, unable to comprehend his words for a second. "No, I haven't spoken to them. They told me when they visited me, when I got out of hospital. When they told me my job was safe, and yes, Max, you are my boyfriend. Someone who is meant to support me, encourage me, want to see me grow and flourish."

Anger explodes from Max.

"And keep you fuckin' safe, but I never managed that either did I?"

Bronagh flinches at his anger, but pulls herself together. Sitting up straighter she tries to make herself look stronger than she feels. "It was not your fault Max! We have been through this." Anger and dismay are laced through her words.

"But because I couldn't keep you... safe, you were abducted and beaten and shit."

Bronagh shakes her head, her anger building.

"So, because you think you've failed, I need to be kept in here. The same way I was kept in that garage only without the chains?"

Max's face contorts like he's been punched in the stomach.

"That's not fair, Bre. I never said that."

"Near enough Max. You said I should stay here, on my own while you go to work. Now to me that sounds very much like I should be kept home, 'for my own safety'." She uses air quotes to drive home her point. Then she stands. "This isn't the forties Max and as I've tried to say many times I wasn't asking for your fuckin' permission to go back to my fuckin' job! Now if you'll excuse me I'm going to phone Erin and arrange my return." She turns to leave, but Max is too far gone in his anger to let her leave with the last word.

"How do you suppose you'll get into your work and back home if I don't let you use my Golf?" Turning back to face him Bronagh swallows deeply. Her anger was peaking, but she held it in, not wanting to give Max the satisfaction of knowing he was getting to her. She realised what Max was really saying and it crushed her. He had started to change when the harassment started all those many months ago. He became possessive and controlling, but now he was holding his possessions over her, it was the last straw. She took a step towards him. Standing toe to toe she pulls herself up to her full height to be the strong, independent woman she knew was still in there and spoke in a very calm voice.

"I'll fuckin' walk!" She turns again and leaves Max standing in the living room, too stunned to move or talk. A feeling of dread washes over him. He may have pushed too far this time, he thinks. He was trying to keep her safe, make up for his failings, but instead he let anger take over. Slumping back onto the couch he holds his head in his hands trying to decipher what he had done and how he was going to fix it.

CHAPTER FORTY-FIVE

Bronagh lies on the bed in the spare room, curled up in the foetus position. She had phoned Erin who was ecstatic that Bronagh wanted to return to work. They arranged for her to go in the next day for a few hours and then agreed that they would take it from there. After that she phoned Gordon asking if he could pick her up on his way to work. Again, another ecstatic response about her feeling ready to return to work. Gordon questions her about Max and his feelings on the subject. She tiptoes around their argument, not wanting to go into the details of how Max had changed, and gets off the phone. She could understand Max's need for her to be safe and his self-blame, but for him to think he could control her was beyond her, and a tactic so low she never thought he would stoop to it. Her head was spinning with all the thoughts of how their relationship should be, with what ifs and self-doubts about the state of their relationship, that maybe she was to blame for some of it, if not all of it. She pulls her thoughts from the dark places they were going and reminds herself that she had no control over Elaine, Stewart or Max's actions. She only has control over her own actions and wellbeing. With thoughts of her future and where it would take her she falls asleep.

Max swithers and worries himself through the next few hours as Bronagh slept. He'd thought he heard her get up and go for a shower. He was desperate to get into the shower with her, make love to her until she forgave him for being such an arsehole, but with the amount of foul language she threw at him he thought better of it. Instead he decides to start preparing dinner, hoping for forgiveness through her stomach.

After her sleep and shower Bronagh feels a renewed energy that everything would work itself out. She would get her life back. Smelling the curry that Max had started to make sends her stomach into a growl. She hopes that they could get themselves back to where they were, that he would loosen his grip on her and realise that she needed to breathe. She also hopes that he's forgiven her for swearing at him... again. She walks into the kitchen and watches Max as he cooks. He looks relaxed moving about the kitchen, the way he did before they were romantically involved.

"Hey you." Not sure of the reaction she would receive she remains standing at the door. She wasn't frightened of Max or his reaction, but she certainly wasn't going to stay to get involved in another argument or listen to any more skewed reasoning of why she shouldn't get her life back. Max turns when he hears her voice. His eyes are soft when he looks at her and his voice gentle.

"Hey yourself." They smile at each other before Max steps forwards. "Bre, I'm sorry. I do want you to get back to your life, our life, together... but I need you safe too." Bronagh slumps. When Max had started to talk she thought he had come to his senses, but now she thinks she's about to hear another lecture on why he needs her safe, and so kept in the house. Max pulls her to him. "I'm going to work on my stressing out and make an effort to get us both back to normal." Max's words are like music to her ears, but like fingernails being drawn down a blackboard to his. He is fighting the inner turmoil that was wanting to lock them both in a bubble and never leave.

"Thank you, Max, that's all I need. Support to get to where I want to be; with you, with my own party and wedding planning business and free from fear." He takes her into his arms.

"You'll get your dreams Bre, and I'll be by your side when you do." Bronagh smiles up at him, hoping he means what he was saying. As the rest of the night unfolds the lovers make an effort to be nice to each other, neither of them wanting another argument.

****

The next morning Bronagh is up and ready before Max leaves for his own work. She knows it's too early, but her nerves were getting the better of her. Max starts to object to her going in, but Bronagh asks him to support her and not bring her down, so he bites his tongue, hard, then leaves, giving her a chaste kiss on the lips as he walks out the front door, his mood matching the weather of the wet Scottish summer's day.

Bronagh, on the other hand, had a nervous excitement running through her. She would've been lying if she said she wasn't worried about returning to work, but she wasn't about to let that stop her from moving on with her life, or let Max know that's how she felt. Hearing the beep of Gordon's car Bronagh takes a deep breath. She walks from the house, reminding herself that this is the beginning of the rest of her life. In the car she gives Gordon a peck on the cheek and thanks him again for picking her up. He waves off her thanks and drives them both to work, chatting aimlessly as he drives.

Getting back into the main planning room with the desks and walls covered in party planning work Bronagh notices the desk she'd been using before was clear. Gordon walks into the room from the staff area with two steaming cups of coffee and hands one to Bronagh. Taking the proffered coffee Bronagh has a bemused look on her face.

"Why is this table empty?" Gordon smiles a secret smile.

"When you were off Erin and David decided to nominate desks to people and they said this one would be yours when you came back." Tears glisten in her eyes as emotion wells up inside her.

"They really believed I would return?" Gordon smiles again, this one sweeter and takes her under his arm.

"Of course, we all did. There was never a doubt in my mind that you'd make your way back. You're a strong woman Bre." The tears that were glistening now fall from their barriers. The ringing of her phone interrupts her tears. She looks at the screen. Max. She swithers about answering it but knows that would be childish and would only make things worse. After the quick call she returns to Gordon's desk and takes a seat. He eyes her.

"Everything all right my princess?" She plasters on a smile and nods, a little too vigorously, then slumps. Not wanting to lie to her friend and needing someone to talk to she decides to open up to Gordon.

"It's Max." Gordon tips his head up. He was glad that Bronagh had opened up. He had had his suspicions that things weren't as rosy as they should be between them, but he hadn't wanted to poke his nose in. "He's not happy that I'm back at work... we had a big argument last night about it. He asked how I planned on getting here if he didn't give me the Golf." Gordon's face is one of shock. He could see that Max was making himself crazy worrying over Bronagh and her safety, but he didn't think he would be so possessive or controlling.

"Oh Princess." Bronagh gives Gordon a sad smile.

"I know. I got really angry and swore at him... at lot actually." Gordon winces at hearing Bronagh had sworn. It didn't take Gordon long to learn Bronagh didn't curse unless she was pushed to it, or drunk. "I accused him of treating me like a forties housewife and that he was keeping me trapped in the house, just the same as I was in the garage only without the shackles." Another wince from Gordon before he turns serious.

"Is that how you're feeling in the relationship, trapped?" Bronagh drops her head into her hands, tears and emotion threaten to overtake her. She takes a deep breath so she can talk.

"I'm starting to." Gordon grabs her hand.

"Bre, I'm so sorry, but hey, listen, you are the strongest woman I know. You will get through this, and if your and Max's love is as strong as I think it could be, youse will get through this. I promise." Bronagh brings Gordon into a hug and thanks him for being such a good friend in such a short space of time. Just as Bronagh composes herself, her phone beeps. Looking at the screen her shoulders slump.

"Another text from Max," she tells Gordon. "This is like the third one since he left for work this morning."

"Let him know you're working and you'll contact him at lunch." Bronagh lets out a slow breath as she types. Putting her phone down she picks up the folder sitting on Gordon's desk and starts to flick through it.

The rest of the morning is taken up with Bronagh helping Gordon with the eighteenth birthday party he had been assigned. She gives him different ideas on how to make the party something more than a 'welcome to the world of drinking legally' party. Gordon is grateful for all her ideas and picks the Cinderella-esque ball idea as the birthday girl was coming across as a princess in the making.

During her three hours at work Max phones and messages a total of eight times. She'd had to decline all but two of his calls as Erin was in the main planning room and Bronagh didn't want to give her boss any reason to regret keeping her job for her. Every time she sent him a message she reminded him that she was at work and she would let him know once she was home, safe. His constant check-ups were beyond grating on her and pushing her to her limits. Putting away her phone after lunch Gordon asks if she was ready to leave.

"Oh aye, I've had enough excitement for the one day!" She was tired and emotional, but happy to be back. The friends drive in silence back to Max's house. Once there Gordon decides that he has to speak his mind.

"Bre, tell me it's none of my business, but... Max needs to get himself under control. He can't be keeping tabs on you like that. It's not healthy." Tears threaten Bronagh again.

"I know. I'm going to speak to him, again, tonight." Worry etches on Gordon's face.

"Listen, just so you know, if you need a break, or some breathing space or anything, I've got a spare room." Bronagh's eyes flash with panic, but it vanishes and a peace settles around her.

"Thanks Gee. I'll remember that." The friends give each other a hug and Bronagh steps from the car. She waves to Gordon as he pulls away then steps into the empty house.

When she was first found in the garage she thought she'd never want to be on her own again, never leave Max's side again, but at that moment, standing in the hall with no one to ask her how she was, if she was coping or where she had been... she felt fine. Not scared or lonely or even panicky. She felt at peace, safe even. Just like she used to feel when she got home to her own flat after a hard day's work. She smiles to herself, praising herself on all the hard work she'd done to get back to that point in her life after her abduction and the quivering wreck she had been. Her phone rings and she huffs. Knowing it would be Max she drags it from her pocket. A quick look at the screen confirms her suspicions.

"Max?" She doesn't bother to conceal her frustrations from her voice.

"Bre, where are you?" She huffs again.

CHAPTER FORTY-SIX

Max had been on tenterhooks all day knowing that Bronagh was out without him. He understood she wasn't on her own, but she wasn't on her own the night she was abducted. So unless she was physically with him he didn't settle. He could tell she was getting pissed off at him with his constant phone calls and messages, but he couldn't help himself.

Walking into the house after work he was desperate to have Bronagh in his arms. He finds her in the kitchen organising dinner with a glass of wine sitting next to her. Approaching her from behind, he wraps his arms around her waist encasing her in his embrace. He feels her tense for a millisecond.

"Hey you." He tests the waters before asking how she was.

"Hey yourself." Her voice is flat even though she answered in their usual way. Max turns her around in his arms.

"Hey, what's wrong?"

Bronagh eyes him, astonishment dancing in her emerald green eyes. "Are you serious? What do you think is wrong?"

Max squeezes his eyes shut, knowing where their conversation was going.

"I know, I'm sorry, Bre, but I just couldn't settle. I needed to know you were safe."

Bronagh takes a hold of Max's arms and removes them from her waist. "I was at work Max. I was safe. I was with people who care about me." She refuses to break eye contact with him, refusing to back down.

"You were with someone who cares for you that night too!" He spits the words out, his tone harsh and laced with anger. Bronagh steps back like she'd been slapped. Anger and frustration flowing through her.

"You still blame Jane for my abduction don't you?" Max shrugs. "For goodness sake, it wasn't her fault. Was she the crappiest friend in the world that night? Aye, but that doesn't mean she's to blame for Stewart and Elaine drugging me and carrying me off!" Max winces at her words, but she continues, warming up to the argument. "You need to get over what Jane did or didn't do. She was dealing with her own stuff, which if you'll remember, ended up being connected to what happened to me. So if anything she was used as a pawn in their sick game against me." Anger flashes in Max's eyes. He couldn't believe Bronagh was letting Jane off with her responsibility.

"She promised me she'd keep you safe, an' she didn't. She told you to fuck off so she could get laid, and not even with someone important. No it was with some random she picked up." This time it's Bronagh that winces. It still hurt that her best friend had picked some random guy in a bar over her, but that didn't make her responsible for Bronagh's abduction.

"Max, you need to start to get over what happened. With Jane, with Elaine and Stewart, and *to* me." Max looks at her desperately.

"How Bre? How am I meant to get over it? You said you would come back to me the next day, but you didn't... you were gone! I thought forever. I thought I would never see you again, I thought you were..." He couldn't give voice to his worst fears over that night. Bronagh's anger lessens at his words. She had thought about how hard it must have been for Max during the days and hours she was missing. Not knowing where she was, if she was safe or alive or maybe he was thinking she had left him. She knew she would have been out of her mind with worry if the tables had been turned. They had spoken about the events of that night and she had suggested Max speak to a counsellor about it all, but he refused, saying as long as he had her in his arms, that was all the counselling he needed. It was becoming apparent to Bronagh that that wasn't working or healthy for either of them.

"Max, I'm sorry you had to go through that worry." Max shakes his head, starting to interrupt, but Bronagh holds up her hand, stopping his words on his lips. "But you need to stop being so possessive and controlling. You are suffocating me. I need to get my life back to being mine. I need to be able to go out and about without my own anxiety overtaking me, and I can't do that when I need to deal with yours at the same time." Max steps forward to take Bronagh into his arms again, but she takes a step backwards keeping the distance between them. Pain lances through his heart.

"Bre?" His tone is almost pleading.

"I need space Max. I need you to let go of the vice like grip you have on me. You need to deal with your obsessive need for me to be safe." Max drops his head.

"I can't." His voice comes out as broken as he was feeling.

"Even if that means you end up pushing me away?" Max's head snaps up, fear dancing in his crystal blue eyes.

"Bronagh, please." It is almost a beg. Bronagh picks up her wine glass. Inside she was breaking, but she knew she needed to stay strong to get her point across. She needed space.

"You need to get help with dealing with what happened. It can't be from me alone." Max nods his head, tears running down his face unchecked.

"Okay, I'll try to calm down on the phone calls and stuff... and I'll look into talking to someone, but Bre, I am never going to stop wanting you safe. I love you, that's never going to change." Bronagh steps forward placing her hand on his arm. The contact is like a lifeline to Max.

"I love you too Max... but I want the Max that I've been in love with forever back. The free, trusting, happy Max not this strung out controlling one. Going up onto her tiptoes she places a gentle kiss on his lips. "Dinner's ready." She walks past him leaving the kitchen and climbs the stairs to the spare bedroom. Once there she phones Jane and arranges for her to pick her up from work for an overdue girls' lunch the next again day. Then she climbs into bed, exhausted physically and emotionally from her first day back at work.

After many beers, no dinner and hours of self-assessment Max climbs the stairs to bed. He'd heard everything Bronagh had said to him, even the warning of losing her. He promises and vows to himself that he would calm down, stop checking up on her, give her the space she needs. But deep down in his gut he knows that was one promise he probably wouldn't keep, just like he knew he wouldn't go and see anyone to talk to. As far as he was concerned he didn't need to; he just needed Bronagh safe and in his arms. Entering his bedroom he expects Bronagh to be there as she hadn't come back downstairs. She wasn't there. His stomach drops, just the way it dropped when he entered her flat that fateful morning. He rushes into the spare room and sighs, relief washing over him as he sees her sleeping form lying amongst the rumpled sheets. Ignoring the reasons why she was in the spare bed, Max climbs in. Taking her in his arms he falls asleep.

****

The next morning Bronagh is up and about before Max. She'd heard him climb into the spare bed the night before, but was too tired to tell him to leave. She had wanted space, hence the reason she wasn't in the bed they shared, but if she was honest with herself she still wanted him there to cuddle into at night.

Max comes into the kitchen and smiles at her. His eyes light up as he kisses her and for a minute everything was back to how it was before, but only for a minute.

"Are you going into work again today?" Max tries to keep his voice neutral but Bronagh hears the worry and maybe a touch of anger in the undertone. She takes a deep breath before answering him.

"Yes, Gordon is picking me up at nine, then Jane is getting me at work and we're going for lunch about one." Max stops making his coffee.

"What? Why? Do you really need to?" Panic lodges itself in his chest and he can't budge it, no matter how many times he tries. Bronagh pinches the bridge of her nose, and breathes deeply, again.

"AYE...! Yes Max, I do need to."

"But..." She slams down her cup the contents slopping out onto the worktop.

"But nothing, Max. Today is going to be hard enough. First time out without you an' all, so don't push it. As I said last night I don't need to be dealing with your shit as well as my own." Panic bubbles up more in Max, but Bronagh doesn't give him a chance to reply. "I will text you when I get to work, and when I go out. You do not need to be keeping tabs on me, do you understand Max?" Her tone is serious and determined. A million reasons run through his head of why she shouldn't go out, either to work or lunch, but panic has stolen his voice. Instead he can only stare as Bronagh walks from the kitchen, the palpable anger in the air dissipating with every step away she takes.

By the time she gets to work Bronagh has managed to calm herself. She had given Gordon a quick rundown of her conversations with Max and her warning that he would push her away. Gordon was supportive of her words and agreed that she had to think of herself and her own healing after her ordeal and that Max had to deal with his.

Erin enters the main planning room and asks to speak to Bronagh in her office. A shiver of panic rushes down her spine. They get into the office and Bronagh takes the visitor seat opposite Erin's behind her desk. Panic and adrenaline mix in Bronagh's veins.

"Bronagh, I know you only came back yesterday, but we got a job request last night and I want to give the job to you." Her panic starts to subside, and it's quickly being replaced by excitement. "In your application and at your interview you commented that this was your dream job." Erin takes a pause and Bronagh thinks she might implode from the suspense. "How do you fancy planning a wedding?" The scream that leaves Bronagh's lips is completely involuntary and she apologises profusely for being unprofessional, but Erin waves them away. "I take that is a yes?" Bronagh nods her head like the proverbial nodding dog.

"Aye, eh, yes. Yes please. Oh Erin thank you. This is exactly what I've been wanting to do and everything that I need at the moment." Emotion overwhelms her as does her tears. Erin continues to talk as she hands Bronagh tissues.

"Now I know you've got a lot on your plate just now, but I think getting back in the saddle of life is the best idea. You can still have your phased return as we won't be giving you any other projects to work on until this one is over. We understand how big this is for one person. Nearer the time we will give you someone to help with the load, probably Gordon, but it's your baby to grow. How does that sound? Bronagh sits stunned for a moment.

"Wow, yes thank you, again. One question, when is the wedding?" Erin coughs.

"Yes, well it's going to be a big wedding, so there's going to be a lot of work involved as it's in six months." Bronagh's eyes widen. Six months isn't a lot of time to plan a full wedding, but she's confident she'll do it to the best of her ability, and she knows it will help her get everything back on track.

"Okay... I'm sure I'll be fine." Erin smiles a warm smile at Bronagh's answer.

"Fantastic. Right, here's the client's details. Contact them and get the ball rolling." Bronagh takes the proffered folder and thanks Erin again.

Gordon looks up from his work and sees the grin on Bronagh's face.

"Wow, look at my princess smiling. What did Erin want?" Bronagh takes a seat at Gordon's desk and goes into detail about the wedding and how he will be involved nearer the end and on the actual day. Gordon grabs her into a hug. "Oh sunshine, that's amazing, and I agree, I think it's exactly what you need." Bronagh goes over to her desk and lifts her mobile. She wants to let Max know her news. "Oh, aye, your phone has been ringing and beeping like fury." The smile slides from her face. She had sent Max a frosty message when she arrived at work, but with her news she had melted some and wanted him to share in her happiness. Looking at her phone she sees that he's phoned her four times and messaged her five in the past hour. Seething at him she fires off a message stating that she was fine, busy, but fine. All feelings of warmth towards him vanishing. Picking up the folder she gets a start on her work, contacting her clients to get meetings organised.

CHAPTER FORTY-SEVEN

Settling into their chairs at the Chinese restaurant, Bronagh takes a deep breath. She'd chosen that restaurant to push herself more in her healing process. She was euphoric at being given the wedding to plan, so wanted to use that euphoria to take another step forward. Jane eyes her as she does her deep breathing exercises, trying to get a hold of her anxiety.

"You okay?" Bronagh nods, not wanting to talk due to concentrating on her breathing. "We can go somewhere else?" Bronagh shakes her head.

"No! I need to do this. I mean, it's only a restaurant and it's our favourite, so I don't want them taking it away from us. I won't let them take anything else away from me... my life is mine again!" Jane smiles with tears in her eyes. She is in awe of her friend. When they had first found Bronagh she was a quivering wreck who clutched onto Max as if she needed him to breathe, but now, after many, many hours of therapy and a whole lot of hard, emotional work she was getting herself back. Making her life hers again, as she had said.

"Good for you!" Jane beams at her friend. Bronagh lifts her phone to message Max when it rings in her hand. Max. Jane looks down, not wanting Bronagh to see her eye roll.

"Max, I was just about to text you... yes... in the Chinese... yes... I'm fine." Jane sneaks a look at her friend. Anger is making her green eyes flash. "No Max, Jane is here and I will let you know when I'm home." Her voice changes to an almost plea. "Please don't keep contacting me, apart from anything else you're going to end up in trouble at work." She sighs. "Goodbye Max." She cancels the call and looks at Jane too brightly. "Food?" Jane agrees.

Once they've had their first round of food Jane decides to broach the subject of Max.

"Things not any better with Max and his obsession then?" Bronagh had turned her phone over to stop seeing the messages Max was continuing to send. He hadn't phoned again, but after five messages she'd had enough.

"No, and if anything I think he's worse today. I spoke to him the other day and again last night about backing off and going to speak to someone, but I think it's fell on deaf ears." She blows out a breath. "I'm so tired with it all. I told him he was pushing me away. I don't want to end things, but..." Jane has sat quiet as Bronagh talks, but hearing that she is thinking of splitting up with Max jolts her to speak.

"You really thinking of leaving him?" Bronagh shrugs then drops her fork to the plate.

"I don't know. I love him with all my heart, but I can't go on like this. I'm feeling more trapped every day. It's like being back in the garage only without the shackles and with heating." Jane places her hand on Bronagh's.

"Aw, Bre, really... that's not good. You know no matter what I'll support you." Bronagh squeezes her friends hand in thanks.

"I know, and thank you. Gordon said I could stay with him if I needed a break, or if the worst happened and I left, but I think I need to get back into my own place. I mean I am paying for it and it's been standing empty for months, so I might be asking if you want a sleepover instead?"

Jane laughs, then apologises. "Sorry... but, a sleepover at our age." She shakes her head with another giggle, then sobers. "Aye, of course I will. Whatever you need to move forward." Jane smiles at Bronagh, and she smiles back, grateful for the support her friends were offering her, and wishing her boyfriend could be the same.

An hour after the friends had started eating, Bronagh's phone rings again.

"Max?" Jane nods towards the ringing phone. Bronagh shows her the screen. "You want me to answer?"

"Oh god no, that would send him into an ever bigger panic." Jane shakes her head and Bronagh answers her phone. "Max I'm fine, what is it...? I'm still at the restaurant, we've been gabbing... No, Max, Jane is taking me home. I'll see you there... bye." She hangs up on him again. The friends continue eating as Bronagh tells Jane her good news of landing the wedding project. Getting home Bronagh heads to the kitchen to make a coffee and send a message to Max.

That's me in, had a lovely day with Jane. See you when you get home. Bre xx

Seconds later her phone rings. She rolls her eyes as Max's name flashes on the screen. She swipes the answer button huffing as she does it.

"Max, what is it?" She can hear worry in his voice as he talks.

"I just wanted to make sure you're okay." She lets out a slow breath, trying to get her anger under control.

"I'm fine," she snaps at him, "I've been fine all day and I asked you not to do this. To not contact me continuously, keeping tabs on me, but you have." A gruff sound comes from Max.

"I told you I wanted to know you were safe. I tried to not contact you, but I couldn't, I needed to know." Bronagh sighs and rubs her tired eyes. She couldn't have this argument again.

"Max, I can't do this any more. You need to let go. You need to get yourself sorted."

"Bre, what are you saying?" Panic laces his words.

"I need to look after myself and not feel trapped any more... I'm going to stay at my place tonight." There is a sharp intake of breath on the other end of the line.

"What? No! Bronagh, no way. You're not ready for that."

Anger flashes through her. "No Max, you're the one that's not ready for this, but I can't be responsible for that." She takes a breath to speak again when Max starts to talk.

"Fine, I'll come with you." Max changes tack.

"No! Max the whole point of me wanting to go to mine is to get space from you and your constant need to know I'm safe. Jane said she would stay with me if I wanted." Another gruff noise comes from Max.

"You've spoken to Jane about this? Have you been planning this?" His accusing tone grates on Bronagh.

"I mentioned today that I wanted to get back to the flat. I told you before the trial finished I would want to do this, so it shouldn't be that much of a shock."

"And I said no." Her anger spikes again.

"You don't get to say no! In fact you don't get to tell me what I can or cannot do Max. Now I'm staying in my own flat tonight whether you like it or not." She takes a breath before continuing. "Please don't push me too far Max." There is warning in her tone.

"What's that meant to mean Bre? I only want you safe."

Bronagh's voice raises slightly. "I know that Max. You've said it on numerous occasions, but it's turning into an obsession and you are making me feel the same way I did in that bloody garage."

"That's unfair Bronagh." Max raises his voice with his every word, "I don't have you chained to a fuckin' wall. All I'm trying to do is keep you fuckin' safe. Why can't you see that? Why won't you let me keep you?" Bronagh's anger gets the better of her.

"Because I'm not a fuckin' possession. I am not yours to keep. My life is mine. I'm doing this Max, I need a fuckin' break. You can either support me on another step forward in my healing, or..."

Max lowers his voice to almost a whisper. "Or what Bronagh?"

There is a heavy pause as Bronagh takes stock of what she is about to say. She calms her heart before speaking again.

"Or I'm leaving you... ending our relationship."

Max makes a strangled noise on the other end of the line.

"Bronagh you don't mean that. Don't do this... Bronagh please."

She chokes back her tears to continue. "I need a break Max, and you need to stop holding on, holding me back. You may not have me chained to a wall, but I feel like you've chained me to you. I can't breathe but you need to know about it, you're constantly checking up on me. I can't do it any more. I'll let you know when I get to my place, then I'll phone you tomorrow, but other than that I don't want you to contact me."

"Bronagh, no." She hears his tears and pain in his voice, but steadies herself, she needs to do this for her.

"Goodbye, Max." She cuts the call before he has the chance to say anything else and slides down the cupboards into a ball on the floor. She starts to sob, her heart breaking, wondering why, just as she gets the chance to work on one of her dreams, her other dream of loving Max for the rest of her life was slipping away from her?

****

Jane and Bronagh sit in Bronagh's living room sharing a bottle of Shiraz. Bronagh was cried out and numb. She'd relayed her conversation to Jane and cried some more when they sat down on her couch. Jane had been shocked, but supportive.

"You sure you want to leave him?" Bronagh snorts sadly at Jane's question.

"Honestly... no. But I can't breathe Jane. He needs to realise he isn't coping with whatever guilt he's feeling about what happened. I want to help him, but he won't help himself, and it's bringing me down." She takes a deep shuddering breath. "He is the love of my life. I will never not love him... but... I can't stay with him if he's going to try an' control me, see me as a possession to be locked away for safekeeping." Her voice breaks as she admits that it would be better for her if she was without Max. Jane wraps her arms around her best friend, her own heart breaking for her friend.

"It'll be okay. Youse are meant to be together." Bronagh's doorbell rings through the flat, interrupting her emotional soul baring. The friends look at each other.

"You expecting anyone?" Jane asks, even though she knows the answer by the fear dancing in Bronagh's eyes.

"No."

"You want me to answer it?" Bronagh nods.

"I'm guessing it's Max, so please could you?"

"No problem." She smiles at Bronagh, then heads to the door. She stops at the living room door. "D'you want to see him?"

"No. I asked him not to contact me after I let him know I was here."

"Okay, wait here." Jane walks the rest of the way to the front door, which is now getting banged on. She checks the spyhole before throwing open the door, anger evident on her features.

Max is standing on the landing looking strung out. His sandy hair is standing on end with the amount of times he'd dragged his hands through it. Pulling at it until it was coming out in his fingers. He had tried to settle himself, told himself over and over again that she was safe, but it didn't work. He'd lifted his phone dozens of times to phone or message Bronagh, but dropped it. He'd had a feeling that she would've ignored his calls or not read his texts, which really would drive him over the edge. So here he was standing on her landing, battering at her door like a madman.

"Max what are you doing here?" Max looks behind Jane for Bronagh.

"I need to see Bre, Jane."

Jane shakes her head. "Nope, not happening."

Max steps back as if Jane had slapped him.

"Why? I'm her boyfriend, I just want —"

Jane rolls her eyes at him then takes a step forward. "Her safe, yes I know Max. You've said that a million times since we got her back. Now, you know fine well she's safe. Just because she's not handcuffed to you does not mean she's in danger."

Max growls at Jane. "That's what I thought the last time, and look what happened." His crystal blue eyes spark like lightening.

"I've apologised for my part in letting Bre get taken. She's forgiven me Max, so why can't you?" Jane keeps her voice calm even though inside she is burning with anger.

"Because I trusted you!" He was shouting now and he knew he was losing the plot, but his life was falling apart.

Bronagh opens the door wider and stands beside Jane.

"Bronagh!" He says her name as a desperate whisper. He looks at her, relieved to see her safe, but shocked at her appearance. She looked exhausted, blue shadows covered the underside of her bloodshot red rimmed eyes. Even the normally sparkling emerald green colour of her irises are dull and tired.

"Max, why?" Max opens his mouth to talk but doesn't get a chance as Bronagh's anger gets the better of her. "And don't you dare say anything about me being safe, or so god help me I will..." She leaves the sentence hanging in the air, not sure exactly what she would do, but knows it wouldn't be pretty. A screaming banshee came unbidden to her mind.

"I couldn't, Bronagh. I tried to do what you asked and give you space and a break and everything else, but I... I couldn't. I needed to see you." His voice breaks and tears flow from both of their eyes. Bronagh steps in front of Jane and places her hand on Max's tear soaked cheek. He turns his face into its warmth and she takes it away, leaving his cheek cold.

"I'm sorry, Max... I can't do this any more." She says the words with pain lancing her heart. "I can't carry both of us. I love you with everything that I am. I will never love anyone else, but I... I can't... I'm sorry. I'm done, we're done. Goodbye Max." She turns to leave but Max grabs her arm and begs for her not to leave him, not to walk away from what they have, what they have both always wanted, what they were only just starting together, but she jerks her arm from his grasp and keeps walking. Getting to the living room door she collapses in a heap in front of the couch. She screams like the banshee she had thought of only minutes before.

Max tries to get past Jane, shouting for Bronagh to change her mind, telling her how much he loves her, begging her not to leave him. Jane places both her hands on his shoulders stopping him in his tracks.

"No, Max, stop. It's over. You need to let her go." She takes a breath. "Let her get through tonight. I'll talk to her, but you need to back off."

He's crying freely, tears coursing down his face. "I need her Jane. I nearly lost her once, I can't go through that again."

Jane nods knowingly. "I understand Max, I do, but Bronagh's right. You need to get yourself sorted. You're not thinking straight. You are holding her captive to you and your need or guilt or whatever it is that's happened to you. She literally escaped being held captive so she doesn't need it in an emotional sense." Max drops his shoulders, the fight draining from him. "Go home Max, and please don't contact her."

He scrubs his nose and eyes. "Tell her I love her."

Jane gives him a sad smile. "I will, but she already knows that... listen Max, for what it's worth I think youse are meant to be together, but not like this. Get yourself sorted." Jane gives his shoulders a squeeze then closes the door on him, leaving him to hear the muffled screams and sobs of his now ex-girlfriend, the love of his life.

CHAPTER FORTY-EIGHT
Six months later

The day Bronagh has been working so hard for has arrived. Her first wedding. Fully organised by her. Her stress levels had been at their highest for the past six months, but that had helped her get through some of her darker moments. The pain and fear she'd felt when she was chained up in the garage had been overpowering and nearly broken her, but none of that compared to the pain she'd felt when she broke up with Max. That night in her flat she'd thought she would stop existing, and she thanked every god she'd ever heard of that Jane was there. She'd lifted her phone countless times to ask Max back, but she knew for her own sanity and healing, and his, she had to stay away. She had to be by herself until it wasn't scary any more (and Max needed to battle his own demons over the incident without her). It took a while for her to be comfortable being in her flat by herself. Even now she still sometimes got panicked, or she woke up sweating and screaming from her nightmares of being locked up and cold and beaten again. These were the nights she desperately wanted Max, but as time went on she was managing to deal with it all better than she ever thought she could. So much so her counsellor had cut back her sessions, saying she was coping well on her own and wouldn't need them for much longer. This panicked her, but made her proud at the same time.

So far the wedding had gone better than planned. The bride was stunning looking in a lace covered, sweetheart neck, princess-cut white gown. The blue, white and silver flowers complemented the crystal blue cowl necked satin dresses of the bridesmaids to perfection. With Gordon's help Bronagh had managed to deal with the few blips that had occurred, the worst being an uninvited guest turning up and demanding to be part of the couple's big day. Between them they managed to guide the unwanted person back outside and convinced them to leave. It brought back memories of Elaine gatecrashing Bronagh's first party, but she pushed that memory to the side so she could cope with the rest of her day.

As the meals drew to a close and everyone was ushered out so the room could be prepared for the evening, Bronagh takes a moment to herself in the ladies' toilets. The day had been hard, stressful, but satisfying, even though the thought of what her and Max's wedding would have been like was never far from her mind. She still missed him, still loved him with every fibre of her being. The last she'd heard he had lost his job and was moving in with his brother in Cumbernauld. It had broken her heart knowing he'd lost everything, partly because of her, but her counsellor reminded her what was and wasn't her responsibility. She had tried to support Max, get him to go to therapy, but he'd insisted he hadn't needed it.

Pulling herself together Bronagh walks back out into the crazy busy world of wedding planning. Within what felt like minutes Bronagh was ushering everyone back into the room where the reception was to take place, the night guests were arriving and she was hunting down the bride and groom for their first dance. The song they picked for their first dance starts up and Bronagh stands at the side of the dance floor watching the married couple as they dance. They only had eyes for each other as people clapped and cheered for them. Gordon stands next to her, wrapping his arm around her waist.

"You okay my princess? You seem far away." Bronagh lifts her eyes to blink away the tears.

"I'm okay." He bumps into her with his hip.

"You thinking about Max?" Her eyes fill again.

"I keep thinking that the colour of the bridesmaids' dresses is the exact colour of his eyes." She takes a deep breath and blows it out, trying to blow away the emotion that's threatening to overtake her. Gordon pulls her into his arms.

"I know I'm not Max, but if you want a dance..." She smiles at her friend as she takes his outstretched hand.

"Even though I don't have the right appendage?" Her eyes glint in humour through the unshed tears.

"I'll make an exception this once." He winks at her as they do a small waltz at the side of the dance floor. "You know princess, I do believe the pair of youse will make your way back to each other." She squeezes her arms tighter around him.

"That's what Jane said."

"Hmm, that Jane is a clever woman." Bronagh lets out a sigh.

"I hope so." She rests her cheek against Gordon's chest and closes her eyes, letting herself believe that there would be a future for her and Max, and that it was him she was dancing with at that moment in time.

****

Max stands behind the bar in the Lock-In pub. After he lost his job he was at rock bottom. He'd lost everything. The job he loved and only girl he would ever love. He knew from the very start of Bronagh's harassment that his behaviour was out of line. After that it disintegrated into obsessive stalking and evolved into the same as everything that Elaine and Stewart put her through. At the time he thought he was doing what was best for her, for them, for their love, but he could see now that that wasn't the case. It took a literal fist fight with his brother and many, many hours of therapy for him to realise that, but eventually he did. During his time at his brother's he'd bought a classic BMW 735 to restore. He always felt calmer when he worked on cars, especially ones that needed proper love and care. Loving the way he felt, seeing the car fully restored and sold on, he decided to start his own business doing it.

Once he felt he was closer to his usual self he decided it was time to get back to his own house. Getting home was bittersweet. The house was empty without Bronagh in it, but that was something he would need to get used to. That grew harder every time he found something of Bronagh's laying about his house. He took the job as barman in the Lock-In for extra cash while his business was growing, getting the bills paid while he picked up another BMW to restore. This one was a 1992 Magenta red 735, which was in bad shape after spending over five years in someone's driveway taking all the Scottish weather had to throw at it. His reasoning for working in that pub was so he didn't bump into Bronagh. He didn't think she would've been back after being abducted from it... but then again maybe he was hoping that she'd overcome everything those two bastards put her through and she would walk through the doors.

He'd heard through the grapevine that Bronagh had pulled off her dream job of planning a wedding in a spectacular vision of winter wonderland. He was so proud of her. Proud of how she'd worked her way back to herself when she could've so easily been broken and lost for the rest of her life. She even managed to do it with the added dependency of his inability to cope with what happened to her.

Dragging himself from his musings he goes to serve some customers. It's the busiest night of the year, Hogmanay. It was going to be the first Hogmanay in years that Bronagh wasn't the first person he reached for at the bells. She wouldn't be his first kiss of the year, and he only had himself to blame.

Stepping out of the taxi, Bronagh, Jane and Gordon stand at the front door of the Lock-In.

"You sure you want to do this?" Jane asks Bronagh as she stands holding her hand with Gordon holding her around her waist. She takes a deep breath and counts inwardly before talking.

"Aye. This is the last thing I need to conquer. I need to take this place back, make it mine again." The three friends smile at each other.

"Well... moan then," Gordon says as he takes the first step, pulling Bronagh into a walk. Getting into the pub takes all of Bronagh's strength. She gets through a group of people standing at the juke box, controlling the music for ten minutes.

She's squeezing Jane's hand to the point she thinks she can feel something pop and Jane yelps.

"Sorry." She smiles at her friend.

"That's okay." Jane grimaces back as she rubs her hand, "You want to grab a table, or come to the bar with me?" Bronagh looks around at the tables then over to the bar. Her breath had been coming quick since walking into the building, but now it catches in her throat and stops altogether, as does her heartbeat. Her eyes have landed on Max. He's smiling at a beautiful blonde. The blonde grins back, a flirtatious grin, and who could blame her. Max was more handsome than Bronagh remembered. He'd always been broad and muscular and now was no exception. He certainly hadn't let himself go over the six months they had been apart. She wonders if he'd kept himself in shape for anyone in particular, maybe even the blonde smiling at him at that moment. A stab of jealousy pokes at her heart. She pushes it aside, reminding herself that it wasn't any of her business, she was the one who walked away. It may have been for a good reason, but it hurt like hell... and it still did.

"It's him." She breathes out. Jane looks at Bronagh, then follows her eye line until she sees Max behind the bar. She turns back to Bronagh.

"Bre, d'you want to leave?" Before she can answer, Max locks eyes with her and she smiles.

Max had finished with the blonde who was shamelessly flirting with him, even asking to kiss him at the bells. He'd gently refused her offer and turned away... straight into the gaze of the love of his life. His heart stutters in his chest as he takes in her beauty. Pride rushes through him, quickly followed by desire and love. He sees her smile and smiles back at her, which quickly turns into a grin. A big stupid grin as she shakes her head at Jane and takes a step towards the bar.

CHAPTER FORTY-NINE

Bronagh takes her first step towards Max. She can see the grin covering his face, which makes her feel more at ease, so she takes that as a good sign. Getting to the bar she can feel her emotions overtaking her and tears threaten, stinging hot at the back of her eyes. She swallows away her fears to speak.

"Hey you." It comes from her lips without thinking and she holds her breath until he answers.

"Hey yourself." They grin at each other. "How've you been?" She relaxes more.

"Good, kinda, still getting there. Although being in here was the last thing I had to overcome... from then." Pain lances through his heart. He acknowledges it then lets it go, letting his pride at how far she'd come take its place.

"Well done you. I'm really proud to see how far you've came... and glad I'm here to see this tonight, even if it is through a twist of fate." Bronagh smiles. She was glad he was there too.

"Thank you. What... about you?" Max gives a small laugh at her hesitant question.

"Better, thank you. I took your advice and went to see someone. You know to talk about everything... well eventually, after my brother beat the shit out of me." Bronagh winces, she knows Max's brother was bigger than him and a training cage fighter.

"That wouldn't have been pretty." Max gives another laugh as he thinks back to the beating he took from his brother and winces at the memory. Bronagh was enjoying how relaxed Max seemed to be with her and how normal they were together.

"No it wasn't, but it worked, so all's good." Gordon and Jane flank Bronagh. "Gordon, Jane." He puts his hand out and Gordon shakes it, Jane gives him a look, then smiles. "Great to see youse. Now what can I get you to drink... the usual?" They all nod and Max goes off to get their drinks. Placing the drinks on the bar Bronagh hands him money but he waves it away. "These are on me, a 'well done' drink." He winks. They all thank him then Gordon and Jane move off to find a table. Max puts his hand on Bronagh's as she lifts her bottle. "Bre." She looks up at him. Her name on his lips sends shivers down her spine and his hand on hers sends electricity shooting through her system. She always wondered how she would react when she saw him again. Now she knew. All the love and desire she had ever felt came rushing back tenfold, from where she'd tried, unsuccessfully, to bury it. "I've missed you... an'... I'm so proud of you." Tears slide down her face.

"I've missed you too Max... so much, and thank you for being here tonight." He winks at her again as she takes her bottle and sits next to Gordon.

"You okay princess?" She nods, dabbing at her cheeks trying to salvage her make-up. "That was a turn up for the books, wasn't it?" Gordon asks and Jane nods and hums. Gordon eyes go into slits as he looks at Jane. "Did you know he would be here?" Bronagh's head snaps up. Jane shakes hers and drinks from her Vodka and Irn Bru.

"No... honestly, no. I heard he was back, but I didn't know what he was doing or if he was staying. Bre I'm sorry, I didn't know he was working here." Bronagh smiles.

"It's fine... honestly. I'm glad he's here. It's like I have a wee bit of extra support and security." Gordon does a dance in his seat and claps his hands.

"I know you still love him, but you still *want* him don't you?" He waggles his eyebrows suggestively. Bronagh's face flushes bright red.

"Gordon...!" She admonishes him then sighs. "Aye... I do." Jane rolls her eyes then mumbles a 'I told you so' under her breath. "Shush you, he probably doesn't feel the same way he did. I mean I'm still not blonde and I dumped him when he was at his lowest." Jane rounds on her friend, trying to keep the anger from her voice.

"Bre, you did what was best for you, for the both of you. You had to. An' you know fine well he was never into blondes, that was just his way of dealing with not having you." Bronagh looks at her friend wide eyed.

"When did you become such a Max fan?" Jane shrugs.

"You know I've always thought youse should be together and that still stands." Bronagh smiles at her friend, wider this time, and looks over at Max. She sees him looking at her with a smile on his face. A ray of hope sparks in her heart.

The ten second countdown starts and Max can't keep his eyes from Bronagh. He'd hardly managed to keep his eyes from her all night. Seeing her again made everything click back into place. It would make all his hard work in therapy worth it if he could win her back. As the clock strikes the five second mark he can see the blonde from earlier make her way over to him. He looks her dead in the eye and shakes his head. He starts towards Bronagh. He was going to have his yearly Hogmanay kiss with Bronagh as usual, even if it was just as friends, as usual. He makes it to the table with a second to spare.

****

Bronagh sees the blonde start to approach Max and him look at her. Her heart sinks, her worst thoughts coming true, but then she sees him shake his head and stride towards her and her heart soars.

"Bronagh?" A cheer goes up as the clock strikes midnight and a new year is brought in. Without any thought they reach for each other and crush their lips together in a longed for kiss. "Happy New Year you," he whispers into her hair.

"Happy new year yourself," she answers. They realise that Gordon and Jane are waiting to wish them a happy new year, so they part, shaking hands and kissing their friends for the new year.

319

The night continues with Max and Bronagh watching each other and smiling as he works. At two in the morning the pub lights go on to groans of all the revellers, and the bouncers start to herald everyone out into the early morning frost of the new year. The three friends go over to the bar to say their goodbyes to Max.

"Max," Gordon shouts, with a sparkle in his slightly unfocused eyes. "We're all heading back to Bronagh's. Why don't you join us once you're finished here?" Max looks at Bronagh questioningly.

"That's up to Bre." All eyes turn to Bronagh.

"Aye... yes, of course. I was going to ask, but someone asked before I had a chance!" She throws Gordon a look but he shrugs it off with a wink.

"That's settled then." He grins to Max, then at Bronagh and back again. Bronagh shakes her head but inside she's jumping up and down with glee. Jane rolls her eyes with a secret smile.

"Right well have a seat and I'll drive us all, seeing as I'm sober an' there'll be no taxis out there."

"Result!" Jane shouts as she high fives Max, but misses. Sending her into a fit of the giggles that leaves her sitting on the floor.

"Result it is!" Gordon says to nobody as he wanders off to speak to the guy he'd been eyeing up all night. Max looks at Bronagh.

"Five minutes, okay?" She nods, then sits on a bar stool to watch him work. Seeing him relaxed and happy again lights her heart up, just as much as seeing his tattoos has it racing again. By the time he's finished she was almost panting, just like she used to when she watched him work on cars and in the house.

The drive over to Bronagh's flat was full of drunken giggles and singing. They all pour into Bronagh's flat, surprised that there was no drunk to climb over on the stairs. Bronagh explains that she'd hardly seen him since the trial, but she'd fully expected him to be there that night. As a passing comment Jane mentions that the trial had changed many people's lives, so it may have changed his. There is an awkward silence for a second until Max stands.

"Beer in the fridge Bre?" breaking it.

"Aye, but sit, you've served us all night, let me get it." She dishes out beers and the four friends relax and talk until the sun rises.

Gordon had fallen asleep on one couch and Jane on the other. Max stands.

"I better be going. You go and get some sleep and I'll phone a taxi." Bronagh stands and walks closer to him. She takes his hand loosely in hers, and takes a deep breath.

"Stay... please?" Max nods and strengthens the grip of their entwined hands and leads them to her bedroom, closing the door behind them.

Early afternoon and the four friends are awake and hugging some of Gordon's amazing coffee.

"Uh, Gee, I've missed your coffee!" Max mutters round his mug. Gordon snorts.

"Obviously!" Gordon spurts out and Max laughs. "Right, I'm going to head. I've got a hot date tonight with the most gorgeous guy from last night." Jane snorts.

"Now that's debatable! An' you said that about the other guy you were dating, what happened to him?"

"That was ages ago, an' he wasn't right, this one is right... I can feel it in my bones!"

Jane snorts then stands.

"Aye, awright then! Give me a minute and I'll grab a taxi with you. I'm guessing these two have shit to talk about." Max chokes on his coffee at Jane's bluntness, but sees the smile Bronagh gives her, so relaxes. Gordon and Jane leave in a flourish of goodbyes, kisses and hand signals for Bronagh to phone them. Sitting back on the couch next to Max, Bronagh turns to face him. She goes to speak but Max takes her hands in his and speaks.

"Bre, let me go first please." She nods her consent. "I'm sorry for everything I put you through. From the blondes you saw me go home with, to making your safety my obsession, my crutch for my own guilt. As I told you last night, I did eventually go to counselling and worked through everything... and you were right, I badly needed it. I've come to terms with the fact that I couldn't have stopped what happened to you, and neither could Jane. Your words, the night we finished, have stayed with me. That you loved me with all that you had, that you'd never love anyone else." Bronagh lowers her head, remembering the night she thought her heart would explode. "I've prayed every day that that's still true." He searches her eyes for an answer. "I've never not loved you Bronagh, and I still want forever with you. So... if we do everything properly this time, date properly, let the natural course of the relationship take place, could we get back together?" Bronagh couldn't breathe. She'd dreamt of this moment, was desperate for it. She could see and feel the difference in Max, but she needed to know there was a definite change.

"Why are you working at the Lock-In?" Max looks at her confused, and a bit defeated.

"I've started my own business, restoring cars then selling them on. But until I have a few more under my belt I need some steady cash coming in. I bought my first BMW during therapy and realised I could breathe and think when I worked on it. So when I was struggling, I turned to the only thing I had left. Cars, and they worked better than the drinking." All the time they'd been speaking Max had been rubbing Bronagh's knuckles, but now she moves her hand. Dismay strikes his heart again until she laces her fingers through his, takes a deep calming breath and starts to talk.

"I'm sorry for everything I put us both through. Even though it wasn't my fault I am sorry. I'm sorry I broke both our hearts, but I think, especially with hindsight, it was the best thing for us... at that moment. I'm glad you found something that helped you and gave you a business. I'm also glad that now you have something to do when you've pissed me off by doing something stupid! Something to work on, to help you work through emotions until we we've both came to our senses and can make up." Confusion covers his face.

"Bre, what are you saying?" She grins.

"I'm saying yes... if we take things slowly, date and not jump in too quick this time, then... yes, I can't wait for forever with you." Ecstasy shoots through him at Bronagh's words. He dives at her, crushing his lips to hers, pinning her to the couch with his weight.

The feeling of being back in Max's arms, feeling his weight on her chest and his lips on her in an all-consuming kiss was more that she'd ever let herself dream. They'd both been to their own private hells, but they'd made it back to each other.

EPILOGUE
One year later

Prison had been hell for Elaine. After the trial she was devastated. That hadn't been part of the plan of destroying Bronagh, but then again, Stewart running away from her and to his death hadn't been part of the plan either. She'd taken to her bed with depression, only moving from it for her antenatal appointments, then to physically give birth.

She gave birth with only the midwives to help her, to a baby boy. Holding her son to her, Elaine broke down. She had been warned that she might not be able to keep her baby, then she'd overheard words of developmental retardation, and foetal alcohol disorder and she knew social services wouldn't hesitate to remove him. She hadn't thought she'd drank to excess once she found out she was pregnant, but then again, she thinks, she didn't find out she was pregnant until she was months into her pregnancy. Their son would be, at best, fostered until she was released. She was told she could have the rest of the night with her son before a social worker came the next morning. She'd spent the entire night holding her son. She named him Stewart Junior, telling him over and over again how much she loved him, how much his father would've loved him, if he was alive, how amazing his father had been and how excited they had been when they found out they were having him.

The morning came as did the social worker. As Stewart Junior was bundled up Elaine sobbed, then shouted, then became hysterical, screaming that they were stealing her baby. She continuously yelled that they had no right to steal her baby, that she had done nothing wrong. Being in prison didn't make her a bad mother. By the time the social worker was finished and her son had been removed, Elaine was in a frenzy of uncontrollable rage. The midwives stayed with her getting her calmed down until eventually, with the midwives' help she got ready to return to prison.

Her depression deepened as she thought about how she had been abandoned all her life. Her parents, her grandparents, Stewart and then her son. Elaine knew somewhere in the back of her rational conscience that Bronagh couldn't be the catalyst for her parents leaving her, or everything else that had ruined Elaine's life, but as the weeks turned into months, and the guards put her on suicide watch, the rational side was gone and Elaine was blaming Bronagh even more than she had when Bronagh had stolen her job. Getting her out of her cell to the breakfast line was a battle and that day was no different. As she stands in the line Elaine furtively looks about her until her eyes settle on one inmate who's standing in a group with other females behind her. They are all talking and giggling. The inmate is small in height with auburn hair. Elaine looks back at her again and glares.

"Stop it!" Elaine shouts at the group, and they all face her. A larger female asks Elaine who she was talking to.

"Her," Elaine spits out, nudging her chin towards the smaller inmate. "You, Bronagh, I want you to shut the fuck up!"

The small inmate laughs. "Who?"

"Don't fuckin' lie to me, bitch. I know fine well it's you."

The small inmate laughs again, and Elaine screams, lunging at her. She lands on the woman with her legs around the woman's waist, knocking her to the floor. Before any guards could get near them Elaine has head butted the inmate four times full in the face. Blood, snot, saliva, teeth and cartilage fly in all directions from the inmates burst nose and face. Still fighting and kicking and hissing like an alley cat the guards drag Elaine from the prone woman. Elaine gets taken to her cell and the other woman to the hospital.

The next time Elaine is out of her cell it's to talk to the governor of the prison. There she learns her and her victim's fate. The woman died after choking on her own blood, so Elaine was being charged with murder.

Hearing that she was to be charged sends Elaine into another rage. She leaps from her chair towards the governor, but is tackled to the ground by the two prison guards that were flanking her before she can get anywhere near her target. They half carry half drag her back to her cell and lock her in, leaving Elaine to think about her life. All she'd wanted was everything that was hers back. Everything that that bitch Bronagh had taken from her, but instead she'd lost everything; her job, her boyfriend, her baby, her freedom... everything, all because of Bronagh. The fact that she couldn't do anything about any of it brought on another fit of rage. Smashing up her cell she slumps to the floor, exhausted and bleeding, waiting on the guards to come and get her to take her to the hospital, this time she hopes for good.

****

Putting the finishing touches to the hall for Gordon's engagement party, Bronagh stands back to look at her work. She couldn't believe out of them all Gordon is the first to dip his toes into the puddle of the grown-up world of marriage. She and Max had spoken about marriage and their future before they had broken up, but since they had made their way back together, they'd been taking things slowly. They'd started dating, going out properly for candlelit dinners, weekends away and even to the Lock-In for drinks, enjoying themselves and each other. Bronagh had admitted to Jane that things felt better this time around. They'd both changed since her ordeal, but only through their break up and a lot of hard work from both of them, they were together and stronger than ever before.

Max cuddles in behind her, wrapping his arms around her waist bringing her from her musings.

"Hey you." He nuzzles into her neck. "This place looks amazing." Bronagh leans her head to the side to give him space to nuzzle.

"Hey yourself, and thank you. I only hope Gordon and his man love it as much as I do." Max turns her to face him.

"I'm sure they will. Listen Bre, I need to tell you something." A shiver runs up her spine.

"What...? Is everything all right?" Max's heart rate increases at the thought of having this conversation with Bronagh.

"Remember, no matter what you think of what I'm going to tell you, I love you and I will always love you." Panic starts to claw at Bronagh's throat.

"Max you're scaring me. Is this something I need to know right now?" Max gives her a kiss.

"I don't want to hide anything from you, so... here goes." He takes a deep breath, "I've heard through the grapevine that Elaine is being charged with murder." Bronagh gasps and holds on tighter to Max hoping her legs wouldn't give out.

"What? How?" She starts her breathing exercises trying to control her heartbeat.

"All I know is she got into a fight in prison and head butted a women breaking most of her face, making her choke on her own blood." A strangled sound comes from Bronagh's throat. "Hey, listen, at least that means she won't be getting out anytime soon." Bronagh nods, unsure how to take the information she has just learned.

"True." She looks over Max's shoulder to see Gordon and his fiancé walking into the hall. She knows she can't give into her panic at that moment so gives Max a quick kiss and smile then walks over to Gordon who's gushing about the decorations. She pushes all thoughts of Elaine and murder to the back of her head and gets on with the rest of the night, partying with her friends. The night ends and she and Max make their way back to her flat. Falling into bed Bronagh cuddles into Max. He'd spent so much time trying to protect her and keep her safe that he ended up trying to control her and keep her like a possession which ended their relationship. Desperate not to let that happen again he'd decided that honesty was the best policy, and deal with whatever the outcome would be. This was why even though he'd worried about telling Bronagh, about Elaine's murder charge, he knew keeping the information from her was wrong.

Bronagh pulls herself closer to Max.

"I love you Mr Stevenson." He smiles against her lips as he takes a kiss.

"I love you too, Miss White. He kisses down her jawline to her neck.

"Hmm, I've been thinking... we're going to need a house that's ours." Max pauses for a second in his kissing, then continues as he talks.

"And why's that?" Max can feel Bronagh's pulse going crazy where he's kissing her neck, making him unsure if he should be worried or not.

"I think I want to be Mrs Stevenson." Max stops kissing her completely and makes a noise.

"Mrs Stevenson?" She grins at his question.

"Hmmm." She starts to kiss him.

"Are you drunk?" Bronagh sits up quickly to look him straight in the eye.

"No... cheeky! I've been thinking about what you told me at the start of the night." Max holds her hand as she talks. "I felt that everything that was mine was taken from me and I needed to get it all back. Get my life back. I've got everything else back, so, now I'm ready for our forever... if that's what you want?" Tears are falling from her eyes as she holds her breath waiting on Max's answer to her sort of proposal.

Max takes her face in his hand and crushes a kiss to her lips.

"Yes, of course I want our forever and everything that comes along with it. House, cars, babies, everything. I've wanted this since the moment I met you." He crushes another kiss to her lips. Breaking the kiss he looks deep into her sparkling emerald eyes. "Bre, I'm so sorry for everything I put you through, but I am glad you were strong enough to make the right choice to end the relationship. You were right, it wasn't healthy for either of us. If you hadn't done that we wouldn't be here now. I am so proud of you, your strength, the love you give me and everyone you care for." He gets up from the bed and reaches into his wallet. "I would be the happiest, proudest man in the world if I could call you Mrs Stevenson... forever." Climbing back onto the bed he holds out a tear drop, claw set, diamond solitaire ring. Bronagh's hand flies to her mouth.

"Max, why do you have that?"

He blushes. "I've had it in my wallet since before we got back together. I bought it a month before, to be exact. It was a 'saw this and thought of you' kinda thing, in the hope that I would find the courage to tell you how I felt." Bronagh smiles and kisses him. "So, are we doing forever? Will you be Mrs Stevenson?"

Bronagh kisses him soundly. "Absolutely!"